P9-DCM-791
EX LIBRIS

Romance
Treasury

THE ROMANCE TREASURY ASSOCIATION

NEW YORK · TORONTO · LONDON

These stories were originally published as follows;

THE PENGELLY JADE
Copyright © 1972 by Lucy Gillen
First published by Mills & Boon Limited in 1972

THE GIRL IN THE GREEN VALLEY
Copyright © 1973 by Elizabeth Hoy
First published by Mills & Boon Limited in 1973

THE BEADS OF NEMESIS
Copyright © 1974 by Elizabeth Hunter
First published by Mills & Boon Limited in 1974

ROMANCE TREASURY is published by
The Romance Treasury Association, Stratford, Ontario, Canada.

Dust Jacket Art by William Biddle
Story Illustrations by Dick Marvin
Book Design by Charles Kadin
Printed by Ronalds Printing, Richmond Hill, Ontario
Bound by T. H. Best Printing Co. Ltd., Don Mills, Ontario

ISBN 0-373-04043-1

Printed in Canada A043

CONTENTS

Page 11
THE PENGELLY JADE
Lucy Gillen

Page 201
THE GIRL
IN THE GREEN VALLEY
Elizabeth Hoy

Page 375
THE BEADS OF NEMESIS
Elizabeth Hunter

THE PENGELLY JADE

The Pengelly Jade

Lucy Gillen

The Jade was a beautiful, priceless heirloom but it had brought ill fortune to the wives of the Pengelly men who had owned it.

"I wish I had the nerve to break the conditions my father imposed against selling it," Uncle Miklas told Bryony when he summoned her to his Cornish home before his death.

But Giles, one of the heirs, discounted the risk and superstition. He wanted the Jade and he wanted Bryony.

Bryony knew her marriage would please her uncle and she was willing. Then her arrogant, forceful Greek cousin, Alex Patinous, arrived. Though he had equal claim to the Jade, he was not impressed by it. But he was by Bryony!

CHAPTER ONE

BRYONY THOUGHT that the impressive stone plaque set in the old church wall looked surprisingly new. Or was it because almost everything else in the tiny gray stone church was so fantastically old that a mere twenty-five years were only a moment in time?

It read, "Matthew Pengelly, Beloved Husband of Maria and Father of Miklas and Merrilyn." Bryony stood alone in the coolness of the aisle, reading the words on the plaque and wondering, not for the first time, just what old Matthew Pengelly had really been like.

He had been her great-grandfather's younger brother and all she really knew of him was that, as a young man, he had been something of a rover, and that he had returned to England at the age of thirty-four with a very young Greek bride and the urge to settle down.

Maria Patinous could speak no word of English, but she made Matthew a loyal and loving wife and gave him a son and a daughter before she died at an early age. Miklas, the son, now lived at Penroyal, the family home, widowed and childless before he was fifty. His sister, Merrilyn, had been over thirty before she married a first cousin, and she, too, was a widow with one son.

When she thought of Giles Pengelly, Bryony smiled. She had seen him quite often as a child, when they had both stayed at Penroyal with Uncle Miklas, less often since they were both older and making their way in the world, and now, thanks to one of old Miklas's autocratic gestures, they were together under the same roof again.

Giles had changed very little since she saw him last. Tall and slim, as he had always been, he had become a very good-looking man. More self-assured, now that he successfully ran the business he had inherited from his father, he nevertheless still retained his quiet, rather solemn manner. He made no secret of the fact that he found Bryony attractive, and that he was delighted to see her again.

They were a very small family, but not especially close in that they did not see each other very often, and sometimes Bryony wished they would keep in closer touch. The old man was, she supposed, some distant sort of cousin, although she always addressed him as uncle, and she was sometimes a little wary of him, a reaction she shared with Giles.

The years had taken a heavy toll of the old man's family and there now remained only Miklas, his sister, and Giles, his nephew, who were really close to him. Bryony herself was admitted only, so she guessed, partly because old Miklas had always liked her and partly because he had inherited his Greek mother's strong sense of family, and therefore even his uncle's great-granddaughter counted as a relative. That he had chosen not to include her father in the invitation did not really surprise Bryony because he had never got on well with him and, as he was not a Pengelly, he did not count as family.

It was a sad fact that, although he was only a little past sixty-five years of age, Miklas Pengelly had been warned by his doctor that he had very little time left; so he had gathered his small family around him while he still could. The old house had not seen so many residents for a good many years and Bryony thought that Mrs. Trevellyan, the housekeeper, would have preferred the local hotel to have housed them. Penroyal was a difficult house to run at the best of times, and with four guests to cope with as well, she felt she was being overtaxed, and showed her resentment in various ways.

The house would, of course, go to Giles as he was the nearest Pengelly male, and heaven knew what the old man would do with the not inconsiderable wealth that both he and his father had accumulated over the years. The main topic of interest would, however, inevitably be who was to get the Pengelly jade.

Matthew Pengelly had brought the small, exquisitely carved, jewel-studded statuette back from the East during his roving years, and he had given it to his young wife after the birth of their son. Miklas had inherited it, in his turn, and soon it would be necessary to hand on the jade to a new owner.

It was reputed to be almost priceless and there was never any question of selling it, for old Matthew had made it a condition that it must remain in the family, although it was considered to be extremely unlucky. First old Matthew had lost his own wife tragically early in life and, only months after he inherited it, Miklas, too, had lost his wife.

Miklas had always maintained a close link with his mother's family in Greece, and particularly with her much younger brother. He had paid for the education of this same brother's son, Alex Patinous, and he had invited him to join the small family gathering at Penroyal.

Bryony frowned when she thought of her fellow guest. Alex Patinous was a curious and uneasy mixture of two worlds. Although he was completely Greek in appearance, the English education provided by his elderly and wealthy cousin had endowed him with a smooth, often discomfiting self-assurance that Bryony viewed with distrust. No one, she felt, who looked so much like an Englishman's idea of an old-time buccaneer had any right to speak impeccable English and look so much at home in an English country mansion.

Of course, Cornwall had its reputation for smuggling and piracy, and Bryony's own ancestors might well have looted and wrecked with the rest, but somehow Alex Patinous always gave her a curiously unsettled feeling. It was not the first time, either, that he had invaded her thoughts, and she impatiently shook her head to dismiss him, returning to her study of the plaque on the wall.

A bright shaft of late autumn sun streaked the gray stone walls through the open doorway and she looked up, vaguely startled, when a dark shadow fell silently amid the sunlight, and in the first moment of turning she experienced that never failing flick of fear as she met the intruder's eyes.

Alex Patinous was tall, taller even than Giles's six feet, and his black hair and eyes and the strong piratical features looked quite out of place in the old church. His smile especially, so white against his dark face, brought to mind things best left unmentioned in such places.

He was lean and strong-looking and always seemed to effuse a dangerous kind of charm which she found very disturbing. The well-fitting gray trousers he wore with a white sweater made him appear darker than ever and she could have sworn that he was well aware of the effect he had on her. Possibly not only on her, but on women in general, for he was a man who would be fully aware of his attraction, she thought, and be prepared to make the most of it.

Whenever she could, she avoided being alone with him, although she told herself more than once that she was behaving quite irrationally by doing so. Just because Giles disliked him, she really had no cause to be avoiding him, except that he disturbed her so strangely.

He stood watching her now from the doorway, feet

slightly apart, one hand in his pocket, that slightly mocking smile glistening in his black eyes. Then he strolled lazily along the stone paved aisle toward her, before he spoke. He came and stood beside her, looking up at the memorial plaque, the smile still in evidence, as if he found her preoccupation both puzzling and amusing.

"Are you studying family history?" he asked in his faultless English.

Bryony nodded, not overpleased to have her peaceful browsing disturbed, especially by this dark, discomfiting stranger who insisted on being so friendly. "I was interested in the plaque," she told him. "I haven't been in the old church since I was a child."

He removed his gaze from the plaque and looked at her instead. "That's not *so* long ago, surely," he speculated, and Bryony shook her head, unwillingly communicative.

"Long enough," she told him. "I'm nearly twenty-three."

He was, perhaps, some ten or eleven years older than she was and looked as if he might take advantage of it. "You look as if you are not long out of the schoolroom," he informed her.

"I'm sure that's meant to be a compliment," she said, trying hard to sound what her father always called prissy.

"Of course." The black eyes studied her for a moment in silent appreciation. She wore her fair hair loose around her shoulders and her gray eyes were wide apart and heavily fringed with brown lashes. Her chin could, perhaps, be a little too firm and stubborn-looking, but there was an exquisite color and softness about her fair skin that would flush so betrayingly whenever she was flustered or angry.

She wore a short wool dress in a soft green color that did things for her gray eyes and clung lovingly to a better than average figure. She was small enough to feel dwarfed when she stood beside him and she knew that the odd, fluttery feeling in her stomach was betrayed by a heightened color in her cheeks.

Alex Patinous looked up at the plaque again, and a small knowing smile touched his lips, as if he suspected just how she felt. "I like to think that we're of the same family," he told her in his deep, quiet voice. "Just how closely are you connected with old Matthew Pengelly, Bryony? It seems to me that the whole family tree is riddled with complications, mostly because the old man found himself such a young bride, I suppose."

"It's not really so complicated," Bryony denied, ready to defend the Pengellys against any criticism. "Matthew Pengelly and my great-grandfather were brothers."

"Oh I see." She could not imagine why he should find that information amusing, but he seemed to, and she hastily lowered her own eyes when she met his slightly mocking gaze. "It's quite distant, isn't it?"

"I suppose so," she admitted. "But my mother was a Pengelly."

"And you're very proud of that."

It was more statement than question and she wondered why she resented it so much when it was true.

"I am," she told him, her chin high.

"And where does Cousin Giles fit into all this?"

He always referred to Giles in that way whenever he spoke of him, and she thought he probably found Giles's dislike of him as amusing as he found her uneasiness.

"That's easy too," she said. "Both old Matthew and his brother, John, were Giles's grandfathers. Aunt Merrilyn married a first cousin."

"Thus complicating matters further," he commented, and she frowned.

"That's not so complicated," she argued. "People do marry first cousins, you know."

"Oh yes, indeed," he agreed solemnly. "And it is not exclusively an English custom either. It happens in my country, too, though not very often, and it does make for rather a complicated family tree, doesn't it?"

"I hadn't thought of it until now," Bryony confessed, "but I suppose it does, in a way."

"Of course, my part in it is further confused by the fact that Maria, old Matthew's wife, was nearly twenty years older than her youngest brother."

"Your father?"

"My father," he agreed. "Actually he's younger than Miklas."

"Oh yes, of course, Uncle Miklas is your cousin, isn't he?"

"He is," he agreed. "Hadn't you realized that?"

He knew perfectly well she hadn't, she thought, and the silent old chuch gave her a strange sense of isolation suddenly. "I—I hadn't realized quite how close you are."

He laughed, and the sound of it added to her uneasiness. "You're wondering why I'm here at the family gathering, aren't you, Bryony?'

"No, no, not at all," she denied, though untruthfully. "I was only thinking how unalike you and Giles are, but, of course, you're not actually related at all, are you, although you're both related to Uncle Miklas."

"If we are related to each other," he told her, "it's far too tortuous a relationship for me to work out at the moment."

Bryony walked on, toward the open door and the sunshine. Somehow, being here with him seemed to make her ridiculously nervous, and she kept hearing Giles's often expressed opinion that he would not like to trust Alex Patinous with anything or anybody. She had never, so far, had cause to complain of his behavior, but she always had the uneasy feeling that that was a situation time would take care of.

She had arrived at Penroyal two weeks ago, and found Alex Patinous already there. Aunt Merrilyn and Giles, when they arrived the following day, had taken his presence at what, they considered, should have been a purely Pengelly affair, very much amiss. Bryony suspected that Aunt Merrilyn had mentioned as much to her brother, too, for she had observed her leaving old Miklas's room one afternoon, looking angry and indignant and almost tearful.

From then on she had been openly antagonistic to the stranger, and Bryony thought Giles was influenced to some extent by his mother's feelings. It was because of the inheritance, of course. The house was entailed and was bound to come to Giles, but there was the money and that priceless, beautiful omen of misfortune, the jade. As long as it was passed to someone in the family, it would not matter who that someone was, and it was true that Alex Patinous was as closely related to old Miklas as Giles was. The old man was much too attached to his younger cousin for anyone's comfort.

Outside the church the air was cool and faintly damp, despite the sun, and the last leaves clung tenaciously to the thinning trees. It would be misty before nightfall. One of those dank, cold mists that clung to brows and eyelashes and crept into the very bones of anyone venturing out into it. Bryony shivered as she listened to the sea crashing against the rugged, gray Cornish rocks some hundred feet below the edge of the churchyard, and marveled at the fascination of the place.

A hand sliding under her left arm, a moment later, forced a small, startled cry from her and she turned to see Alex Patinous smiling at her reaction. "You don't mind if I walk back with you?" It was more statement than question and Bryony wondered what he would have said if she had answered him in the affirmative. Instead, however, she shook her head briefly and started on the short walk back along the cliff top to Penroyal.

It was a lovely walk even at this time of the year, and the gray, restless expanse of the sea looked endless under pale blue autumn sky just streaked with clouds, yellow-edged with sun. To the west, the wide curve of Marby Bay still held the warmth of past summer days, its ragged, rocky shoreline hemmed with white sand and a retreating tide.

Eastward, the wilder, unpopulated Marby Head held past associations with smugglers and shipwreckers, and looked as if it still waited for more victims to crash helplessly onto the rocks where the local people stood patiently with darkened lanterns.

Cornishmen were traditionally dark, and her own father was much less typical than the man walking beside her. There was strength and assurance in the hand that supported her elbow as they walked, and she thought again what a strange mixture of savagery and sophistication he was. His manners were invariably impeccable, and yet when she looked at the dark face above the high collar of a white sweater she could better see him as one of her own more disreputable ancestors than the well-educated man she knew him to be.

As if he sensed the gist of her thoughts, he looked down at her and smiled. "There's quite a history attached to this part of the world, so Miklas tells me," he said.

"Yes... yes, there is." She still found it difficult to get used to his familiar use of the old man's Christian name, and she knew he recognized it, for he smiled again and displayed those incredibly good teeth.

Bryony had never been to Greece in her life, and her

whole concept of the place was based on some rather lurid and only half-remembered tales she had read as a girl about wild mountains and even wilder men who lurked the mountains and waylaid innocent travelers.

Alex Patinous, she thought, fitted perfectly into these preconceived ideas, and with what she had heard about the way Greek men treated their women. It was not at all difficult to imagine him subjugating any woman he married and then taking his pleasure, wherever, in any way, he chose.

It was probably quite wrong of her, of course, but the belief persisted. That dark face with the black hair curling just slightly in the nape of his neck, and the arrogant black eyes below expressive brows, set her imagination racing out of control.

"You must show me some of the old smugglers' hideouts," he told her. "Miklas says you know most of them."

"I...I used to," she admitted. "I used to spend most of my school holidays here, and we used to explore the old caves."

"We?"

She nodded. "Giles and I."

He was smiling again, in such a knowing way that she felt her cheeks burning with resentment. "Oh yes, of course, Cousin Giles."

"Giles stayed here, too, with his parents. Uncle Miklas enjoyed having his family here, especially the children, and we loved it here."

"I can imagine you would," he told her. "But somehow I can't quite visualize Giles being a Pengelly, not in the same way as you and Miklas. He's too...." His free hand made some vague gestures in the air, but left no doubt just what he meant to convey, and Bryony felt herself stiffen in resentment. She was very fond of Giles and she would not have him maligned, however vaguely, by this arrogant stranger.

"I don't know what you mean," she told him. "Giles is a credit to the Pengellys. He works very hard, too, running his company."

"Exactly," Alex agreed. "He's so respectable I simply can't fit him in with the family history. Your ancestors were a real gang of brigands, weren't they?"

"Were they?" Her face showed quite plainly that she resented the criticism.

"Shipwreckers," he said. "Surely not the most gentle of characters."

Bryony knew she was being unreasonably sensitive about it, but she disliked hearing him talk so disparagingly about her Pengelly ancestors. "It...it was considered fair game in those days," she informed him, ignoring a certain lack of accuracy.

"Not by the customs and duty officers," he retorted. "Or the poor devils they lured onto the rocks."

It was unfair of him, she thought, to make what she had always considered a rather romantic history sound so horribly cruel and heartless. "The Pengellys weren't the only ones, you know," she told him. "Practically every family along this part of the coast did it."

"And common practice makes it okay, is that it?" he asked, laughing softly when she flushed.

"It was wrong, I know that," she said, "but...well, it was something that happened in those days and the sentences they got if they were caught were just as savage as the crime itself."

"You sound like a lawyer," he said, as they strode the last few yards toward the house, and she could not completely resist a smile.

"I used to work for one," she told him. "Perhaps that's why."

His surprise, she thought, was genuine, and he looked at her curiously. "Just imagine," he said. "We both serve the same profession. I've known you two whole weeks and I never knew that."

Bryony shrugged. "It's not so surprising," she declared. "After all, we've scarcely been on familiar enough terms to discuss our private lives, have we?"

His hand tightened on her arm briefly and the black eyes looked down at her with a disturbing intensity. "That's easily remedied," he told her. "Always providing Cousin Giles lets me get a word in, of course. Has he a firm claim to you?"

She bit on her lip for a moment, tempted to make her answer as stingingly acid as possible, but he was a fellow guest and more or less a stranger, so she thought better of it. "If you mean what I think you mean," she said shortly "no—he hasn't."

He hugged her arm again briefly as they went into the house. "Good," he said. "I'm glad to hear it."

Penroyal had been built long before the Pengellys got possession of it *via* a very propitious marriage, but they had had it now for well over a hundred and fifty years and the wide stairway displayed rather stylized portraits of the last few owners and their families. A large likeness of old Miklas looked down, rather self-consciously, from the topmost position. Bryony loved the old house, and she felt that a hundred years of respectability gave her every right to be proud of being a Pengelly on her mother's side, no matter what this impudent interloper thought.

It was, possibly, because the latter thought was uppermost in her mind as she freed her arm and went toward the stairs that she unconsciously put on a certain air of arrogance. "If you'll excuse me," she said, "I have to write a letter before teatime."

His brief bow, she felt, was more a gesture of mockery than politeness and there was a most discomforting glitter in his eyes when he looked at her. "Of course, Miss Foster." He invariably used her Christian name, so it was obvious he was taunting her for her manner, and she felt the color rush warmly into her cheeks as she turned away from him and went upstairs.

As she was about to pass Miklas Pengelly's room, she hesitated whether or not to look in on him. Mostly the old man was flatteringly glad to see her, but at times he could be quite short with her. She knew it was due to his illness, however, that his temper was variable, and she made allowances. The answer to her knock was encouraging this time, and she smiled as she opened the door.

Miklas Pengelly looked far older than his sixty-five years and, Bryony thought, far more Greek than he had as a younger man. His hair was now completely gray, but still had a strong curl and showed no signs of thinning, despite his illness. His eyes were sharp and black as ever, as he smiled on seeing her. The eyes, she thought, were exactly as Alex Patinous's would be in about thirty years' time.

He held out a hand to her and she went over and stood beside his bed. "Have you been out walking?" he asked, and she nodded.

"Just as far as the old church," she told him. He looked out of the window at the light blue sky and the pale sun, then shook his head. "It'll be misty by nightfall," he said, echoing her own earlier guess.

"That's what I thought. It's quite shivery, despite the sun."

"I saw you come back," he told her. "With Alex."

She nodded. "I saw him in the church while I was looking at the plaque, and he walked back with me."

Thick gray brows rose expressively. "I never knew

Alex was interested in old churches," he remarked.

"I don't think he is," Bryony told him. "I think, perhaps, he saw me in there looking at the plaque, and was curious enough to come and see what I was doing."

Surprisingly, he chuckled. "Quite likely," he allowed. "He's got a strong streak of inquisitiveness and he isn't backward about displaying it."

She remembered something suddenly and frowned thoughtfully. "I didn't know he had anything to do with the legal profession," she said. "He remarked about us being in the same profession."

The old man smiled, shaking his head. "He's a rather bigger cog in the wheel than you are, Bryony dear. Alex is a fully fledged lawyer with his own practice, but I suppose you *are* both in the same profession."

"I see." She tried hard to visualize that dark, piratical face on the side of the angels in court, and failed. He looked far too much like an old-time buccaneer to be *that* respectable.

She blinked a moment later when the old man spoke again. "I haven't seen Giles for a couple of days," he said. "Is he still here?"

"Yes. Oh yes, he's still here." It must be very trying for him to be confined to the one room all the time, and he looked forward too much to visits from his family when he was well enough. It was bad of Giles to have neglected him for two days, and she must speak to him about it. "He probably doesn't realize you're well enough to see anyone," she told him, attempting to excuse Giles's omission.

"Well, he should know," old Miklas retorted, unpacified. "You've been to see me every day, and so has Alex."

She disliked Alex being made the example for Giles to follow and she frowned over it. "Maybe he thought you didn't want to see him," she suggested. "I... I believe he said something about you having a disagreement about something, last time he came in and saw you. He's rather sensitive, Uncle Miklas."

"Sensitive!" The old man scorned the idea. "A nephew of mine has no business being sensitive. I'm not a man who watches my words, like my father. I can't think where he gets it from, unless it's from that stupid sister of mine. Comes of marrying a first cousin, I suppose," he added. "Bad for the character."

"Uncle Miklas, you shouldn't talk about them like that," Bryony told him, surprising herself with her firmness. "Aunt Merrilyn is very fond of you, and so is Giles."

"Merrilyn's an interfering old busybody," he retorted. "She's so afraid of what I'll do with the money that she'll stoop to anything."

"Oh no, Uncle Miklas!"

"Oh yes," the old man insisted. "Do you know she actually came and demanded that I send Alex packing. Have you ever heard the like? Alex is as much family to me as she and Giles are."

"Oh, not quite, surely," Bryony felt bound to protest. "They're your sister and your nephew, and—"

"And Alex is my cousin," he retorted swiftly.

"But it's because he's not a Pengelly," she insisted. "I know Aunt Merrilyn is thinking about the... the jade as much as anything, Uncle Miklas. After all, it *is* known as the Pengelly jade, isn't it?"

The old man nodded slowly. "I'm not sure that damned thing is such a desirable acquisiton," he told her. "I only wish I had the nerve to break the condition father made, and sell the wretched thing, for it's got a curse on it."

It was something of a surprise to hear him speak in

that way, for he had always been such a severely practical man, that curses and superstitions seemed so out of character for him. "It certainly doesn't seem to have brought anyone much luck so far," she allowed, "but surely it *can* only be superstition, can't it?"

"Can it?" The wrinkled brown face looked so wise and sad suddenly, and the black eyes so brightly inscrutable that she felt he was somehow alien in this pleasant, homely room.

"Well, of course it is," she said firmly, in an effort to convince herself as much as him.

"Its history should have been a warning," the old man went on, as if she had not spoken, and Bryony looked at him curiously. "It belonged to a Chinese Emperor, you know, or so the story goes, and it was stolen from him by one of the warlords. When the Emperor discovered its loss, he put a curse on it and, from what we hear, it must have been a pretty effective one, because it was quickly handed on from one owner to another for hundreds of years until someone got cold feet and tried to break the curse by giving it to a temple."

Bryony nodded; hearing the old story again reminded her of her childhood. "And your father took it from the temple when he was in the East," she said.

Old Miklas smiled ruefully. "It was typical of my father to do such a thing," he told her. "For a Cornishman he was notoriously unsuperstitious, and he was determined to prove that there was no such thing as a curse, or at least that it didn't work."

"And his wife died very early in life," Bryony mused softly.

"And my wife too," he reminded her. "That cursed jade is a heavy responsibility, Bryony."

"But it's only a superstition," she urged, hating to see him so worried about it.

"Perhaps you're right." He sighed, and she realized how quickly he had tired.

"I must go and let you rest," she told him, as she got to her feet. "If Nurse comes and finds me here and you looking so tired, she'll scold me and you too, and I won't blame her."

He held on to her hand for a moment, his expression thoughtful and a little worried, as if his mind was still on the problem of the notorious jade statuette. "I like to see you, Bryony," he told her. "Don't *you* neglect me, will you?"

Impulsively she bent her head and kissed him, her eyes suspiciously bright. "Of course I won't, Uncle Miklas. I'll come and see you every day and so will Giles. I'll tell him you're not still angry with him."

"He should know it without being told," the old man said. "But I suppose he has other fish to fry, hasn't he?"

"I...I don't quite understand you," she told him, and he shook his head.

"You've grown into a very beautiful girl, Bryony," he said softly, "and however stupid that nephew of mine may be, he isn't blind."

It was not a subject Bryony was prepared to discuss at the moment and she shook her head slowly. "Giles and I have always got on well together, Uncle Miklas. It's no different now."

"Hmm." The bright, black eyes looked at her speculatively for a moment, then he smiled. "If you say so, my dear."

CHAPTER TWO

IT WAS SOMETHING to think about, Bryony thought, when she woke fairly early next morning and lay watching the pale sun filter through her bedroom curtains onto the wall. Certainly Giles had shown a kind of proprietary manner toward her since his arrival at Penroyal, although she had taken little notice of it until Miklas Pengelly had mentioned it.

Giles was very good-looking and she was very fond of him, but she was definitely not prepared to commit herself to being anything more at the moment. Aunt Merrilyn, she thought wryly, would not take kindly to the idea either, for she was very possessive with her only child and had always looked upon Bryony as not really a Pengelly at all, although her mother had been one.

She got up hastily, after a glance at the clock beside her bed, and made her way down to breakfast. The rest of the household were already there and accepted her murmured apology with brief nods and varying degrees of friendliness. Giles smiled at her and said a rather restrained good morning, while Aunt Merrilyn merely muttered a short good day before returning to the more inviting subject of her breakfast. Aunt Merrilyn's appetite had always been a source of endless speculation to Bryony when she was a child—how such a small woman could consume such vast quantities of food without apparent discomfort.

The only really fulsome greeting came from Alex Patinous, who looked up with a broad smile, left his chair and saw her seated and then poured her some coffee. It was just as usual, but this morning, with the old man's opinion still fresh in her mind, she found herself noticing it more closely.

"Thank you." She sat down next to Alex and accepted her coffee with the usual smile. A rather absent smile, for her attention was on Giles as she wondered why he did not perform these little niceties instead of leaving it to a stranger. Then, seeing Aunt Merrilyn's small, tight mouth, she knew why and mentally shrugged resignation. However much of an efficient businessman he might be, Giles was till an obedient son, and while he was with his mother he took care not to offend her.

"Are you going to be busy this morning?" Alex Patinous asked her, so unexpectedly that she was lost for an answer, for a moment, and merely blinked at him.

"I...I don't know," she said, at last, glancing instinctively at Giles, who caught her eye and drew his brows together in a small frown.

"I was hoping to take you into Penryn this morning, Bryony," he told her, and she noticed the hasty tightening of Aunt Merrilyn's mouth.

"I thought you were taking me to Marby this morning, Giles," she said, her harsh voice slightly muffled by a mouthful of toast. "I do hope you hadn't forgotten about it, darling."

"Oh! Oh, no, of course not, Mother." He looked across at Bryony apologetically. "I'm sorry, Bryony. I *had* forgotten I'd promised to take mother shopping this morning."

"And I'm sure you'd be quite horribly bored, Bryony dear," Aunt Merrilyn told her with a smile. "I know how you hate shopping in Marby. It's so old-fashioned for you, isn't it?"

"I don't mind Marby sometimes," Bryony told her, hoping to hear Giles put forward an argument for her coming with them despite his mother's obvious dislike of the idea.

"But you wouldn't want to come all that way just to be bored, my dear." The harsh voice was insistent, and Giles showed no sign of arguing with its decision.

Alex Patinous's black eyes were watching her with a strange mixture of sympathy and curiosity, and his wide mouth was not quite smiling. "That means that you're not going to be busy this morning, Bryony, after all," he said quietly. "So, before you think of anything else, may I speak up and ask for your services as local guide and expert?"

She knew Giles was annoyed about having his own plans thwarted, but she doubted if he would summon enough courage to openly defy his mother, and she nodded in answer to Alex's question. "I'm not sure that I'm an expert on anything," she told him. "But if you care to entrust your safety to my guidance, I'll show you some of the places Giles and I discovered as children."

"Such dangerous places for children to play," Merrilyn declared. "If I'd had my way, Giles would never have been allowed to play in caves and over rocks. He could have been hurt or—" she shuddered realistically "—even worse."

It was probably quite true, Bryony knew, but if Giles's father had still been alive he would, no doubt, have been more venturesome and less ruled by his mother's will. She had liked Giles's father and he had proved an excellent accomplice in their childhood games.

Giles obviously hated being shown up in front of the man he disliked so much and he frowned at his mother's fears. "Nonsense, mother," he told her, brusquely for him. "We were in no danger at all. Father looked after us and we had some wonderful times running in and out of those old smugglers' hideouts, didn't we, Bryony?"

"Wonderful," she agreed, smiling at him. "I always enjoyed my holidays down here with Uncle Miklas."

"You were very lucky to be invited so often," Aunt Merrilyn informed her with her sugar-sweet smile that deceived no one, least of all Bryony. "My brother was always notoriously generous and open hearted."

"Always," Bryony agreed. "I was very grateful to him. Even small as I was, I realized that if it had not been for Uncle Miklas I wouldn't have had such a wonderful time during school holidays."

"Of course," Aunt Merrilyn insisted, as if determined to keep the record straight, "he isn't really *your* uncle, he's Giles's."

"Oh, Mother, surely that's a minor point," Giles objected. "Uncle Miklas liked—likes—Bryony to call him uncle, and she could hardly call him Miklas, could she?"

"As I do," Alex interposed quietly, and Bryony almost giggled aloud when she saw Aunt Merrilyn's tight, disapproving mouth.

"I dislike hearing young people refer to or call older people by their Christian names," she told him stiffly. "It shows a sad lack of respect, I think."

Alex seemed unperturbed by the opinion and merely lifted one eyebrow to show his surprise. "I know there's nearly thirty years between us, Merrilyn," he told her, being outrageously familiar, "but Miklas is my cousin, not my uncle, and he likes me to use his Christian name."

"I find it unpalatable," Aunt Merrilyn informed him in a voice as chill as ice, "as I do your use of *my* name, Mr. Patinous."

"I'm sorry." He bowed almost to the level of the table, but the black eyes were glittering wickedly when he looked across at Bryony and she hastily lowered her own so that he should not guess how much she enjoyed seeing someone score off her irritating relative.

Aunt Merrilyn finished her coffee, so disturbed by his impudence that she actually overlooked a slice of toast still in the rack. "If you're ready, Giles," she said, "perhaps Bryony will excuse us. I don't want to be too late getting to Marby, in case it gets crowded. I do so much hate crowded shops."

She made her exit with all the dignity at her command, but somehow, because Alex Patinous's black eyes followed her progress, she looked pompous and rather ridiculous, and Bryony felt almost sorry for her.

Surprisingly he did not say anything after Giles and his mother had gone, but merely poured himself some more coffee, while Bryony got on with her breakfast. That strange, disturbing uneasiness stirred in her again, and she wished she could have left with Giles and Aunt Merrylin, rather than be left here alone with him.

She glanced up at him when she sensed him looking at her. "Do you disapprove of my calling Miklas by his Christian name, also?" he asked, and she shook her head.

"No. No, of course not; if Uncle Miklas himself doesn't mind, I don't see why anyone else should."

"I am so glad that, for once, you approve of me," he told her, with pseudo solemnity. He seemed not in the least disturbed by Aunt Merrilyn's dislike, in fact he would probably thrive on it, she thought.

She declined to be drawn by the obvious bait and gave her attention to her meal again, wishing she could feel less like a nervous schoolgirl whenever she was with him. He looked, if anything, even more attractive this morning, with a thick, creamy Arran sweater showing up the dark features, and slim-fitting navy blue slacks. He always looked so right, she thought, not a little annoyed at the idea of being unable to find anything amiss. She tried not to notice the way his black hair just touched the high neck of the sweater at the back, or the way the broad shoulders tapered down to a slim, narrow waist.

"Why do you always look as if you're expecting something to happen, when you and I are alone together?" he asked suddenly, and Bryony felt the color flood into her cheeks.

"That's a ridiculous thing to say," she accused, when she could find words.

"Not at all," he argued. "Whenever I am alone with you, I get the feeling that you expect me to...." He spread his hands expressively and Bryony dared not look at him for fear of what she might see in his eyes. He really had no right to try and make her feel so small.

"You're very much mistaken," she assured him, trying to steady her voice which insisted on trembling horribly. "I expect nothing of you, Mr. Patinous, except normal good manners."

For a moment she could almost have believed that his expression of shocked surprise was genuine, but then she saw the glitter of amusement in his black eyes and hastily lowered her own. "I hope I am always good-mannered," he said. "Would you rather I called you Miss Foster, instead of Bryony?"

"No. No, of course not—that isn't necessary."

"Then will you be equally agreeable and call me Alex?"

"Yes, if you prefer it."

"I do." He looked at her for a moment in silence,

then smiled again. "You don't like me very much more than your aunt and Giles do, do you, Bryony?'

"I...I didn't say that," she protested.

He shook his head, slowly, still smiling but with an air of arrogant self-assurance that dismissed her opinion and anyone else's as unimportant. "You do not have to say it," he told her. "But it's true."

"Alex—"

He held up a hand. "No, please don't deny it."

There was a long meaningful silence which Bryony felt she had to break. "Do...do you *want* me to show you the caves?" she asked at last.

"Will you?"

She nodded. "But I'm not the expert you think I am."

"I'll take that chance." His smile challenged her. "As long as you're not incurring Giles's wrath by coming with me."

She bit her lips on the retort that rose to her tongue, and instead tried to sound matter-of-fact. "Giles knows we're going," she told him, "and he's not likely to say anything about it if you don't."

He looked at her, narrow-eyed and speculating, across the breakfast table, his cup of coffee held in both hands. "Does he ever defy his mother and speak up for you?" he asked softly.

"Yes. Yes, of course."

He smiled slowly. "You surprise me."

Bryony flushed angrily. Even if Giles's actions did lack stamina when it came to dealing with his mother, there was no excuse for this arrogant stranger to make such pointed remarks about him. "You have no right to talk about Giles like that," she told him. "He's my cousin—well, a sort of distant cousin, and I won't have you run him down to me."

"He's my cousin too," he reminded her softly, his

eyes glittering. "But he is a Pengelly, of course, and the Pengellys are all-powerful, and must not be criticized. Is that what you are telling me, Bryony?"

She lifted her chin, her cheeks pink. "If you like," she told him. "In this part of the world the Pengellys are very important people."

"And in the part of the world where I come from," he said quietly, "it is important to be a Patinous, but you and your family never think about that, do you?"

She was silent for a moment, realizing for the first time that this seemingly easygoing, impudent man had a fierce pride at least equal to her own family's. It was something that none of them had considered, except possibly Uncle Miklas who knew them so much better than anyone else.

"I'm...I'm sorry...." She could find no words to say what she felt, and he smiled recognition of it.

"Family pride can cause more wars and heartache than anything," he told her, "so I shall not start a vendetta, much as I'm tempted by your formidable aunt, or whatever the lady is. I shall call a truce unless she attacks without provocation and then I cannot guarantee my reaction." He drained his cup and put it down, smiling across at her. "How soon can you be ready?" he asked.

"In a few minutes." She looked down at the light shoes she wore. "I shall have to put something more substantial on my feet if we're going rock climbing."

He nodded. "You'd better wear slacks, too," he told her. "They're more suitable for that sort of thing."

She felt rather inclined to argue with him, mostly because she objected to the rank arrogance of his manner. It had not been so much a suggestion as an order and she resented it bitterly. He had absolutely no right to tell her what to wear, and she had a good mind to tell him so. She made no comment, however, but merely got up from the table and walked out of the room with her chin in the air and a dark, stormy look in her gray eyes.

Had it not been that she was forced to agree that slacks were far more suitable for rock climbing and exploring caves, she would have told him what she thought of his instructions and gone as she was. But he was right and, unless she was prepared to suffer the embarrassment of being quite unsuitably dressed, she had little option but to comply.

It was no more than ten minutes later that she left her room, wearing walking shoes and blue denims, as he had suggested, with a soft sweater to keep out the sharp wind that would almost inevitably be blowing from the sea.

She had not been very long changing and she thought it would not matter too much if she kept Alex Patinous waiting for a little while, so she paused before Miklas Pengelly's door, wondering if he was ready to see a visitor this early in the day. Her question was answered a few seconds later when the nurse came out, and smiled encouragingly at her, standing to one side to allow her to enter.

The room smelled strongly of disinfectant and looked spick and clean with the sun shining in through the windows, so that Bryony wondred at Giles's dislike of sickrooms. The old man looked fresh and much brighter this morning, having rested well all night, and he looked up with a smile of welcome when she came in. "Hello, Bryony my dear, come in."

"Hello, Uncle Miklas." She sat on the edge of his bed. "How are you this morning?"

"Better, my dear, better." He nodded his gray head and smiled. "Sometimes I feel so good first thing in the morning that, I think, I'm a fraud for staying in my bed."

"Nonsense, no one thinks you're a fraud," she assured him, "but we'd love to think you could come down and join us."

He shook his head slowly. "It's not possible, Bryony, much as I'd like to." He looked at the way she was dressed and smiled a query. "Where are you off to all dressed up so practically?" he asked. "Are you and Giles going walking?"

"Not Giles," she told him, looking down at her hands. "I promised to take Alex exploring some of the caves this morning."

"Oh, I see." He sat thoughtfully silent for a moment. "So it *was* Giles's car I heard go off just now?"

She nodded. "He's taken Aunt Merrilyn into Marby for some shopping."

He sighed and shook his head slowly. "That woman," he said with certainty, "is a fool."

Bryony smiled understanding. "She doesn't like me very much," she told him, without malice she hoped, "and she likes Alex even less."

"Then she can just lump it," he declared stubbornly. "I ask whom I please to my home and she can put up with it."

"Poor Aunt Merrilyn," she smiled, remembering Alex's exchange with her earlier. "She means well."

"She means well for herself and her precious Giles," he retorted. "She's ruined that boy since his father died."

"It's natural, I suppose," she said. "There's only the two of them, after all."

"Until Giles marries," the old man said quietly. "*Then* the fur'll fly, you take my word for it."

"Yes." She avoided his eyes again. "I imagine it will."

A knock on the bedroom door made them both look

up, and the old man called out a welcome. It was Alex Patinous, as Bryony had half expected it would be, and she hastily lowered her eyes when he looked straight at her, one brow arched as if he questioned her being there at all.

"I was under the impression that you were getting ready to come out with me," he told her, with such unpardonable arrogance that she felt her color rising as she glared at him.

"As you can see, I *am* ready," she told him. "I just came in to have a word with Uncle Miklas before we went."

"As I did." He seemed quite unperturbed that he had offended her, and smiled at the old man cheerfully. "Bryony is to show me some of your smugglers' haunts this morning," he told him. "Did she tell you?"

"Said she was showing you some of the local history," Miklas agreed. "But be very careful down on the rocks, Alex. It'll still be pretty misty lower down, and you can miss your footing if you're not used to it."

"I understood Bryony was something of an expert," he told the old man. "So I shall have no fears."

"I'm not an expert," Bryony denied impatiently. "But you will keep insisting that I am."

"I'm sorry." He bowed his head in mock humility and she could cheerfully have hit him.

"I just hope you won't blame me," she told him, "if we get stuck or break our necks. I haven't been in those caves since I was about thirteen years old, and I've forgotten most of what I knew about them."

"But you'll soon remember when you see them again," he assured her confidently.

"I hope so."

"I'm prepared to risk life and limb if you are," he told her, and she heard Uncle Miklas chuckling to himself quietly. "I'm not unused to rock climbing myself," Alex added. "I did quite a lot when I was younger."

"Then you'd better lead the expedition," she retorted, and he laughed.

"I will if you're afraid to do so," he told her, and she bit her lip as she met the challenge in his eyes.

"You have nothing much to worry about," old Miklas told them. "As long as you remember about the mist and where the tide comes in, but be careful just the same."

"We will."

The assurance came from Alex Patinous, and Bryony wondered for a moment if he was ever in doubt about anything. Such self-confidence was almost frightening.

"I'm always careful, Uncle Miklas," she told him. "I won't get into any trouble, I promise." She bent and kissed him gently on the forehead. "Maybe Giles will come in and see you when he gets back with Aunt Merrilyn," she told him.

"Hmm, and maybe he won't," the old man retorted.

"Uncle Miklas, he...."

"All right, my dear." He held her hand for a moment. "Never mind Giles, you go and show Alex our caves, hmm?"

"And I'll make sure she doesn't do anything foolish," Alex Patinous promised confidently. "Don't worry about her."

The old man, she thought, was quite pleased that she was going with Alex, for neither of his other guests were very friendly toward him, and he was genuinely fond of his much younger cousin. If only for Uncle Miklas's sake, she told herself, she must try and be a bit more amiable toward the unwelcome visitor.

It was even more windy than she had anticipated when they started down the rock face, down toward the beach nearly fifty feet below, where the sea pounded remorse-lessly at the ragged gray teeth that straddled the white sand.

It was fine so far, but the wind was like a blustery warning of rain to come and she wondered, briefly, as they went down the rocky incline, if it would have been wiser to postpone their exploring until another day. As the old man had said, remnants of mist still hung in wispy veils around corners of rock and, at times, floated across to partially obscure their view of the sea.

There was no easily recognizable path down the rocks, but it was fairly easy descending if one was surefooted and not put off by heights. Alex Patinous, she noted wryly, was as agile as a mountain goat, and her mind dwelt uneasily on stories she had heard of brigands in the Grecian mountains. With his dark face, rugged and unconcerned above the thick white sweater, he looked like something out of a boy's adventure story and not at all like the respected lawyer his cousin claimed he was.

Once he caught her looking at him when he turned his head unexpectedly, and he grinned as if he could guess at least something of what was in her mind and found it very amusing. "Nearly down," he called back.

She realized that since she was the supposed expert in the matter, she should have been in the lead, but he had firmly insisted on going down first and she had complied willingly enough in view of her lack of practice.

"Just to your right," she called down to him as he paused on a narrow ledge. "There should be an opening somewhere there, if I remember," she told him, and he peered around the protruding rock, then nodded.

"You're right, there is."

It was only a second later that he disappeared from sight and she hesitated for a moment before going on. He had obviously stepped around the corner into the first of the caves that opened off the rock face. She negotiated her way down and a moment or two later stood on the same ledge he had occupied, peering into the cave she had not seen for nearly ten years.

It smelled dank and somehow sickly, but she swallowed her dislike of its dark interior and stepped inside. The roof was low and beaded with moisture, probably partly due to the lingering mist, and for a moment she shared Aunt Merrilyn's dislike of the caves as a safe place to play. Her younger self, she thought, must have been far more brave than her grown-up one.

"Come right in," Alex invited.

"I'm...I'm not sure I want to," she told him, her voice echoing flatly on the damp rock. "It's horribly damp and dismal."

"But exciting," he assured her, his black eyes gleaming. "I can imagine your cut-throat ancestors hiding their ill-gotten loot in here out of sight of the Customs men," he told her, less precise in his speech than usual.

"My ancestors were no more cut-throat than... than...than anyone else's," she said, hastily changing her mind about naming his.

"Than mine?" he suggested softly, and laughed. "Probably you're right, but I know nothing about mine, and you do." He looked around the high cavern. "Do you think their ghosts might still be here?" he asked, in a deep, hollow-sounding voice that reverberated around the rocky walls. Then he laughed like a maniac, and Bryony let out a squeak of protest, putting her hands to her mouth.

"Don't *do* that," she complained. "It sounds awful in this place."

"It's full of atmosphere," he insisted, looking around at the long, low dome of a roof and the ragged, damp walls that disappeared into the darkness at the back. "We shall go on a little further, I think."

She was not to be consulted, it seemed, and she wished most fervently that she had never consented to come on this foolhardy expedition. "We can't go any further," she said, not without satisfaction, and he looked back over his shoulder at her. "We haven't got a torch," she pointed out, "and it's as black as pitch back there. Worse still, further back."

"You may have come unprepared," he told her with a smile, "but I did not."

She stared at the torch he produced from a back pocket and felt her heart sink dismally. The thought of walking into the dark, primeval nether regions of the caves with him gave her a feeling of panic, and she felt sure he must at least suspect it because of the way he was smiling.

"It... it isn't very safe," she ventured, and he laughed softly, sending a shiver along her spine.

"Nonsense," he told her. "I don't take chances, Bryony. You'll be perfectly safe if you're sensible."

"I—"

"Are you coming with me?" he asked impatiently. "Or are you going to stay here and shiver until I come back?"

"I'll... I'll stay here."

He stood with the torch in one hand, his hands on his hips, feet planted firmly apart and a look in his eyes that she disliked intensely. "You call yourself a Pengelly," he jeered softly, and laughed. "They would not own you, those old Pengellys."

Bryony flushed, her chin lifted in defiance. "I'm not frightened," she denied. "I just don't want to go trailing around in the damp. It's silly when there's nothing to see."

"How do you know?" he challenged. "Have you been?"

She nodded. "When I was a child."

His eyes swept over her in one insolent, expressive glance that brought furious color to her cheeks. "You must have had more courage then," he told her, and turned away.

"Wait!"

She followed the small yellow glow of the torch to the far end of the cave, and he turned at her call, waiting for her to join him. His left hand reached out as she came closer and grasped hers tightly, leading her on further into the darkness where the walls dripped wetly and the silence was full of echoes.

"Hello," he said suddenly. "Some steps going down." His face turned to her, darkly shadowed in the yellow light of the torch. "Do you know about these steps?" he asked, and she nodded.

"They go down into another cave at beach level."

"Then we'll go down that way, shall we?"

She doubted if she had much choice in the matter now that she had come so far, but she nodded her head and felt herself drawn along to the top of the steps. They were crudely cut in the solid rock and worn with the passage of time, running water and, perhaps, passing feet, and they looked as if they descended to the very bowels of the earth.

"I...I don't know if they're safe," she demured, and he turned and looked at her shrewdly.

"Is it the steps or your courage you are not sure of?" he asked softly, his voice echoing eerily around the walls.

"The steps, of course," she said, her eyes wide and shiny in the torchlight, and looking almost as black as his.

"Then I shall go down first," he told her. "Will that reassure you?"

"No, please don't." She clung to his hand, still holding hers. "If... if they aren't safe and you... I wouldn't know what to do."

His smile was startlingly white in the dark features. "I won't break my neck," he assured her, "but I am flattered that you care whether I do or not."

"I don't," she retorted shortly. "I just don't fancy having to rescue you, that's all."

"Oh, sweet as honey and soft as down," he quoted softly. "You stay here, little rabbit, while I see where they go to."

"No, Alex!" He turned his head again. "I'll come with you."

"I thought you might," he said quietly.

The steps were much steeper than Bryony remembered them and they felt horribly slippery underfoot, so that she hung on grimly to his hand, her other hand feeling its way cautiously along the wet, cold walls.

"There's a gallery about halfway down," she ventured, when they had gone part way.

"In the wall?"

She nodded, then realized he could not see her. "Yes, it was a sort of... of look-out place, I think."

He shone the torch around for a while, then switched it off momentarily, making her cry out in protest. "I can see a little patch of daylight around the next corner," he informed her, and shone the torch again.

It was, as Bryony had said, probably an old look-out post, really no more than a small hole in the rock face, but giving a breathtaking view of the sea and the bay in the distance. As children, she and Giles had climbed out onto the ledge of rock beyond the hole and perched there like kings of the castle, with Giles's father holding on firmly to the pair of them.

She looked on dubiously, however, when Alex climbed out and then reached back to help her out too. "I..." she began.

"It's quite safe," he assured her.

"I know. I've sat out there often with Giles."

"But you don't trust me?"

"I didn't say that!" Se wished he did not always make her feel as if she was being unduly bigoted towards him.

He still held out his hands and, without another word, she grasped them and allowed herself to be pulled out on to the ledge. "Now—wasn't it worth it?" he demanded, when she stood beside him, and she nodded.

"It's a wonderful view," she agreed. "I always felt as if I was above the whole world when I was up here."

"King of the castle," he said softly, then laughingly corrected himself. "No, that's Giles, isn't it? You're queen of the castle."

"Something like that," she agreed cautiously. "It's an exciting feeling."

He was looking at her intently, his black eyes heavy-lidded against the wind. "Did Giles enjoy it, too?" he asked.

"Yes. Yes, I think so." She was puzzled as to why he had seen fit to mention Giles at this particular moment, and in such a tone of voice. "Why do you ask?" she added, and he shrugged.

"Curiosity," he confessed. "I can well imagine Giles would like being king of the castle, in the same way he'll enjoy owning Penroyal when he gets it."

"Of course, he loves Penroyal, as I do." She could not have put her finger on her reason, but she suspected he was being critical of Giles again and, as always, she resented it. "He has every *right* to inherit Penroyal, you know," she told him. "He's the nearest male Pengelly."

"Of course." He was silent for a moment, his expression thoughtful. "But I rather think he's just as anxious to get the jade too, isn't he?"

"The jade? You know about the jade?" Of course he knew about the jade, she thought a moment later. It had belonged to his aunt until she died. He would be as familiar with the history of the jade as she was herself and probably more superstitious about it, too, but she was suspicious of his current interest in it.

He looked at her steadily, as if he expected her to deny or at least argue his right to know of it. "You forget it belonged to my father's sister until she died," he reminded her. "I know it's considered unlucky."

"But you hope Uncle Miklas leaves it to you?" she guessed, without really knowing why she said it.

He smiled wryly, his wide mouth looking slightly crooked, and the white teeth scarcely in evidence. "I thought you suspected my interest in it," he declared, "but I'm not at all sure I want it."

"But—" She wondered how honest he would be in his reply. "Suppose *you* get the jade," she said. "What would you do with it?"

The black eyes held hers for a moment before he shook his head. "Rather than risk the life of the girl I married," he said quietly, "I'd throw the cursed thing into the sea."

Bryony stared at him, startled by his apparent seriousness. "But it's beautiful," she objected. "And valuable."

"But neither as beautiful nor as precious as the girl I shall marry," he told her. "It may be only an old superstition, Bryony, but I'd never dare take the risk."

"I see." She raised her eyes and looked at him, half shyly. "She must be very beautiful, this girl you're going to marry."

He smiled, the wind tossing his thick black hair over his forehead. "Oh, she will be," he assured her softly. "When I find her."

"Oh. I see."

She felt as if she had ventured beyond the bounds of discretion, become too embarrassingly personal, and she felt a small cold shiver run along her spine as she tried to avoid his eyes and failed.

"I'm sure you don't." His voice was so quiet that she only just heard it above the sound of the wind and the waves. "Will Giles have the same fears, I wonder," he said, "or will he be prepared to take the chance?"

"I... I don't know." She could not answer more truthfully on Giles's behalf, although there was no doubt that Aunt Merrilyn would have something to say if he *did* attempt to refuse it on any grounds at all.

"Aren't you afraid?"

"Afraid?" She looked at him wide-eyed and uncertain. "I... I don't understand you."

His head was shaking slowly and there was a hint of mockery in the way he was looking at her. "No," he said, "you really don't, do you?"

"If you—"

"If Giles gets the jade, and you marry Giles," he pointed out, without waiting to hear what she had to say, "you have plenty of reason to be shivering in your shoes."

She stared at him for a moment, seeing her own possible involvement for the first time, then she shook her head. "I don't know where you get the idea from," she told him, "that I've any intention of marrying Giles."

He laughed then. A short, disturbing sound that was snatched away by the wind. "From Giles himself," he told her. "That's where I got the idea."

"You mean...he told you that I was going to marry him?" She could not for a minute imagine such a thing happening, but even Giles, she supposed, could be pushed to the brink of indiscretion by this provoking and, at times, maddening stranger in their midst.

He shook his head, but it was obvious from his expression that he thought it more than likely it would happen. "Not so far," he said, "but I've seen the way he looks at you, and that's evidence enough for anyone."

"No evidence at all without fact," she retorted, appreciating the use of legal language, that they both were familiar with.

"*Touché.*" He inclined his head in a mock bow, his more usual smile in evidence again. "But I have my instincts too, Bryony, and they tell me that poor old Giles is getting rather a bad case of heart disease."

"That's ridiculous!" she argued. Almost as ridiculous, she thought a second later, as the two of them standing up here, high above the sea, arguing about something that had nothing to do with Alex Patinous at all.

"It's true."

"Even if it is," she declared, lifting her chin and looking down her nose at him, "it need not concern you. You have no right at all to speak about...about Giles and I—"

"Giles and me," he corrected her softly, his black eyes gleaming wickedly as he recognized her resentment.

"How dare you correct me!" she fumed. "I know my own language well enough, thank you."

"And being a foreigner I don't, eh?" he asked, apparently unperturbed by her anger or her bigotry.

"Will you stop picking on me?" she said. "I'm trying to be...to be nice to you because you're a visitor, but—"

"So are you," he pointed out quietly, and laughed when she flushed pink with the frustration of trying to get the better of him.

"I'm going back," she told him, turning back to the small exit they had used, and shaking off the hands that immediately proffered help. "I can manage, thank you."

He followed her through the hole again, saying nothing until she hesitated on the narrow, dark steps, wondering whether to go up or down. "I'll go first." Once again the decision was made for her and she had little option but to follow him down the rest of the way to the lower cave, one hand, again, held firmly in his.

The sound of the sea grew louder and she was thankful for it in one way, for it made conversation virtually impossible. Her left hand groped its way along the cold dankness of the rock and she breathed an almost audible sigh of relief when, a moment later, a faint gleam of daylight showed up just around the next bend.

He turned briefly and looked back at her, his smile wide in the yellow light of the torch, lending his face the piratical look she found so disturbing. "Faint heart wins through," he taunted. "You'd never have made a good smuggler, Bryony."

She refused to be wheedled into laughing at her own fears and instead of smiling, lifted her chin again and did not answer. Only one more curve in the stone stairway, and they would be in another shallower cave that opened onto the rock-strewn beach where the sea raced up to the entrance every high tide, only to draw back again before it had done more than leave a tracery of damp sand, and a few bits of flotsam.

So anxious was she to end their precarious descent,

and so concentrating on keeping her chin high in defiance of his taunt, that she was less careful how she went down those last few steps. She felt herself falling and cried out, almost at the same moment as she caught her first glimpse of the welcome yawn of daylight in the cave's mouth.

Her cry was faint and almost lost in the roar of the approaching tide, tossed and tumbled in the wind, but before she had recovered her breath, she was caught and held against something warm and soft that threatened to smother her. It took her a second or two to realize that it was his sweater and that she was held with heart-stopping tightness in his arms.

A pulse in her forehead was throbbing wildly as he set her on her feet again, holding her at arm's length and smiling at her. "Okay?" he asked briefly, and she nodded.

"Yes—thank you." She sounded as breathless as she felt, and hoped fervently that he would not attribute it to other than her fall. She pushed at his hands that now rested on her shoulders, either side of her neck, but he resisted her, and his fingers moved caressingly against her skin.

"Did this happen the last time you were here?" he asked softly, and she felt the hot color in her cheeks as she sought to free herself.

"Let me go!" she said, breathless with indignation and something else she could not quite identify. "Let me go!"

"Of course." She had quite expected him to comply in view of his answer, but before she realized what was happening, he pulled her face closer to his and kissed her with such force that her head was pushed back against the fingers that now twined in her hair and held her still.

"Alex!"

She should have resisted, she knew, but there seemed little she could do but allow herself to be swept against him, her fingers spread over the strong, steady beat of his heart.

"If Giles does not make the most of his chances," he said throatily, a moment later, "I *do.*"

CHAPTER THREE

BRYONY KNEW it was inevitable that Aunt Merrilyn would make something more than there was of her visit to the caves with Alex Patinous, if only to show Giles what an unreliable and fickle creature she was. It was at dinner that evening that she chose to raise the subject and Bryony almost sighed audibly at the inevitability of it.

"Where did you and Mr. Patinous go this morning, Bryony dear?" she asked, after their coffee had been poured and they sat talking.

"Only to see a couple of the caves," Bryony told her, offhandedly, and glanced at Alex to see if she could rely on him not to be too forthcoming about the trip.

His expression was not very encouraging, but she thought he would probably not say too much, as much for his own sake as for hers, because he would not want to give Aunt Merrilyn the satisfaction of having something to crow about. "It was very interesting," he said, and only a raised eyebrow made the statement more meaningful to Bryony than it was to Giles and his mother.

"This area is full of interesting history," Aunt Merrilyn informed him rather loftily, not realizing what dangerous ground she was treading on. "The Pengellys have been here for hundreds of years, you know."

"So I believe," Alex said. "Miklas has told me quite a lot of the family history. I found it fascinating.

"Oh?" Finely marked brows expressed not only

surprise but dislike of the idea. "I hope you didn't get the wrong impression, Mr. Patinous. My brother is inclined to romance about the old days at times, and make things sound more—" she spread her hands delicately. "I hope you don't take too seriously everything he tells you."

"Oh, I think he knew what he was talking about," Alex told her quietly. "He takes a great deal of interest in the family history—he always has—and there's nothing wrong with his faculties, Mrs. Pengelly."

Aunt Merrilyn looked rather taken aback at being told so firmly that any effort to try and disguise the less reputable side of the story was useless. But Aunt Merrilyn was not to be defeated for very long, and her smile was deceptively sweet when she looked at him.

"I imagine your own ancestry is quite interesting, Mr. Patinous," she suggested. "One hears such stories of Greece that one wonders just how much of it could possibly be true."

"Oh, most of it, I expect," Alex allowed quietly, his black eyes holding her gaze steadily. "You should visit Greece one day, Mrs. Pengelly—after all, it's your own history, too, isn't it?"

Aunt Merrilyn always preferred to forget that she, too, was half-Greek, like Miklas, and her thin cheeks flushed a bright pink at being reminded of it. If Miklas was more than ready to acknowledge Alex as his cousin, Merrilyn was not prepared to.

"I never think of myself as anything but English, I'm afraid," she told him. "I don't remember my mother at all, and my upbringing was completely English. I count myself completely Pengelly."

"I see." Those unnerving black eyes surveyed her for a moment before flicking briefly to Bryony. "According to Miklas that makes for a pretty interesting ancestry, too."

"Whatever my brother may have told you about our family in the past," Aunt Merrilyn told him stiffly, "I advise you not to take it too seriously."

"You mean they *weren't* wreckers and smugglers?" he asked softly, looking unbelievably innocent despite the piratical features.

Aunt Merrilyn bit on her lip, her thin face expressing exactly what she thought of such impudence from an outsider and a stranger, even if he did claim kinship. "The Pengellys have nothing to be ashamed of, Mr. Patinous," she informed him coldly. "I have my doubts as to *that* part of our history."

His gaze flicked unerringly to Bryony and a faint smile touched his mouth as he sought her support. "Bryony believes it," he said. "Don't you, Bryony?"

"I...I'm not sure," she said. She had never felt so guilty in her life, she thought, and there was really no reason for her to. Even if it was true, it was scarcely logical for the descendants of those less law-abiding Pengellys to be held responsible for the sins of their forefathers.

"You said it was all right because everybody else was doing it," he insisted relentlessly. "Don't you remember?"

Bryony looked across at Giles and met a curious and not altogether encouraging gaze. "I...I didn't quite know what to say," she told her tormentor. "I suppose they could have been smugglers and probably wreckers, but it *was* generally accepted in this part of the world, and I don't quite see why I should be made to feel guilty about it two hundred or so years later."

"Oh, not that long, surely," Alex protested, a wicked grin making the most of her discomfort, until she could cheerfully have hurled her coffee at him, cup and all.

"I don't care how long ago it was," she declared. "It's not important in this day and age."

"Of course it isn't," Aunt Merrilyn said. "No one bothers about things that happened so long ago."

"Unless it's creditable," he said softly, and Bryony, who was possibly the only one who heard him properly, glared across at him angrily, her not inconsiderable temper showing itself in the brightness of her gray eyes.

They looked storm-dark in her flushed face and she was determined to defend her precious family heritage. "I wish you'd keep such...such insolent opinions to yourself, Mr. Patinous," she told him. "We have a lot to be proud of in our family and we don't take kindly to strangers trying to belittle us."

"Not belittle you," he denied, and his tone was just as polite and much less angry than her own. In fact, Bryony thought wildly, he was actually enjoying the exchange. "I'm sure none of us can bear too close scrutiny into our backgrounds."

"You speak for yourself," she retorted, and saw that even Aunt Merrilyn was aghast at her reaction.

Her antagonist, however, seemed quite willing to exchange insults with her, if that was what she wanted, and his black eyes gleamed at her. "Now we're getting down to basics," he said softly, and laughed.

"Bryony!" Aunt Merrilyn's sharp voice pulled her up short before she could deliver the retort she had ready and, much to her own surprise, she subsided as meekly as Giles might have done, her cheeks pink with anger and embarrassment.

"If you'll excuse me," she said, her voice throatily harsh, "I think I'll go and see Uncle Miklas before he gets too tired."

"Will you come for a walk with me after you've seen him?" Giles asked, and Bryony nodded.

It was impossible to guess what it was that made her angle her chin defiantly at Alex Patinous as she answered him. "Yes, I will, Giles," she told him, braving Aunt Merrilyn's frown of disapproval. "I won't be very long."

It was, in fact, nearly half an hour later that she left old Miklas's room, and the sky outside was already dark and scattered with crisp autumn stars that glittered above a now calm sea. She let out a sigh of sheer pleasure and peace as they strolled along the cliff top, the ground dropping steeply toward the old church. Her face huddled in her coat collar against the sharp autumn wind that ruffled her fair hair into dishevelment.

"Tired?" Giles asked, hearing her sigh, and she shook her head.

"No, I'm not tired, Giles. I was just thinking what a lovely night it is, and how I love being at Penroyal."

"So do I." He had a hand under her arm and his fingers curled tightly, almost possessively they walked in silence for a moment or two, then he looked down at her, as if trying to judge her reaction. "I just wish Patinous wasn't here too," he said at last.

Bryony smiled, guessing what was on his mind. "I don't let him bother me to that extent," she told him, not quite truthfully. "You should do the same, Giles."

"I can't. Not while he behaves the way he does with you."

She looked up at him, but could judge nothing of his expression in the starlit darkness. "How does he behave with me?" she asked, curious to hear his opinion.

"As you'd expect, Giles retorted. "For heaven's sake, Bryony, you must know the way he... he flirts with you every chance he gets."

"Does he?" She was surprised to hear him be so outspoken and suspected that Aunt Merrilyn had been the orignator of the suggestion. "You're imagining things, Giles."

"No, I'm not," he insisted, sounding very sure of

himself, as he usually did when he was out of earshot and sight of his mother. "He's a...a seducer if ever I saw one, and I wish he'd leave you alone."

She was glad of the enveloping darkness to hide the color that was in her cheeks, and wished they could have discussed almost any other topic but their fellow guest. "He does leave me alone," she informed him. "And I'm quite capable of taking care of myself, you know, Giles, I'm not a baby."

"You're very beautiful," Giles declared firmly, "and Patinous isn't the type to ignore a beautiful girl. It's his nature to be predatory—I've seen his sort before."

"So have I," said Bryony, wondering how the subject could have become so serious. "Don't worry about me, Giles, I can manage Alex Patinous if need be."

"If you can't, I damned soon will," Giles threatened darkly.

"I'm sure it won't be necessary." She had never known Giles to be so determinedly masterful before, and the experience was not unpleasant.

"What *did* you do this morning, Bryony?" he asked after a few minutes' silence, and she looked up at him, again, trying to see his face and judge what he expected her to say.

"We did as I told you," she said. "We went down the rock path and into the cave entrance, about halfway down. You remember the one your father used to take us to." He nodded. "Then we went down through the cave, down the steps and out onto the beach from the lower cave."

"Did he behave himself?"

"Yes." She had never been a very good liar, and she knew he would not fail to notice it.

"Bryony?"

"He...he did catch me when I fell down the last few steps in the cave," she told him, hoping it would not be necessary to go into details. Giles had never ben so curious about her activities before, and she felt quite sure that Aunt Merrilyn had been putting ideas into his head.

"You fell down some steps?" He sounded anxious now. "I didn't know that. Were you hurt?"

"No. No, of course not. He caught me before I actually fell and hurt myself."

"How very convenient," he jeered, then suddenly hugged her arm closely, in case she thought he was blaming her. "I wish you hadn't gone with him," he said. "If I hadn't had to take mother into Marby you could have come with me, but I had promised her, and there was nothing I could do about it."

"You could have asked me to come with you," she suggested.

"But you more or less said you didn't want to come with us," he protested. "If I'd known, Bryony, I'd have asked you."

"Aunt Merrilyn said I didn't want to," she reminded him. "I wasn't given a chance to say one way or the other, because you didn't ask me."

"I'm sorry."

"Oh, don't worry about it now," she told him. "It isn't that important. But when you don't even bother to ask me to come with you, Giles, you can't very well complain if I get roped in to act as guide to Alex Patinous."

"Didn't you enjoy it?"

She wondered just how honest she could be and still be tactful. "It was quite an experience," she said. "I'd forgotten how spooky those caves can be."

"Were you very frightened?" He looked very anxious about it and very serious. "I wish I'd gone with you now."

"I know, Giles, I wish you had, too." She thought she never remembered him being so serious as a boy, but then, of course, his father had been alive and he had not been the sole object of his mother's devotion.

"You know I'd much rather have been with you, don't you?"

"Would you?" She smiled up at him, although she knew he could not see her clearly. "We used to have some good times together, didn't we, Giles?"

"Marvelous," he agreed, and sounded so wistful that she thought he, too, was remembering his father. "And we could again," he said.

"I'm sure we could," she said softly. "Even if we're not children."

They were high up on the most exposed part of the cliff now, and the wind was more blustery, sighing around the old church as it stood, dark and ghostlike, only a couple of hundred yards away. Giles turned her around to face him and stood for a moment with his hands on her arms, his face a pale, uncertain blur in the darkness.

"We weren't really children the last time we were here," he said, and she wondered why her heart was beginning a hard, rapid beat under her ribs. Something in his voice warned her that Giles was seeking words as he had never sought them before, words that would make everything different. "I haven't seen you for such a long time," he said slowly, "but I've never forgotten you, you know."

"We had such a lot in common," Bryony said softly. "We shared so much of our childhood, Giles, we couldn't forget each other."

His hand lifted her chin and he looked down at her. "I thought you'd be beautiful when you got older," he said, his voice a little husky with emotion, "but I never realized how lovely you'd be. I can scarcely believe my eyes, every time I look at you."

"Giles. . . ." She was unsure if she wanted him to go on, although she felt only pleasurable excitement at the prospect of his feeling so deeply for her. It was her own feelings she was unsure of. Whether she would be in love with Giles as he was now, or the Giles she remembered, rather sentimentally, from her childhood.

"No, don't stop me," he begged. "I'm in love with you, Bryony. I suppose I always was a little in love with you, especially that last time."

"The last time," Bryony said with a reminiscent smile, "we were allowed to go to the caves on our own, weren't we?"

It was a little unkind of her, she supposed, to mock Aunt Merrilyn's possessiveness, but even then, when Giles was nearly twenty, she had disliked them going off on their own, and it was only the intervention of his father that had made their few trips together possible. Not that there had been any suggestion of anything serious between them, for Bryony had been far too young, but Aunt Merrilyn had been suspicious of her even then.

He was silent for a moment, and she wondered if he realized just how possessive his mother was, or if he was now so used to her ways that he did not even recognize that she was smothering him. "I'm afraid mother isn't always the easiest person to get on with," he told her, speaking slowly, as if he chose his words with care. "But she means well, Bryony, and it hasn't always been easy for her, you know."

"No, I suppose it hasn't," Bryony allowed, although she could not help thinking how much less easy it had been for her widowed father to provide a home and enough love for two parents, and without the help of a large income such as Aunt Merrilyn had.

"Things will get better," he said. "I mean—I know you think that mother is sometimes a bit—well, overpowering, and I suppose she is, but it'll be different when I have Penroyal."

"You're bound to have the house," Bryony agreed quietly. "But will it make all that much difference, Giles? Won't Aunt Merrilyn expect to come and live here with you?"

"Here at Penroyal?" He looked as if the idea had not only not occurred to him, but did not please him either.

"It was her home," she reminded him.

"Well, she has her own home now," he said, and his tone of voice left no doubt as to his intention. "Penroyal will be mine, and I can't have mother here, I'm afraid. It wouldn't work."

"You get along together, don't you?"

He laughed shortly. "Oh yes, we get along very well, but mother isn't going to take kindly to the idea of me having a wife, I'm afraid, and I shall be getting married, Bryony, as soon as you make up your mind to say yes."

"I... I don't think that will be yet," she told him, trying to sound as if she saw it only a long way in the future.

"You've known me long enough," he objected. "It shouldn't take you long to decide whether to marry me or not."

"You'll give me time to think about it, though?" she asked, and he nodded.

"Yes, of course, there's time yet."

Talking of marrying reminded her of the conversation she had had with Alex Patinous that morning, and she wondered what Giles's feelings were in connection with the jade and its reputation of bad luck. "I... I was wondering what will happen to the jade," she ventured, feeling her way carefully. "Will Uncle Miklas leave that to you as well, do you suppose?"

She knew he was frowning over the question even though she could not see his face. "I can't see that he has many people to leave it to," he said slowly. "There's only me, mother or you that have any right to it, surely."

"And Alex."

He made a sound somewhere between a short and a snarl and she flinched at the sound of it. "Patinous doesn't come into it," he said shortly. "It's the Pengelly jade and he has absolutely no right to it at all." He peered down at her suspiciously. "Does he claim he has?" he demanded.

"Not exactly," Bryony admitted. "But it did belong to his aunt, you know, and he's as closely related to Uncle Miklas as you are, Giles."

"He's not a Pengelly," Giles insisted stubbornly. "He has no right to it."

"Actually, he doesn't want it."

She had known that would have some such effect, and she could not help but feel a small prick of satisfaction at the soft intake of breath he gave, and the short silence that followed. "You seem very well informed about that," he told her. "But I doubt if he'll have the chance to refuse it. Uncle Miklas has too much family feeling to leave it to an outsider, and a foreigner."

"His cousin and your mother's," she reminded him again.

His silence was filled with meaning, and she thought that, until now, he had not even considered Alex Patinous as a likely inheritor of the jade, even if his mother had. "How do you know what he feels about the jade?" he asked, then.

"We... we talked about it, among other things, this morning," she said.

"Fishing, probably," Giles suggested shortly. "Wonders if he's going to get it."

"I told you, he doesn't want it. He said so."

Giles laughed harshly. "Sour grapes," he jeered. "I'll bet he'd keep it quick enough if it was left to him."

"Would *you*?"

"Keep it?" He sounded puzzled. "Yes, of course I would. What else would you imagine I'd do? It's a very valuable piece, even if we can't sell it."

"You...you wouldn't feel you were taking rather a chance when...when you married?"

"No, of course not," he informed her. "Good heavens, you don't actually believe that claptrap about it being unlucky, do you?"

"I don't know," Bryony demurred. "It hasn't been very lucky so far, has it?"

"It's nothing but coincidence and old wives' tales," he retorted. "I don't believe in superstitions and, quite frankly, Bryony, I'm surprised you even think about it."

She shrugged, made more uneasy by his attitude, although he had voiced no more than she had said to Uncle Miklas on the same subject. "Uncle Miklas more than half believes it," she told him, and he laughed shortly.

"It could be that Uncle Miklas listens to his Greek relatives too often," he said. "Alex Patinous has probably been filling his head with all that old rubbish, and he believes it."

"His mother died young," Bryony reminded him, determined to make her point, "and so did Uncle Miklas's wife. You wouldn't feel you were risking the life of your...your wife by keeping it?"

He shook his head vehemently, so that she felt the movement of it. "Absolutely not," he said, and raised her chin with one finger. "I wouldn't ask you to marry me if I thought there was the slightest danger attached to it," he added softly.

"I...I know."

"It won't influence your answer?" he asked, and she thought he sounded anxious.

"I—no, I don't think so."

"If it did, I *would* think about refusing it," he told her.

"You mustn't do that." She laughed softly. "Aunt Merrilyn would *never* forgive me then," she added.

"Then mother had better have the jade," he told her. "That way we both get what we want, don't we?"

"Do you?"

He bent his head and his lips were only inches from hers when he spoke. "I want you, Bryony, even if I have to give up the jade to have you, and from now on I want you to spend *all* your time with me. Don't let Patinous come between us."

Bryony blinked at the idea of that, ready to deny it. "Of course he won't do that," she declared.

"I hope not." He sought her mouth and kissed her in a way that she would never have believed him capable of, and when he released her she was far too light-headed to say anything more than his name. "I love you," he told her, close to her ear. "I love you, Bryony."

"You...you said you'd give me time to think about it," she reminded him, and he nodded, seemingly quite self-confident about the outcome.

"Think about it," he told her. "But remember I love you, whatever else you forget."

"I'll remember," she promised, and remembered, too, that if Giles did inherit the Pengelly jade he would expect her to accept the fact that he did not believe in its sinister reputation, and the shiver that trickled along her spine did not only stem from the chill wind blowing in from the sea.

CHAPTER FOUR

It was perhaps rather silly of her to have come out and to have walked so far when it looked like being misty, Bryony thought, but she had been convinced that it would come to nothing much until later in the evening, and she felt she really had to get out of the house for a while.

Aunt Merrilyn had been extra trying today, probably because she suspected that Giles's feeling for her had become something more than youthful nostalgia. Aunt Merrilyn would make a formidable enemy and an even more formidable mother-in-law.

Even Uncle Miklas had been less welcoming today than usual when she looked in to see him, and Giles had been obliged to go back to London unexpectedly. There were, he explained before he went, certain things that one could not delegate to a deputy, and he was obliged to go, or there would be a minor crisis. Bryony felt rather more lost without him than she cared to admit, and she had, perhaps, been a bit out of temper herself.

She had rather huffily refused Alex Patinous's company and set off on her own, enjoying the brisk wind and the sharp nip in the air as she strode along, hands in her pockets, head up, hair flying behind her. It was almost guaranteed to improve her disposition, a walk along the cliff tops and back, and that was what she planned to do.

She planned to walk along the cliff top as far as Marby Bay, and then back along the beach, taking her time and only getting back in time for a quick change and clean up before dinner. There was plenty of time, she told herself, and the mist would not come down until late evening at the earliest.

She discovered her mistake when she was a little more than halfway back along the white sandy beach and the mist began to descend rapidly. She shivered, even in her warm sweater, and got the impression that she had been cut off from the rest of the world by the thick, swirling white mist that clung to her face and hair.

She walked doggedly on, for the simple reason that there was little else she could do. If she turned back she would have to wait for a bus out of Marby Bay and that would take nearly as long as it would for her to walk back, and the journey itself was long and slow. Much better to keep on going.

She could hear the sea on her left, and would have been unworried except that she was getting uncomfortably damp and chill and she knew there was a high tide soon. She was obliged to slow her pace because visibility was very low and, where she would normally have had plenty of time to beat the tide to the highest points, she was now cutting things a bit fine.

The mist got thicker as she left the lower-lying area and it swirled around the high rock cliffs, making it almost impossible to see at all. The coldness of it crept into her bones and clung in moist drops to her eyelashes. It seemed to her that the sound of the sea was growing uncomfortably close, but as yet she could see nothing of it, and for that, at least, she breathed a sigh of relief. Keeping close to the rocks, she made her way carefully, having to detour around some of the bigger outbreaks that marched across the beach and impeded her way.

At last she thought she recognized something familiar and smiled her relief, only to pull a wry face a moment later when the first wave rolled up to the mouth of the cave and momentarily blocked it. The only solution was to wait until there was time between the waves and then run into the cave before the next one came.

A small roller surged up to the mouth of the cave and, after a second, retreated. Bryony ran as fast as she could, her feet slow and dragging on the damp sand, and just failed to beat the next arrival. It broke soakingly over her feet and legs and sucked at her feet as it drew back, leaving her only a few seconds to gain the comparative dryness of the cave.

The steps that she had so laboriously climbed down with Alex only a couple of days before looked so easily accessible, but she hesitated to use them alone and in the dark. No doubt her former companion would have been very disparaging about her lack of courage, but, somehow, the idea of climbing that interminable stairway alone daunted her as little else did.

It was not the way she had planned to return, but she knew that trying to negotiate the cliff path in this mist was far too dangerous, and the steps up into the cave were the only alternative unless she was to stay down here all night. At least on the steps she would have the walls to guide her upward, even if she was in darkness.

It was rather spooky once she had left behind what little daylight there was, and she already regretted her decision not to chance the cliff path. The sound of her own footsteps made her think of the tales about her less reputable ancestors and she had the uneasy feeling that they were watching her and passing judgment on her lack of courage.

She remembered, as she toiled upward, that she had told Uncle Miklas her intention of returning along the beach and up the cliff path. She was later than she had meant to be, by now, and she hoped he was not worrying about her; if he was, there was little she could do about it except prepare for a lecture on her foolishness when she got back.

The gallery that she had visited with Alex gave her a few minutes' respite from the daunting darkness, and she sat on the edge of the small exit hole for a few minutes, even though it meant her getting more wet from the mist that swirled in through the opening and wisped, ghostlike, as far as the poor daylight extended up the rest of the steps.

It took even more determination to start on the second part of her climb and she clenched her teeth as she started upward again. For a few feet the dampness of the mist followed her, then it was still and completely dark again. Once, she thought she heard the sound of a voice somewhere above her and she stopped, wide-eyed in the blackness, staring upward but seeing nothing, her heart thumping heavily against her ribs.

It was nothing but her own fancy, of course, but she felt more afraid than she had ever done in her life and she prayed that the first glimmer of gray daylight would appear soon on the wall above her. Around another turn in the tortuous stairway, she stopped again, her breath tight in her throat, listening as other footsteps came down toward her.

"Bryony!" She put her hands to her ears, knowing she could not really hear her name being called, her heart thudding rapidly as her name echoed round the rock walls.

"Bryony!"

Again that deep, slightly unreal voice bounced and echoed against the dark walls and she covered her mouth and stood there, rooted to the spot. There was silence for a while, even the footsteps had stopped, and she put her hand to the wall again, feeling she needed its support now more than ever as she began, cautiously, to climb again.

A faint gray light on the wall above her brought tears of relief to her eyes and she was perhaps a little less careful how she walked, for, a second later, a small piece of loose rock slid from under her left foot and sent her flying back against the wall, while a cry of despair echoed all around her.

For a second or so she merely clung to the damp wall, trying to recover her breath, then she turned her head sharply as something else drew her eyes. A yellow light flickered on the wall briefly, first one side, then the other, and she closed her eyes hastily.

All the stories she had ever heard of her smuggling ancestors came into her head in one terrifying jumble and she opened her eyes again to watch the shifting yellow light, unable to move or cry out. It came slowly down the steps, and she was almost ready to scream when the face came into view. A dark-visaged, piratical face with the yellow light playing on the rugged contours of it and making it appear like something out of a nightmare.

"Bryony!"

It was seconds before she sobbed her relief and flopped limply into the arms that waited to catch her. "I—I thought you were—were—" She could not go on, but buried her face against the soft dampness of his sweater feeling as if her legs would give way under her at any minute.

"Take it easy, now, take it easy." A hand stroked her hair and at the same time soothed her frayed nerves, and she was content to cling to him for as long as it took her to realize the position she was in, then she leaned away from him and rubbed a hand over her dirty, tearstained face.

"You frightened the life out of me," she accused, her voice still shaky and uncertain, and she saw the whiteness of a grin light the dark face.

"I thought it was you," Alex told her. "Now I know it is."

"How...how did you know where I was?"

"Miklas told me you were planning to come back along the beach and when there was no sign of you, I concluded that even you had enough sense to give the cliff path a wide berth in this mist. So I fetched a torch and came down here to see if you were coming back this way."

He shone the torch full on her face, so that she turned her head away sharply from the brightness of it after being so long in the dark. "Don't do that!" She realized she was probably being very petulant and childish, especially when he had taken the trouble to come and find her.

Reaction, she told herself, was taking its toll. First the mist, then the long dark climb up the cave steps, and his sudden and frightening appearance were enough to make anyone edgy. She need not have worried about his being offended, however, for he was till smiling at her, the light of the torch playing on the wall behind her.

"Are you all right?" he asked. "I thought I heard you cry out just now."

Her legs were still trembling and she felt a bit tearful still, but the worst of her ordeal was over and she must make an effort to pull herself together. "I stepped on a loose piece of rock," she explained. "And I nearly went backward down the steps again."

"You're sure you didn't hurt yourself?"

"Quite sure," she said. "I—I'm fine."

"Hmm." He sounded as if he doubted it, and put a hand under her arm to support her. "If you can manage it now, we'll go on." She nodded, and she started up the steps again, this time feeling more confident, with the torch to guide them and with Alex following.

There was still the rest of the cliff path to negotiate and she looked upward into the mist, her heart sinking as she faced it. "Are you feeling up to it?" he asked.

Bryony looked at him, dark and rugged as the rocks behind him, and slightly unreal in the swirling mist. "I haven't much option, have I?" she asked.

"I could go up and get a rope if it would make you feel better," he offered. "Would you rather wait here, while I go?"

She shook her head hastily, dreading the thought of being abandoned on this lonely ledge. "No," she said. "No, please don't leave me, I'll...I'll be okay."

She did not understand the word he replied, but concluded that it was something in his own tongue, and it must have been complimentary, judging by his expression. Then he reached for her hand and led the way up the steep path as surely as a mountain goat, his long legs making little of the climb.

She should have been the one who led the way, she thought, as she followed him upward. She was the one who had been here so often as a child, and knew these paths so well, yet it was this dark, self-confident stranger who took the initiative and held tightly to her hand to reassure her.

He strode up the steep rocky path as if he had spent all his life here, looking back once or twice to see how well she was coping with the climb. "Would you like to stop for a moment?" he asked once, and Bryony shook her head without speaking. His smile told her that it was the answer he had expected and he said something in his own tongue which seemed to be amusing, for he smiled to himself as he turned away again.

Her relief was so great as they reached the top of the

path and stood once more on firm, flat ground that she closed her eyes for a moment, feeling horribly unsteady on her feet. At once the ready arm was around her waist again, strong and reassuring, and she instinctively leaned against him.

"Bryony!" He sounded anxious. "Are you all right?"

She nodded, trying to smile, wishing she did not feel so much like a forlorn child. She had never considered herself a helpless little female, and yet whenever she was with Alex Patinous, it was the feeling he gave her. Her hair was damp and clung to her head, darker than its usual light gold color, and wisps of it stuck to her cheeks giving her a sad, gamin look that, had she realized it, made her look very appealing.

"I'm okay," she told him. "Just glad to be on terra firma again."

"I thought you had been brought up to clamber up and down these rocks," he said. "Have you lost your nerve, now that you are older?" A smile took the edge off the gibe, but she still resented it and frowned at him.

"It's a long time since I was here," she told him, ready as ever to defend her behavior. "I'm badly out of practice, and, also, I'm not a schoolgirl any longer."

The black eyes swept over her swiftly and eloquently so that there was no mistaking his meaning, and he put a hand under her arm again. "I had noticed that," he said quietly. "Come—the sooner you can get out of those wet clothes the better." She was once more urged along at a pace which left her a little breathless, even though the faster movement sent the blood tingling through her body and warmed her.

"I...I'm all right," she insisted.

"So you keep telling me," he retorted. "But you look like an abandoned orphan and very cold. We must get you home and out of those wet things."

"But I can't keep up ith you," she protested. "You're walking much too fast."

He stopped then, and looked down at her as if she was indeed a child, and a fractious one at that. "Very well," he allowed at last. "I will walk a little slower, and you will put on my jacket to keep you warm."

He took off the thick tweed jacket he wore and put it around her shoulders. She snuggled into it gratefully, hugging the warmth of his body to her while he smiled enigmatically as they started toward the house once more.

There was no sign of Aunt Merrilyn when they walked into the hall, and Bryony thanked heaven for it, for she would have been neither sympathetic nor understanding, and she would almost certainly have made something of her return with Alex Patinous and the fact that she was wearing his jacket.

"Go upstairs quickly and change," Alex urged as they crossed the hall, and she nodded, willing enough this time to do as she said without argument. "I'll make some coffee for you."

"There's no . . . ." she began, and he raised an imperious hand to silence her.

"There *is* need," he told her firmly. "You are cold and wet, and we do not want a pneumonia patient to look after. Now go, quickly."

"You are the most—arrogant man I've ever had the misfortune to meet!" she told him shortly, her face aflame, her eyes glinting angrily at his summary manner.

"That may be so," he told her, apparently undeterred by her criticism. "But you still need hot coffee when you have bathed and changed. Now, if you will excuse me, I'll see to it."

She watched him walk away from her across the hall, his straight back and arrogantly held head uncaring for her anger and disapproval. Alex Patinous was a law unto himself, it seemed, and he cared nothing for anyone's opinion.

She started to climb the stairs to her room, remembering suddenly, as she went, that she had not even thanked him for coming to look for her, and she leaned over the banister, the heavy jacket still held around her tightly.

"Alex!"

He turned, one brow raised, his black eyes curious and disconcertingly steady as he looked at her. "Thank you for... thank you for coming to find me."

He smiled slowly. "You are welcome," he told her in a voice more solemn than the laughter that lurked in his eyes. "Now will you please go and get out of those wet things?"

She smiled instinctively at the change of manner and looked at him from under her lashes as she started up the stairs again. "Certainly," she agreed, "and I look forward to that coffee."

She bathed and changed into dry clothes, reveling in the pleasure of bodily comfort again, and thinking almost longingly of the coffee she had been promised. She smoothed down the yellow wool dress she had put on and looked for a moment at her reflection. An idle study, she nevertheless noticed that her cheeks were still warm and pink and her eyes still brighter than normal. She was none the worse for her ordeal, although she would not easily forget it.

Through the mirror she caught sight of Alex Patinous's jacket lying on a chair and frowned thoughtfully. There seemed little point in taking a damp jacket downstairs to him, since it was unlikely he would want it again at the moment. Also if Aunt Merrilyn was in the sitting room, as was likely, she did not want to be seen returning the jacket.

Much better, she decided, to put it in his room for

him, as she passed. If she draped it over a chair it would be easily found and, at the same time, dry out before he wanted it again.

She rapped softly on his bedroom door a few minutes later, then opened it cautiously when there was no reply, feeling oddly shy as she stood in the doorway for a hesitating second or two with the coat clutched to her chest. There was a chair standing just inside the door and she draped the coat on the back of it.

She came out as quietly as she had gone in and almost cried out with surprise as she closed the door. "Bryony!"

She turned startled eyes. "Aunt Merrilyn!"

The shrewd, sharp eyes were narrowed and the small mouth pursed suspiciously. "What on earth," she asked in a dangerously sweet voice, "are you doing in Mr. Patinous's room?"

"Nothing, Aunt Merrilyn." She knew her cheeks were flaming and cursed her luck at having to meet the one person she wanted most to avoid at this moment.

"Really?" The thin brows rose doubtfully. "How very odd to go visiting other people's rooms for no reason."

"I should have said, nothing important," Bryony amended, wishing she did not feel so guilty. There was something about Aunt Merrilyn that always made her feel she was doing something she shouldn't have been doing.

"Is Mr. Patinous out?"

Bryony shook her head. "No, he's downstairs in the sitting room."

"I see."

She was not being believed, that was obvious, Bryony thought, and wished she had not bothered returning the darn jacket until some other time. "Actually," she said, "I was returning Alex's coat. He loaned it to me earlier because I was so cold."

Aunt Merrilyn looked at her for a moment in silence, then she turned her around slowly so that Bryony stood with her back to her. "Do let me help you with your dress, my dear," she said sweetly. "You haven't zipped it properly. Perhaps you dressed in rather a hurry."

"Thank you." The zipper on her dress was undone for about three or four inches, because she was never able to reach it properly. It was only when she turned back again and saw the meaningful look that Aunt Merrilyn gave, first at her and then at the closed door of Alex Patinous's room, that she realized which direction Aunt Merrilyn's thoughts were traveling in, and she looked at her with stormy eyes, her hands clenched tight at her sides.

"I can't reach that zip properly, Aunt Merrilyn," she told her. "That's why my dress was undone."

"Of course if you say so, my dear Bryony, you know best."

"I *do* know best," Bryony insisted. "And I dislike your implication, Aunt Merrilyn."

"My dear child, I made no—implication, as you call it."

"But you...."

"The implication was yours, Bryony." The hard, dark eyes dared her to argue the point.

"Aunt Merrilyn—" she shrugged resignedly. It was pointless arguing with her, since she would never be believed, except when her aunt saw Alex downstairs for herself.

"Have you been out in this mist?" Aunt Merrilyn asked, and Bryony nodded. "You must have got very wet. It's really a silly thing to do. Has Mr. Patinous been out in it too?"

"He has," said Bryony. "He's downstairs now, getting me some coffee, I hope."

"Oh, yes?"

The ramrod back made its way downstairs, and Bryony

followed, feeling quite murderously inclined. Really, there was no limit to Aunt Merrilyn's imagination when it came to thinking the worst. Well, the appearance of Alex in the sitting room would soon put her firmly in her place. She followed Aunt Merrilyn into the room, fully expecting to see him there, and bit her lip when he wasn't.

Aunt Merrilyn curled her lower lip. "He *isn't* here, as you can see," she told her. "He isn't down yet, as I thought."

"But—" Bryony stared wide-eyed at the empty room, then back at her tormentor. "He should be here," she insisted, but faintly.

"But he isn't."

Bryony met the sharp, suggestive look in her eyes and turned and fled, closing the door noisily behind her. She would have gone back upstairs, but as she made her way across the hall, the door into the kitchen opened and Alex came out, a wide smile on his face, one finger beckoning to her.

She hurried over, her cheeks flaming, her hands clenched at her side, ready to blame him for her embarrassment. "Where were you?" she demanded, and he looked momentarily surprised.

"Where was I, when?" he asked, his eyes already showing a hint of laughter as he looked at her flushed face and stormy eyes.

"Where were you when I came downstairs with Aunt Merrilyn?"

"I expect I was in the kitchen making your coffee," he told her. "Mrs. Trevellyan's out for the afternoon. Didn't you know?"

She shook her head, following him into the cosy warmth of the kitchen, her face a picture of doubt. "No, I didn't know," she said.

Alex looked at her curiously as he poured out two cups of coffee. "Why does it matter where I was when you came downstairs with Aunt Merrilyn?" he asked.

"Because I've just had the most awful five minutes with her," Bryony told him. "And if you'd been in the sitting room where I expected you to be, it wouldn't have been so bad."

He was definitely laughing at her now, and she glared at him stormily. "I'm sorry," he said. "But, perhaps, if I knew what you were talking about, I might be more sympathetic."

"I doubt it," she retorted, sipping the hot coffee gratefully. She knew he was watching her, waiting to be enlightened, and at the moment she was feeling far too angry to explain anything to him.

"May I ask why I was supposed to be in the sitting room at the given time?" he asked, in his precise English.

"I've never been so humiliated in my whole life," Bryony complained. "I quite expected you to be there."

He looked at her over the rim of his cup, his eyes gleaming wickedly. "If you don't come to the point," he told her, "I shall probably go berserk."

"It's Aunt Merrilyn," Bryony explained at last. "She caught...saw me coming out of your room."

"Indeed?" His brows shot upward and he laughed softly, his eyes studying her face thoughtfully. "That sounds very, very interesting."

"Aunt Merrilyn thought so too," Bryony retorted, more angry than ever because he thought it amusing.

"Would you mind enlarging on that?"

"Do I have to?" she asked shortly, and he nodded.

"If you please." He sounded, she thought wildly, as if he was in court.

"I was taking your jacket back to your room. I thought

if I hung it over the back of a chair," she hastened to explain, "it would dry before you wanted it again."

"Thoughtful of you."

Bryony flushed. "You've no need to be sarcastic," she told him. "I didn't think it was worth carrying it all the way downstairs."

"And risking Aunt Merrilyn seeing you?" he suggested softly.

Bryony nodded ruefully. "As it was, she came along just as I was leaving your room."

He shook his head, but she thought it was more as a condemnation for her carelessness than regret for her being caught. "And knowing Cousin Merrilyn, she put it in the worst possible light," he guessed, and she realized he was still quietly laughing to himself at her predicament.

"Of course she did," Bryony said, not sharing his amusement. "And that—" She bit her lip hastily.

He raised a black brow at her questioningly. "And that was not all?" he guessed. "Am I right?"

She glared at him angrily, reluctant to give him anything else to laugh at. "No, you're *not* right," she denied.

His gaze was disconcertingly steady and she hastily lowered her eyes. "I think I am," he said quietly. "Please tell me the rest, Bryony."

He could be very persuasive, she thought wildly, and bit her lip hard, because she knew he would find the rest of the episode even more to his taste. "To make matters worse—"

"Can they get worse?" he asked softly. "Do tell me. I think I have a right to know if I am involved in something." His shoulders added to the expressive use of his hands. "I like to know what it is," he said.

"It—it was my dress," she began, feeling horribly

gauche as she sought for the right words. "I couldn't reach the zipper to do it up properly and—and it was open a few inches when Aunt Merrilyn saw me." Her cheeks were bright red, she knew, and she was furious when she realized he was laughing again.

"Mmm," he said softly. "You were in a predicament. Is that why you hoped I would be in the sitting room?"

"Yes, of course it is," Bryony said shortly. "If you'd been there she'd have known you couldn't have been in your own room when... well, when I came out of it."

"And now she will never know, will she?" he asked, seemingly unconcerned either for his own reputation or hers. "After all, I've had plenty of time to come downstairs since then, have I not?"

"You have," she declared. "And Aunt Merrilyn will have thought of that too."

And you are worried about it, hmm?"

"Of course I'm worried about it," Bryony told him. "At least, I don't like her getting the wrong idea about me, not in that direction anyway."

"It is all rather making a mountain out of a molehill, isn't it?" he suggested with a smile that dismissed the whole thing as much too trivial to worry about.

"I suppose it is," she admitted.

"Then why not just ignore it?" He looked at her and laughed softly to himself at her fears. "You look so solemn," he told her.

"Alex, I don't think it's funny!"

He made a wry face. "No, I don't suppose *you* do," he allowed. "And I'm quite sure Cousin Giles will have something to say about it."

"Aunt Merrilyn will be sure to tell him," she said. "I... I think Giles will believe me, but he *won't* think it's funny." She glared at his smiling face reproachfully.

He drank another mouthful of coffee and smiled.

"Well, I don't see things in quite the same light," he told her, "so you'll have to forgive me if I *do.*"

"If it wasn't for wasting good coffee," Bryony told him darkly, "I'd tip this all over you."

His laughter echoed around the old kitchen again and she looked at him, her eyes stormy gray. There was no doubt at all that Aunt Merrilyn would relay the episode, as she saw it, to Giles, and that idea was discomfiting enough, but what worried her most was if she also saw fit to tell Uncle Miklas about it.

She thought he was only as moral as most elderly men are, but whether he would tolerate what Aunt Merrilyn implied was another matter, and, apart from anything else, she hated to have the old man's liking for her destroyed by a stupid mistake.

"Alex." She got to her feet, unwilling to face anything sitting down.

"Hmm?"

"Will you—I mean, could you tell Uncle Miklas about it?"

He, too, got up from the table and perched himself on the edge of it, his eyes watching her curiously. "Why?" he asked. "Do you think she'll tell him?"

"I know she will."

"Hmm." He reached for her hands and drew her closer to him, his eyes searching her face. "I won't ask why you don't want Miklas to think the worst of you," he told her softly. "I know it isn't because you're afraid of being cut off without a penny, so I'll tell him. Okay?"

She nodded. "Thank you, Alex."

"Any time." He smiled at her solemn face and squeezed her hands gently. "Cheer up," he told her. "Aunt Merrilyn isn't all-powerful. I have a certain amount of pull with Miklas, too, you know. He'll know who to believe."

"I know—I know he will."

"Then smile, hmm?" He leaned forward and planted a kiss on her mouth just as Aunt Merrilyn opened the kitchen door and put her head around, missing nothing of the scene nor failing to make the most of what she saw.

"I'm *so* sorry," she apologized sweetly. "I didn't realize.'

Bryony could feel the warmth of color in her face and guessed she must look both embarrassed and guilty, however little reason there was for her to. It was Alex, self-assured as ever, who answered her.

"No need to apologize, Mrs. Pengelly," he told her blithely. "Did you want Bryony for something?"

Bryony hated the look of sharp satisfaction in her eyes and she found it difficult not to make a hasty and brusque explanation. However that would have made matters worse, and she had no hope of being believed anyway.

"I only came to tell you," Aunt Merrilyn said, in her very sweetest voice, "that Giles is coming back tonight, but I don't suppose it matters to anyone but me, really, does it?"

CHAPTER FIVE

DINNER THE NIGHT BEFORE had not been a very enjoyable meal, thanks to Aunt Merrilyn's obvious pleasure at having seen Bryony with Alex in the kitchen and Alex's refusal to be contrite about it. In fact, she was almost as angry with him for refusing to treat it seriously as she was with Aunt Merrilyn. She was not looking forward to breakfast this morning at all.

Not that she wouldn't be glad to see Giles back, but she disliked being misjudged on anything and particularly on her moral behavior. However innocent that kiss had been, Aunt Merrilyn would never believe it anything but proof positive that Bryony was having an affair with Alex Patinous. It was really too bad, she thought, that everyone seemed determined to make things difficult for her.

She was quite concerned, too, as well as curious, to know just how much Aunt Merrilyn had told Giles last night. He had arrived back rather late and most of the household had already gone to bed, but Aunt Merrilyn had insisted on waiting for him, and there was no doubt in Bryony's mind what her reason was for doing so. She had heard Giles's car arrive, but it was nearly half an hour later when she heard him and his mother come upstairs.

Bryony lay there, awake early, watching the first pale fingers of sun sneak in between a gap in the curtains, and thought ruefully that today was going to be one of those days. She could feel it in her bones and, not for the first time, she pondered on possible reasons why Aunt Merrilyn disliked her so much. It made things very difficult both for her and Giles, and it would make them even more so if Giles was to tell his mother that he intended to marry her.

She left it until the very last minute before she bathed and dressed and went down to breakfast, rather vainly hoping that everyone else would have already breakfasted and gone. When she walked into the room, however, three pairs of eyes looked up, and she could tell from the expression in Giles's that her guess had been right. Aunt Merrilyn had wasted no time.

Giles did not, however, give Alex the opportunity to perform his usual service of seeing her seated and pouring her coffee, but took on the duty himself, but after only the most perfunctory greeting. Alex, deprived of his chores, looked at her with an exaggeratedly raised brow, but said nothing beyond his normal cheerful greeting.

"Was...was your trip successful?" Bryony asked Giles, aware of Aunt Merrilyn's sharp eyes fixed on her.

"Yes, thanks."

"I'm glad you didn't have to be away too long."

"Are you?" Again his answer was brief, monosyllabic, and she began to feel the first prick of resentment at his manner.

It was obvious that he did not intend to enlighten her further either about his trip or anything else, and she realized she was fighting a losing battle against Aunt Merrilyn's gossiping. It was most unfair of him, she thought, to judge her on that alone, without giving her a chance to speak for herself.

"He saw an old friend while he was in London, didn't you, Giles?" his mother asked, and it was obvious Giles did not like the question, for he looked distinctly uneasy.

"I saw quite a few people, mother, but I had very little time to say much to any of them. I was too anxious to get back." The last was addressed directly to Bryony and she was a little puzzled by his attitude. He seemed almost as if *he* was feeling guilty about something, and the reason for it perplexed her. He looked sheepish, she decided, after another hasty look, instead of showing disapproval as she had expected. It was rather disconcerting.

"Oh, but it was lovely, you bumping into Sylvia like that, dear, wasn't it?" Aunt Merrilyn insisted in her pseudosweet voice. "Such a happy coincidence."

Bryony looked across at Giles, realizing at last the reason for his discomfiture, and feeling a bit sorry for him. Apparently his visit to London had not been without incident or confined to business, but his mother's attempts to convey as much to Bryony was obviously not to his liking, and he frowned.

"Mother, bumping into Sylvia *was* coincidence and that's all," he said shortly. "We exchanged a few words and then parted."

"Sylvia Greenaway is *such* a nice girl," Aunt Merrilyn assured Bryony with a smile. "So well bred and not a bit modern or... or loose-living as so many girls are now." *That*, Bryony thought, was a direct gibe at herself, and she felt the color in her cheeks as she fought to remain quiet. "She's the goddaughter of Lady Coulson, you know," Aunt Merrilyn went on remorselessly, "and very attractive."

"Is she?"

It was obvious that Aunt Merrilyn had plans for Giles and the desirable Miss Greenaway, whoever she might be, and wanted Bryony to know about it. Giles, on the other hand, seemed not to share his mother's enthusiasm, and he was apparently worried in case Bryony thought he did.

"Lady Coulson is a friend of mother's," he explained, his eyes watching Bryony anxiously. "Sylvia spends quite a lot of time with her. That's how I met her, and what with dinners and charity things all the time, you know how it is. I suppose I see quite a bit of her, one way and another."

"Giles—" his mother intervened determinedly—"don't sound so much as if you're apologizing, dear. I'm sure Bryony understands that things are different for you and Sylvia. I mean, I don't suppose she goes to dinners and charity gatherings very often, do you, Bryony dear?"

"Not very often," Bryony agreed, her eyes bright with resentment for the way she was being treated as a poor relation. "I'm usually too busy earning my living, although I have been known to go to a theater sometimes."

"Bryony—" Giles looked at her anxiously, but Aunt Merrilyn was satisfied that she had the upper hand now and she meant to make the most of it.

"I expect Sylvia is missing you, isn't she, Giles?" she asked, and Giles frowned at her.

"Of course she isn't, mother," he snapped. "Why on earth should she be?" Bryony had never heard him speak so sharply to his mother before and she saw the look of surprise on Aunt Merrilyn's face.

"Giles dear, you *do* sound cross," she reproached him, then smiled. "But I expect you're tired. You were rather late last night, weren't you? You should have stayed in town overnight again, instead of rushing back."

"I wanted to get back to...." He looked at Bryony for a moment, then shrugged and gave his attention to his meal again. "I suppose I needn't have bothered," he added grimly.

As much for her own benefit as for his, Bryony wanted to speak to Giles alone and she eventually managed it during the morning, although it was difficult to give Aunt Merrilyn the slip. She seemed determined not to let Giles see her alone and kept him busy for as long as she possibly could.

They sat at last, on the cliff top in the sun, hugging their knees and looking down at the gray blue sea that rolled restlessly under a brisk wind. It had been a favorite place of theirs in the old days, and Bryony hoped that in some way it would help to make her task easier.

"I don't know quite how to begin, now that it comes to the point," she confessed. "I wanted to talk to you, Giles, because I know—I can guess, that Aunt Merrilyn's told you about what she *thought* she saw yesterday."

He turned his head and looked at her steadily, his brown eyes uncertain and rather unhappy. "I don't want to believe it, Bryony," he said. "But what else could I do when mother told me?"

"You could have waited until you'd listened to the truth," Bryony suggested. "I'd like you to hear my side of it, Giles, if only because I object to having my reputation shredded for no reason at all."

"*Did* mother catch you coming out of his room?" he asked, and she frowned.

"She *saw* me coming out of Alex's room," she corrected him quietly. "And as Alex wasn't in there at the time, I couldn't quite see what all the fuss was about."

"But he wasn't downstairs, as you claimed, either," Giles insisted, willing to be convinced, but unsure if he was.

"He was in the kitchen making coffee," Bryony told him. "We were both pretty wet after being out in that wretched mist, but I was soaked through and shivering with cold. Alex volunteered to make me some hot coffee and I wasn't going to argue with him. I was too glad of his help."

"You'd had to change your clothes?"

She smiled wryly. Obviously Aunt Merrilyn had omitted nothing in the telling. "That's right, and I couldn't reach the zipper in my dress properly to do it up," she said. "If Aunt Merrilyn had been really observant, she'd have noticed that I wasn't wearing the same clothes I'd gone out in. As to why I was in Alex's room," she added, when she saw the question looming, "he'd lent me his jacket because I was so cold, and I was returning it. Also, as I'm sure your mother will have told you," she went on relentlessly, "he took it into his head to kiss me."

"Why?"

She laughed shortly, lifting her chin and letting the wind blow through her hair and cool her cheeks. "I could take exception to that question," she told him. "It's not very flattering, especialy when you tell me I'm pretty. I don't quite know why he kissed me, but it was an extremely chaste and passionless kiss and by way of being a sort of reassurance, I think. He'd promised to let Uncle Miklas know that there was nothing to the story, before Aunt Merrilyn told him otherwise," she added.

Giles looked almost startled for a moment, then he sighed and shook his head. "Yes. I suppose it's inevitable, isn't it?"

"It wouldn't be so bad if it was true," Bryony claimed. "I couldn't say much about it then."

"But it isn't?"

She shook her head vehemently. "No, of course it isn't."

He was silent for quite a few minutes. Obviously weighing up the evidence, she thought dryly. Then he reached out and took her hand in his. "I didn't think I knew you so little," he said softly. "I'm sorry I ever doubted you, Bryony."

"I dislike being maligned for something I didn't do," she told him with a rueful laugh. "If I was really promiscuous, I suppose, I'd take Aunt Merrilyn in my stride."

Giles sighed. "I know," he agreed, "and I'm sorry about it, darling, but—"

"But Aunt Merrilyn would rather you showed more interest in Sylvia Greenback, or whatever her name is, and less in me."

He looked uneasy again, his eyes downcast, his fingers twined tightly with hers. "Mother likes Sylvia," he told her, "and I think—I'm sure—she and Frances Coulson would like nothing better than to see something come of our friendship."

Bryony studied his good-looking face, with its brown eyes and square chin, the thick brown hair untidied by the wind and wondered if there might not have been a good chance of his becoming more than friends with the other girl, if it had not been for Uncle Miklas's invitation.

"What about you, Giles?" she asked softly. "Would you like to see it become more than just a friendship?"

His fingers tightened over hers and he looked at her earnestly, so that she was bound to believe him. "You know I wouldn't," he said.

"I—I suppose she's very rich?" she guessed, and smiled when he looked surprised at the question.

"I'm afraid so," he agreed. "That's very important to mother, of course."

"But not to you?"

"Not where you're concerned," Giles assured her. "I'd marry you even if you were in rags, Bryony. I love you."

"Well, I'm not exactly in rags," she protested laughingly, "but I doubt if I could compete with your Sylvia in your mother's eyes, even if I was as rich as Rockefeller."

Giles frowned. "I wish I could do something about that," he said. "It's quite ridiculous the way she dislikes you."

"I've been thinking about that," Bryony said after a moment or two of thought. "I could be quite wrong, of course, but—well, my mother said something once that could explain why Aunt Merrilyn dislikes me."

"*Your* mother?" He looked doubtful.

"Yes. It was something I remember her saying once, when she was talking to a friend of hers, and I wasn't supposed to be listening. She said that Miklas had never forgiven her for marrying Piers Foster. I didn't understand it much at the time, but now, putting two and two together, it could be the reason, couldn't it?"

It was obvious from his face that the idea did not appeal at all, and she wished she had not spoken so freely. "You're suggesting that mother and your—" He spread his hands, disliking to put it into words.

"It seems likely, I think," she said. "Don't you?"

"I suppose so." He admitted it reluctantly, she thought. "I know mother knew Piers Foster, your father, quite well for some time, but I'd never realized there was anything like that."

"I could be quite wrong," Bryony said hastily. "But she's only a couple of years or so older than daddy and I'm very like my mother was, or so they tell me. It would explain quite a lot, wouldn't it?"

"I suppose it would." He was silent for a moment, then he shrugged. "Anyway, whatever her reasons, mother is going to *have* to accept you."

"Maybe," Bryony said, not very hopefully, and wondered if Aunt Merrilyn was the only one that had yet to be convinced.

IT WAS WARM and bright for late September, and Bryony was enjoying her stay at Penroyal, even if Aunt Merrilyn made things uncomfortable for her whenever she had the opportunity. She enjoyed her visits to old Miklas and knew he welcomed her. They talked for hours and sometimes Giles got impatient with her for spending so much time with the old man.

"But he likes to see me, Giles," she told him, more than once. "He gets very lonely up there on his own and he loves company."

"Well, Patinous spends enough time with him," Giles declared. "He knows what he's doing, I don't doubt."

"Is that why you think I spend so much time with Uncle Miklas, too?" she asked, and he shook his head hastily.

"No, of course not, darling. I know you're fond of the old man."

"I wish you were a bit more fond of him," said Bryony. "He'd like to see you more often, Giles, and you very seldom go and see him."

"I suppose I should," he allowed grudgingly. "But I've always hated sickrooms. They make me feel ill just being in them, I can't help it."

Another reason he disliked her spending so much time with his uncle was because, quite often, her visits and Alex's coincided. At first she would go out of the room again whenever she found Alex there, but they had both insisted that she stay and she had had little option with the two of them pressing her.

It was no secret that old Miklas was not getting any better, nor would he, but Bryony found Aunt Merrilyn's attitude very hard to understand. She seldom had a good word to say for her brother and it was obvious that she was interested only in how he would leave his money.

Giles's interest in the old man was less mercenary, she thought, although he, too, had mentioned more than once that he disliked his uncle's affection for Alex, and Bryony knew he was jealous of him.

It was quite late one evening when she left Miklas and decided to go for a walk alone. It was a long time until bedtime, and Giles and his mother were playing cribbage in the sitting room, a game she hated and which Aunt Merrilyn adored. Unwilling to have company, she was careful to let herself out through the front door without being heard.

Old Miklas's increasing weakness worried her, mostly because she was very fond of the old man and she knew she would miss him probably more than his immediate family would. It was because she had so much on her mind at the moment that she was not in the mood for company.

It was late enough for there to be a full, bright moon that gave the sea a luminous look and made the rocks and the white sanded beach look almost disturbingly romantic. Even the wind blowing in from the sea felt warmer than of late, and she let her topcoat fly open as she walked.

With no special destination in mind, she made her way along the cliff top, the way quite plainly visible in the moonlight, and the sound-deadening turf still springy under her feet. She could hear the sea below on the rocks, sighing and whispering with the retreating tide, and it somehow fitted in with her own rather sad mood perfectly.

Almost unknowingly she walked in the direction of Marby Head, although it was rather a foolish thing to do at that time of night, and the sudden realization of where she was brought her to a sudden halt just above a path down to the beach.

Marby Head had always had a special attraction for her, probably because the original Pengellys had lived in what was, now, little more than a grassy ruin, standing right at the top of the cliff. It was conveniently close to that path leading down to the beach. No doubt, she thought wryly, Alex Patinous would have made something of that fact, had he been there.

It was wild and unpopulated up here, and the moonlight gave it an even greater air of romanticism than its history had endowed it with. It was not difficult to imagine those old Pengellys waiting, silent and patient, in the shadows, and for a moment Bryony shivered, though not with cold.

She stood for a moment, tempted by the moonlight shining on the sea, and the white sand which seemed to have a luminiscence of its own. It would be easy enough to walk along the beach and then climb back to Penroyal via the other cliff path. She was familiar enough with it to find her way without coming to any harm, as long as the moon remained as bright and illuminating as it was now.

She had already decided to yield to temptation when she suddenly spun around sharply. Her breath caught in her throat as she heard someone coming up behind her. The figure was tall, too tall to be Giles, and the moonlight casting shadows on the dark face soon identified him.

He was wearing dark slacks and a dark sweater, but no jacket, and she thought he fitted discomfitingly well into his surroundings. There was something dark and potentially dangerous about him that she felt sure the old Pengellys would have approved of. For herself, she would rather have seen anyone else at that moment.

"Hello," he said, as he came within earshot. "Did I frighten you?"

If that was what he was hoping for, she thought, he

was going to be disappointed. It was not fear of him that had startled her, but fear of the unknown, and now that he was identified, fear was not the emotion that disturbed her. It was something strange and discomfiting that set her pulses racing wildly and brought a warm flush of color to her cheeks.

She shook her head. "No, you didn't frighten me, I was just surprised, that's all."

"Are you visiting the haunts of your ancestors?"

The allusion was a little too near the truth for comfort, and she shivered briefly as she looked at the few dark humps of mossy stone, which were all that remained of the original Pengelly home. "In a way," she told him. "These ruins were once the Pengellys' home."

"Mm. Interesting." He walked nearer to the few reminders of her forefathers and stood for a moment in silence as if they gave him food for thought. "Of course," he said at last, turning back to her, "they haven't always lived at Penroyal, have they?"

"Not always," she agreed. "Although it's been a long time since they first came here."

"I've never been here before," he mused. "I'm glad I came."

"Why *did* you come?"

He studied her for a moment, and she thought he found her curiosity amusing, as almost inevitably he would. "I saw you leaving the house as if you were trying not to be seen," he informed her. "And, I thought, I would come too."

"Oh? What for?"

His black eyes had a curious luminosity in the moonlight and she thought that, for the first time since she had known him, he resented being questioned.

"Would you believe that I wanted to make sure you came to no harm?" he asked quietly.

She hesitated over her answer. Her heart was behaving in the most erratic way and she could not look at him without her hands trembling. "I—I don't know why you should think I'm incapable of looking after myself," she told him.

"Are you capable of looking after yourself, Bryony?"

"Yes. Yes, of course I am."

He was silent for a moment. "Miklas saw you from his window," he told her then, "and he wasn't very happy that you should be out here alone." He looked around at the ruins of the old stone house and the lonely, quiet expanse of Marby Head. "He would have been even less happy had he known you were up *here* alone," he added, and raised a brow curiously. "Why did you not ask Giles to come with you?"

Her gray eyes looked almost as dark as his in the deceptive moonlight and she had no intention of being questioned about Giles. She looked at him meaningly. "Because I didn't want company," she told him. "I wanted to be alone."

"I see." He said something else, too, presumably in Greek, since she could not understand it, and she eyed him suspiciously.

"What does that mean?" she demanded.

He shrugged, a smile showing briefly white in his dark face. "Moody," he said, "is as near as you will get to it."

She stood there for a moment, undecided now whether to go on as she had planned, or whether to go back, her hands thrust into her coat pockets, her fair hair glinting almost silver in the moon light. "I'm not moody," she denied. "I just wanted time to think."

"About you and Giles?" She might have known he would jump to that conclusion, she thought, and that he would make her private thoughts his business.

She shook her head and moved away from him and

toward the path leading down to the beach. "Not about me and Giles," she denied. "There's nothing to think about there." It was, perhaps, not strictly true, but she had no intention of confiding in him, especially about anything as personal as her relationship with Giles.

He put out a hand to guide her down the first, steep part of the path, and she made no demur about that, but allowed him to take the lead. "I would have thought that the advent of another woman on the scene would give you quite a lot to think about," he informed her, and Bryony frowned.

"You can think what you like," she retorted, refusing to be drawn. "What Giles and I do, doesn't concern you."

"So you've told me before," he said, undeterred. "But it concerns Miklas, I think."

She said nothing to that, but followed him down the path to the beach, the white sand soft and shifting under her feet after the solidity of rock, so that for a brief second she clung tightly to his hand.

"You don't have to come with me," she told him, as they started to walk along the smooth, silvery stretch of sand.

He turned a smile on her, still holding her hand although she did not for the moment realize he was. "You cannot lose me as easily as that," he informed her. "I am your self-appointed guardian angel."

"Guardian *angel*?" She laughed lightly, freeing her hand and walking a little way ahead of him, the peaceful, quiet beauty of their surroundings already changing her rather sober mood to one dangerously like excitement.

"Do you not think I'm on the side of the angels?" he asked, and she turned her head to look at him over one shoulder.

"Uncle Miklas says you're an important legal eagle,"

she told him, "so I suppose you must be on the side of the angels."

"A legal eagle." He tried the unfamiliar phrase and nodded as if he approved of it. "Is that what Miklas claims I am?"

"Those weren't his words," Bryony admitted, "they're mine."

He laughed. "I thought they must be."

"But he did tell me that you were a much bigger cog in the wheel than I am, presumably with the idea of letting me know that I should treat you with the proper respect."

"Which you do not!"

She flicked him another glance over her shoulder, a smile recognizing his feelings in the matter. "Do you think I should?" she asked. She had not meant to be provocative, but there was something in the air that made her feel a little light-headed—some atmosphere created by the softly swishing sea and the brilliance of the moonlight, that had a dizzying effect, and she thought he felt it, too.

"Should I call you Mr. Patinous or sir?" she asked, and laughed softly.

"You should," he retorted, his black eyes glowing darkly. "But it's unlikely you ever will."

"Very unlikely," she agreed, and laughed again as she ran still further ahead of him, going as near go the receding tide as she safely could, while he came more slowly, his hands in his pockets, watching her.

"Come here," he told her imperiously when she narrowly escaped getting her feet wet.

Bryony laughed, looking back at him where he stood some yards away on the damp sand which held their dark footprints. "Are you afraid of getting wet?" she taunted, feeling almost dizzily light-hearted. Her eyes were bright and shining in the soft oval of her face and the warm wind lifted her fair hair and blew it across her eyes, so that she brushed it back with one hand.

"I'm not afraid of anything," he told her quietly. "But I have more sense than to want to get my feet wet, when I have to walk back home."

Bryony shook her head, her mouth softly reproachful. "Oh, you're too practical for me," she told him, and stretched out her arms toward the huge yellow moon. "Oh, it's such a beautiful night!"

"It *is* beautiful," he agreed. "Now come here before you are caught by the next wave, Bryony."

He held out a hand to her and, without hesitation, she put her own into it and walked beside him again. "You should see the Mediterranean on a summer night," he said suddenly, and she looked at him, struck by an unmistakable note of wistfulness, touched by it, too, for she had never thought of his ever being homesick.

"I'd love to see it," she said softly. "It must be wonderful, especially on a night like this."

He smiled, and she found herself, for the first time, in complete sympathy with him. It was the first time she had ever felt so close to him and the feeling gave her a pleasantly warm glow, her heart skipping lightly as she looked up at him.

"You must visit Greece sometime," he told her. "you'd love it."

"I expect I would," she agreed, "but visits to Greece don't happen to girls like me, Alex. Not unless we're very, very thrifty," she added with a smile, "which I'm not."

"Then you should find some other way to go," he told her. "A beautiful girl should not be thwarted by lack of money, surely."

"This girl is," she told him briefly, and he looked

down at her for a moment in silence, then he smiled and said something in his own tongue, which she frowned over.

"And what does that mean?" she asked, without much hope of being told, judging by the expression on his face.

"Wouldn't you like to know?"

He sounded as if he was returning to normal and she had to admit that she regretted it. "Alex!"

He shook his head, smiling at her, looking so dark and excitingly dangerous that she felt her stomach turn over. His strong fingers squeezed hers tightly until she cried out in protest. "I shall teach you Greek," he told her. "Then I shall not have to keep translating for you."

"Would you?" she asked curiously, her huge shiny eyes looking up at him, and he laughed softly, turning her to face him, his hands pressing her close until she was forced to lean back her head to look at him.

"With pleasure," he said huskily, his mouth brushing softly against her chin. Then he found her mouth and kissed her, gently at first, then with increasing ardor until she felt as if she had stopped breathing and her knees were so weak she felt she would have fallen if he had let her go.

"Alex!"

They were, neither of them, aware of anything but themselves until a voice, hoarse with anger, spoke her name and she gave an audible gasp as she turned and faced Giles.

"What the hell do you think you're doing, Patinous?" He sounded almost ridiculously melodramatic and Bryony was still trying to recover her breath sufficiently to answer him.

Alex, however, had no such difficulty and he faced

Giles, unbelievably calm and self-possessed. "I was enjoying the moonlight with Bryony," he informed him. "I hope you do not object, Giles."

"Damn you!" Giles's face writhed angrily as he sought for words to express just how he felt about this arrogant, unflappable stranger . "You have no right to behave like that with Bryony. She and I are going to be married."

"Are you?" Alex sounded so unconcerned that Bryony found it hard to believe that this was the same man who had kissed her so disturbingly only seconds ago.

"Giles," she ventured, finding her voice at last, "I—I was only—"

She knew Alex was watching her, and she knew he was finding the whole incident very amusing, as she should have known he would.

"Do you want to stay here?" Giles asked her, more calmly now. "Or are you coming back to the house with me?"

She hesitated, looking at Giles and then Alex, who merely smiled sardonically and thrust both hands into his pockets. "By all means go back with Giles," he told her blandly. "After all, isn't there an old saying in your country? Two is company, three is a crowd?" he laughed softly. "I do not like crowds, Bryony."

CHAPTER SIX

"I JUST CAN'T UNDERSTAND you," Giles told her the following morning, after breakfast, and Bryony sighed.

She had refused to discuss her being with Alex Patinous the night before, but had gone straight up to her room, her chin high and her eyes defiantly bright. Aunt Merrilyn had already gone to bed when they came in, so at least she had not been there to add fuel to the threatening flames, but this morning her sharp, dark eyes had watched Bryony all through breakfast until she had felt like shouting her defiance at her.

As soon as the meal was over Giles had taken her arm firmly, ignoring his mother's frown, and walked her to the door without asking whether she wanted to go with him or not. She had gone willingly enough, although she knew what was on his mind.

A night's sleep had given her the opportunity to see things more clearly, and she had come to the conclusion that there was nothing so very terrible about a stolen kiss on a moonlit beach. It happened all the time, and obviously Alex Patinous did not take it seriously, so why should she? She had, however, avoided his gaze across the breakfast table this morning and had spoken to him only when she had been directly addressed.

She walked with Giles now, down to the beach via the path they had climbed together last night, and she thought how very different the setting was this morning. It was still beautiful, with the white sands stretching for miles, and the sea a gray-green color under the autumn sun, but there was none of the magic that the full moon had given it last night, and none of the heady atmosphere that had sent her into Alex Patinous's arms.

"You weren't even making an effort to resist," Giles was complaining, his voice sharper than usual, and reminding her irresistibly of his mother.

Bryony frowned, her hands thrust deep into her coat pockets, her hair blowing wildly in the brisk wind. "For heaven's sake, Giles," she said, "you're making a mountain of a molehill. There was a full moon last night, it was a beautiful night and I—well, I suppose I felt a bit crazy, that's all. It was only one kiss, after all."

"One kiss," Giles retorted, "is all *I* saw."

Bryony flushed, her shoulders hunched against the criticism. "There was no more *to* see," she told him. "Just one kiss."

"It didn't need an expert to see what sort of a kiss it was either," Giles replied sharply. "Damn Patinous! Why can't he stay away from you?"

"I don't know why you're making so much fuss, Giles," she told him. "If we'd been—well, been doing anything we shouldn't, we'd hardly have been down on the open beach where anyone could find us. As you did," she added.

"And just as well," he told her shortly. "Heaven knows what would have happened next, judging by the bit I saw." He walked in silence for a while, his face set firmly into self-righteousness, his brows drawn into a straight line. "Why did you go with him, anyway?" he asked, after a while.

"I didn't—he followed me."

"Damn him!"

"Only because Uncle Miklas saw me from his window

and asked him to come after me," she told him. "He didn't like me being out on my own at night."

"Neither do I—" said Giles "—and if I'd known *I'd* have come after you. Why didn't Uncle Miklas ask me to come, if he was worried?"

"Probably because you didn't go near him last night," Bryony retorted. "Alex did."

"Alex!" He curled his lip disdainfully. "Patinous is up to something, Bryony, I know it. He wants the jade, unless I'm very much mistaken, and he's keeping in with the old man to get it, but he doesn't fool me or mother."

"I don't think he's trying to fool anybody," she said, believing it, although perhaps it was not very tactful to say so at the moment.

"Bryony!" He brought them to a halt suddenly, and turned her around to face him, his eyes searching her face, anxiety as well as anger in them now. "You...you're not falling for Patinous, are you?"

"No, of course not!" She tried to sound indignant, but she avoided looking at him when she answered.

Alex Patinous was without doubt a very attractive man, but she doubted if he would ever be serious about anyone. Certainly he had been momentarily serious last night when he had spoken of his home, but it had been quickly dismissed, and it had had nothing to do with the way he felt about her. He was perhaps four or five years older than Giles and he was, as far as she knew, still unmarried, so he was evidently in no hurry to marry.

Giles, of course, was single too, but he was a different matter altogether. For one thing, he had told her that he had been in love with her for a long time, and that would account, in part, for his single state. Also there was Aunt Merrilyn. It would take a brave girl to outface Giles's formidable mother long enough to get serious enough to marry him, unless she was hand-picked, like Sylvia Greenaway.

She was sorely tempted for a moment to bring up the subject of the girl he had met in London, but she remembered how embarrassed and apologetic he had been the last time the girl had been mentioned and she decided it would be rather unkind. She liked Giles too much to hurt him deliberately just to pay him back for suspecting her.

He looked down at her for a second or two, then suddenly bent and kissed her mouth; almost as if he was trying to erase the kiss that Alex Patinous had given her last night. When he released her, she was a little breathless, but felt none of the blood-stirring excitement she had felt last night. She could not help experiencing a brief flicker of disappointment, but then she thought that last night it had been the effect of the moonlight on the sea and the other trappings of conventional romance, including a very attractive Greek.

"I love you," Giles said, his voice a little unsteady, his arms tight around her. "I love you, Bryony."

"Giles—"

"Don't you care about me at all?" he asked plaintively, forestalling the expected protest.

"Yes, of course I do. You know I'm very fond of you, but—well, at the moment I don't love you the way you want me to, Giles. I'm sorry."

"Is it Patinous?"

"I've already told you it isn't," she told him. "Why won't you believe me, Giles? I'm not in love with anyone at all. I'm as fond of you as I always was, but, at the moment, it's nothing more."

"Then I shall go on hoping," he said, hugging her close to him again, and brushing her forehead with his lips. "I won't give up, Bryony."

It had puzzled Bryony for some time, how Alex Patinous could have a successful legal practice in Greece and yet be staying in England for so long, and she mentioned as much to Miklas one day. The old man looked at her, sharp-eyed, and smiled.

"He's left his practice in other hands at the moment," he told her, and Bryony looked doubtful.

"But...but that's not very wise, surely," she objected. "I know enough about the legal profession, in England at least, to know that a solicitor or a barrister couldn't afford to leave his practice for several weeks as Alex has. He'd lose all his clients."

The old man smiled knowingly. "Alex knows what he's doing, Bryony," he told her. "He's thinking of giving up his practice anyway, shortly, and the Patinouses aren't paupers, you know."

But—I thought *you* paid for—I mean, you sent Alex to school over here, didn't you?"

He nodded. "I did, but not because the Patinouses couldn't afford to. Although Alex is my cousin he's thirty years my junior, and you know I always got on very well with my mother's people." He laughed quickly. "I was always much more Greek than Merrilyn and I was always proud to admit it. I never had a son of my own and Niklos was very generous. He allowed me to share his."

"I see."

"Niklos Patinous has a very prosperous shipping business, you know, but he's getting into his sixties now and Alex is his only son, so he wants him to take over from him."

She wondered how Alex felt about giving up his own career to run his father's business, and if he was as obedient, in his way, to parental wishes, as Giles was. Somehow she could not imagine him doing anything he did not want to do. "I didn't realize they were so...." She spread her hands, and the old man smiled.

"You hadn't realized that the Patinouses were as wealthy—in fact, much more wealthy than the Pengellys," he guessed. "It's the impression Merrilyn likes to give. She likes to think that my father married beneath himself but in fact he didn't—far from it. Mama came from a very good family and a rich one, too."

"I see."

"How are you and Giles getting on?" The question was so unexpected that she blinked at him for a moment uncertainly.

"We—we get on very well, Uncle Miklas, we always have."

The sudden switch from Alex to Giles puzzled her, but sometimes it was difficult to follow the old man's train of thought. He was frowning over his nephew, as he often did. "I wish he had a bit more go in him, that lad," he said. "He's been too mollycoddled by his mother, that's the trouble."

"Giles is all right," she declared, unwilling to see him, yet again, compared unfavorably with Alex. "He's quiet and sometimes a bit too self-effacing where Aunt Merrilyn's concerned, but he's nice and uncomplicated."

"Is that what you like in a man?" Miklas demanded, his dark eyes watching her closely, and Bryony felt the warm flush of color in her cheeks as she sought an answer.

"I like Giles," she told him cautiously. "So I suppose I do."

"Huh! You're more Pengelly than he is, even if he has got it from both sides. You've got spirit, Bryony, and most men like that in a girl."

"Not in a wife, surely," she smiled. "Isn't it better to have someone quiet and obedient?"

The sound he made was somewhere between a snort and a laugh, and his bright, dark eyes glittered brightly. "Not for a Pengelly or a Patinous," he denied. "We like our women with spirit. My wife...." he began, then shook his head, looking older and more tired suddenly. "She was a wonderful woman," he said softly, and Bryony reached for his hand and squeezed it gently in her own.

"I wish I could have seen Aunt Mary," she said. "I've often wondered what she was like."

The old man shook his head slowly. "That cursed jade," he said. "I wish I'd never seen it."

"Oh, Uncle Miklas, you can't blame the jade!" she cried, her hands tight over his. "It *must* be superstition, it wouldn't bear thinking about if it wasn't. Giles says it's only superstition and old wives' tales."

"*He* would," the old man remarked sardonically. "It's valuable."

Speaking of the jade reminded her of Alex's words, and she held the old man's hand gently in hers, not looking at him when she spoke. "You...you won't leave the jade to Alex, will you, Uncle Miklas?" she asked.

The sharp black eyes looked at her shrewdly for a moment. "Has Giles asked you to beg on his behalf?" he asked, and Bryony hastily shook her head, horrified that she had given such an impression.

"No, of course not," she denied.

"Oh? Then why are you asking me not to leave it to Alex?"

"Because...." she hesitated to tell him the reason, for obviously Alex had not spoken of it himself to the old man and she was possibly being very indiscreet. "He—he doesn't want it, Uncle Miklas," she said at last, and looked up in time to see his eyebrows flick upward in an expression that reminded her of the man they were discussing.

"Did *he* tell you that?"

"More or less," she admitted. "He said—he said that he wouldn't dare take the chance of having it because it was bad luck."

Surprisingly, he chuckled, shaking his head. "Superstitious devil," he said, evidently amused by the idea. "I'd never have thought it of Alex." He turned bright and curious eyes to her. "When and why did he tell you that?" he demanded.

She shrugged, seeing herself probably involved in something she would rather have avoided, now that it was too late. "It was when we were talking about the jade once," she told him. "He said he wouldn't want it and rather than risk the life of the girl he's going to marry, he'd throw it into the sea."

"Oh...ho!" He narrowed his eyes and studied his fingers thoughtfully for a moment. "So there's a woman involved, is there? Well, it's time he got himself a wife, he's nearly thirty-five and he's played around long enough. If he's going to take on the Patinous business, he'll need to have sons of his own to pass it on to. Did he say who this lucky girl was that he was going to marry?"

Bryony shook her head, feeling oddly uneasy for some reason she could not explain. "I gathered he hasn't met her yet," she told him. "He spoke as if he hadn't."

"Aah, I see."

"Uncle Miklas...." she bit her lip uncertainly, wondering if she had said too much. Alex Patinous would not take kindly to being discussed in his absence, she thought, and especially about anything as personal as this. "You—you won't tell Alex I said anything, will you?" she begged.

"About the girl he's going to marry?" he asked, and she saw a hint of Alex's black-eyed amusement in his expression, despite the drawn, tired face. "Don't worry, Bryony, I shan't give you away."

"Thank you." She got up and gently disengaged her hands, looking down at him affectionately. He looked so tired and ill, but still those bright black eyes glittered with mischief at her secrets. "I'd better go and let you rest for a while," she told him. "I'm tiring you."

"Of course you're not," he argued, and she shook her head over his refusal to admit it, bending to kiss his forehead.

"I am, and I have to go and write to daddy, anyway," she told him. "I'll see you again, Uncle Miklas."

"Bryony!" He called to her as she reached the door and she turned and smiled curiously. "Where's Giles?"

"I don't know for sure," she confessed. "You know he bought himself a boat, don't you?"

"I know Merrilyn said something about him getting one." He grinned. "She tried to talk him out of it. I'm glad she didn't manage it—shows he's got *some* mind of his own."

"It arrived yesterday," she told him, "and it was moored down on the docks. He wanted me to go out with him this morning, but I'm not a very good sailor and I told him I'd rather not."

He looked out at the overcast sky and the rising sea in the distance. "Let's hope he can handle it in rough weather," he said. "It'll be blowing a gale out there before long."

Bryony, too, looked at the gathering clouds and shook her head. "I hope he's back before it breaks," she said. "He's gone alone."

"Idiot." The old man's opinion was brief and concise. "He should have taken Alex with him. He knows all there is to know about boats and he's used to handling them."

"Is he?" She could not imagine why it should come as such a surprise that Alex knew how to handle a boat. After all, he lived by the sea and always had done as far as she knew. No doubt, she thought wryly, he did it well, as he did everything else, rough weather or not. "Oh well," she added, with another look at the dark sky, "maybe Giles will be back before the storm breaks."

But Giles was not back before the storm broke and Bryony watched the heaving sea anxiously, wishing he would come. She felt rather helpless and told herself more than once that she was probably making a lot of fuss about nothing. Giles was probably quite capable of handling a boat in bad weather, despite Aunt Merrilyn's fears, and he would surely not have gone too far out on his first trip in a new boat.

By the time the storm had been blowing for nearly half an hour, however, she was feeling anxious and she turned hopefully when the door opened behind her. She had thought it was probably Aunt Merrilyn with some news, although she had not heard the telephone ring, nor seen Giles coming across the cliffs as he would have to.

It wasn't Aunt Merrilyn, however, but Alex Patinous, and he smiled encouragingly when he saw her worried face. "You are worrying about Giles?" he asked, and she nodded. "Thank heaven you had enough sense not to go with him."

"I—I almost wish I had," she told him, biting her lip. "At least I'd know what was going on out there."

"I told him there would be a storm before very long, when he started out," he said, joining her at the window. "But—" he shrugged "—you know Giles."

"I know how he'd react to being given advice by you," she told him, and he frowned.

"You are criticizing me for speaking of it?" he asked brusquely, and she lowered her eyes hastily. He did not take kindly to being criticized, especially when he had been proved right.

"I... no, not really," she said. "I just wish you hadn't said anything to him, that's all. He was bound to go as far as he could, just to prove to you that he was quite capable of handling his boat in a storm."

"He isn't," he told her bluntly. "He had never been out with this boat before, it was a foolhardy thing to do, even to prove to me that he was a good sailor."

She stood for a second or two watching the storm, feeling a cold, heavy uncertainty in the pit of her stomach. Something awful was happening to Giles and she could do nothing about it.

Alex...."

She thought he had been about to say something, but he looked down at her with a half smile when she turned to face him. "You would like me to go and look for him?" he guessed, and she stared at him for a moment.

"Would you?" She held his gaze, her own eyes wide and appealing and darkly gray. "Uncle Miklas says you're an expert sailor and you—you might find him."

"I might," he agreed. "Although I'm not sure he would welcome my help, even in this."

"Oh, I'm sure he would under the circumstances," she assured him, and hoped she was right.

She turned back again to the window and looked at the wildly tossing sea beyond the cliffs and whipping white horses that sped towards destruction on the rocks. Her stomach muscles contracted suddenly when she thought of him setting out in such dangerous weather just because she had asked him to go and look for Giles, and she spun around, a hand clutching at his arm as he turned to go.

"No, Alex!" The black eyes looked at her steadily, and she hastily lowered her own, shaking her head slowly. "I—I don't think you should go," she said, her voice shaky. "I—I know Giles is out there and he may be—he may be hurt or something, but if you go and something happens to you—I...I asked you to go—I shouldn't bear it if anything happened."

His hand covered hers and there was a gentle look in the black eyes. He was quite serious, although he was smiling. "Nothing will happen to me," he told her, self-confident as ever, "but I'm delighted that you look so anxious on my behalf, Bryony."

"Don't joke at a time like this!" she told him, close to tears with anxiety and uncertainty. She was unwilling to have him risk his neck on that vicious sea just because she had asked him to look for Giles, but she disliked having him take her anxiety for more than it was.

"I was not joking," he told her. "And you have no need to feel guilty about asking me to go, if that is what is on your mind. I came in to tell you that I was going down to borrow a boat and go out and look for Giles. You merely forestalled me."

"You...you were?"

He nodded. "I was. Does that make you feel better?"

"I don't know."

He squeezed her fingers gently, then put a hand to her face, his fingers caressing her cheek. "I was going to look for him, Bryony, truly."

He smiled at her briefly, then turned and walked away, and she let him get as far as the door before she called out to him. Crossing the room on legs that felt incredibly weak, she hesitated only a second, then tiptoed and kissed him lightly on his chin. "Please be careful," she whispered.

"Of course I will." He added some word in his language, and then he was out the door and across the hall while she still stood there uncertainly.

It was only minutes later that she saw him from the window as left the house, his dark sweater covered by an oilskin and his black hair tossing wildly in the wind that forced him to bend before it. Until he was out of sight beyond the dip in the cliffs she watched him, and her heart felt so heavy that she put a hand to her ribs and stared out of the window with anxious eyes.

When Aunt Merrilyn joined her some time later, she thought she had never seen her look so drawn and worried. Her face was a pasty white and her usually sharp eyes had a curiously blank look, as if she was sleepwalking. Bryony took her hands gently and seated her on the long wooden window seat, her expression kind and understanding.

No matter what Aunt Merrilyn had done or said in the past, now she was a very worried mother whose only son was somewhere out there on the sea, riding out a storm. It was impossible not to feel for her, and Bryony was nothing if not compassionate.

"He'll be all right, Aunt Merrilyn," she said softly, wishing she could believe it herself. "He'll be all right, I'm sure he will."

Aunt Merrilyn's hands were clasped tightly together and she seemed unable to take her eyes off the storm outside. "I knew something would—would happen," she said, her usually sharp voice trembling and uncertain. "I begged him not to buy that boat. I've never wanted him to have one, I knew something would happen."

"He's—he's quite a good sailor," Bryony said, trying

to sound convincing, although, in truth, she had no idea just how good Giles was. Aunt Merrilyn's blank eyes flicked briefly into an expression of impatience, more like her usual self. "He isn't," she denied, refusing consolation. "He hasn't been in a boat since he was a boy, when his father took him. George always liked boats—such dangerous things."

"Alex—Mr. Patinous has gone out to look for him," Bryony told her, trying to bring some sort of comfort, however poor. "He's an expert sailor, so Uncle Miklas says."

"That man!" The eyes lost their blankness at last and glittered hatred for a moment at the mention of Alex. "I blame him for this. If he hadn't told Giles there was going to be a storm and that he shouldn't go out, he would never have gone at all. I'm sure he wouldn't."

"Oh, Aunt Merrilyn," Bryony protested, "you can't blame Alex for it. Giles shouldn't have gone out, especially if he knew there was a storm rising."

"It was Alex Patinous's fault," Aunt Merrilyn insisted. "Although I don't expect *you* to admit it." Her voice rose to near hysteria. "You know Giles couldn't let him get away with a challenge like that. That man probably did it on purpose. If he dared Giles to go, he *had* to go."

"He did *not* have to go," Bryony denied firmly. "Giles is a grown man, Aunt Merrilyn, not a child. He can think for himself."

"He's too easily fooled," Aunt Merrilyn argued, determinedly aggressive. "Anyone can take advantage of Giles. He needs me to see that he isn't made a fool of." The hard-eyed reproving look she gave Bryony left no doubt that she included her in the ones seeking to make a fool of her son.

"But he's thirty years old," Bryony objected impatiently, her sympathy rapidly evaporating before such foolishness. "He can think for himself, surely, make up his own mind."

The sharp, unhappy eyes held her gaze and Bryony thought she had never seen such open dislike for herself before, and shivered, almost without realizing it. "Oh yes, you'd like that, wouldn't you?" Aunt Merrilyn said harshly. "If I left Giles to make up his own mind, he'd be fooled by every little gold digger that made eyes at him. But I'll make sure it doesn't happen. I'll see that he doesn't marry just anybody." Her eyes filled with tears suddenly and the set face crumpled like a child's. "If he ever comes back," she sobbed. "If he ever comes back again."

Despite her berating her, Bryony could not bring herself to ignore such obvious agony of mind as Aunt Merrilyn was going through, and she put an arm around her shoulders and comforted her as best she could. She held her close while the thin body shook with grief and patted her back soothingly. Giles was the be-all and end-all of her existence, and Bryony dared not think what would happen if he did not return from that foolhardy trip.

IT WAS NEARLY TWO and a half hours later that Bryony, back again in the window, saw two figures coming across the cliffs toward the house and breathed a sigh of relief when she recognized them. She ran into the hall and called up the stairs. "Aunt Merrilyn! Aunt Merrilyn, they're back!" then ran to the telephone to call the doctor.

Aunt Merrilyn, she knew, would be interested only in Giles being back, but she could have cried her own relief to see Alex Patinous with him and supporting him as if Giles had been hurt, or was suffering from exhaustion. It had been the sight of Giles dragging himself along supported by his companion that had prompted her to call the doctor.

Aunt Merrilyn came down from her room, her eyes streaming with tears when she saw Giles, limp and pale faced, and she looked as if she was about to collapse, as well as her son. She completely ignored Alex, and took over Giles herself, leading him upstairs, oblivious of everyone else.

"The doctor's been sent for," she told him as they left. "You must go to bed at once, Giles, and get warm."

For a moment Bryony watched them go upstairs, then she became aware that Alex was watching her and when she turned to him, he smiled. A wide and totally unexpected smile under the circumstances, and more than usually striking because his dark face was streaming water and his hair dripping wetly onto his nose and forehead.

"I would be very grateful for some of that hot coffee I know you have waiting for me," he told her, and Bryone smiled. It was mostly relief, she told herself, that made her stomach churn so crazily at the sight of him standing there.

"It's already made," she told him. "I'll go and turn up the heat while you change into some dry clothes."

She stirred the fire into more vivid life while he was gone and had the pot of hot coffee ready in the sitting room when he came down again, looking none the worse for his experience. The coffee was spiked with some rum she had found in the buffet, and had had no qualms about helping herself to.

The doctor came, quite some time after he was sent for, and Bryony showed him up to Giles's room, passed the good news on to Uncle Miklas, then came downstairs again to find Alex standing in front of the fire, his black head still shinily wet, but with none of Giles's pale-faced limpness about him.

He smiled across at her when she came in and swallowed his coffee in great, steaming mouthfuls, sighing his pleasure at the additional fragrance of rum. "That was very good," he told her, setting down the empty mug, and refusing a refill.

"You must have been cold," she said, but in fact he looked so little affected by the experience that she might almost have believed he had not been out.

"Cold and wet—" he shrugged "—but both are easily disposed of once it is over."

She thought he was alluding to Giles's condition and felt the inevitable prick of resentment as she unconsciously lifted her chin and looked at him. "Giles was less fortunate," she said, and flushed when he smiled.

"Cousin Giles is even less of a sailor than I thought," he told her.

Bryony frowned. "Is he very badly hurt?" she asked, disliking his easy, rather disdainful manner, and he smiled again.

"He's not hurt at all," he told her, and Bryony frowned at him over the rim of her own coffee mug.

"But—but he looked so pale and he was—limp and only half conscious. He must have been hurt."

His smile was sardonic and he shook his head. "As I told you," he declared, "Giles is not a good sailor."

Bryony stared at him for a moment, unbelievingly. "You—do you mean he's—he's seasick?"

He nodded and smiled again, seemingly amused at the idea. "I should say that he is just about the worst sailor in Britain."

"But that's ridiculous," Bryony objected. "Giles was a good sailor. We used to go sailing with his father when we were quite small, and he was never seasick then." She raised her challenging chin again and her eyes had a dark gray, stormy look as she prepared to defend Giles from his taunts. "I don't believe you," she told him shortly. "You're making it up."

"If you wish to believe that." His eyes looked bright and glittered with something she thought was quite probably anger, although he shrugged as if it could not matter less to him what she thought. He disliked being criticized or argued with, she thought, and could not prevent a swift flicker of excitement at the idea of having bested him.

"Then why is the doctor so long with him?" she asked, and he shrugged again.

"Possibly because Aunt Merrilyn is making rather a lot of fuss," he suggested. "She sounded hysterical."

"She's been very worried," Bryony told him, again defensively, and the black eyes looked at her steadily for a moment.

"But you have not?" he suggested softly, and she flushed.

"Not—not in the same way as Aunt Merrilyn," she told him. "Giles is her only son—her only child, she has no one else."

"And you have been consoling her." It was a statement, not a question, and she turned away rather than meet the look in his eyes that was both curious and understanding.

"I—I did my best," she admitted. "I'm not very popular with Aunt Merrilyn, so it wasn't very easy."

"No, it wouldn't be," he said quietly. "But that would not prevent you from letting her touch your soft heart, would it?"

She suspected sarcasm and swung around to accuse

him of it, but as she turned he raised a hand to brush back the heavy, wet hair from his forehead and she noticed for the first time that a long piece of sticking plaster decorated his left arm and disappeared into the sleeve of his sweater.

"Alex, you're hurt!" She walked across to him, her eyes anxious, fearing she had misjudged him. "I didn't know."

"I am not hurt," he denied, but she would have none of it, and took his arm, turning it to reveal the plaster.

"Why didn't you tell me?"

He seemed to find her anxiety amusing, for he was smiling again and the black eyes teased her. "It is a small cut, nothing more," he told her, pulling down the sleeve of his sweater to cover it.

"Let me see it."

"Why?" His brows elevated into the hair that had flopped over his forehead again. "There is nothing very much to see."

"But it's still bleeding—" Bryony insisted "—and I think the doctor should see it while he's here. It may need stitching."

"It does not need stitching," he insisted firmly, but still smiling. "And I will not have a fuss made over such a small cut."

"Well, whether you want to or not," she told him shortly, "I'm going to tell the doctor when he comes down, and get him to look at it."

"If you do, Bryony," he warned darkly, "I shall be very angry."

She stuck her small nose in the air and smiled derisively. "Is that supposed to make me tremble in my shoes,?" she asked. "Because you're angry with me?"

"It should." He looked down at her from his position

against the tall mantel, and his eyes glowed like coals in the reflected firelight. "If you knew me better you would be trembling in your shoes," he told her. "I do not often lose my temper, but if I do I shall make even you tremble."

"I doubt it!" She dismissed the idea with a toss of her head, but her heart was racing wildly and the color warm in her cheeks. He would, she thought, have a quite impressive temper once it was aroused.

"You will not tell the doctor, Bryony, do you hear me?"

"I hear you—" she allowed "—but it doesn't mean to say I shall take any notice of you."

"You...." The sound of footsteps on the stairs silenced him, and they both looked across the room.

"The doctor," said Bryony, and was out of the door before he could intervene.

The doctor looked at her standing in the hall, and smiled ruefully when she asked after Giles. "There's nothing much the matter with him," he told her. "Seasickness can be very nasty, but it's never proved fatal yet. He'll survive."

"You...you mean he isn't hurt?"

The doctor smiled again. "Only his pride, I think," he told her, and Bryony suspected that his unusually offhand manner had been provoked by Aunt Merrilyn's fussing.

"I'm very glad."

The doctor was the same one who attended Uncle Miklas and he was also a friend of the old man's, so she guessed he had called in on him before coming down. "Is there another patient?" he asked, looking across at the sitting room door she had left ajar.

She hesitated, knowing Alex Patinous was listening for her answer, and she was very tempted to mention that he had the cut on his arm. "Not really," she said at last, and the doctor raised a brow in query.

"Not really." He repeated her answer and a smile doubted the truth of it.

"Mr. Patinous cut his arm," she told him, sensing the atmosphere from the sitting room even out here in the hallway. "But he says he doesn't need attention, Doctor."

The doctor chuckled, nodding his head as he glanced at the open door again. "I can imagine that's just what he would say—" he told her "—from what I've seen of Mr. Patinous with your uncle." The sharp but friendly eyes looked at her shrewdly. "And what do you think, Miss Foster? Does he need my attention?"

Bryony glanced at the door again and bit her lip. "I—I suppose he knows what's best," she admitted cautiously. "So perhaps he doesn't need anything done to it."

The doctor nodded his head, picking up his hat from the hall table. "Perhaps," he agreed. "If he does, he knows where I am."

Bryony saw him to the door, then went back into the sitting room to meet Alex's black-eyed gaze uneasily. "You did exactly what I told you not to do," he told her, and she flushed indignantly.

"I don't *have* to do as you tell me to," she declared. "I mentioned that you'd hurt your arm but that you didn't want anything done about it." She shrugged with a nonchalance she was far from feeling. "If you want to be stubborn about it, it's up to you."

"Thank you. You also heard that there is nothing wrong with Giles, as I told you, although you insisted I was wrong about it."

"Oh, all right," she said shortly. "You were right, yet again, I'll allow that. It's becoming quite monotonous the number of times you're right."

She looked up and saw a bright glitter of anger in the black eyes. Hastily lowering her own she walked across to the window where she had spent so much time watching for him and Giles to come back.

"But you will not apologize for calling me a liar?"

"I didn't call you a liar," she denied indignantly, turning to face him.

"You told me I was making it up," he insisted. "Though for what reason, I am at a loss to understand. But you did say that you did not believe me, and that is calling me a liar, if I understand your crazy language properly."

"And you expect me to apologize?"

"It would be polite."

She flushed, hating the idea of being made to say she was sorry for such a trivial thing, and she was quite sure he was serious about it, although it could have been laughter that glittered in his eyes now and mocked her uncertainty. "I think you're making an awful fuss about nothing," she declared. "But if you want me to say I'm sorry I didn't believe you—all right, I will."

"Come here."

She blinked at him for a moment, wondering if she had heard him correctly, but he was looking at her quite sternly and she shook her head. "I—"

"Come here," he insisted.

She went, although she wondered at her own compliance, and stood beside him before the fire, her hands feeling suddenly weak and trembling. He looked down at her for several seconds in silence then he put out a hand and raised her chin. "I will not insist on an apology—" he told her softly "—on one condition."

"Condition?" She raised her eyes and saw laughter in his, her pulse racing wildly.

"Will you admit that you worried about me while I was out there looking for your weak-kneed lover?" he asked, and Bryony stared at him for a moment before knocking his hand away and glaring at him angrily.

"I'll do no such thing—" she declared, her face flushed and angry "—and Giles *isn't* my lover!"

He laughed softly, his black eyes taunting her, then he bent his head and kissed her mouth lightly. "That's all I wanted to know," he said.

CHAPTER SEVEN

IT WAS MORE than a week since Giles's disastrous trip in his new boat, and he had not been out in it since. Whether it was because he realized that he was less of a sailor than he had thought, or whether Aunt Merrilyn had discouraged him, Bryony did not know, but she thought it more discreet to say nothing about it until Giles himself raised the subject.

It was not Giles, however, who mentioned the boat, but Alex, one day at lunch, and Bryony glanced warily at Giles, wondering how he would reply. His seasickness was a sore subject and he disliked having it mentioned at all, however obliquely.

"If you want to sell your boat—" said Alex, without preamble "—I would be pleased to buy it from you, Giles."

Hasty looks were exchanged by Giles and his mother, and then Giles shook his head. "I don't want to sell it," he said. "I've only just bought it."

Alex smiled, his black eyes glistening. "I thought perhaps after your experience last time out—" he told him "—you might be considering giving it up."

Giles's good-looking face flushed, and he looked across at Bryony, hating to have the subject raised in front of her. "That was a bit of a mountain out of a molehill," he said, seeking to make as little of it as possible. "There was a bad storm and I was exhausted coping with the boat, but I've certainly no intention of giving it up."

"I wish you would, darling," Aunt Merrilyn told him, and Giles scowled.

"Well, I shan't, mother, so you may as well face up to the fact."

"But I'll worry every time you take the wretched thing out," his mother objected. "You *know* how I worry, Giles. Bryony will tell you that I was nearly out of my mind."

The unexpected appeal made Bryony stare at her for a moment before she nodded agreement. "Aunt Merrilyn was *very* worried, Giles."

Giles brown eyes narrowed slightly as he looked across at her. "Were't you worried too?" he asked, and her glance at Alex was quite involuntary.

"Of course I was," she said. "Anything could have happened."

"That's exactly my point, Giles," his mother told him, before Giles could reply. "*Any*thing could have happened, and I shall be worried to death every time you go out in the wretched thing."

"That's ridiculous, mother!"

"It's true," Aunt Merrilyn insisted, unyielding, and Giles looked uneasy.

"But I enjoy sailing."

He was weakening, Bryony thought, and surprised herself by speaking up on his behalf, even though she foresaw quite a few more episodes like last week's looming in the future. Giles's stubbornness would probably outweigh common sense every time, but she longed to see him stand fast against Aunt Merrilyn—just once.

"It seems rather a shame to part with the boat after you've had it such a little time," she said, and Aunt Merrilyn's sharp, unfriendly eyes fixed themselves on her, her thin lips compressed tightly.

"I wouldn't expect you to be in sympathy with my

point of view, of course, Bryony," she told her, her voice harshly condemning.

"Oh, but it isn't that I'm out of sympathy," Bryony denied hastily. "But Giles does enjoy sailing, Aunt Merrilyn, and he hasn't had the boat very long."

"I'd much rather he'd *never* had it," she was told adamantly. "I dislike the idea of Giles out on the open sea with nothing but a frail motorboat."

"Oh, mother, for heaven's sake," Giles protested. "It isn't frail and not in the least bit dangerous."

"Thousands of people sail that type of craft," Bryony told her, still supporting Giles. "And very few come to grief."

"I have no desire to see my only son become one of the very few who do," Aunt Merrilyn declared. "I don't expect you to understand how I feel, you weren't as worried as I was during that awful storm. Not about Giles, at least." The brief meaningful glance she gave to Alex brought the hot color to Bryony's cheeks. *Dear God,* she thought, *she'll do anything to drive the wedge further in between us.* Alex's expression was scarcely comforting in the circumstances, and she viewed the sardonic lift of his eyebrows and the small, knowing half-smile he wore with dismay.

"That isn't true, Aunt Merrilyn," she denied, wondering if Giles had noticed the byplay. "I was worried about Giles, you know I was."

"I know you seemed concerned about someone—" Aunt Merrilyn agreed "—but I wasn't sure which one of them it was. In view of your subsequent behavior, it can hardly have been Giles, I think."

Bryony looked puzzled. As far as she knew she had treated Giles no differently since the incident. "Subsequent behavior?" she echoed. "I don't quite understand, Aunt Merrilyn."

"I mean that you were scarcely sympathetic when Giles was recovering from his ordeal," Aunt Merrilyn stated firmly. "You acted as if nothing had happened."

"Mother—"

"But he wasn't ill or hurt," Bryony insisted. "He was only...."

"He was ill," Aunt Merrilyn declared inflexibly. "And I consider you were extremely unfeeling in the circumstances." The thin mouth tightened ominously and she looked across at Alex, her expression full of meaning. "I suppose your attention was elsewhere."

"You—" Bryony began, but was silenced by a raised hand, and she looked at Alex's dark face curiously.

"Bryony's concern was for both Giles and myself," he told Aunt Merrilyn quietly. "It does not matter to what degree she was concerned for either one or the other. Worry is natural at a time like that and Bryony is extremely softhearted, as you will have realized."

"Indeed?" The sharp eyes looked at him a little warily.

"She did her best to console you, did she not, Merrilyn?"

The familiar Christian name seemed to inflame her further and her thin face flushed an angry red, her hard dark eyes glittering as she looked at him. "You will not address me in such familiar terms," she told him, her voice razor-edged. "And you can't possibly know what happened here during that storm."

"Bryony told me what happened—" Alex informed her, unperturbed "—and I chose to believe her."

Aunt Merrilyn's lip curled. "No doubt," she said. "But consolation costs nothing and Bryony knows when to be suitably sympathetic, as she is with my brother."

"Aunt Merrilyn!" Bryony's gray eyes widened in disbelief. Never before had Aunt Merrilyn been so virulently antagonistic and she wished Giles would do more about it than merely sit there looking unhappy and rather sheepish.

"I'm not deceived by your look of innocence, even if Giles is."

"Aunt Merrilyn, you're wrong."

"I am not! You've been planning to marry Giles ever since you were at school." Her dark eyes blazed and she threw discretion to the winds, apparently uncaring who heard her accusations. Her face was an alarming shade of red and Bryony wondered if she was about to suffer some sort of a stroke as she glared across the table.

"No! I. . . . "

"A penniless, conniving little opportunist!" Aunt Merrilyn went on relentlessly. "You made up your mind to marry Giles as soon as you were old enough to realize the difference in your circumstances, and you would have succeeded by now, if I hadn't kept Giles out of your way."

"No, no, no!" Tears of anger stood trembling on her lashes and she shook her head despairingly, unable to believe it was happening. If only Giles would come to her aid. Say or do something to stop this vicious tirade against her. But he still sat there, stiff and rather blank-faced, as if he too only half-believed what he saw and heard. "I've never planned any such thing," she insisted, her voice tight in her throat. "And you've no right to say I have."

"Rubbish! You want to marry Giles so that you can have the house and the money *and* the jade. But you shan't have them. I swear it. You—"

"Silence!"

It was almost as if a bomb had dropped and Alex was on his feet, tall and unbelievably stern, with his brows drawn into a straight line above the glittering black eyes. Never had Bryony seen anything so impressive as the depth and fury of his anger, and he stood over Aunt Merrilyn as if he would strike her. He was a figure to inspire fear and awe, but it was not fear that Bryony felt when she looked at him, but a strange kind of excitement that shivered through her body and made her limbs shake.

All eyes were fixed on him as if hypnotized, and Aunt Merrilyn's mouth was half-opened and looked rather foolish. Giles had gone pale and his brown eyes had a bemused look as he stared at Alex.

"You have nothing to fear, Merrilyn," Alex's deep, authoritative voice broke into silence, daring to use that familiar christian name again. "Bryony will not be marrying Giles. It's out of the question."

"Alex!" Bryony attempted to protest, but he ignored her.

"I will not have any further speculation on the subject," he declared shortly. "Bryony cannot marry Giles because she is betrothed to me." Aunt Merrilyn opened her mouth to speak, but a raised hand stopped her. "We will have no more talk of it," he commanded.

"You—" Giles was driven to protest at last, while Bryony stared at Alex, huge-eyed, a baffling mixture of fury and excitement churning in her breast.

"We *will* talk of it," she managed at last. "You have no right to—"

"Be silent!" The curt command cut her short and she subsided though her eyes blazed at him stormily. "There has been too much prevarication," Alex went on, thoroughly in command of the situation. "This—this pathetic schoolboy crush you profess to have for Bryony, Giles, is pitiful in the extreme, especially with a girl like Bryony." His usually undetectable accent was more noticeable, Bryony thought dizzily as she listened to him. "She needs a man who knows what he is about and has no hesitation in letting her know it, not a half-man, clinging to his mama's apron."

It was a cruel judgment, but near enough to the truth to make it even more unpalatable, and Giles clenched his fists on the table, his face flushed and angry, his eyes blazing furiously. "Damn you, Patinous! Damn you, damn you!"

His futile curses were the last words Bryony heard distinctly as she found her way to the door and banged it shut behind her. She cared nothing for the sharp east wind that blew across the exposed cliff-top, but hurried out of the house and down the slope without pause, anxious only to put as much distance as possible between her and Penroyal.

Down the springy turf incline she fled, past the little church and on into the village, her heart racing wildly, her cheeks hotly flushed despite the chilling wind. Never in all her life had she felt so furiously angry or so helpless to do anything about the cause. After such a declaration as Alex Patinous had made, how could she stay and argue that there was absolutely no truth in it? Aunt Merrilyn would never believe her and even Giles would be unconvinced without a good deal of persuasion, and this she was not prepared to provide at the moment.

He had absolutely no right, she fumed as she hurried on, to embarrass her like that. No right at all, and as soon as she had gathered her wits about her and recovered from the shock she would tell him exactly what she thought of him.

The pier was deserted and she halted her headlong flight at last, where the little black trawlers bobbed against the sea wall on the advancing tide, her breathing hard and labored. Her hands were clenched tightly, gray eyes dark as storm clouds as she picked out Giles's shiny white launch further along the pier, dazzling and rather ostentatious among its drab, more practical neighbors.

It was almost without thinking that she walked toward it and stood for a moment on the pier, looking down at the polished wood and brass, and the shiny white paint. Then she cautiously climbed aboard, and studied the instrument board in the cockpit.

During his enthusiastic first flush of ownership Giles had shown her every minute detail of its operation and she thought she could remember enough of what he had told and shown her to get it started at least. It would serve them all right, she decided, if she disappeared for a while and let them worry about her. There was Uncle Miklas, of course, but perhaps he would not need to know until she came back, and she was quite sure he would understand.

The sudden roar of the engine startled her at first, but no one came to question her right to be there and she took the boat, carefully and warily, out into the bay, feeling it respond, all too easily, to a mere touch of her hand. Her heart was hammering uneasily against her ribs as she took the boat out further and she recalled that last voice she had barely heard before she obeyed her instinct to flee. As she had slammed the door she thought someone called out her name, but the resulting bang had drowned it and she could not even be sure whose voice it was. Most likely it had been Alex, and at the thought of Alex her fury was renewed.

There was a slight wind and the air felt damp, but the sea was not too rough and, so far, her stomach had not rebelled. She remembered Marne Rock from her childhood, a small island of rock some five hundred yards off the shore, and she steered towards it. It was small and lonely and quite deserted, exactly suited to her present mood.

There was room, she remembered, on the far side of the island to moor a boat and space to sit in the shelter of the many outcrops of rock that would break the worst of the wind. A good place to hide herself for half an hour or so until she felt more like being sociable toward her annoying family.

She maneuvered the boat around to the far side of the tiny island and was just wondering if she had not been rather ambitious in hoping that she could get close enough to moor it, when, after a few protesting splutters, the engine went dead. "Oh no!" She stared at the gauge and it confirmed her worst fears. The boat was out of fuel and she rued her carelessness in not checking before she set out.

Determined to do other than drift aimlessly in on the tide, she balanced herself precariously on the bow of the boat and was able to reach far enough to throw the painter over a rock and draw the boat in near enough for her to step ashore. She would still be stranded there until someone came along and saw her, but there were usually plenty of boats about, she remembered, when she had been here with Giles and his father.

After nearly two hours Bryony was shivering with cold, and the wool dress that had seemed so cosily warm now felt sticky and damp from the spray and the dampness in the air. She huddled close under a rock overhang and for the first time felt a flicker of fear.

At this time of the year there were no summer visitors, as there had been when she and Giles were staying at Penroyal before, and there would be no pleasure boats leaving Marby Bay—something she had overlooked until now. There would be no craft passing this spot until the trawlers left harbor on the night tide, and that was not for several hours yet.

Reluctantly she left what little shelter she had and climbed to the top of the highest rock from where she could see the deserted pier, and it looked so much further away than she had realized. Also the daylight was going and soon the long, late autumn evening would set in, leaving her alone and invisible to anyone.

Something else caught her eye, too, and made her shiver with something other than the cold. A mist was rising along the shoreline and already the first gray wisps of it drifted between her and the shore. There was little she could do to attract attention to her plight, except stand on the rock and wave her arms, hoping she would be seen. Her dress was a soft, pale yellow and that would help to make her visible against the gray sea and the sky, but she could distinguish no one moving on the pier at the moment.

Her arms were aching and she felt near to tears after half an hour on her cold, precarious perch, and still there had been no answering wave from the shore, although she thought she saw figures moving about. But it was almost too dark now to see anything at all that distance, and the mist was closing in.

Despairingly she sank down onto the cold rock, hugging her arms about her in an effort to stem the chill that was rapidly creeping over her whole body. No one would see her now, with the mist and the darkness both obscuring any attempt she might make to attract attention.

The thought of spending the night on that chill, inhospitable rock island was too much for her, and she began to cry. Great warm, rolling tears that were no consolation at all as she sat in the shelter of the overhang, hugging herself to keep as warm as she could. To be found suffering from exposure because of her own carelessness, after everything else, would be too much to bear.

She was uncertain whether having a watch was a comfort or not, for she could see how slowly the time was passing and it was difficult to believe that it was barely an hour since she had left her perch above, and given up any hope of being seen tonight. Her stomach too was protesting and she realized that she had missed tea and dinner too.

She was so sunk in self-pity that the first sounds of an approaching engine went unoticed. It was only when a voice was raised above the sound of the sea crashing on the rocks that she lifted her head, a sudden wild hope surging in her breast. A boat! It must be a boat, for nothing else would make that rough, chugging wheeze that was rapidly drawing nearer, and she scrambled to her feet, her tear-stained face stiff and chilled but eagerly expectant.

Then she heard the voice again. "Bryony!"

She bit on her lip, some of her eagerness vanishing before embarrassment and uncertainty. Of course it *would* have to be Alex Patinous who found her. She emerged from the shelter of the overhang and was stunned to see how thick the mist was. Combined with the darkness of night she could see almost nothing of her rescuer but a faint yellow light in the bow and two smaller ones of red and green on either side.

"I'm here!"

"Where, for heaven's sake?" He sounded sharp and impatient and she hoped he wasn't alone, as the feeble light turned slowly toward her.

"Here!" A further movement, precariously near to the edge of the rock, and he spotted her yellow dress.

"Don't come any nearer or you'll fall in," he instructed. He avoided colliding with Giles's boat, though heaven knew how, for the light was virtually useless in such a mist, and a moment later the painter came hurtling in her direction, accompanied by a curt order to tie it up to a rock, then he stepped ashore.

He looked huge, looming out of the mist like that, and she stepped back involuntarily, able to distinguish the dark, glowering anger on his face only with difficulty, and then only because she was so close to him. He was dressed in a thick, high-necked sweater of some dark color, and a dark, knee-length jacket, and to Bryony he looked menacingly villainous.

She merely stared at him, her voice dry in her throat, her eyes wide and unconsciously appealing, and for a moment he looked down at her with a gaze that was deep and unfathomable. Then he said something in his own language, unexpectedly soft voiced.

"Alex!"

She was longing now to run into his arms and be held close while his warmth penetrated her chilled body, but she received no encouragement. "You have behaved with unpardonable recklessness," he informed her sternly. "Do you realize that?"

She nodded miserably. "P... please... take me home," she begged, horrified to find her teeth chattering and her legs feeling as if they were about to collapse under her.

He seemed to Bryony to be holding himself unnaturally stiff and there was none of his usual air of mocking non-chalance about him as he looked down at the pale oval of her face. "That will not be possible, I'm afraid," he told her coolly.

She stared at him, uncomprehending for a moment, then the color rushed to her cheeks and she felt the wild, erratic thudding of her heart under her ribs. She must surely have heard him wrongly. "But—but we can't stay here," she protested, searching the dark face for some sign of the familiar taunting smile. But even in that dim, uncertain light she saw nothing but gravity in the black eyes and straight mouth.

"I am afraid we have to," he informed her. "I cannot take the boat back in this mist, it is much too dangerous. As it was, the man who rented me the boat refused to come with me because the mist is getting so thick."

"But, Alex—"

"It is useless to argue, Bryony." He sounded impatient again. "It was by mere chance that I saw you in the first place. It was almost dark and I had searched everywhere else. I saw Giles's boat was gone and guessed you would have been just foolish enough to have taken it out on your own."

"I—I wanted to get away for a while," she explained reproachfully. "I couldn't know it would run out of fuel."

"If you had been careful you would have checked the gauge first," he told her shortly. "I supposed it was something of the sort when I saw you waving for help."

"That was hours ago," she said, grudgingly.

"It took me nearly an hour to find my way here in the mist and the darkness," he informed her. "I was warned I was asking for trouble to come, but I couldn't let you stay out here all night alone."

The risk he had taken in coming to fetch her only now came home to her and she lowered her eyes, a little ashamed of the ungraciousness of her reception. "Thank you for coming, Alex. I really am grateful."

"I'm glad to hear it."

His tone almost brought her anger back again, but she had made a voluntary truce for the time being and she did not want to be the one to break it if she could help it. "I—I'm worried about Uncle Miklas," she told him. "If I—we're out all night, he'll be worried sick."

"We have to be here all night," he said adamantly. "We have no choice."

"But you *got* here."

"And I have no intention of making the return journey in such conditions just to salve your maidenly conscience," he told her, an edge of steel in his voice. "So do not attempt to persuade me, Bryony."

"But Uncle Miklas—"

"He won't know," he told her confidently. "I gave instructions that he was not to be told anything about it, and Nurse Carter will see that I am obeyed."

"Obeyed!" The gibe was torn from her, due to the anxiety she felt for the possible effect on Miklas's health if he found out they were missing all night, and from the bitter resentment aroused by his autocratic manner. "You always take it for granted that you'll be obeyed, don't you?"

"I usually am." He sounded so calm and matter-of-fact it was unbearable. He was always arrogant and sure of himself, but it seemed to Bryony that there was a new and inexplicable aloofness about him now that puzzled her.

She shivered, and her teeth were chattering again as the mist crept into her bones. "I'm s...so c...cold," she complained.

Without comment he took off the thick jacket he wore and wrapped it around her, pulling the neck of it close under her chin, while Bryony closed her eyes to the ecstasy of its warmth. "I should have known you would come without a coat," he told her as she hugged the jacket to her, uncaring about anything else at the moment.

She bit on her lips and looked up at him, her emotions too confused to sort out anger from relief. "I was too upset by...by your...your ridiculous announcement," she informed him between shivers, and she saw a hint of a smile crook one corner of his mouth.

"I don't think you were as much upset as surprised,"

he declared confidently. "I was interested to see what Giles would do, and I was not disappointed. He did nothing."

"You—" She stared at him in the feeble yellow light from the bow of the boat. "Oh, you—you despicable, unfeeling brute! How could you do anything so—so underhanded and callous?"

He shrugged briefly. "I don't consider I did," he informed her. "If Giles had really cared for you, he would have done something more constructive than emit a few mild curses."

She shrugged down further into the enveloping jacket and wished she had more grounds for arguing with him, her eyes downcast, her mouth softly reproachful. "Where—where's Giles now?" she asked, and he laughed shortly.

"Out searching for you," he told her. "We had no idea which way you'd gone, so Giles looked along the Marby Head direction and I came the other way. Of course it was some time before we realized that you'd left the house at all."

"I—I suppose I should have told someone I was going," she admitted.

"It would have been more thoughtful, but less characteristic," he said, and raised a silencing hand when she would have protested. He looked behind him where the two boats were moored and nodded. "I think we'll use Giles's boat," he decided.

She looked at him uncertainly, her heart suddenly skipping nervously again as she clasped the heavy jacket to her throat. "Why only Giles's boat?" she asked. "There are two."

"There are two," he agreed quietly. "But you've been out in the cold and damp too long already and we do not want you down with pneumonia. There is more protec tion in Giles's from wind and spray so we will use his."

"B—but I'm quite w—warm now," she protested through chattering teeth. "I'll be all right, Alex."

"You will do as I say," he told her shortly, and lifted her off her feet as easily as if she had been a child.

"No!"

He deposited her none too gently in the cockpit of Giles's boat and stepped down after her. "Go as far under as you can get," he instructed. He pulled the two long leather cushions from the side seats and put them in the bottom of the boat, side by side. "Now sit down."

"No, I—"

"Sit down!" His voice was thunderous and she could see him well enough to be deterred from further argument by the glitter in his black eyes. she sat down, as near the edge of the cushions as she could get, his coat huddled around her, her face half-buried in the upturned collar.

It was certainly more sheltered, and she wondered why she had not considered doing the same when she was on her own, but she had no intention of trying to sleep even if she was obliged to stay there all night.

He came and sat beside her, forcibly close because of the narrowness of the boat, and she watched the small flame of his lighter longingly as he lit a cigarette. She did not usually smoke, but there was something comforting about the red glow of the cigarette, and she pursed her lips over his lack of courtesy in not offering her one.

"I'd like a cigarette too," she told him.

He turned his lead in her direction, but the light was less use down here in the depths of the boat and she could only guess at his expression. "You do not smoke," he declared.

"But I—I'd like one now."

He made no move to take out his cigarette case again

and the glowing tip traveled once more to his lips before he spoke. "I do not like women to smoke—" he informed her then "—and I do not want you making yourself sick from sheer bravado."

"I . . . ." she stared at the dark outline of him in frustrated anger. "Oh, you—I *hate* you!"

"I do not believe that—" he told her calmly "—and as you have to have my company for the rest of the night, you might as well try to stop fighting me, at least for a while."

She glared at his shadowy bulk angrily. "Why couldn't Giles have come for me?" she complained. "Why did it have to be you?"

He laughed shortly, and drew on the cigarette again before he answered. "It was a matter of luck," he informed her, and she knew he was looking at her steadily even though she could not see him very well. "Also, he is not sure at the moment whether he wants to find you. No doubt he will have decided one way or the other by morning."

"And that's your fault," Bryony accused. "For making that—that ridiculous statment about—about our being engaged."

Surprisingly he chuckled, and the sound of it was so comfortingly familiar that, for the moment, she was grateful for it. "Under the circumstances it is as well that we are considred betrothed," he told her. "Then it will not seem quite so compromising if we spend the night together."

"Spend—" She held her breath for a moment, realizing for the first time that that was just the phrase that Aunt Merrilyn would use. Giles would never forgive her for allowing herself to become so compromised, however much of an unwilling partner she was.

"Do you not feel slighted that the man who professes to love you allows you to be so ill-used by his mother?" he asked, ignoring her half-formed protest.

She found it difficult to answer that without being untruthful and she hesitated for several seconds while she sought an answer. "Giles—well, Giles is different, away from Aunt Merrilyn," she explained, and he laughed shortly.

"Such a valiant lover," he jeered. "Who trembles when his mother calls."

"Oh, stop it! Leave Giles alone!" She felt near to tears again and bit on her lip anxiously. There were many times when she had wished Giles could have been less ruled by his mother, but she hated to hear him so maligned by this man who had no fear of anything or anybody and cared little or nothing for the opinions of others. He could not possibly understand.

"I am quite willing to do so," he told her quietly. "But can you?"

"I . . . I'm going to marry Giles," she told him, feeling obliged to put on a bold face. "I—"

"Do you love him?" The question was short and autocratic and she was silent for a moment before she answered.

"That has nothing to do with you," she said at last, and subsided into silence.

"It has if you are engaged to me." His voice was low and held something that quickened her pulse and made her hug her arms to herself closer than ever. She would refuse to rise to his provocation and ignore him for the rest of the time they were there.

At the thought of the long, dark, silent hours before her, she shivered and closed her eyes, but refused to even consider making herself more comfortable. The luminous face of her watch told her how slowly the time was going, and she would have sworn that a whole night had passed when an anxious check revealed it to be only half-past ten.

"Why don't you try to sleep?" His voice sounded soft

and persuasive and she turned her head briefly to see him propped up on one elbow, apparently quite at ease on the improvised bed.

"No, thank you."

"You cannot stay awake all night," he argued, and she shrugged herself into the coat collar.

"I can if I decide to," she told him.

She did not understand the foreign word he said, but its meaning was pretty plain from his tone of voice and she felt the warm wetness of tears in her eyes again, biting her lip as it trembled warningly.

"Leave me alone," she said, her voice shaking betrayingly.

"Of course." It was obvious that he had interpreted her remark much differently than she had intended it, and she turned her head to berate him. But she was tired and cold and her head ached abominably, so that instead of retorting sharply as she had meant to she made a small, sobbing sound and crumpled her head on to the cushion, her shoulders hunched despondently under the thick coat.

Crying was a relief and the tears came fast and uncontrollably. She no longer cared if he thought her a baby or not as she sobbed, her face buried in the rough coat collar. The cushion was almost as hard and unyielding as the bottom of the coat would have been, but she did not care about that either as she lay there, a tearful and pathetic bundle in the darkness.

The cushion beside her whispered softly when he moved and his hands lay on her shoulders for a moment before they slid across her back and down to her waist, pulling her close to the lean, hard warmth of his body. "Sshh!" His mouth was close to her ear and his face buried in her hair.

The words he spoke so softly were indecipherable to

her, but there was comfort and reassurance in the sound of his voice and she buried her face in the warm hollow of his shoulder. "Don't cry, please don't cry," he begged softly in English, his voice muffled against her hair, then his lips brushed briefly against her forehead, and softly on her tearful cheeks.

"I...I didn't want to."

His laugh was deep and warm and reverberated through her body. "Then stop it, *mikros eros*."

"I...I'll try."

He held her close and before she realized it, her tears had ceased and she felt a glowing warmth running through her whole body. She was never quite sure how it was that she suddenly found herself clinging to him as if he was her one hope in life, her arms clasped behind his neck, her fingers twined in that curl of rough, black hair that touched his collar.

"Bryony!"

There was an urgency in the deep, soft voice suddenly, and the arms that held her tightened like a band of steel around her. Another whisper of movement and she was swept into a hold that threatened to crush the breath from her. His breath stirred the damp tendrils of her hair as he murmured more words in his own language, then his mouth sought and held hers in a fierce possession.

She responded instinctively, as to some wild, uncontrollable longing, the blood singing through her veins, unconscious of her surroundings and everything else except that she needed him more than any other living soul at that moment.

It was all the more hard to believe, therefore, a few minutes later when she heard that soft whisper of movement again and the arms that held her were withdrawn. He was on his feet by the time she recovered her breath, standing upright, his tall shape looming like a dark figure-head against the gloomy mist.

She sat up, her legs curled under her, the coat clutched to her throat, uncertain what the true state of her feelings was in the turmoil of emotions she felt. Then he turned his head and spoke over his shoulder.

"Job's comforter, isn't that the name you use?" he asked. The flame of the lighter flicked and died before she spoke, and she watched the red glow of cigarette rise and fall as he drew smoke into his lungs and expelled it, adding to the swirling mist.

"I... I'm sorry, Alex." It seemed almost ludicrous to apologize so formally to him after the last few minutes, but she felt that she was in some way to blame for what had happened. Perhaps even more than he was.

He turned then and, although she could not see them well, she knew that the black eyes were peering at her speculatively in the darkness, and it was not too difficult to imagine his more usual self finding the situation very amusing.

"Are you blaming yourself?" he asked, and she nodded, then realized he could not possibly see it.

"I... in a way, yes," she admitted, and he laughed, a soft, deep sound in the clinging mist. A sound that sent new shivers along her spine and curled her fingers as they held the coat tightly to her chin.

He said nothing for a moment and she wondered at his not denying it. "In the circumstances—" he said quietly, a moment later "—I think it might be best if I stay at this end and keep watch in case the mist clears and someone comes to find us."

"You think they will?"

He shrugged. "The man I rented the boat from knows that I came out here to fetch you," he said, "and he will no doubt rouse someone to come here if the mist lifts, even if only because he fears the loss of his boat."

"I see."

"Try to get some sleep."

"What about you?"

He laughed softly. "I don't need sleep," he told her. "I'll sit in the stern and keep watch." The cigarette tip made a glowing arc as it curved toward the water and she sat still looking at him, uncertain and sleepless.

"I...I shan't sleep."

"You can try."

He turned away from her again and took out another cigarette, the lighter flaring briefly to reveal the strong, dark features. Piratical, she had once thought of them, and she watched for as long as the small bright flame lasted, then hunched her shoulders in the thick jacket and settled back to wait, a curious and inexplicable feeling of disappointment pouting her lips as she closed her eyes.

CHAPTER EIGHT

It was to the gentle rocking of the boat that Bryony awoke next morning and it took her a moment or two to realize where she was, then she instinctively raised her head and looked down to the stern of the boat to see if Alex was still there. He would be, of course, he could not have gone and left her without her knowing it, but the sight of him reassured her.

He lay full length on one of the wooden seats, his long arms stretched above his head as he yawned lazily. She sat upright on her bed of cushions and glanced down at the thick coat she still wore, putting a hand to her tousled hair. It was not the most flattering state to wake up in and she rued the fact that she had nothing with her that would help to make her more presentable, not even a comb for her hair.

She looked across at him again. "Hello."

Lazily he turned his head and looked at her for a moment before he smiled, noting her dishevelment, then he sat up and ran his fingers through his hair. "Good morning." He yawned again and stretched with an animal-like grace, easing his long limbs from the cramped confines of the seat. "Did you sleep?"

"I...I suppose I must have done," Bryony agreed, and looked at the hard wooden seat he occupied. "You should have taken one of these cushions," she told him. "I didn't really need them both, and I had your coat too."

He smiled again, quirking an eyebrow at her. "I could hardly take it from you," he said. "And I'm quite happy as I am, thank you."

Now that she could see him plainly for the first time since last night, she felt a sudden sense of shyness and avoided his eyes carefully as she touched her hair again. "I must look a terrible mess," she said. "I suppose it's too much to hope you have a comb?"

"It is," he agreed. "I don't carry one in this sort of outfit, but you don't have to worry about the way you look." The black eyes swept over her boldly and lingeringly, laughter lurking in their depths. "You would look beautiful even after a shipwreck."

She got to her feet, stretching as he had done, looking across to where Marby Bay was just becoming vaguely discernible in the growing light. "Will someone be coming out to see if we're all right, do you think?"

He shrugged. "I should think not. The mist has cleared and I have enough fuel to take us back to shore."

"Giles's boat too?"

He smiled wryly. "Giles's boat too, if you like. We can tie it astern and tow it in." He stood up, looming large in the gray light. "You're worried as much about what he will have to say about you taking his boat as about... us. Hmm?"

She kept her eyes downcast and made some effort to brush the creases from her dress and the jacket.

"I—I don't know what to say about—about being here," she said slowly. "Giles will never understand, mostly because Aunt Merrilyn will give him all sorts of ideas about me." She glanced up briefly. "It wouldn't have been quite so bad if you hadn't been here too," she told him.

"I'm sorry." His features were composed into an expression of regret, but the laughter still glittered in his

eyes. "Would you rather I had left your here alone?"
"Oh no, of course not!"

"Then there was only one alternative," he pointed out. "And much as Giles will disapprove, I cannot think that he would have done any differently in the circumstances."

She stared at him for a moment, surprised to hear him giving Giles the benefit of the doubt in anything. "I'm sure he'd have done the same thing," she agreed.

"So—" he spread his hands in the first really Greek gesture she had ever seen him use "—how can he blame me for doing as he would have done himself?"

"I...I don't know that he'll blame you, exactly," she said. "After all, it was *my* fault it happened at all."

His brows shot upward. "Your fault?" he said softly. "I was under the impression that I was to be the villain."

"Well, it was you initially." She felt the color rise in her cheeks again and wished she could just for once, get the better of him. "If you hadn't told that—that awful lie about—about us being engaged, it would never have happened."

"Ah!" He nodded his head. "I thought I would eventually—what is your slang expression—carry the can?"

"Only because you deserve to!" she retorted. She looked across at the gradually emerging shoreline and thought about Uncle Miklas. If only she could think of some credible-sounding reason that would console Uncle Miklas for her behavior she would be content, no matter what Giles thought. "Can we leave now?" she asked. "Before it gets too light?"

"Before there are too many people about?" he guessed, and laughed softly at the color that flooded her cheeks.

"Please can we go?"

"Of course." He tried the painter of Giles's boat to

the stern of the borrowed one and helped her aboard, his eyes smiling wickedly at her as he lifted her in beside him.

"You're enjoying this," she accused, as he started the engine and shattered the stillness of the early morning with its racket.

"Am I?" he asked.

"You know you are. You might almost have planned it the way you've...."

Something in his manner and the way he turned a frowning brow on her made her stop in mid-sentence. "I could not have planned it and you know it, Bryony. It was your own foolishness that left you stranded on that rock and I was the one that happened to find you. Anything that happened last night can be put down to circumstances, and left unmentioned once we are ashore."

She glared at him reproachfully, the coat held almost defensively around her. "I suppose you're not new to this sort of situation," she guessed, and again the black brows flicked upward as he turned and looked down at her.

"I have been in somewhat similar situations before," he allowed quietly. "Although scarcely in such discomfort or with such disappointing results."

Bryony felt her cheeks flaming, and she looked straight ahead at the approaching coastline of Marby Bay, a choking sensation in her throat suddenly. "I'm—I'm sorry you were put to so much trouble only to be disappointed," she told him, her voice trembling horribly. "But I'm not used to...to...."

"Spending the night with a man?" he suggested softly, and to her dismay, laughed when she lifted her chin in defiance of his opinion. He must have thought her a silly and gullible female for surrendering so easily to the comfort of his arms.

She refused to say another word but stood stiff and withdrawn beside him until they came alongside the pier in Marby Bay. He helped her ashore, holding her longer than was necessary, a faint tantalizing smile around his mouth when she pushed his hands away and stalked off indignantly along the pier. She would never again feel at ease with him because she could not forget the way he had kissed her, the way his arms had held her as if he would never let her go.

She was a fool, she told herself, as she walked toward the green and gray rise of the cliff, but she could not help the persistent skip her heart gave every time she thought of being with him in Giles's boat. She should have repulsed him from the moment she felt his hands on her shoulders, instead she had turned to him, lain against the lean hard curve of his body and allowed him to kiss her as no other man had ever done before. Alex Patinous was a practised and experienced lover and no doubt he had thought her easy prey, but unexciting. It was the last thought that made her bite her lip.

His long legs made little of the distance between them, and before she had gone very far up the incline he was beside her again, looking down at her flushed face as if he guessed something of her thoughts and found it amusing.

The turf was springy underfoot and wet too, with the heavy dew. The first glimpse of sun sat hazily on the horizon and she unconsciously registered the fact that it was going to be another fine day.

She had never before approached Penroyal with such reticence, but she hated the thought of facing Giles and Aunt Merrilyn. Probably Giles would already be up and wondering why she had not come in before now. She could scarcely believe that she had slept at all in the circumstances that had existed—that she had slept so well was astounding, although, no doubt, the gentle rocking of the boat had had something to do with it.

Her companion seemed even less affected by his uncomfortable night. It must have been incredibly hard on that wooden seat and yet he showed no after-effects at all. True, his black hair was tossed and untidy and his chin showed the need to shave off the first dark shadow of a beard, but he seemed otherwise quite normal.

She studied him for a moment from under her lashes and decided that he looked, if anything, even more piratical and disreputable than ever, but there was a spring in his step as he walked beside her and he looked almost as if he faced the prospect of a family storm with pleasure.

He glanced around suddenly and smiled when he caught her watching him, murmuring something in his own tongue that she had no hope of understanding. One hand rubbed over his stubbly chin. "I'll probably frighten the housekeeper to death," he guessed with a laugh, and cocked one brow at her quizzically. "Do I frighten you with my early morning face, Bryony?"

She shook her head, feeling that wild hammering of her heart again at the sudden intimacy of his voice. "No," she denied. "Although you do need a shave, certainly."

"I could grow a beard and become the buccaneer you think me," he suggested, and laughed when she looked discomfited. "You do think of me as an old-time buccaneer, don't you?" he asked. "You told Miklas so."

Bryony bit her lip. "Oh, he shouldn't have told you that," she protested. "It wasn't fair."

"All's fair in love and war," he quoted surprisingly, and she glanced at him, startled by his use of the proverb.

"This is neither," she told him, and he laughed again,

one hand reaching for hers as they climbed the steep rise toward the house.

Mrs. Trevellyan was getting breakfast when they came in, and she looked at them in such a way as left no doubt as to *her* opinion of people who stayed out all night, her small suspicious eyes reminding Bryony of Aunt Merrilyn.

Bryony would have liked to run straight up to her room, but Alex's hand holding hers precluded any idea of immediate flight, and she felt herself coloring furiously when he smiled a greeting to the housekeeper.

"Good morning," he said, but she merely nodded her head. "Is there hot water for baths?"

"There is," she allowed grudgingly. "But Mr. Giles is using the near bathroom at the moment."

"Very well." He smiled down at Bryony. "You go and use the other bathroom, Bryony, and I'll follow Giles when he has finished."

"I'm very hungry," she explained. "I've had nothing since lunch yesterday."

"Then the sooner you get out of those damp things and come down for your breakfast the better," he told her.

"I...."

She knew the housekeeper was watching her, waiting for her to argue with him, but instead she shook her head and fled up the stairs, wondering what newly acquired meekness had made her do as he told her without demur. She passed Uncle Miklas's room and heard a murmur of voices, hesitating whether to go in and see him first, but then she remembered that it was possible he did not yet know she had been out all night, and she did not want to be the one to tell him. It was only as she was undressing that she realized that, yet again, she was doing exactly as Alex Patinous had wanted her to.

She stripped off every stitch and wrapped herself in a

warm dressing grown, armed herself with a sponge and set off toward the bathroom, her slippered feet swishing softly on the carpeted landing. It was as she passed the door of the occupied bathroom that the door opened and Giles came out.

He looked fresh-faced and newly shaved and smelled of some spicy lotion that tickled her nose pleasantly. When he saw her he stared for a moment, as if he was not quite sure what he should do, then his brows drew together and he drew himself up to his full height and looked down his nose at her.

"Good morning, Bryony."

The conventional greeting was loaded with suspicion and innuendo, and Bryony felt her cheeks burning furiously. "Good morning, Giles."

He continued to look at her for a moment, then shifted uneasily when she said no more. "Are...are you all right?"

"Yes, thank you."

He would never realize, she thought wonderingly, how much he could have achieved if only he had taken her in his arms and told her how worried he had been about her. But it was useless to expect so much of him when Aunt Merrilyn had had her say first.

"I...we were worried about you."

"Were you?"

"Of course, anything could have happened to you."

"I'm sorry." She looked up suddenly, thinking of Uncle Miklas. "Uncle Miklas doesn't know, does he?"

He shook his head swiftly. "No, we didn't tell him. We thought it best not to worry him."

"I'm so glad. I was so worried about him knowing and perhaps having an attack because he was upset about us—me being missing, but Alex said...." she stopped then, realizing how tactless she had been.

The darkness gathered in Giles's brown eyes and for a brief second he looked incredibly like Alex. "Alex said!" he echoed harshly. "Patinous thinks he owns Penroyal, but he's going to discover his mistake before very long. As soon as Uncle Miklas has gone, Patinous is getting out of this house and he'll never come into it again."

"Giles, don't!"

He had sounded so unfeeling in his reference to his uncle and Bryony hated to think of Penroyal without the old man. It would never be the same again once he was gone, and she doubted if she would be any more welcome there than Alex. Aunt Merrilyn would see to that.

"I'm sorry." The apology was instinctive and he put out a hand to her while Bryony suddenly realized that, away from Aunt Merrilyn, she could probably have as much influence over him as his mother did. "Bryony!" He touched her arm, tentatively, as if afraid she might repulse him, and his expression was anxious rather than condemning now.

"I...I shall hate it without Uncle Miklas," she told him. "I'm very fond of him, Giles, and I hate to hear you talk as—as if he didn't matter."

"I didn't mean it to sound like that," he insisted. He put a hand to his brow and pushed back a thick fall of brown hair that hid his forehead. "I was just so furious about you and Patinous yesterday that I'm not thinking straight yet. I just don't understand, Bryony."

"Neither do I," she confessed ruefully. "But I didn't enjoy being out all night, Giles. It was cold and cramped and very uncomfortable."

"Where *were* you? I gather Patinous must have found you since he was out all night, too."

She felt an utter fool as she answered him. "I was on Marne Rock," she said.

He stared at her, suspicion stirring again. "But how on earth did you get out there?"

She looked down at her hands, remembering Alex's suggestion that she was as concerned about Giles's reaction to her taking his boat as she was about being with him all night. "I...I took your boat," she confessed, and glanced up in time to see the horrified expression on his face.

"My boat! Good heavens, Bryony, what on earth possessed you?"

She was uncertain which he was most concerned about, the idea of her being in danger or the fate of his boat. "I was angry and fed up," she told him. "I saw your boat by the pier and...well, I just took it."

"Where is it now?"

"Back at the pier. We towed it in this morning behind the boat Alex borrowed."

"Towed it?" He looked as if he suspected the worst. "Why? How much damage have you done?"

Bryony looked at him reproachfully. Obviously the boat was his main concern at the moment. "There's no damage done," she informed him a little stiffly. "I ran out of fuel, that's all. Fortunately, Alex spotted me waving for help fromm the top of Marne Rock, and he borrowed another boat and came out to me."

Giles looked as if his worst suspicions had been confirmed. "If he saw you waving to him, it must still have been daylight," he said. "So why was it necessary for you to spend all night out there?"

"Because it was almost dark when he saw me," she explained, rapidly losing patience with him. "By the time he could find another boat and persuade the man to rent it to him, the mist was coming down pretty thick and it was getting darker all the time. The man refused to come with him because the mist was so bad, and it took him hours to find me. It would have been completely foolhardy to attempt to return journey with conditions as they were."

"So you slept in the boats, I suppose?"

She nodded. "We slept in the boats," she agreed, bending the truth a little for the sake of peace.

He looked at her for several seconds, his brown eyes dark and unhappy, then he shook his head and put his hands on her shoulders. "I...I still don't understand about...about yesterday at lunch time," he said slowly. "Why on earth did Patinous make that statement about you and him being...being engaged or betrothed or whatever he calls it?"

She lowered her gaze, unwilling to look at him because she wished she *knew* exactly why Alex had done it. "I don't know," she confessed.

"It couldn't be true, could it?" he begged, and she felt her color rise, her pulse quickening.

"Of course it isn't true," she said. "Though I've no doubt Aunt Merrilyn wishes it was."

"Bryony!"

"It's true, Giles." She looked up at him again, her gray eyes bright with determination. "You know Aunt Merrilyn will never feel any differently about me, and I don't feel inclined to have to face her on my own every time she chooses to—to launch an attack."

"Oh, darling, it'll be different when we're married and living here at Penroyal. She won't be able to interfere then."

Bryony sighed, suddenly very tired and hungry. "I wish I could believe that—" she told him "—but somehow I can't, Giles."

"But don't...." He looked at her anxiously, seeming lost and helpless somehow and not at all like the self-confident business man she had first thought him. "Don't say no, Bryony, please," he begged. "Not a definite no. Give me a chance to try and change."

She studied his face for a moment, then smiled slowly. "I'm not sure it would work, even if you did stand up to Aunt Merrilyn," she told him frankly. "You were ready to suspect the worst of me because I was stranded last night."

"Oh, darling, please! I'm sorry."

"I believe you. I suppose it was Aunt Merrilyn again," she added wryly, and saw the blood come into his face as he admitted it.

"I tried to argue," he told her, "but everything was against you, darling. The fact that Patinous had made that...that idiotic statement about the two of you, and then you were both missing last night. It did *look* bad, Bryony, you have to admit it."

"I do admit it," she told him frankly. "But I would appreciate it if you spoke up for me sometimes, Giles. Told Aunt Merrilyn that you believe me, for a change, and aren't prepared to let me be browbeaten."

"I know, I know!" He ran his fingers through his hair, his brow creased. "I will try, darling, I promise."

"Oh, Giles!"

She reached up a hand and touched his face gently, her fingers caressing his cheek, her eyes warm and understanding. She could not have realized how appealingly lovely she looked in the enveloping blue robe, with her golden fair hair tumbled and wisping about her face.

Giles's arms reached for her and he made a soft moaning sound as he pulled her into his arms, burying his face in her hair. "Bryony! Bryony, I love you!"

She was surprised to find herself less appreciative of his display of affection than she had ever been before, and she held her body rather stiffly in resistance, avoiding too close a contact with him. Remembering how easily and willingly she had gone to Alex's arms last night, she thought only of resisting another such incident with Giles and she used her hands to push herself away from him.

He looked pained and would have protested, she thought, but there were footsteps coming up the stairs and they did not belong to the housekeeper. It was only seconds before Alex appeared and his black brows shot upward at the sight of them, a hint of smile on his mouth.

"Good morning, Giles."

Giles merely glared at him, but Alex was unconcerned and the black gaze came to rest on Bryony's tousled head and the enveloping robe. "You have not had your bath yet, *mikros eros*," he said to her. "And you said you were hungry, so why don't you bathe and dress and get some breakfast, hmm?"

"I...I've been talking to Giles," she explained, and Giles glared at him angrily.

"Why don't you mind your own damned business, Patinous?" he demanded hoarsely, his face flushed, the brown eyes looking almost as black as Alex's.

"But it is my business if Bryony stands around and catches pneumonia or dies of starvation," he argued quietly, a glint of wickedness in his eyes. "I went to a great deal of trouble to rescue her and I would hate to see my efforts wasted."

"I can guess how much trouble you went to—" Giles retorted "—and I'm damned glad your efforts *were* wasted."

"Oh, I don't think they were entirely wasted, were they?" he asked softly the black eyes fixed on Bryony's mouth in a way that set her pulses racing wildly and gave her the urge to flee back to her room and hide herself.

"You mean...." Giles began, his face an alarming shade of red that reminded Bryony irresistibly of his mother, and he looked at her sharply.

"I mean—" Alex told him firmly "—that rescuing your beautiful cousin from a watery grave was not wasted time or effort, as I'm sure you'll agree."

"Oh...oh yes, of course." Giles looked sheepishly at her and his eyes begged forgiveness again.

"I expected to find you jumping to all the wrong conclusions," Alex informed him calmly, ignoring the black frown on Giles's brow. "But you have no cause to be so insulting toward Bryony, surely. Don't you trust her?"

"You...." Giles fumed, his hands clenched at his sides. "If you had an ounce of decency, Patinous, you'd leave this house after the way you behaved yesterday at lunch."

"Leave the house?" Alex's black eyes hardened and the arrogant head came up sharply. Despite the night's growth of beard, Bryony thought hazily, he still looked as proud and arrogant as Lucifer and she put a hand to her breast to still the lurch it gave before skipping crazily against her ribs. "You do not own Penroyal yet, I think," he said quietly, and Giles had the grace to look ashamed.

"Not yet," he admitted, his voice harsh with anger. "But when I do, Patinous, you'll be out of here so fast you'll wonder what hit you!"

Alex's black eyes encompassed Bryony again and she bit her lip as she hastily lowered her gaze. "Not until I have what's rightfully mine," he said softly, and strode off down the landing to his own room, laughing quietly as he went.

"Damn him!" Giles fumed, watching the tall lean figure disappear. "Damn him, damn him!" And Bryony, turning to go on her own way, sighed resignedly to hear history repeating itself.

CHAPTER NINE

BRYONY TRIED TO AVOID being alone with Alex whenever possible, although most times it was difficult. If Aunt Merrilyn had been trying to play matchmaker, Bryony thought wryly, she could not have done more to ensure their being together.

She made sure that Giles was not available by having him take her into Marby shopping so often that Bryony was quite sure it was unnecessary. She demanded that he accompany her when she went for her walks too, always carefully omitting to invite Bryony to come with them. So far Giles had done little to resist the deliberate campaign, merely shrugging helplessly when his mother commanded his company again.

One afternoon, however, she had accepted an invitation to visit an old acquaintance in the district whom she had not seen since her girlhood and, since Giles had not been included in the invitation, she had gone off alone, although she had not liked the idea, obviously.

It was a lovely day. Bright as only autumn can be, with the trees wearing the last of their glowing colors and the sun clear and bright in a pale blue sky. Giles greeted Bryony at lunch time with a smile of triumph while his mother's attention was taken up with her meal, and Bryony could not help experiencing a twinge of impatience at his attitude.

How could a man of thirty, who successfully ran a prosperous business, be such a child when it came to dealing with his own mother? Certainly Aunt Merrilyn was a formidable woman by anyone's standards, but surely Giles must realize that if it came to the point, she would never insist on her own way to the extent of losing him. He had the upper hand, if only he could see it.

She responded to his smile, however, and quite looked forward to spending the afternoon with him, although she had no idea what plans he had in mind. Probably they would do nothing more strenuous than walk along the cliff as far as Marby Bay, or perhaps in the opposite direction to the haunts of their mutual ancestors. Whichever it was, Bryony had no objections, for she loved the area wholeheartedly and never tired of seeing it in all its different moods and variations.

Involuntarily she looked across at Alex, and felt a brief touch of pity for him, although the idea seemed ludicrous, on reflection. Alex Patinous was the last person on earth to need anyone's pity. It was simply that she had suddenly remembered her earlier vow to be pleasant and companionable to him because he was in a strange country. Lately she had been bent on avoiding him rather than being friendly and she felt rather guilty about it.

He had been obliged to take solitary walks because certainly Giles or Aunt Merrilyn would not invite him to join them and she thought he was a man who enjoyed company, although, possibly, of his own choosing.

Sensing her watching him, he looked up suddenly and caught and held her gaze so that she hastily sought a distraction. His black eyes were unfathomable and, after a moment, he smiled, a raised eyebrow quizzing the reason for her interest. Perhaps, after all, it would be better to leave things as they were.

"I THOUGHT WE might have dinner in Marby," Giles suggested as they walked down to the cliff's edge after lunch, and Bryony looked at him curiously, sensing an air of excitement about him that could not be entirely due to his mother's absence. "It would be fun, Bryony."

"Is it possible?" she asked. "I mean won't Aunt Merrilyn be expecting to see you at dinner here?"

He frowned, sensitive to the gentle gibe, and thrust both hands into his pants pockets. "Mother's staying out for dinner as well," he told her. "And anyway, I'd still have asked you, Bryony, you don't have to make snide remarks like that."

"I'm sorry. But I know Aunt Merrilyn wouldn't have been very pleased if she *had* been coming back here for dinner and found you missing. You don't usually like crossing her, do you?"

"No," he agreed, surprisingly frank, "I don't."

"Where are we going?"

"Tonight?" She nodded. "I thought we might try that new place that's just opened in Codden Street. I've not been there and it's supposed to be very good, I believe."

Bryony smiled wryly. "That," she informed him dryly, "has a hint of big city condescension about it, my lad, whether you intended it or not."

"I didn't," he said. "But I do want to take you somewhere especially decent tonight, darling."

"Do you?" She looked up at him curiously. "Why especially tonight?"

He looked for a moment as if he was going to tell her his reason, then he shook his head and smiled. "Wait and see," he told her.

Something in his voice, in the way he looked at her, gave her a clue to the reason, and she bit her lip anxiously. She was not prepared to tell Giles that she would marry him yet, nor did she relish the idea of the alternative, and she was pretty sure that a romantic evening followed by a proposal was what was in his mind.

"Giles."

"Hmm?"

She had her arm through his and she felt the muscles in it tense under her fingers, suspecting what she was going to say, evidently. "I—I hope you're not going to—to ask me, again, to marry you."

He looked down at her, a shadow of doubt between his brows. "As a matter of fact I was," he said, sounding disappointed already and a bit put out by her frankness. "I was going to suggest that this afternoon we go into Marby and choose a ring and then celebrate the occasion tonight with dinner."

So her guess had been right, Bryony thought ruefully, and shook her head slowly. "I'd much rather you didn't, Giles."

He was silent for a moment and she began to feel rather mean and unkind. "Do you mean you're not willing to marry me?" he asked, and she flinched from the disappointment in his voice.

"I...I can't, Giles."

"But I thought...you *aren't* tied up with Alex Patinous, are you? You said you weren't."

"I'm not," she agreed. "I'm not...tied up with anybody at the moment, Giles, and I'm not sure I want to be. I'm quite happy as I am."

"Well, I'm not," Giles retorted sharply. "But I suppose that doesn't matter, does it?"

"Oh, Giles, for heaven's sake, don't feel so sorry for yourself! Of course it matters. I'm very fond of you and I hate to see you unhappy, but the remedy's in your own hands, not mine."

"That I should stand up to mother?" he guessed bitterly, and kicked at a stone lying in his path. "That really bothers you, doesn't it, Bryony?"

"It does," she admitted. "You're an intelligent, good-looking man, Giles, and you could have the world at your feet, if only you realized it. You have looks, money, charm and brains, a combination most men would give their right arms for, and yet, you let Aunt Merrilyn treat you as if you were not a very bright child. It *does* bother me... I wish you'd do something about it."

"But I'm trying to," he insisted, missing the point entirely. "If you marry me, we shall live here at Penroyal and mother will stay in her house in London. I shall insist."

She could not resist a faint smile at the idea of Giles insisting on anything in the face of Aunt Merrilyn's determination, but she hoped Giles would not see it. "That's simply putting the onus on me," she objected. "You must do it on your own, Giles, and not depend on me to make sure your mother doesn't move in with you. She's *your* mother; you must let her see that you have a mind of your own."

"How can I when you refuse to cooperate?" he demanded. "I love you and you say you're fond of me, though God knows what that's supposed to mean."

"It means I'm fond of you," Bryony insisted. "I love you, Giles, but not in the way you'd want me to. I'm sorry, but that's how it is."

He walked in silence for a while, his head down, a suggestion of sulkiness at the corners of his mouth. "Oh, God, what a damned mess!" he exclaimed suddenly, kicking viciously at the tufts of turf. "If Patinous hadn't come on the scene with his... his great lover act, you'd have married me the first time I asked you. I know you would."

"I wouldn't," she argued, refusing to lose her temper, although she was very near to doing so. "I wouldn't marry anyone if I felt only a... a sort of sisterly affection for him as I do for you. Alex has nothing whatever to do with it—I make up my own mind."

"And you've made it up against marrying me," he said bitterly. "*Now* what do I do?"

"Do?" She looked genuinely puzzled.

"I was relying on this to—to give me a lever against mother," he confessed. "If we'd got the ring this afternoon and been already engaged by the time she came back, there'd have been nothing she could do about it. Now I'm back where I started."

Bryony stared at him in disbelief. "Do you mean to say—" she said slowly "—that your prime concern in asking me to become engaged to you was simply so that you could flaunt it as an act of defiance against Aunt Merrilyn? I'm not very flattered, Giles."

"No, no, of course not!" He looked so genuinely shocked at the idea that she was forced to believe him. "But it would have helped."

"Well, I'm sorry." She looked up at the good-looking face with its brown eyes, now hidden under lowered lids, and the thick brown hair, so much lighter than the Patinous Pengellys'. He had inherited his coloring more from his father's side than his mother's, and there was little of the darkness in him that Maria Patinous had brought to his mother's looks.

"Oh, Giles," she said, suddenly contrite, "please don't look so... so unhappy. There'll be other chances."

"Chances that you'll change your mind about marrying me?"

She shook her head. "Not necessarily that," she said. "But if you can run a business, handle men and complicated business matters, surely one woman isn't going to defeat you, is she? Even if she is your own mother."

"Perhaps it's because she *is* my mother that she *does* defeat me," he said ruefully, and sighed deeply. A moment later he put his hand over hers where it lay on his arm, and squeezed her fingers, a wry smile touching his mouth as he looked down at her. "I refuse to be done out of my dinner—" he told her "—even if the cause for celebration didn't materialize. So we'll go anyway... if you're still prepared to come with me."

"Of course I am." She smiled up at him affectionately, and squeezed his arm. "I haven't been taken out to dinner for far too long," she told him. "I'm looking forward to it."

ALTHOUGH SHE SAW old Miklas every day, Bryony could not help noticing, when she called on him that evening before she went out with Giles, how much weaker the old man seemed. He lay back on the pillows instead of being propped up and his hands looked almost transparent and uncharacteristically still.

Bryony bent and kissed him gently on his forehead, and he smiled, opening tired eyes to look at her admiringly. "Who's the lucky man?" he asked. "You look good enough to eat, my dear."

His voice too, she noticed, was much less strong and he drew each breath as if it pained him. "I'm going out to dinner with Giles," she told him, sitting on the edge of the bed as she always did. She brushed a soothing hand over his forehead where the curly gray hair flopped, and felt the skin moist and cold. "Uncle Miklas, you don't seem at all well. Shouldn't we get Doctor Short to call and see you?"

"No, no child," he waved a frail hand. "The nurse is quite capable of doing all that can be done for me. I don't expect to be around much longer." He reached up a hand and touched her cheek. "You're such a lovely child," he said softly, and half to himself. "I'd like to have seen you settled."

"Oh, Uncle Miklas, I'm settled enough." Her eyes were bright with threatening tears and she held on to his hand, suddenly afraid of losing him.

"You should have a good husband," he insisted, his thin fingers still caressing her cheek. "A good man who'll work for you and love you, for you deserve to be loved."

She was blushing, she knew it, and the old man smiled to see it, a hint of the old mischief in his sharp black eyes as he shook his head. "You will have to say 'yes' to someone soon," he told her. "No man in his right mind is going to allow a lovely girl like you to remain single for very long." His gaze was almost as sharp as normal, as he looked at her. "Have you someone in mind, Bryony?"

She shook her head, eyes downcast. "No, Uncle Miklas, although...." she hesitated, but his hand on her face encouraged her. "Giles wants to marry me," she told him, and he smiled wryly, the gesture emphasizing the lines of pain around his mouth and eyes.

"But you can't face the idea of Merrilyn," he said, and shook his head. "With Giles you'll always have to, my dear, for he's incapable of standing up to her."

"I just don't understand it," Bryony objected. "He's a successful businessman. How can he be so good at his job and still be such a...a...."

"Mammy's darling?" the old man suggested softly, and Bryony shook her head hastily.

"I wasn't going to say that," she denied.

"But it's true."

She was silent for a moment, forgetting all about her date, intent on trying to understand the puzzle that was Giles. "Oh, I wish I knew," she said at last. "I wish he'd make a stand, just once, Uncle Miklas."

"Instead of letting Merrilyn insult you and browbeat

you," he said, and Bryony looked at him suspiciously.

"How do you know she does?" she asked, knowing the answer full well.

He smiled again. "Alex and Merrilyn don't exactly hit it off," he said. "He doesn't tell tales out of school, Bryony, but he was so furious one day because of the way Merrilyn had spoken to you, and because Giles had done nothing about it."

She kept her eyes lowered, feeling the color warm in her cheeks. "I can stand up for myself," she declared. "I don't need a champion."

"But you're entitled to one," the old man told her softly. "A beautiful woman should never have to fight her own battles."

She looked up and smiled, taking his hands in hers and holding them tightly in her own, suddenly aware that she would probably be the only other person besides Alex who would miss him when he was gone.

"Giles does his best," she said, but knew she wasn't believed, by the ironical quirk at one corner of his mouth—an expression that reminded her of Alex. Lately she had noticed so many things about Alex that reminded her of Uncle Miklas and the recognition made her uneasy.

"Doesn't Alex?" he asked softly, and she looked at him for a moment before she answered.

"Alex is different," she said at last. "He has more...more self-confidence than Giles, and he's—well, he's more conceited, he *knows* he's always right."

"Oh dear!" The pain-circled eyes glittered with laughter for a moment. "That can be a drawback, can't it?"

"It's infuriating," Bryony admitted bluntly.

"But reassuring?"

She studied his thin, lined face for a moment, seeing

those black eyes watching her, just as Alex often did. Speculative and knowing and very discomfiting. "You and Alex are too much alike," she told him then. "You're bound to see eye to eye on everything."

"Most things," he agreed, rather complacently, she thought.

"Uncle Miklas, I...." she stopped then, shaking her head and looking down at their clasped hands. "I'd better go—" she said, "—before Giles thinks I've forgotten him."

"Where are you going for your dinner?"

"A new place in Marby. Giles heard it was good."

"And expensive, I hope," the old man said, and chuckled despite the pain it caused him. "Enjoy yourself, Bryony."

"We will." She bent and kissed his forehead gently. "Try and rest, Uncle Miklas, you look very poorly and you worry me."

"Don't you worry about me," he whispered. "You go out and have fun, my dear."

"Good night, Uncle Miklas." She turned at the doorway and smiled, waving a hand in farewell. "Sleep well."

DINNER WITH GILES, Bryony discovered, was something of a revelation. He seemed to shed his reticence, and became as she had imagined he would be in his role of business executive. Faced with waiters and menus he became the polished, self-confident man she had visualized when she first saw him after their last childhood visit.

He was self-confident and the perfect escort, and his manner made his attitude toward his mother even harder to understand. By the time they were halfway through their dinner, she had quite decided that he was something of an enigma.

He ordered dinner for her and kept her wineglass

filled, so that she was very uncertain just how much she had actually drunk. The food was excellent and the service swift and discreet, and Bryony found herself viewing not only Giles, but the whole world, much more favorably.

"To my beautiful cousin," he said, raising his glass, and Bryony immediately remembered the last person who had called her that. Alex Patinous came all too easily into her mind and she frowned over it as she sought to dismiss him yet again.

"Don't you like being called my beautiful cousin?" Giles asked anxiously, seeing her frown, and she smiled.

"Of course I like it," she told him. "No woman objects to being called anyone's beautiful cousin."

"No one else could possibly lay claim to quite such a beautiful one," Giles informed her solemnly, his tongue made glib by the wine, a sparkle of self-confidence in his eyes.

"Flattery is music to my ears."

"You don't have to be flattered," Giles assured her earnestly. "Oh, Bryony!"

He took her hand in his, but she successfully released it and picked up her wineglass again, feeling her heart hammering uncomfortably hard against her ribs. At all costs she had to stop Giles from proposing again. "I think I've...." she giggled softly and put a hand to her mouth to smother it. "I think I've had too much to drink, Giles, I feel all sort of floaty and funny."

"You haven't had *that* much," Giles protested, his brown eyes glowing darkly in the shaded light. "It must be the company you're in."

"You think so?" She looked at him, trying to treat it as a joke, but her eyes were wide and lustrous and her cheeks flushed softly and she looked incredibly lovely.

He leaned across the table and managed to capture her

left hand in his again, raising it to his lips and kissing the tips of her fingers. "I'm sure of it," he told her. "You should come out to dinner with me more often."

She looked at him demurely from under her lashes, and her smile teased him. "You should *ask* me more often," she said softly.

"If I did, would you come?"

Despite the headiness of the wine and the way the blood was pounding away in her head, she recognized that it was the wine talking. In the cold light of day and faced with Aunt Merrilyn's opposition, he would think differently. Now, however, it seemed rather cruel to undermine his self-confidence when he was enjoying himself.

"I might," she told him, and he kissed her fingers again.

"Then I shall ask you. Over and over again, until you get so used to the idea of being with me that you won't feel right without me." He kissed the palm of the hand he held, his lips lingering gently before he closed her fingers over his own to enclose the kiss, pressing their clasped hands to his cheek. "*Then* perhaps you'll marry me," he added in a whisper.

There was a full moon as they drove home, and Bryony thought she had seldom seen a bigger or more beautiful one. It shone into the car and lent a certain shadowy arrogance to Giles's profile as he concentrated on his driving. His eyes looked darker, and his hair appeared black in the semi-darkness, little dark shadows flicked over his face and gave it a less smooth and more rugged look.

"You look like Alex," she said, without thinking and saw the dark brows draw together, while his mouth tightened with dislike at the idea.

"I don't know that I'm flattered," he told her

brusquely, then turned his head briefly to look at her. "You *have* had too much wine if you can see any similarity between me and Patinous!"

"Well, I'm sorry, but I can," Bryony declared recklessly. "And I don't know why you have to be so touchy about it. After all, it's not *so* odd that you should look alike, is it? You both have Patinous blood in your veins."

"Well, very little in my case," he declared.

Bryony leaned her head back against the seat, looking at him curiously. "Why do you hate them so much, Giles?" she asked. "You and Aunt Merrilyn. You really hate the Patinouses, don't you?"

"Do we?" His shoulders lifted in a shrug. "I suppose we just don't like to think of ourselves as anything else but thoroughbred Pengellys. We know we're part Patinous, but we prefer not to remember it."

"Half Patinous in Aunt Merrilyn's case," she asserted. "That's what makes it so difficult to understand. What did poor Maria ever do to her to make Aunt Merrilyn so ashamed of her own mother's family?"

"That's not quite true," he objected. "Mother doesn't—she doesn't hate her mother's family and neither do I, but Alex Patinous is enough to put anyone's back up, you must admit."

"He's arrogant and very sure of himself, certainly," Bryony allowed.

"And he never gives up trying to—to make an impression on you."

Bryony looked at him despairingly. "Oh, Giles, why do you have to keep bringing up that subject? It's idiotic and you know it. Alex has absolutely no interest in me in that direction."

"No?" He looked at her steadily, the bright moon lending a glitter to his eyes. "Do you know what that name means...the name that he called you?"

"Name?" She frowned for a moment, then remembered that Alex had used the same words to her—when she was talking to Giles outside the bathroom the morning they came home together—as he had used to comfort her when she was crying. "I don't even remember what it was," she told him, bending the truth, just a little. *Mikros eros*, he had called her.

"Well, I do, and I took the trouble to ask Uncle Miklas."

She looked at him indignantly. "Why for heaven's sake?"

"Because...well, because I suspected it was some form of endearment, and I was right. It means love—*now* do you say he has no interest in you?"

"But good heavens, Giles, people use words like that for no reason at all. Why, if you think like that, you'd be suspicious every time a...a bus driver called me 'love' and *that* happens often enough, even to old ladies of eighty."

"It sounds so...so damned possessive, the way he says it," Giles objected.

"Well, it isn't, I assure you." She considered she had successfully countered that accusation. "Anyway, whatever he may do, it doesn't excuse Aunt Merrilyn insisting on his calling her Mrs. Pengelly. He *is* her first cousin, after all."

"I know that, but look how he throws his weight around. Somebody has to put him in his place."

She sighed. "He's a proud man, Giles, and he doesn't take kindly to being treated as an interloper where he has as much right as the rest of Uncle Miklas's family. He's not the type of man to take anything lying down, even Aunt Merrilyn's regal manner."

It was, she realized too late, a very provocative speech

to make, and she could not imagine what had possessed her to make it. She heard Giles's sharp intake of breath and saw his knuckles showing white where he gripped the steering wheel more tightly. He was driving quite slowly and there was no traffic on the road, but she wished he was less intense and giving more attention to his driving.

"I know you're an admirer of the great lover," he jeered. "I always suspected as much."

"Oh, don't be ridiculous!" Bryony retorted. "You're so good at making mountains out of molehills, Giles. It must be an inherited talent."

"How *dare* you!"She realized that she had gone too far, and he spat the words from between his teeth, his hands taut and white-boned on the wheel. "How dare you make snide remarks about me while you defend Patinous as if...as if he was—"

"Giles!" Her voice carried a warning, and he stopped, taking the car up onto the grass border beside the road and braking sharply to a halt.

They were only yards from the entrance to Penroyal, but he seemed not to have noticed that, as he turned in his seat and looked at her, his eyes glowing angrily in the moonlight. It had not been her intention to quarrel with Giles, or to provoke him into losing his temper. It was the last thing she wanted, and when she looked up at him she was genuinely contrite.

"I'm—I'm sorry, Giles, I shouldn't have said that." She put a hand to her forehead, and smiled ruefully, her eyes appealing. "I can only plead extenuating circumstances."

He did not respond to the overture, but merely sat stiff and straight in his seat for a moment, saying nothing, and she could feel him trembling with anger still. "You meant it, Bryony," he said at last, and surprised her with his quietness. "Please don't pretend you didn't. You haven't much time for me, really, have you?"

"Oh, Giles, don't...." She was anxious now to placate him. He was too much a part of her life, her childhood, for her to want to risk a permanent quarrel with him.

"I have to face it sooner or later, I suppose," he said, apparently bent on making a big issue of it. "You'll never feel as much for me as I do for you."

"I...I'm very—"

"If you say once more that you're fond of me—" he interrupted shortly "—I shall begin to hate you, Bryony."

"Oh no, please don't do that!"

He looked at her steadily for a moment. "Would it matter *so* much?" he asked, and she nodded.

"You know it would. We've been such good friends all those wonderful years we came here. You're—you're almost like part of me. You, Uncle Miklas, and Penroyal—you're all part of the happiest times of my life and I love you all."

He was silent again for a few seconds, and she felt him easing out of the tension that held him stiff and unbending beside her. Then he took her face between his two hands and leaned forward to kiss her gently on her mouth. It was almost like a kiss of goodbye, and for a moment she felt the warning prickle in her eyes that threatened tears.

"I'm not sure I like being classed with an old man and a house—" he said ruefully "—but I'm glad you love me, anyway, at all." He kissed her again, more lingering this time, as if he was reluctant to release her. "I refuse to give up hope," he added softly. "I love you too much."

"Even if I'm mean and bitchy?" Relief made her

lighthearted again, and she touched his face gently, her eyes bright and shining the in the moonlight.

"I'd forgive you anything—" he vowed. "—and I hope you'll look on it as something in my favor."

"You have a lot in your favor, Giles," she said softly. "As I've already told you."

"But not enough."

"Please—"

"All right, all right!" He held up his hands, and smiled as he turned to restart the car. "Subject closed—for now."

CHAPTER TEN

Aunt Merrilyn made herself even more unpleasant than usual when she discovered that Giles had taken Bryony out to dinner in her absence, and for nearly a week she took every opportunity to find fault with everything she did or said.

Bryony was unwilling to have a full-scale confrontation with her, fearing the effect it could have on Uncle Miklas if she was driven to leave Penroyal, as she would surely have to do after such a quarrel. Aunt Merrilyn, however, seemed bent on forcing the issue, and Bryony was not sure that she could contain her temper for very much longer.

It was true that Giles had spoken up in her defense on a couple of occasions, but his mother had made such a scene about his lack of support for her that he had eventually subsided into his more usual speechless inaction, leaving Bryony to defend herself. None of these incidents, she noticed, happened when Alex was within earshot. Apparently Aunt Merrilyn had learned that he was one person she could not get the better of.

It was after one particularly virulent attack that Bryony left the sitting room, unable to trust herself any longer. Her cheeks were flaming and her eyes blazing stormily, and she was not looking where she was going as she came out of the door in headlong flight. She saw nothing and no one, until strong hands gripped the tops of her arms and brought her to a sudden halt.

"Let me go!" Her reaction was instinctive, and she did not even realize it was Alex who held her until she looked up and saw his black eyes regarding her with speculative amusement.

"What has happened?" he asked, refusing to release her, despite her efforts.

She looked at him for a moment with stormy eyes, her breathing deep and erratic, tears of anger and frustration trembling on her lashes. She would have given anything to have had Giles speak up for her, say something in her defense; instead he had merely looked at his mother reproachfully and made some half-hearted protest that was soon drowned in the tirade against Bryony. For the first time she was forced to recognize that he would never be any different, no matter how often he protested to the contrary, and the realization made her feel utterly disgusted with him.

"It's... it's nothing I can't handle," she told Alex, but wondered why she found herself wishing *he* had been there when Aunt Merrilyn had berated her so cruelly.

"I think not," he said quietly. "Is it Merrilyn?"

She nodded. The taunts and insinuations had been too much to bear, and she had been forced either to run from the room or do something violent to Aunt Merrilyn. Now she felt like crying her heart out, and to her dismay the first warm, fat tears rolled slowly down her cheeks. Alex smiled understanding. "Was it very bad?" he asked.

"It was awful!" She choked on the words, and felt her temper still simmering, ready to break out and explode. "She hates me so much it's almost—psychological."

"You mean psychopathic," he argued, gently, and she glared at him through a haze of tears.

"I know what I mean," she retorted. "And will you let me *go*?"

She wriggled against his grip, but he released only one of her arms and with the other one spun her around so that she was forced to walk with him across the width of the hall to the stairs. "I suspect it is more anger than hurt you are feeling," he told her confidently, right as usual. "And the best remedy for that is fresh air. A long walk will do you good. Get a coat and come with me."

She frowned her dislike of the arrangement, particularly the latter part of it, and she tugged at her captive arm in vain. "I will *not* get a coat," she informed him. "And I'm not going anywhere with you. Now let me go!"

He stood with her by the stairs, his black eyes studying her flushed, tear-stained face. "Sometimes—" he said at last in his immaculate English "—I am in sympathy with Merrilyn. You can be an infuriating child, Bryony Foster, and I shall lose patience with you in a moment."

"I don't care! I'm tired of being told what to do—and stop calling me a child."

"Then stop behaving like one, and go and fetch a coat. Or I shall take you out as you are and see if the cold air will cool down your temper."

"You—"

"Bryony!"

She took another look at the expression in his eyes and decided that discretion was the greater part of valor. After all, there was nothing to prevent her staying in her room once she was free of him. "All right," she agreed, suddenly and unconvincingly meek. "I'll fetch a coat."

Something in her manner, or, perhaps, her sudden capitulation, must have made him suspicious, for when she went upstairs she found him following her. "I do not trust you when you are so suddenly obedient," he informed her, a smile touching his mouth when he saw her frown. "I will come with you and make sure that you return."

"I won't have you coming into my room," she told him shortly. "Aunt Merrilyn has enough to gossip about now, without adding fuel to the flames."

His brows shot upward into his black hair. "You fear for your reputation?"

"Someone has to," she retorted, and he laughed softly.

"Then I shall wait out here for you."

She stuck her chin in the air and refused to be drawn further on the subject. Really, after a session with Aunt Merrilyn at her worst, she could well have done without Alex Patinous's arrogant insistence. Between the two of them she was as badly scalded as burned.

When they reached the landing, he halted beside Miklas's door and smiled at her wryly. "Bowing to your susceptible reputation—" he told her "—I shall go in and see how Miklas is. You usually call in on your way out, don't you?"

She nodded. "Usually," she agreed, wondering just what he had in mind now.

"And you will do so this time?"

Again she nodded. "I expect so, why?"

"I shall go in and sit with Miklas while you fetch your coat, hmm?" His smile challenged her to argue the point. "You will come in on your way back and fetch me."

She was sorely tempted to click her heels and salute smartly, but she resisted the temptation and instead walked along to her room, while he stood there and watched her. A faint smile touched his mouth when he saw her stiff back and the defiant tilt of her fair head.

She forgot, almost at once, her intention of staying in her room once she was free of him, and she took a thick red wool coat from a cupboard and turned the dark fur collar up around her face. There was a fierce east wind blowing today and it was bitterly cold. The fact, that she was doing exactly as he had said and going for a walk to cool off, did not occur to her as she left her room and closed the door quietly behind her.

The carpeted landing deadened her footsteps and it was as she raised her hand to knock on Miklas's door that she realized she could probably get out of the house alone, without her self-appointed escort. It would serve him right if she did, and Uncle Miklas would understand. She had to show Alex Patinous that she had no intention of doing as he told her, just because he told her.

She salved her conscience about Uncle Miklas by thinking that she could go in again later and see him, as she had intended anyway. She had seen him once today and she always went in to see him each evening before he went to sleep.

If she was to walk in the fresh air to cool off her temper she did not require company, in fact she would do better without it—especially Alex's, and the thought of deliberately going without him pleased her enormously. There were far too many people telling her what to do, for once she would please herself.

She pulled on warm gloves and pulled the collar of her coat further up around her face. Now, all that remained was to get out of the house without his seeing her. The fact that he would probably see her from Miklas's window, once she had left the house, merely added spice to the idea.

She tiptoed the rest of the way along the landing, and suddenly felt the desire to giggle uncontrollably when she thought how furtive she must appear. The heavy front door presented no problems, for it slid quietly behind her with not a squeak from its ancient hinges.

Once free of the house, she took several deep breaths,

the cold wind catching at her throat, but clearing her head miraculously. Almost without thinking she turned to her left and the direction of the church and the village, the turf springy and damp underfoot after yesterday's rain, and the sky gray and overcast as if there was more to come.

Far from looking the golden, gentle place that holiday-makers knew, the rocky Cornish coast had a bleak, savage look about it that sent shivers along her spine, and set her heart racing as she faced the wind blowing out from the land and lashing her hair around her face. This was her country, Pengelly country, and she loved it just as much, perhaps even more, at this time of the year when it lost its gentleness and showed the more ruthless side of itself.

The sound of the sea dashing against the rocks was loud even from this high up, and the lower down the slope she went the louder it became. Seeing the pier below her, however, and the huddle of little houses and hotels, she stopped in her tracks suddenly, the fierce wind lifting her hair and tossing it into wild confusion.

Her mood at the moment demanded something a little less safe and conventional than the fishing village presented. The wild, unpopulated sweep of Marby Head was much more to her liking and, without a second thought, she turned around and made her way back up the incline, passing Penroyal without a second glance.

Hands thrust deep into the pockets of the red coat, shoulders hunched into the warm fur collar, she climbed the hill toward Marby Head, and the old Pengelly house. The wind blew harder as she climbed and her head bowed before it, her breathing deep and stimulating. Up on the bleak, open expanse of Marby Head itself it whistled and moaned through the grass-covered ruins of the old house.

It was blowing offshore and her position could have been dangerous, but she gave it not a thought, although once or twice she was almost blown off balance. Despite, or perhaps because of, the cold blustering of the wind, however, there was an air of savage excitement about the place which, in her present mood, she responded to.

She walked as far as the undulating cliffs went before they swept down to become open beach, then she stood for several minutes looking out at the gray, surging expanse of the sea, letting the wind whip her hair forward around her face. Nothing could ever stir her blood as this rugged, rocky coast did, and no matter where she went, it would always have a very special place in her heart.

Almost reluctantly she turned away at last and made her way back across the cliffs, feeling far less tense and angry than when she had set out. Alex had been right, fresh air was what she needed. Right as usual! She pulled a wry face, one gloved hand pushing back the strands of hair blown across her face. If only he could be wrong for once!

She paused briefly at the old Pengelly house and found herself remembering the bright moonlit evening when Alex had followed her from the house and found her here. To make sure she came to no harm, he had told her, because Uncle Miklas was worried about her being alone.

She touched her lips instinctively and remembered another time when she had been with Alex, then shrugged hastily to dismiss the memory of his lean, hard strength holding her close against the cold and the mist. The thought of those few moments turned her stomach over and she clenched her hands into fists as she stood there in the ruins, her heart thudding wildly suddenly.

She could remember no time with Giles that had excited her as those few minutes in Alex's arms, and she covered her mouth with her hands suddenly as the truth struck her like a physical blow. She was in love with Alex! How she could have failed to realize it so far, she could not imagine, for it was so obvious.

The way her hands and kees trembled every time he was close, even when his black eyes looked at her. Even now—just thinking about him—everything pointed to it and she had not realized it until now. One thing she was certain of, however—he must never know how she felt. It was impossible to believe that he could ever feel the same way about her, for their worlds were miles apart both geographically and materially.

He was a clever, educated and wealthy man of the world and experienced with women too, by his own admission. He would find her a poor substitute for the wealthy, sophisticated women he was used to. She shook her head, remembering that night on Giles's boat. That should be proof enough for her, for he had left her after only a few minutes and spent the rest of the night on the hard wooden seat rather than stay with her. She only wished she could dismiss it as easily as he apparently could.

She had been thinking so deeply about him, and was so preoccupied, that to see him so suddenly in the flesh as she walked down the incline was something of a shock, and she stared at the tall, dark figure for a moment unbelievingly.

He stood perilously near the edge of the cliff. some fifty yards below her, opposite Penroyal, and he wore no coat despite the bitter wind. The dark, hip-hugging slacks he wore with a creamy sweater emphasized his height and his darkness and, as she watched, she saw his right arm lift into the air something held in his hand.

At the very moment she recognized the soft, green beauty of the jade statuette he released it at the height of his throw, and it curved outward and downward toward the rocks and the sea below.

"Alex!" She ran down the gentle slope, her eyes watching the glittering beauty of jade and emeralds and swallowed by the hungry gray water.

He turned at her cry and his face shocked her into stillness for a moment, some yards from him. The normally darkly tanned skin had a grayish tinge, and the black eyes looked blank and expressionless, wide open like those of a sleepwalker. He did not speak but simply looked at her and Bryony felt a cold hand clutch at her heart suddenly as she recognized the reason, as surely as if he had told her.

"Oh, no!"

It was so painfully obvious, as soon as she saw his face. No one else would have been so affected by Uncle Miklas's death, for Alex had loved his cousin, as she did herself. He nodded slowly, shrugging his shoulders as if to throw off some weight that was too great to bear.

"Only a few minutes ago," he told her, his deep, quiet voice unwavering but filled with such sorrow that she felt the tears filled her eyes.

"Oh, I wish—I wish I'd known," she said choking on the words, thinking how she had carefully sneaked out of the house without seeing Uncle Miklas.

"I would like to have... Alex?" She looked down at the gray, uneasy sea, remembering the scene she had witnessed. "The... the jade?"

For a moment he looked as if he had no idea of her meaning, then he, too, looked down at where the statuette had disappeared into the gray water.

"Are you greedy for that thing too, Bryony?" he asked softly. "I had taken you for the exception to the rule."

"No, no, I didn't want it." Tears ran unashamedly down her cheeks, turned icy by the cold wind, and she longed for comfort, his comfort. Her heart ached for it.

"Miklas asked me to—dispose of it. He hated it and...." He lifted one shoulder and used a hand to make his meaning, and Bryony thought he had never looked more strange, or more remote. She was almost ashamed to realize that her first thought was that Alex would have to leave Penroyal. Giles had threatened as much.

Giles! Her head lifted and she looked at him questioningly. "Do—do Giles and Aunt Merrilyn know about Uncle...." She swallowed hard, and he nodded.

"I sent Mrs. Trevellyan to fetch them when I left the house."

"They weren't with him when—when—"

He shook his head, his strong mouth smiling bitterly. "Miklas was never a hypocrite," he said. "He did not want to see them at the last. He wanted to see you, but you weren't there."

The words, the hint of accusation, were too much for her and she looked at him for a long reproachful minute, then turned and fled up to the house, her feet stumbling on unseen obstacles, her eyes flooded with tears.

UNCLE MIKLAS WAS BURIED in the churchyard on the cliff, beside his father and mother and his wife, while the bleak north wind blew across the gray skies and moaned sadly around the little church.

Aunt Merrilyn looked suitably bereaved for the sake of the many local folk who came to bid the old man goodbye. It meant something in this part of the world to be a Pengelly, and Aunt Merrilyn intended no one to forget it.

Giles, Bryony thought, was more affected by his uncle's death than he had expected to be, and he stood beside her in the cold inhospitality of the churchyard, his brown eyes downcast, his face pale above dark overcoat.

No one had seen anything much of Alex since the old man died, but Bryony suspected he spent a good deal of his time walking alone, and she felt so helpless that she could not console him. Once or twice she had seen him leave the house to walk along the cliff-tops, and just as often she had been tempted to offer him her company.

Only the hunch of his shoulders as he faced the blustering wind, and that look of remoteness on the formerly friendly face had deterred her. She hesitated to intrude into his grief, although she longed for his comfort in her own.

At the funeral he stood apart, tall and looking somehow older in a formal dark suit and overcoat, his black head bared to the wind, his strong hands clasped as in prayer while his cousin was laid to his rest.

It was on the following day that Giles asserted his new ownership rights, and Bryony suspected that Aunt Merrilyn was behind the gesture. They had breakfast quite early, and Giles suddenly looked across the table at Alex, his knuckles white-boned as he put aside his plate.

"I presume you'll be leaving today, Patinous?" he said, and Bryony stared at him.

"Giles, no!"

Alex looked up slowly. His black eyes had lost their blank look and, for a moment, Bryony could have sworn there was a glimpse of the old devilment in them as he studied Giles carefully before answering.

"I can leave Penroyal as soon as you like—" he said quietly "—but it will be necessary for me to stay in England for a while yet. You see, I am my cousin's executor."

"You?" Aunt Merrilyn's sharp eyes looked at him suspiciously.

Alex nodded. "Me, Cousin Merrilyn. Does that shock you?"

"Frankly, yes!" Her tight mouth closed on the words and she bristled indignation.

"I am sorry, but it was Miklas's wish and there is nothing I can do about it. I shall be required to stay until the will has been proved which, since it is a simple, straightforward document, will not take very long."

"You seem well informed," Giles jeered suspiciously, and Bryony held her breath when she remembered the fate of the jade statuette. What would happen, when Giles and his mother discovered that the Pengelly jade they both coveted so much had been consigned to the sea, did not bear thinking about.

"I think I am," Alex said, unperturbed by the obvious hostility of them both. "Miklas showed it to me. I *am* a lawyer, you know, and his executor. There were things he wanted to make sure I understood."

"He had a perfectly good lawyer," Aunt Merrilyn declared sharply. "*Our* family lawyer."

Alex bowed acknowledgment of the fact, ignoring the gibe. "And Mr. Jarvis will be handling everything Merrilyn, have no fear. There is little that needs understanding, however, as the house is entailed and therefore will come to you automatically, Giles, and the money is divided equally between you and Bryony."

"Bryony!" Aunt Merrilyn almost hissed her name and the bright dark eyes glared maliciously.

Alex's dark brows shot upward in challenge. "You have some objection?" he asked softly, and Merrilyn bit her lip angrily but said no more.

"There's still the Pengelly jade," Giles reminded him, and Bryony looked at Alex, almost afraid for him.

"The Pengelly jade no longer exists," he told them quietly, and poured himself fresh coffee, while Bryony marveled at his composure. Nothing seemed to disturb that urbane self-confidence.

"No longer exists?" Aunt Merrilyn echoed harshly, while Giles stared at him open-mouthed.

"I destroyed it," Alex told her calmly. "At Miklas's request."

For the moment Aunt Merrilyn, too, was stunned into silence, then her sharp, dark eyes blazed furiously, her hands clenched before her. "You're lying!" she accused, her voice crackling with anger.

"I assure you I am not," Alex told her. "Miklas hated that jade for the misfortune it brought to him and his father and he did not want the responsibility of handing it on to anyone else in the family. He has put it in his will that it should be destroyed, but he wanted to be *certain* that it would be, so he made me promise that I would destroy it as soon as he was gone—which I did."

"I don't believe you," Aunt Merrilyn insisted harshly. "You've kept it for yourself!"

"Oh, no, Aunt Merrilyn!" Bryony's cry was instinctive and she felt the impact of three pairs of eyes turned on her. "I saw Alex throw the jade into the sea, the day Uncle Miklas died."

"You...." Contempt and disbelief blazed at her. "You and this...this man have kept the jade! You always meant to, and now Miklas is dead you think you can get away with it. Well, you can't. I don't believe *anyone* would throw such a valuable object into the sea, I refuse to believe it."

"It's true!" Bryony insisted desperately, defending Alex as fervently as she had ever defended the Pengellys against his gibes. "You must believe me! Why should I lie about it?"

Aunt Merrilyn's nose twitched and her eyebrows rose. "Because you've been besotted with Alex Patinous right from the start, of course."

"No!" She dared not look at Alex and see the amusement in his eyes at the very idea, for he must inevitably find it amusing.

"Of course you have," Aunt Merrilyn went on remorselessly. "Anyone could see it and no doubt he made the most of the fact—to get what he wanted."

It was no longer possible to avoid tht black-eyed gaze and she looked at him wide-eyed, her hands trembling and so very near to tears that they trembled on her lashes. The very thing she had wanted to avoid letting him know, Aunt Merrilyn now had told him; she had made her look small and foolish in front of him when she desperately wanted to remain calm.

She could stand it no longer and she stumbled to her feet, and ran for the door, uncaring where she went as long as it was away from that room and the three pairs of eyes, each with its own expression—Aunt Merrilyn, pleased to have made her look foolish, Giles, unbelieving as always, and heaven alone knew what Alex was thinking at this minute.

She climbed the stairs to her room, glancing longingly at the closed door of Miklas's empty room as she passed, wishing she could go in and talk to him, seek his comfort. Uncle Miklas would have understood.

She stood for several seconds by the window, her tearful face pressed against the coolness of the glass, unable to stop thinking of what Alex must be thinking of her—a silly, impetuous young girl who threw herself into his arms at the first opportunity. Perhaps he would pity her, but he was probably used to such episodes and would take it in his stride as he did everything else. His pity for her predicament was something she could not face, and she cried softly as she pulled out suitcases and began cramming her things into them.

Nothing mattered now except to get away from Penroyal, as quickly as possible, before she had to face him again. She brushed a hand across the blinding tears as she turned to take more dresses from a cupboard and turned back, her arms full, just as the door opened without a preliminary knock and Alex appeared.

The black gaze looked at her for a moment in silence, his long frame bent slightly as he leaned against the jamb of the door.

"Are you going somewhere?" he asked softly, and she bit another flow of tears as she turned away from him.

"Away," she told him huskily. "Anywhere away from here."

"I think not."

The familiar flush rose to her cheeks as he walked across the room and began tossing the things out of her cases onto the bed.

"Stop it, Alex, leave me alone! Please leave me alone!" The plea had a heartrending appeal and she knew that she could not stand much more.

"This is unnecessary," he told her firmly. "You will unpack again at once."

"You...you don't understand," she whispered, her heart turning over at the sight of him standing there, so determined and so heart-achingly familiar.

"I think I do."

"No, no, you don't, you can't!" She picked up some of the things again and began cramming them back into the case. "I can't take any more, Alex, I just can't take any more. I'm going."

"You will do as I tell you." He spoke quietly but with such authority that she looked up at him uncertainly. He was closer suddenly, and she could feel the frantic, almost painful thudding of her heart when his hands touched her arms, then slid down to encompass her waist. He pulled her closer to him and touch of his lean hardness against her reminded her of that other time when she had been so tempted to surrender to him.

Her hands curled into tight little fists on his chest and she looked at him appealingly.

"Please, Alex!"

"You are going to have to learn to do as you are told," he informed her quietly, his black eyes glowing and watching her in a way that was at once exciting and a little frightening. "I will not have my wife disobey me, however small the issue."

She spread her hands over the strong steady beat of his heart. "Your—your wife?" Her huge gray eyes had a bewildered and almost childish look and his arms tightened around her until she could not have moved away even had she wanted to. "Alex—"

"You are too impulsive, *mikros eros*," he said softly. Little love—she smiled at the sound of it and remembered how Giles had declared that he used the endearment with an air of possessiveness.

He bent his dark head to seek her mouth and she lifted her face to him eagerly. His lips were gentle at first, growing more ardent, almost savage in their demands as he kissed her face, her eyes, and the soft, pulsing hollow at the base of her throat. His face buried in the golden fairness of her hair, he spoke, softly against her ear, words which she did not understand but which she knew were ones she wanted to hear, and she closed her eyes as a deep glowing warmth ran through her when he sought her mouth again.

She looked up at him at last, her eyes shining with a kind of gentle triumph. "I love you," she said softly.

"Aunt Merrilyn with right. I always loved you, only I didn't know it."

"But *I* knew it, my little love," he told her, smiling as if he had never doubted it, and she pouted her mouth at him.

"Of course—" she teased "—you're *al*ways right, aren't you?"

He laughed and held her close again, and she remembered how he had left her so suddenly that night on Giles's boat. She had been so willing to give anything he asked of her, but he had turned away and she had thought he found her unexciting. Now his reason puzzled her and she leaned away from him, looking at him curiously.

"Alex... that night, the night we... I was stranded on Marne Rock. You—"

He was shaking his head, smiling in gentle mockery as he anticipated her question. "I wanted you then as I do now, my darling," he said softly. "I've wanted you since the first moment I saw you, but a frightened child seeking consolation was not my idea of the right circumstances, and I did not want you to hate me for being too impatient." That irrepressible self-confidence showed again in his smile. "I could afford to wait," he told her. "I knew you'd never marry Giles, you had too much of the real Pengelly blood in your veins—Miklas knew it too."

"Uncle Miklas," she said softly. "I shall miss him terribly, Alex, as you will."

"I shall," he agreed. "But I shall have so many things and so many places to show you, my darling. You told me once that moonlit nights in Greece did not happen to girls like you, but you see...." He smiled down at her. "We shall have so many of them, Bryony. You will love my country."

"Won't . . . won't your family mind you marrying a—a foreigner?" she asked, suddenly shy at the thought of a whole new way of life.

He laughed, kissing her mouth, his black eyes glowing darkly. "We have married foreigners before," he reminded her. "I am my father's only son and he will be so relieved that at last he is going to have grandsons to carry on his name that he will adore you—as I do."

She laughed, a little breathlessly, imagining small boys with Alex's black hair and fathomless black eyes. "I'll do my best," she promised, and he hugged her close again, his voice muffled against her ear.

His fingers held a handful of her golden fair hair. "And for me, all our daughters will have golden hair like their mother," he said softly, and she murmured agreement without words. There would be little use disagreeing with him, she thought happily, as he kissed her again—he was always right.

THE GIRL IN THE GREEN VALLEY

The Girl in the Green Valley

Elizabeth Hoy

The nursing job in a French ski resort couldn't have come at a better time for Marnie. Robert, tall, dark and handsome, with whom she had so easily fallen in love, had put other interests ahead of her.

"See you on the ski slopes," she had said flippantly to cover the hurt of their parting. Words she had forgotten until he suddenly turned up there to remind her of them.

His arrival proved very inopportune, for Marnie had discovered that working with Dr. David Harford more than compensated for her earlier disappointment. He was dedicated and selfless; could she live up to his high standards? Certainly not with an old love in the background!

CHAPTER ONE

"HOW WOULD YOU LIKE to go to a ski resort in the French Alps?" Jane Barton asked across her paper-littered desk.

"Ski resort?" Sally Marnhem echoed, the words coming out in an astonished squeak.

"A ski resort," Jane confirmed, smiling. "At a village called Arbois in the Haute Savoie." She riffled through a pile of papers before her. "Here's a request from a Doctor Harford; obviously English and apparently practicing in Arbois. He asks for a nurse with a sympathetic personality to look after an elderly lady who's recovering from a mild stroke."

Sally—Marnie to her intimate associates—gave a gusty sigh. Another geriatric case! "What's an old lady doing having strokes in the middle of a ski resort?"

"It seems she's staying with her son, a Mr. Mark Rotherham, who, with his family, is having a skiing holiday at Arbois. He's rented a chalet there for the February-March season, Doctor Harford explains. Grandma went along with them. Then tactlessly the poor old girl had this stroke."

"I wonder how ill she is?" Marnie mused, visualizing the heavy nursing so often entailed in cases of this kind.

"She's not too seriously ill, I imagine. 'A slight stroke,' Doctor Harford emphasized when he phoned."

"He phoned!" Marnie exclaimed. "All the way from Arbois?"

"Only because the family is on holiday and obviously

doesn't want to be tied to a sickroom. Harford had already been on to the Langbury Agency in London and was a bit fussed, I think, because they had no one available to offer him. They advised him to try me. They've sent me clients before."

Marnie digested this information in silence, still a little doubtful. She had never before been asked to travel so far. A village in the Alps sounded dauntingly remote. What was an English doctor doing there?

"What did he sound like on the phone?" she asked.

"Oh, all right. Deep voice, very masculine. Manner a bit abrupt, pehaps; sounded as though he's accustomed to giving orders and having them obeyed without question. Autocratic. But then young doctors often are."

"How do you know he's young?"

"I looked him up in the Medical Directory. I wasn't going to send you off to work with some doubtful character. But Harford is all right. Age thirty, qualified brilliantly in Edinburgh, and is now a resident physician at the Arbois Clinic. I checked on this, too; an expensive establishment for chest cases. Twenty-five private rooms, so there'll be plenty to interest our Harford and keep him busy, though he apparently finds time to take the odd outside case, as well."

"Hmmm!" Marnie mused.

Jane pushed her papers aside with an impatient hand. "Okay, Marnie, if you aren't keen on this case I can find you plenty of needy souls nearer home...and your glamorous boyfriend, if that's what's worrying you."

Marnie didn't miss the underlying sneer. Jane had never approved of her friendship with Robert Tallant. Good old Jane, with her head so firmly screwed on the right way. They had trained together at St. Chad's Hospital in London and later met again here in Seafleet, where Jane was running her successful agency, while Marnie had taken up free-lance cases in preference to the more restricted routine of working in an institution.

She said with a forced little laugh, "Glamorous boyfriend indeed! You surely don't think I took the great Robert's attention seriously? Or that I'd miss a trip to a winter sports resort because of him? Honestly, Jane!"

Had Jane noticed that she spoke of the glamorous boyfriend's attentions in the past tense? In fact, the trip to Arbois couldn't have come at a more opportune moment, Marnie reflected.

Robert's image floated before her—tall, dark and handsome; the worn-out cliché fitted. But it didn't include his warm quick smile, his air of solicitous tenderness, his wit, his ready laughter. With Robert it was never a dull moment. Perhaps because personality was his stock-in-trade as leading actor at the large repertory theater of the busy south-coast town of Seafleet. A progressive rep with a varied program, it catered to summer visitors who only wanted to be entertained, and to the more selective audiences of residents who were proud to be allowed to see experimental plays tried out before being shown in London. And Robert played the lead in most of them. Marnie had met him six months before when she had been called to a local hospital to "be a private nurse" to him while he spent a week recovering from a not very serious car accident.

Since then she had never missed the opening night of one of his performances, for which he invariably sent her complimentary tickets, perhaps at first as a grateful patient. But later he had taken to inviting her to join him after the show at the Actors' Club next door to the theater, where she had met members of the cast and listened to the excited chatter that inevitably follows a first night successfully negotiated. Marnie had found it all very novel and amusing. Something more than just amusing when Robert began taking her for drives into the country on his free Sunday evenings, in his high-powered sports car. They would stop at some Downland village inn where they would eat a simple meal, lingering to talk—mostly of Robert and his ambitions. He wanted to direct plays as well as act in them, and Marnie was a sympathetic listener. It was all such a change from her life in a series of sickrooms. And Robert's charm was compelling. But she kept her head...and her heart, refusing to be too deeply stirred, even when on the way home in the late dusk of those summer evenings he stopped the car in some sheltered spot to kiss her and tell her how sweet she was. Perhaps, she could think now, there had been something lacking in those kisses. They did not convey the ultimate message. And, she would remind herself, she was not a naïve schoolgirl. Actors, she told herself, never stopped acting. She was nobody's fool, even if she did hail from a remote valley in the Lammermuir Hills.

Then something happened that destroyed all her carefully guarded defenses.

"How did the weekend in town with Robert's people go?" Jane was asking.

"Oh, it was super," Marnie answered a trifle too emphatically, and hurriedly changed the subject. "How do I get to Arbois?" she asked.

"Plane to Geneva," Jane replied with her usual crisp competence. "Right away. I can book a flight for you tomorrow. Sure you want to go?"

"Absolutely sure."

Jane gathered her papers together again. "You won't regret it, I'm certain. Arbois, according to the advertisements, is at its most beautiful in the early spring. Sun and snow and cloudless skies. I read all the package tour adverts in the Sunday supplements," she ended a little wistfully.

But Marnie's thoughts were back with that agonizing, embarrassing weekend in the big Chelsea mansion. "Come home with me and meet my people," Robert had suggested over one of their tête-à-tête suppers. A casual invitation, she was to realize later, but at the moment it had seemed a significant step forward in their relationship. In her circle boys didn't take their girlfriends home unless matters had arrived at a fairly serious stage. In the intervening days her carefully controlled emotions got somewhat out of hand. And Robert was so fatally easy to fall in love with!

Driving to London with him that crisp wintry Saturday morning she had been full of suppressed excitement.

His home was the first shock for her. It was so large, so magnificent, and it was a manservant who opened the door to them. Though she knew Robert's father was a distinguished Q.C. she hadn't expected quite such an imposing background. The spacious hall that they entered, deeply carpeted and furnished with antiques, breathed luxury and wealth. With a hand under her elbow Robert guided her toward a lofty double door, opened for them by the manservant, and leading into a long, beautiful room where a bright fire burned on an immense marble hearth. Tea was in progress, and a sprinkling of guests sat on the deep settees and comfortable armchairs. The air was full of chatter and gently modulated laughter. The woman who rose to greet Marnie seemed, at a first glance, young enough to be Robert's older sister. Faultlessly elegant, she held out a welcoming hand.

"This is Sarah Marnhem, mother," Robert introduced Marnie. "The nurse who was so kind to me when I was in hospital."

"Ah, yes, of course," Mrs. Tallant replied a trifle vaguely. "How nice of you to come and see us, my dear. I'm sure you would like some tea after your drive up from the coast. Robert's open sports cars are so uncomfortable, I always think." She indicated an armchair into which Marnie sank, wishing that in this overheated room she could have been rid of her tweed coat. Mrs. Tallant, before returning to her seat by the fire, had murmured an introduction to a smartly dressed middle-aged woman in the chair next to Marnie's. Robert, having turned her over to his mother, had left her, taking his seat on a settee beside a dazzlingly pretty girl—about seventeen years of age, Marnie guessed, and with a sinking heart she saw the familiar Tallant charm come into action.

Following her glance, the woman to whom she had been introduced said, "That's Hermione Garland, the child who's making such a hit at the Royal in that weird new play, *Whom the Gods Love.* You'll have seen it, of course?"

"No, I'm afraid I haven't," Marnie murmured, accepting a cup of tea from an immaculately clad parlormaid.

"Most of the people here this afternoon are theater folk," her informant went on. "Are you theater?" she asked, and hastily corrected herself. "Ah, no, of course not. I heard Robert say you'd looked after him in hospital. A nurse!" She stared at Marnie in disbelief, as if she had been an Eskimo or a Hottentot, then dismissively turned away to continue a conversation she had been having with a rather faded blond beauty on her other side. The parlormaid had returned by this time with a cake stand on which were arrayed an assortment of little cakes and wafer-thin sandwiches. Marnie said, "No thank you," to them and gulped her tea.

For what seemed an eternity she sat there, ignored, until Mrs. Tallant once more became aware of her and with a glance at her hot, unhappy face said, "I expect you would like to go to your room and freshen up, my dear. Simpkins!" she addressed the hovering parlor-maid, "will you take Miss Marnhem upstairs. I think Mrs. Jeffers has put her in the blue room."

Mrs. Jeffers. So there was a housekeeper as well as a parlormaid, and doubtless, downstairs a cook and a kitchenmaid. This was high society life-style with a vengeance, and Marnie was not sure that she liked it. It made Robert's home seem more like a hotel than a home, and Robert, as soon as he entered it, had become part of its cool impersonality.

Stifling the ache in her heart, she followed the maid up the shallow, richly carpeted staircase. The blue room, when she reached it, though small, was the last word in comfort. Her humble suitcase had already been unpacked, the simple dinner dress she had brought hung up in the wardrobe. In the mirror over the dressing table she saw her flushed, unhappy face; the wide gray eyes, looking back at her, held bewilderment. She felt dashed, diminished, disappointed. Robert's home was so... *unwelcoming*; why had he brought her here? She wished she had not come.

The discovery that the blue room possessed its own private bathroom did something to restore her morale. She had a long luxurious bath to steady her nerves and then lay down on the invitingly comfortable bed and tried, without much success, to concentrate on one of the bedside books that had been provided. It was almost seven o'clock when she went downstairs. Rested and refreshed, looking her best in her dinner frock, Robert would come to her and their easy relationship would be restored.

But it didn't turn out that way. When she entered the drawing room the teatime crowd had been replaced by another assortment of guests, having cocktails and sherry. Once more Mrs. Tallant introduced her to one or two of the least obviously occupied of her visitors. And Robert was still engrossed with Hermione Garland who was looking absolutely fabulous in a filmy white dress trimmed in silver, her golden hair floating around her bare shoulders. Like a fairy on a Christmas tree, Marnie thought cattily. But cattiness did not help. The whole evening was a nightmare of awkwardness and loneliness...and not fitting in, although Robert's august father, who turned out to be rather a dear, tried to put her at her ease in the odd moments when he was not in demand by his other guests and his exigent wife. There were, of course, brief contacts with Robert, but for the most part, like his father, he was preoccupied with the comings and goings of his dazzling friends—and especially preoccupied with Hermione. "An amusing crowd, aren't they?" he flung breathlessly at Marnie at one point. But he did nothing to help to incorporate her with them and she was dismally conscious of being an outsider.

The next day, Sunday, was even worse. Sitting now in Jane's office, Marnie smothered the thought of it, remembering only the final blow it had been when Robert apologized that he couldn't drive her back to Seafleet because 'something had cropped up.' (Hermione, Marnie decided bitterly.) "My old man's chauffeur will take you in the Bentley, which will be far more comfortable for you than my open Jag."

Why, Marnie wondered once more, had he bothered to invite her to his home if it was only to neglect her? The question had buzzed in her brain in the fortnight that had elapsed. Answers presented themselves; he had perhaps wanted to show her that while he enjoyed her companionship in the provincial circles of Seafleet, she would never fit in with the world he was aiming for in the higher regions of theatrical London. In a telephone call from him since her return to Seafleet he had revealed that during the unfortunate weekend he had been approached by a leading London stage director who had offered him an important role in a forthcoming West End production: *Nought Else is Living.* So it hadn't been altogether Hermione monopolizing him—although she was very much involved, since she was to play the very young leading lady opposite Robert in the new play. Naturally he had grasped the opportunity and moved into the higher echelons of his profession. Seafleet had been simply his place of apprenticeship, Marnie realized, a period of training, which she had enlivened with her friendship. For it was nothing more than the most casual friendship he wanted from her.... The carefully built-up explanations for her unhappy weekend fell away. The invitation to his home had been as casual as everything else in their relationship.

"Doctor Harford himself will meet you at Geneva airport," Jane was announcing. "I'm to send him a telegram with your flight number."

The young man with the abrupt manner and autocratic air. Marnie's thoughts swung to him reluctantly. Anything less like Robert's irresistible and compelling charm. But it would make a change—it would be good for her, like a great splash of cold water in the face to bring her to her senses.

"He will, he says, be carrying a copy of *The Lancet*, Jane was continuing.

"How original!" Marnie sneered.

"But practical," Jane defended her client. "He's got to give you some sign by which you'll recognize him. And what could be more opposite than the good old *Lancet*?"

"As long as we find one another..." Marnie said.

"You will," Jane confirmed hearteningly.

EXACTLY TWENTY-FOUR HOURS later Marnie, sitting in one of the aisle seats of a well-filled jet, heard a disembodied voice announcing that they were losing height and would be landing at Geneva in fifteen minutes. Glancing across at the window on her left she caught a glimpse through breaking clouds of needle-sharp mountain tops. The Alps. Last night when she was packing in the room of the hostel where she lived, Robert had phoned to ask her in his casual way if she would be "doing anything" the following day around lunch time.

"Yes," she had delighted in informing him crisply. "I shall be taking off for Geneva on my way to Arbois, a ski resort in the French Alps."

That shook him, as she had hoped it would. "Good heavens! Do you mean you're going there to ski?"

"No. To take a case. But I shall be able to get some skiing in, as well," she was careful to add. "It doesn't seem too demanding an assignment. Just somebody needing a spot of therapy and care." She wouldn't say anything about old ladies and strokes, or point out that she didn't know one end of a ski from the other.

"Well, well!" There was a trenchant pause. "Good luck and all that, my dear. How long do you expect to be away?"

"I have no idea. Some time, I imagine."

"I shall miss you."

No doubt he would. He still had a month of his contract at the Seafleet theater to work out and her acquiescent, admiring presence would have helped him to endure the repetitious work in an environment he had suddenly outgrown.

"You'll soon be in London rehearsing for *Nought Else is Living*," she reminded him.

"Yes, of course!" His voice came to life. "Hermione will be playing the lead—did I tell you?"

"Yes,' she snapped back. "Several times. I'm sure life will be very pleasant for you at the Sheridan Theater."

There was another long pause. Had he hung up, annoyed at her tone? But no. The ingratiating voice, when it came, was soft with remorse. "You're mad at me, aren't you, Marnie? I don't wonder. I'm afraid you didn't have very much of a time at my people's place the other weekend. It was just unlucky... Terrington turning up to make me his fabulous offer. I had to play along with him."

And with Hermione, Marnie thought. But aloud she said, "Of course you had to, Robert. Don't give it a thought."

"My people liked you awfully," he offered.

Marnie laughed. "You tell a pretty fib, don't you, Robert? But not to worry—about the lost weekend, I mean. You have your life to live, and I have mine. I must ring off now... have masses to do getting ready to leave. See you on the ski slopes!" she ended jokingly.

"That's a thought, Marnie. Here's to our meeting in Arbois," he replied quickly. Competent theatrical repartee; nothing more. To go in one ear and out the other. But at least he had had the grace to offer a tardy apology for the way he had neglected her during their London weekend. How much did the hurt still rankle? Not as much as it had done a few days ago. Here on the threshold of what promised to be an interesting new world the wound Robert had dealt her was already easing, a wound to her pride, perhaps, rather than her heart. It had been stupid of her to get all worked up at being invited to his home—letting her carefully maintained guard slip.

There now was the illuminated notice about fastening seat belts. She fumbled with hers and felt the slight subsequent jerks as they rapidly lost height, as if the great plane was bumping its way down a flight of stairs. Then came the amazingly gentle impact as they touched down, and the swift race along the runway, the first real sensation of speed since they had left Heathrow.

Geneva at a first glance was disappointingly like any other airport. There was the usual feeling of unreality as they crossed the tarmac to customs and immigration, the journey at high altitude having done something unspecified to one's legs, or was it one's head? But whatever it was, the feeling soon wore off and by the time Marnie emerged into the exit hall with the porter who carried her luggage she felt perfectly normal again. Her fellow passengers all seemed to be certain where they were going; only Marnie hesitated at the final barrier, scanning the small crowd who waited there for arriving friends.

For a moment Marnie hung back, shrinking a little from her encounter with the unknown quantity that was Harford, clinging to her anonymity.

Then she saw him, a man of medium height, bareheaded, wearing a rough-textured car coat, holding a medical magazine to his chest. Like a poultice, Marnie thought with an inward nervous giggle. Scanning the crowd with an air of impatience, he waited for her to announce herself.

Moving toward him she was, for the first time on her journey, conscious of her appearance, hoping she looked all right and would make a good first impression. Perhaps she ought to have worn a hat, and her tweed coat was a season out of date. Still, she wasn't competing in a fashion parade, she reminded herself, and defiantly tossed a soft fair lock out of her eyes. Approaching the well-displayed *Lancet*, she suppressed a desire to say, "Dr. Livingstone, I presume!" But it was a correct and somewhat timid, "Dr. Harford?" that came out. "I'm Sarah Marnhem."

"Ah, Miss Marnhem." The keen eyes that swept over her held disapproval. Hazel eyes under level brows. The thick brown hair that lay close to his head had a hazel glint to it. He was deeply tanned; it was a strong face, well cut, tight-lipped, as if at this moment of assessment he found something lacking in her. "I thought you would have been wearing a uniform," he said with a withering glance at her blown fair hair and tweed coat.

"Uniform!" Marnie echoed. How fuddy-duddy can you get? "One doesn't usually wear an outdoor uniform nowadays," she reminded him gently, and would have liked to add that they weren't living in the 1930's. But he had taken her suitcase from the porter and was moving so rapidly ahead toward the parking lot that she practically had to trot to keep up with him. Strong, silent man, she decided ruefully. And bad-mannered into the bargain. Not a normal word of greeting. "Did you have a good flight, et cetera?" Just that snarl about her missing uniform.

"We have a two hours' run before us," he offered as he opened the car door for her. It might have been an apology for his curtness, or at least an explanation of his unceremonious haste. Yet, oddly, though his hand was on the handle of the door he did not open it for her, but stood by her side in a strangely arrested way, looking down at her. The sharpness had gone from his eyes now; they held what seemed more like a question, a sort of wonder. The pause was so long that it was embarrassing. Then as if rousing himself with an effort he passed his free hand across his brow and flung the car door open. A moment later they were out of the airport and speeding along a wide busy road, with a vista of mountains at the end of it. She was in Geneva, Marnie reminded herself, and saw the great lake with the boulevards of houses and high-rise apartments all around it.

"You'll have had a meal on the plane," the doctor stated, rather than asked.

"Yes, of course," Marnie agreed rather shortly. Because now it was teatime and she would have loved a cup of tea... as well as a longer look at the famous city. They were cruising along one of the lakeside boulevards now. Pavement cafés presented themselves invitingly. In the late afternoon sunshine the people at the little tables looked out over the ink-blue waters and toyed with delectable pastries. Envying them, Marnie was whisked away, leaving the lake behind. A level road bordered with trees soon brought them to a customs barrier. Dr. Harford, obviously well known to the officials, was waved on and the striped poles came down behind them. A little farther on there was a second barrier, where the procedure was very much the same.

They were now in France, the doctor announced. "Do you know this part of the world at all?"

"No," Marnie answered. "My few trips abroad have been to sunspots like Spain and Majorca."

"Humph," grunted her companion, unimpressed by trips to Majorca. He hadn't, it emerged, been thinking about holidays. "I was wondering what experience in private nursing you've actually had," he said. "I thought you would have been older."

And clad in an ankle-length navy blue coat with bonnet and veil to match, Marnie thought.

"I'm twenty-five," she informed her companion, mentally adding the few months that would bring her to this respectable-sounding age. "And I've been doing private nursing ever since I finished my training at St. Chad's three years ago."

"A St. Chad's nurse!" He sounded impressed, as well he might be. St. Chad's as a teaching hospital had no rival among the great hospitals of London. The glance he flicked at her was almost respectful. Then he spoiled it by saying, "You don't look twenty-five, more like nineteen, a rather foolish nineteen at that, with all that greenish stuff on your eyelids. Why do girls nowadays feel that they have to go about looking as if they've just had a couple of unfortunate rounds in a boxing ring?"

Marnie colored angrily. She had put the merest smear of eyeshadow on her lids today. Who on earth did this rude young man think he was!

"Aren't you being a little personal?" she demanded hotly. "Also strangely out of date. Don't nurses in France go in for a discreet touch of makeup, especially when they're off duty?"

"Not my nurses," he answered. "You see, they happen to be exceedingly serious people who take their work as part of their vocation."

"They sound like nuns," Marnie said, with a hint of mockery.

"They are nuns," the doctor returned unexpectedly. "I'm resident physician at the local chest clinic, which is run by a nursing order. Wonderful women!" he ended reverently.

"I'm sure they are," Marnie murmured, deflated, but unable to resist the impulse to add, "I'm afraid I'll never be able to live up to them." It was intended sardonically, but Dr. Harford didn't seem to have a very perceptive sense of humor.

"As long as you wear your uniform when you're on duty," he said.

"Of course I will," Marnie all but shouted at him. What sort of a nurse did this poker-faced young man think she was?

The car swung around a sharp bend and began to climb steeply. There was snow everywhere now, the frozen road crackling under the chain-encrusted wheels.

They drove on in silence and presently Marnie became aware that her companion was giving her a series of purposeful sidelong glances. "I get the feeling that I've seen you somewhere before," he said at last. "Where do you come from?"

"My home is Scotland," Marnie told him. "Border country. The north corner of Berwick to be exact, at the foot of the Lammermuir Hills. My father farms there." As she spoke she could see in her mind's eye the low granite building with its neat barns and huts—surrounded by rich green fields.

"Indeed! I did part of my training in Edinburgh, which I suppose would be your shopping center?"

"On special occasions, yes," Marnie agreed. "So you may have sat opposite me in a bus one day. "Once seen, never forgotten," she added flippantly.

Obviously disapproving of flippancy and uninterested in the possibility of a bus encounter, the doctor offered no comment.

They were out of the pine-tree belt now, the road growing ever steeper. Marnie caught her breath at the beauty of the panorama revealed; mountain peak after mountain peak, white against the rosy evening sky; one dominating peak lifting itself in majesty to pierce the blue bowl of heaven.

"Mont Blanc," the doctor announced on a note of almost personal pride. "It reigns over Arbois, which is tucked away in that high altitude valley ahead of us."

They were back in the shadow of a pine wood again, a turn in the road having robbed them of the vista of mountains, and the doctor was talking about Marnie's prospective patient.

"Mrs. Rotherham needs encouragement, gentle therapy, carefully graduated exercises. It won't be hard nursing, but it will require patience and understanding. Mrs.

Rotherham is in her mid-seventies, and having lived an active life, mostly free from ailments, she finds her present disabilities a trial. I hope you'll contrive to get on with her...."

Once more that underlying note of doubt in her competence, Marnie thought with a sinking sensation. It wasn't going to be easy to work with this Harford man if he had so little confidence in her.

The black pines were thinning, the road began to level out. There were houses at intervals now, Christmas-card houses with steeply pitched roofs on which snow lay in thick white cushions, icicles hanging in sparkling rows from the eaves.

Then they were entering Arbois, cruising slowly down a long snow-covered street. Marnie looked in fascination at the smart shops and hotels, all brilliantly lit up. Canned music poured from a background skating rink, the inevitable "Skaters' Waltz." Skiers returning from a day on the slopes, their skis balanced on their shoulders, thronged the narrow pavements. A horse-drawn sleigh came gliding toward them with a gay clatter of ringing bells. It was all so novel, so animated.

"Arbois warming up for its usual evening whoopee," the doctor said, and leaning over her pointed out the fifteenth-century church standing back in the wide central *place.* For an instant his shoulder lay lightly against her own. Faintly disturbed at the unexpected physical contact, she scarcely saw the historic church, rapidly left behind as they climbed a steep rough lane flanked with the inevitable pine trees and high banks of snow.

"Les Trois Chasseurs," the doctor announced as they drew up before a large chalet-type house built of rough mountain stone, with the usual steeply pitched Alpine-style roof and wide pinewood balconies. There was no garden approach—just the rough snow-covered ground that bordered the lane. In a rocky cleft nearby a mountain torrent raced, the sound of its rushing water filling the air—tingling air, that seemed to sparkle on the lips like champagne. Marnie drew in a deep breath as she followed the doctor through a thick wooden door, which hc had opened unceremoniously.

"Anyone at home?" he called out. But there was no reply. Peering around her in the dim windowless hall, Marnie saw parkas and coats hanging on the walls, which also supported propped-up skis. A bare pinewood staircase led to an upper floor where, Marnie was to discover, the dwelling space proper really began. The ground floor, apart from being a dumping place for skis, merely housed a laundry room, a garage and a space to store the stacks of pine logs that would burn at all hours in the living rooms above.

The doctor led the way up the stairs, swinging her heavy suitcase effortlessly in his hand. There was the same air of urgency about him that she had noticed at the airport. A sort of suppressed energy—as if he were supercharged. An emanation of physical strength came from the broad shoulders under the rough fur-fabric jacket.

They reached a wide upstairs hallway, bare pinewood like the stairs, a series of doors opening off. Dropping the suitcase, the doctor entered a large, bright living room, where a deep settee was drawn up before a roaring fire. Here, too, Marnie noticed in a lightning glance, the decor was almost all the same golden, shining pinewood: the walls, the floor, the long dining table set in a picture window at the far end of the all-purpose room. There were rugs and comfortable armchairs to relieve the stark effect.

From out of the settee's depths a young girl extricated herself, an open book in her hand. She was wearing ski clothes, her glinting fair hair half veiling her lively, vivid face.

"Hello, David!" she greeted the doctor familiarly. "Mummy and daddy are doing the Varens-Alp today. I expect they'll be home any minute now."

"Meanwhile here's Nurse Marnhem," the doctor said, and more formally murmured, "Stella Rotherham, Nurse Marnhem."

"Hello!" Stella offered automatically, making no attempt to hold out a welcoming hand. "Granny is waiting for you," she added. "She's been on tenterhooks all afternoon."

"Most inadvisable," the doctor growled. "We'd better go along to her at once."

Crossing the hallway, Marnie noticed her suitcase had disappeared, whisked away by some servant, she supposed. The room they now entered was large and brightly illuminated with the last rays of the setting sun. An old lady, muffled in shawls, was sitting by an open French window, her small face peering sharply above the folds of her wraps. An arresting face, which might once have held the ethereal loveliness of her granddaughter's. The bright undaunted eyes, quick, inquisitive, held a hint of laughter, as though even at the age of seventy-five, with a mild stroke hovering, life could still be amusing.

"Ah, David," she welcomed the young man. "What have you brought me?" She held a fragile white hand out to Marnie, her bright eyes keenly assessing the stranger. "Young," she pronounced in a tone of satisfaction, "and quite pretty. Also she looks good-tempered, which she'll have to be with me as her patient." Her tinkling laughter rang out. "You've done well, David! I like your Nurse Marnhem. Though I'm not going to call her nurse all the time. It sounds so hospital-like. What is your Christian name, my dear?"

"Most of my friends call me Marnie," Marnie said, her spirits rising. What a delightful old girl! Anything less like a grumpy invalid it would be hard to imagine.

"Your hand is cold." The doctor was feeling her pulse. "You ought not to be sitting here by the open window at this hour. Nurse—" he turned to Marnie "—will you help Mrs. Rotherham to get into bed? Then you can join me in the lounge where I'll give you your general instructions."

"Let the poor girl get her outdoor things off first," the old lady protested as the doctor left them. "Your room is through there, my dear." She pointed to a door opening out of her own room. "Denise, that is my daughter-in-law, thought you would be best in there so that you will be near me at night. But I promise not to disturb you. I sleep well, thanks to David's pills and potions."

Entering the room indicated, Marnie found her suitcase on a chair by the comfortable-looking bed. Hurriedly unlocking it, she took out her white uniform and linen coif, so that when she returned to her patient she was professionally attired, her hair hidden demurely under the linen folds of the coif.

Old Mrs. Rotherham peered at her. "How quick you've been! But must you wear that white thing on your head? Your hair is so pretty, and the less you look like a starchy nurse the happier I shall be. So just be your own charming self and try not to think of me too much as an invalid. I think that will help."

"I'm sure you're right," Marnie agreed, and swept the coif from her head. "But perhaps Dr. Harford will disapprove. He seemed especially keen on my wearing correct uniform."

"Dear boy," the old lady murmured. "Such a clever doctor, but inclined to fuss over details, I tell him. Don't take him too seriously, he needs to relax. He works far too hard... ought to spend more time on the ski slopes. He's a marvelous skier, wins those terrible, swift races, slaloms, or whatever they're called, and in the summer, when he can't ski, he climbs. Mountains are his passion. He's my great-nephew, you know. That's one reason we always come to Arbois, where he's been practicing for the past three years. Adores the place, has bought himself a delightful small chalet the other side of the valley."

"Perhaps it's time I was helping you into bed," Marnie suggested, fearing a garrulous flow of family history. And the doctor was waiting for her in the lounge, she remembered.

"Before we close the window do let me creep out onto the balcony," the old lady pleaded. "The sunset is so beautiful."

A little doubtful of the wisdom of the proceeding, Marnie helped the old lady out of her chair and supported her across the window's threshold onto the balcony.

"There!" she announced in a rapturous tone. "Look to the left, right down the valley."

Turning her head obediently, Marnie stood transfixed. The light had faded from the hollow of the valley now and the lesser mountains were shrouded in cold blue twilight. But soaring above them, alone, supreme, against a sky of gold, was the majestic summit of Mont Blanc bathed in a glow of purest rose pink.

"Isn't it beautiful!" the old lady whispered. "Every evening I try to get out here to look at it. If there's no one to help me I hold onto the window frame and lean out. My beautiful Mont Blanc, every night it speaks to me. And do you know what it says? 'At eventide it shall be light.' It gives me such courage, for my evening I know is growing short, and it is very precious."

CHAPTER TWO

WHEN HER PATIENT was comfortably settled in bed, Marnie returned to the lounge to join the doctor and receive his instructions. He was alone when she entered, Stella having vanished, leaving a crumpled handkerchief and an open book flung down on the settee. Beyond the uncurtained picture window at the far end of the big room the twilit, snow-covered valley was a ghostly white, splashed with the inky blackness of fir trees. In the darkening room the piled-up logs on the hearth burned with a golden and crimson brilliance, throwing a dancing light across the pine-paneled walls and highly polished floor. The tangy smell of the burning wood spiced the warm air.

Turning from the window, where he had been standing, the doctor greeted Marnie's entrance with a glance that held once more a hint of disapproval. The absence of her white linen coif, of course, Marnie decided, and put a defensive hand to her hastily bundled-up hair, locks of which were escaping over her brow and ears.

"Mrs. Rotherham asked me not to wear my cap," she found herself explaining on a note of apology for which she despised herself. Why should she apologize to this autocratic young man who was taking advantage of his professional seniority to make her feel small? Yet she had to go on with her faltering explanation. "She wants me to look as little as possible like a nurse."

David Harford laughed. "I'm sure you'll be only too happy to oblige."

Marnie colored angrily. "Surely it's a good thing to minimize the invalidish atmosphere?" she challenged. "Mrs. Rotherham says she hates being treated as an invalid...even more than she dislikes being regarded as old, since she doesn't *feel* old."

The doctor shrugged. "Like most women, my great-aunt prefers make-believe to reality. Did she, by the way, mention to you my connection with the family?"

Marnie nodded. "She told me you're her great-nephew."

"A great-nephew to be gently laughed at rather than her medical adviser to be obeyed."

Medical dictator would be more like it, Marnie thought.

Motioning to her to sit down on the settee, the doctor leaned an elbow on the mantelpiece and began giving her her instructions—which were all more or less predictable. At least she didn't have to stand to attention to listen to them, Marnie congratulated herself.

Mrs. Rotherham's seizure had not been serious, the crisp voice reiterated; time and patience would alleviate her condition.

"Time?" Marnie echoed. "Does that mean this is to be a case of long duration?"

"Would it matter to you if it were?" His tone was sharp.

"No, of course not. I shall be glad to help Mrs. Rotherham as long as she needs me...and," she couldn't help adding impulsively, "Arbois is very beautiful." Then, seeing the inevitable displeasure return to his glance, she added hastily, "Though that's hardly the point."

"It certainly isn't." His tone was sardonic. "No doubt

you find the idea of a ski resort attractive, and of course you must have reasonable free time. But I hope your first interest will be to get Mrs. Rotherham on her feet as soon as possible: massage, gentle exercise... the usual routine for such cases. She will, I hope, be fit to travel when the family returns to England in about a month's time. My uncle is an exceedingly busy man with many interests in the city; furthermore, he has the tenancy of this chalet for a definitely limited period. So you can see how important it is that my great-aunt make, approximately, a complete recovery."

"But supposing she doesn't?" Marnie asked.

"In that event she might have to put in a spell at the clinic. Or I could have her at my chalet. In which case I would have to find someone to look after her, either yourself or one of the nurses from the clinic." There was a pause. "We must see how it works out."

So he wasn't committing himself; she was to be on trial, Marnie concluded. So be it! She wasn't at all sure she would want to live at close quarters in the chalet of this dogmatic young man. Yet old Mrs. Rotherham was a dear, and once she became involved with her it might not be easy to become disentangled. For the moment Marnie made no comment. There was, indeed, nothing she could usefully say.

Silence fell upon them. The only sound in the room was the crackling of the logs on the hearth. From his stance by the mantelpiece, oddly illuminated by the rosy firelight, the doctor looked down on her. It was a long, unfaltering and vaguely disturbing look. Trying to return it with equally impassive steadiness, Marnie was vividly aware of every detail of his appearance. He was wearing a rough tweed jacket with leather patches on shoulder and sleeves, and he gave the impression of being taller than he actually was. His hair, she thought, was the color of mahogany, and the firelight was doing strange things to his eyes, giving them an odd bright eagerness... almost a hungriness.

Self-consciousness engulfed her, and once more she put a nervous hand to her hair. She felt her cheeks grow hot and the room with its roaring fire seemed suddenly insufferably warm.

If only he would stop staring at her with those merciless hazel eyes! Was he trying to hypnotize her, she wondered ridiculously. Then to her horror she heard herself blurt, "Is there something wrong with me?"

He seemed to come to life, as if wakening out of a dream. "I'm sorry. Was I staring at you? It's just that you look so like someone I once... met. And yet you're not really like her. Something is missing. I was trying to work it out."

"The time you sat opposite me in a bus in Edinburgh," she suggested with an unsteady little laugh.

He shook his head. "No, not that. If indeed I ever did sit opposite you in a bus in Edinburgh. In some strange way you stir a chord of memory. But it's all very indefinite... cloudy...." He passed a hand across his brow.

"In other worlds I loved you long ago, Love that has no beginning, has no end...." Whatever put those words into her head, Marnie wondered, and heard the sound of footsteps on the stairway beyond the open door... ski boots clattering against bare uncarpeted wood.

A moment later Mark and Denise Rotherham entered the room. There was a small flurry of introductions.

"I'm so glad you've arrived, nurse." Young Mrs. Rotherham held out a welcoming hand. "It will ease things enormously having you. Although my mother-in-law isn't really very ill, I haven't felt I ought to leave her.

I only went out this afternoon because I knew you would be arriving, and she had that to look forward to. Also Marie, our kind housekeeper, was having an eye to her." The rather guilty little explanation trailed away and it was Mark Rotherham who now took Marnie's hand.

"I hope you had a pleasant journey," he offered politely.

"Where's Stella?" Denise Rotherham broke in anxiously before Marnie could answer the inquiry about her journey.

"She was here when we came in," the doctor said. "Then a little later she said something about having a date in the village.'

"Oh, dear, she knows I don't like her hanging about the cafés at this aperitif hour."

"Oh, she'll be all right," the doctor assured her lightly. "I'll send her home if I see her. I'm just on my way now. . . ."

"You won't stay for dinner?"

"Good lord, no!" he flung back with the lack of ceremony permissible among close relatives. "I've still got a round to do at the clinic. Heaven knows when I shall be through."

"Well, join us a little later if you feel like it," Denise Rotherham insisted. "You'll find us at the Splendide. We shall be going down there as usual later on."

"Right-oh!" He was off then without further ceremony, clattering down the noisy stairs.

"This dim, religious light," Denise grumbled, and switched on a bright overhead chandelier, which made Marnie blink. With brisk movements Denise was pulling the curtains across the now completely blank windows. She was tall and dark haired, her very blue eyes set in a heart-shaped piquant face. Stella, it seemed, took after her large fairish father, and though she was more classically beautiful than her mother, she would never have the same dynamic appeal. Denise Rotherham was one of those strikingly positive people who know what they want and usually contrive to get it. She was dressed in a dark skiing costume, her snow-encrusted ski boots leaving puddles on the floor. Marnie began to understand the scarcity of rugs and carpets in the big room, the preponderance indeed in the whole house of bare polished pinewood underfoot.

Excusing herself, she returned to the sickroom to see how her patient was getting on. She was sitting up with piled pillows behind her, and a tray before her on the hospital-style bed table.

"Marie has just brought my supper," she remarked. "Stay and talk to me while I eat it."

Marnie's professional eye made certain that the food that had been given to the old lady was in keeping with the strict diet Dr. Harford had prescribed. It was. All was well. Sitting in an armchair drawn close to the bed, she chatted in an easy fashion while the old lady ate, grumbling at the absence of exciting dishes. "All this nonsense of David's about my keeping to steamed chicken and grilled fish and milk junkets! When am I going to be allowed to have some of the lovely French food and wine I'm missing?"

Marnie, uttering reassurances, wondered where she herself would be expected to eat. Would she be dining with the family? Or would her meals be served to her in her own room? To her relief she found later that she was to dine with the Rotherhams, Denise making it clear during a brief visit to her mother on her way to bathe and change.

"You must change for the evening, too," old Mrs. Rotherham advised Marnie. "You won't want to spend all your time in that white overall thing. Go and put on something pretty. And if you'd like a bath you'll find a bathroom for your exclusive use in the passage, beside your bedroom. There's a plethora of bathrooms in this house—that's one reason Mark always rents it. You need lots of baths when you're skiing," she added. "It's hot work. I know." She shook a regretful head. "I used to do my share of it before *anno domini* caught up with me." A remark that launched her on to a spate of reminiscences—names like Davos, St. Moritz, Kitzbühl rippled from her tongue. "All the handsome ski instructors! And the Austrians are the cleverest and the most dangerous...far too attractive to be safe." She gave Marnie a wicked glance. "As you'll no doubt find out! But go carefully. We already have one romantic problem on our hands in this family!"

An obscure remark, which Marnie pondered as presently she changed her dress, missing out on the bath. She was not sure how much time she ought to spend away from her patient. She would need some attention after her supper and there were tablets to be given....

Dinner, she discovered, was to be served in the same long, wide room that housed the outsize settee and the roaring fire. The bare pinewood table at the end of the room had been laid with mats and glass and silver by the time Marnie joined the Rotherhams. Denise was serving drinks from a cart drawn close to the settee where her husband had settled himself. He rose politely as Marnie entered.

"Do sit down, nurse," Denise Rotherham pointed to one of the roomy armchairs. "What will you have to drink? There's sherry, Dubonnet, Cinzano," she rattled off a list of unfamiliar French aperitifs. Marnie chose sherry, playing safe.

The door opened with a defiant flourish and Stella came in, still wearing her skiing gear.

"Stella!" her mother greeted her in an exasperated tone. "Where have you been? You know I don't like you hanging about the village cafés alone at this hour...and you haven't even given yourself time to change. Marie is just about to serve the soup."

"Good, I'm starving!" Stella returned, taking her place at the table as the housekeeper entered carrying a steaming tureen.

"And I wasn't hanging about the village, as you so elegantly put it," she shot at her mother, "making me sound like a lost puppy. I was with Dolores in La Belle Piste."

"Only Dolores?" her mother pursued suspiciously.

"Rudi turned up, if you must know."

"And Dolores tactfully disappeared, while Rudi brought you home, making it a lingering walk beneath the stars...."

"Oh, for heaven's sake!" Stella cried out.

"Exactly," her father broke in. "Let's have our meal in peace."

A strained peace at first, but as the excellent meal progressed Denise was giving an animated account of the afternoon she had spent on the demanding slope of the Varens-Alp. "The snow was quite perfect, the run not overcrowded." She turned to Marnie: "Do you ski, nurse?"

"I've never had the chance to learn," Marnie deplored. "Even though I come from Scotland, my home is in the Border country, miles from the snowy slopes of the Cairngorms."

"Then you really must learn while you're here," the older woman urged, and added generously, "I could lend you a pair of ski pants and you could rent skis and boots at the ski school. Stella," she ended, darting an oddly warning glance at her daughter, "could take you there tomorrow morning when she goes for her lesson."

"Only that I'm not here to play about on ski slopes," Marnie pointed out regretfully.

"But you must have some time off," Denise insisted. "You can't spend all your time hanging about the sick-room; my mother-in-law would hate it. She's an independent soul. Once you've helped her with her morning routine and treatments there's no reason why you shouldn't have a couple of hours off duty before lunch, learning what you can on the nursery slopes. Stella, I'm sure, would be pleased to have you with her."

Stella greeted this remark with a scowl, but said nothing.

"Stella," her father began dryly, "is an addict of the nursery slopes. She ought to have been done with them long ago, trying the higher runs. But she is, it seems, a slow learner."

"I'm not a slow learner," Stella flung at her parent indignantly. "But it's no use rushing things. The fundamentals of skiing are all-important, Rudi says."

"I'm sure he does!" Mark agreed sardonically.

Stella went scarlet. "You're just being horrible about him! Why can't you leave him alone? You said we were to have dinner in peace."

"And so we shall," Denise declared, and firmly changed the subject.

So there was a disturbing ski instructor in the background—Austrian by the sound of his name. Marnie remembered old Mrs. Rotherham's hints at a romantic problem in the family. And it was Rudi rather than Dolores, Stella had gone down to the village to meet before dinner. Her parents didn't approve... no wonder; the girl, by the look of her, would be hardly fifteen.

Was that the reason Denise Rotherham was so anxious for her to take up skiing, Marnie wondered. Was she to be a mixture of spy and chaperone? Even so the thought of learning kick turns and balancing and stemming, all the complicated maneuvers that went into the control of a pair of skis on a slippery incline, filled her with excitement. What would Dr. Harford think of such frivolity?

A question she put to Denise Rotherham when after dinner she took Marnie to her own room and produced a shabby but serviceable windproof parka and a pair of tapered pants, which could be held taut under the instep with an elastic band.

"Oh, David won't mind," Denise dismissed her relative. "He adores skiing himself and is awfully good at it after three winters here. I'm sure he'll approve of you taking it up during the hours my mother-in-law doesn't need you."

Marnie had her doubts, but Denise was hurrying on, offering advice now about gloves—which could be purchased in the village. "Don't let them talk you into having mitts. You must have your fingers free to grip your sticks. Woollen or leather gloves with a pair of silk gloves inside are the best...." she rattled on amiably.

"It's so kind of you," Marnie murmured, a little overwhelmed by the urgency of young Mrs. Rotherham's manner. "But really I don't like to embark on all this without consulting Dr. Harford."

"Don't worry; I'll talk to him. We shall be seeing him at the Splendide this evening. It's quite the nicest of the several night spots in the village—a dance floor and a bar, as well as an excellent restaurant where we sometimes eat. The night life here is so lively. We must introduce you to it some time."

A Doctor Harford who enjoyed skiing and the lively night life of Arbois—this was certainly not Marnie's first impression of him.

When she had settled old Mrs. Rotherham for the night she returned to the now empty living room. The dinner table had been cleared, the fire replenished. She sank into a corner of the enveloping settee and gazed into the heart of the piled-up logs. It was very quiet—only the ticking of the beautiful little carriage clock on the mantelpiece and the small silken sound of the flames on the hearth disturbed the silence. Indoors and out the hush of the snow-filled valley seemed to prevail. Was it only this morning she had left Heathrow? Marnie closed her eyes and let her thoughts drift back drowsily over the day's experiences: her uneventful flight with its one glimpse of the high Alps; her arrival at Geneva where the doctor awaited her—his critical eyes not altogether liking the look of her; then the drive up the twisting mountain roads to the enchanted village of Arbois. A village full of light and music...and the strange cold smell of snow. For snow on the Alpine heights did have its own pungent stinging breath, she had discovered on that soaring enchanted drive. She thought of her arrival here at Les Trois Chasseurs, and her meeting with the unexpectedly charming old lady who was to be her patient.

The recollections grew blurred, drifted together... She slept, her fair hair with its golden lights spread out on the cushion behind her; her lashes long on her flushed cheeks, her lips slightly apart.

Was it the sense of another presence that aroused her? She stirred and opened her eyes drowsily to find with a sharp pang of shock that Dr. David Harford was standing at the end of the settee, looking down at her with a contemplative smile on his lips. "You must," he said, "be either very tired or very bored to fall asleep at this hour of the evening."

She jumped to her feet, conscious of her rumpled

dress, her untidy hair, angry with herself for appearing at a disadvantage before this domineering young man.

"It's the heat...the snow," she offered in confusion. "This great hot fire, after the snowy air outside...."

"All right, all right!" He waved her back to her seat on the settee again. "Don't work yourself up. I'm sorry I disturbed you, you looked so pretty in your sleep; much too pretty, if I may say so, to be dozing by the fire in the early evening, missing all the delights of this lively Alpine resort."

Compliments! Now what possessed the man? And what possessed *her* to color at the personal tone of his remarks? "I'm not here in Arbois because it's a lively Alpine resort," she reminded him sharply.

"Quite. Which is rather hard on you, I feel. Perhaps all nurses ought to be nuns like my nursing Sisters at the clinic. Wholly dedicated...free from the distractions of being young and beautiful."

"You can be dedicated without being a nun," Marnie pointed out, adding with some asperity for fulsome compliments: "Nor am I all that young and beautiful—if your remarks were intended to be personal."

"Not altogether," the doctor admitted. "I was partly generalizing. Caring for the sick, whether as a doctor or a nurse, leaves little time or energy for one's own pursuits and interests."

An exaggerated viewpoint, she felt, and it didn't altogether tally with what Denise Rotherham had revealed of the young man's very satisfactorily filled off-duty hours on the ski slopes and in the cafés.

With a dismissive shake of his shoulders he changed the subject. "What I really called in for was to bring you a bottle of Mrs. Rotherham's sleeping tablets." He took a small phial from his pocket and handed it to Marnie. "One or two last thing at night—as she needs them. I've just looked in on her and found her playing patience. I turned on her television for her."

Something I ought to have been doing for her, Marnie thought, once more getting to her feet. "I should go and watch the television with her, perhaps...."

"I'm sure she would like that."

Was there implied reproach in his tone?

"She seemed to be dozing when I left her," she added a little guiltily.

The doctor offered no comment. *Letting my own conscience be my judge*, Marnie thought wryly.

Turning the fur collar of his short coat up around his ears, the young man followed her out of the room, saying he was off to the Splendide to join the Rotherhams.

"I shouldn't let the old lady watch the television for too long," he advised as he started down the stairs. A moment later Marnie heard the chained wheels of his car crunching away over the frozen snow.

IN THE MORNING the household came to life slowly. Denise Rotherham appeared in the living room at nine o'clock, hugging a utilitarian woollen dressing gown around her, as Marnie was breakfasting on hot coffee and croissants. She had been up some time settling her patient for the day.

"Wouldn't you rather have had a cooked breakfast?" Denise offered, ringing for Marie and more coffee.

Marnie said the French breakfast was fine. "I never eat a large meal in the morning."

"We have lunch at noon," Denise told her. "So that we can have a long afternoon on the ski slopes. Usually I'm up much earlier than this so I can work in a morning skiing session as well, but we were very late getting back from the Splendide last night; there was a specially amusing cabaret show. I'm afraid," she offered at a tangent, "there'll hardly be time for you to start your skiing lessons this morning. But perhaps you could go down to the school with Stella—if she ever gets up—and see about your ski boots and skis."

Marnie said uneasily, "It's very kind of you to want me to have some skiing, Mrs. Rotherham, but I really feel I ought not to leave my patient."

"Oh, that's all right," Denise's tone was offhand. "I mentioned your off-duty time to David last night and he said he was sure he could leave it to your discretion. Once you've got mother up and dressed and settled in her chair by the window she'll be perfectly happy on her own. Marie is used to looking in on her from time to time."

"But there are her graded exercises, her massage, which will take up most of the morning," Marnie insisted.

Denise looked put out. "Oh, dear, how tiresome. I was hoping you would have been able to go to the slopes with Stella both morning and afternoon. But perhaps it had better be in the afternoons only . . . starting this afternoon. If you change into your skiing gear before lunch you'll be ready to start off with Stella as soon as we've had our meal. And, incidentally, do feel free to call me Denise if you like, and may I call you Marnie as mother does? It's so much less formal than nurse."

"But of course," Marnie agreed, and though she was warmed by the friendly overture and the anxiety over her skiing lessons she couldn't help feeling it was all just a little bit excessive. Why should Denise Rotherham care so much what she did with her off-duty time? Did the handsome Austrian really have anything to do with it—a mildly melodramatic possibility confirmed by Stella later as they walked down to the village. All around them the snow-clad mountains soared in splendor against a bright blue sky. The afternoon sun was hot, the air filled with the musical drip-drip from the thick sparkling icicles that hung from every steeply pitched roof. They crossed the little bridge that spanned the stream that raced down from the ravine by Les Trois Chasseurs. How strange it was not frozen over, Marnie marveled.

"It's too full and too fast to freeze," Stella deigned to explain. She hadn't spoken a word since they left the house, sulking, as she had done all through lunchtime.

"Mother is impossible," she burst out at last. "Pushing you into this skiing business when you've never done any skiing before. You'll break an ankle or something, and David will be furious."

"Why should I break an ankle?" Marnie returned, a trifle nettled at this assumption of her clumsiness. "It's very kind of your mother to want me to learn skiing; lending me a ski suit, and making sure I have free time."

Stella uttered a derogatory exclamation. "Mother isn't being kind. She's just using you. You're being sent to the ski school to keep an eye on the erring daughter. Mum is terrified over my friendship with Rudi Praxmann. He's the ski instructor at the school." She threw Marnie a wickedly sparkling glance, her eyes, her whole face coming vividly alive. "Dishy!" she breathed ecstatically. "And how! You'll see...."

Marnie, engaged in keeping her balance on a particularly slippery patch of snow, could find no comment to offer to this outburst. But inwardly she was dismayed at the role for which she had been cast—a peeping duenna! She had suspected as much, but the confirmation of her fears spoiled the happiness she had been feeling about the kindly atmosphere at Les Trois Chasseurs. All the same, she told herself, young Mrs. Rotherham's anxiety over her lovely and very young daughter was natural enough. A conclusion that was strengthened when she found herself face to face with the redoubtable Rudi.

The ski school proved to be a large wooden hut on the edge of the gentle incline known as the nursery slopes. Apart from a rough desk on which lay record books of some kind, the only other objects to be seen were untidy heaps of boots, tangles of ski poles and the skis themselves standing in sheaves against the bare wooden walls. A medley of warmly clad aspiring pupils came and went, finding their own particular pair of skis and putting them on. The clatter of skis and voices was overwhelming, the whole animated scene dominated by a tall young man with butter-colored hair—more gilt than merely blond. He was deeply tanned, the brightness of his hair and the blue of his eyes making an almost startling contrast. Above his close-fitting ski pants he wore a well washed, rather shrunken white jersey, a row of multi-colored badges sewn across the chest, trophies no doubt from his racing success. Rudi, the handsome Austrian; there was no mistaking him. And there was charm as well as good looks. No wonder, Marnie thought, that the teenage Stella was dazzled by him.

Leaning against him familiarly, she introduced Marnie, not stressing her function in the Rotherham household; just saying, "This is Miss Marnhem, who's staying with us, Rudi. She's never done any skiing before and wants to learn."

"Then you have come to the right place, Miss Marnhem," Rudi smiled, displaying a row of very white teeth. He held out his hand and Marnie, putting her own into it, was surprised by its size and strength. A skier's hand—overdeveloped from the endless gripping and manipulating of the ski poles which were so vitally a part of his sweeping swooping races down impossible snow gradients. Marnie found herself wishing she could see him in action.

For the next few minutes he devoted himself to the task of fitting her out with the right-sized boots and skis.

"Short skis are best for beginners," he told her. "They give you a better balance. Hold up your arm." He took her hand again, lifting her arm straight above her head, then measured several skis against it until he found one that came to the tips of her outstretched fingers.

"Long skis for maneuverability, short skis for safety," he quoted.

"When do I get on to long skis?" inquired Stella, who was hovering at his side, ignoring the group of learners who were already practicing their initial skills on the easy gradient outside the hut.

"When you move up to the next grade; the group led by Anton le Farge," he told her. "Which you seem in no hurry to do." The smile that accompanied this observation was indulgent and smugly male—a conqueror's smile.

Stella colored. "I'm just making sure."

"Of what?" Rudi challenged mischievously.

Stella's blush deepened, but she made no reply.

"Comme tu es belle!" Rudi whispered, gently tweaking one of the curls that hung over her ears. Then, turning back to the waiting Marnie, he gave his attention to the matter of boots. They had to fit perfectly, he explained, if they were to hold the skis. After that there were the safety bindings to be negotiated.

Equipped at last, clutching her ski poles desperately, Marnie moved awkwardly out of the hut in Rudi's wake. How on earth was she ever going to balance on the slippery snow shod in these impossible pieces of laminated wood?

"Come and join my novices," Rudi invited.

"I'll take you first," he told a waiting group of about

half a dozen people of all ages and sexes. There was even one elderly gentleman, wrapped to the neck in clumsy woollens, an old-fashioned Balaclava helmet pulled down over his ears. Somehow Marnie waddled her way into line with these raw recruits, Stella coming to stand beside her.

"*Tiens!*" Rudi exclaimed impatiently. "You don't have to stay with this lot, Stella. Go along and try out some traverse climbing on your own until I am ready for your group."

"I'd rather stay here," Stella declared obstinately.

Rudi gave it up with a shrug. "You are crazy, *ma petite*!"

Crazy indeed, Marnie reflected pityingly, while she balanced gingerly on her unfamiliar footwear. Crazy enough to do all the running after her handsome instructor. Poor Stella! And she didn't even have the sense to know that throwing yourself at a man's head was just about the last way to get into his good graces.

"First we learn to walk," Rudi was saying, moving with enviable grace and ease toward his timorous pupils. "*Allez*! Round in a circle. Push your skis, don't lift them. And always use your poles. Put your hands through the leather thong and grip firmly. Never... but never let your poles dangle—out of control."

Marnie worked hard, concentrating desperately, and by the end of her first session at the school was able to make a very slow and cautious descent down a barely perceptible slope. But it was a beginning.

She returned to Les Trois Chasseurs in a glow of achievement and delicious fatigue. It was the sunset hour and already the village street, as she passed through it, was thronged with skiers returning from the cable cars and ski lifts, eager for their cups of tea or hot chocolate. Marnie, hurrying back to her invalid, felt a small pang of jealousy. A cup of hot chocolate would have been a pleasant climax to her strenuous afternoon. Indeed the old gentleman in the Balaclava had actually invited her to join him over a cup of that delicious beverage. But she was not, she reminded herself, a carefree holidaymaker. To have a couple of hours off in the afternoon was as much as she had any right to expect.

SHE WAS GLAD when she returned to the chalet to find that tea awaited her. Denise Rotherham, seated before the inevitable roaring fire with the well-laden tea cart in front of her, called to her as she came up the stairs.

"A cup of tea before you go in to mother," she suggested. "She's perfectly all right. I've just come from her room. I only did the lower slopes of the Jolyon this afternoon, so I got in early.

"How did your first lesson go?" she inquired, as Marnie sank gratefully onto the comfortable settee.

"It was absolutely super," she pronounced, at a loss to describe the afternoon's sensations. "Fabulous! I can hardly wait until I can skim down the mountainsides like the real skiers I glimpsed from my humble nursery slope."

Denise laughed. "I know exactly how you feel. I was just the same the first year we came out here. It all seems so utterly impossible. But one soon gets the hang of it."

"Stella didn't come back with you," she remarked then, rather sharply.

Marnie, drinking a heartening swallow of hot tea, didn't answer for a moment. Then she said cautiously, "I think she went to La Belle Piste."

"With that ski instructor?" Denise put in sharply.

"Well, yes," Marnie admitted reluctantly, resenting being made to tell tales out of school.

"They were alone?"

"I think so. I wasn't really noticing."

"Well, I wish you *would* notice," Denise said in an odd shrill voice, not quite under control. "I'm not asking you to spy on Stella, or anything like that. But if you could just keep an eye on her.... She's completely lost her head over this young man and I'm worried stiff about her. She's only fifteen and this is her first attack of puppy love." Denise shook her head despairingly. "It would have to happen with a totally unpredictable foreigner!"

"Herr Praxmann strikes me as a responsible person," Marnie offered in comfort—and might have added that, if anything, he seemed mildly embarrassed by Stella's infatuation for him.

"Yet he encourages this child, taking her off alone to tea, or whatever," Denise said. "Puppy love," she groaned, "it used to be funny, a little pathetic, but quite harmless. But now!" She shrugged. "With all this permissiveness, the eternal stressing on sex wherever you turn; plays, television, cinemas, and most of all perhaps in schools among the older children themselves. It makes one wonder what things are coming to. Nobody cares anymore. There are no standards any longer. And," she summed it up bitterly, "having a fifteen-year-old daughter in this day and age is... hell!" She turned to Marnie at her side appealingly. "If you could talk to her, try to put some sense into her. You're much more her generation."

"I'm ten years older than she is," Marnie pointed out.

"But you're still closer to her than I am, in this context. Couldn't you try to make her see that being a charmer is part of Rudi's stock-in-trade, that he chats up every female who joins his classes, no matter what age she is? In fact I'm sure he'll try it on you. Indeed," Denise added with a little laugh, "it might not be a bad idea if you were to divert some of the charm-boy's attention to your attractive self. *That* would give Stella something to think about!"

Shocked at this suggestion, Marnie said nothing. But Denise was desperate, she reminded herself. One had to make allowances for her.

When she spoke again it was to say the doctor had called during the afternoon. "Mother said he seemed quite put out that you weren't here to receive him."

"But I thought you'd told him I was going skiing...discussed it with him, and got his approval," Marnie said anxiously.

"We didn't exactly mention skiing when I talked to him at the Splendide last night," Denise said evasively. "I simply pointed out to him that you were entitled to a certain amount of fresh air...and exercise."

Marnie accepted her second cup of tea in silence. She was so sure Doctor Harford had been told of her afternoon enterprise, and had given her venture on to the snow fields his blessing. It was a shock to find that this was not so. Marnie remembered with a pang what Stella had said this afternoon when they were on their way to the ski school—that David would be "furious" about her skiing, fearful that she might have one of the accidents which were all too common among foolhardy beginners, rendering her useless to old Mrs. Rotherham. Perhaps that was why Denise hadn't been more specific with him about his nurse's skiing aspirations, fearful of encountering his veto. It was clear she hadn't been quite straight either with Marnie or the doctor about this. All that mattered to her was finding a kind of unofficial "private eye" who would keep her informed as to her daughter's indiscretions with the handsome Austrian.

"Mother isn't being kind, making it easy for you to go skiing with me. She's just using you." That was what Stella had said as they walked to the village after lunch.

And it seemed as if Stella was right.

CHAPTER THREE

THE FOLLOWING MORNING Marnie was occupied with the routine of the sickroom. She put her patient through her gentle exercises, and they were both delighted at the progress she was making. The limbs which had been affected by her seizure were noticeably more mobile. By eleven o'clock the sun was shining onto the balcony and straight into the room.

"It's so tempting!" the old lady exclaimed, stretching her thin hands out to the golden light. "I'm sure I would be perfectly all right sitting on the balcony for a while this morning."

"Hadn't we better wait until we've asked the doctor?" Marnie suggested.

"Young David? I don't have to have his permission for every move I make," was the scornful reply.

"But he *is* your doctor."

"Oh, I know all about that." The old lady's shrug dismissed all doctors. "After all, it is my own body we're talking about. I've had it for a good many years and managed it with tolerable success. I think I can be trusted now to do what's best for it."

Defeated by the questionable logic, Marnie gave in, and for the first time since her illness old Mrs. Rotherham, fully dressed and warmly wrapped up, was installed in a lounge chair on the balcony. Beyond the snowy waste ground that surrounded the chalet, the road descended to the village—an animated highway this morning, dotted with colorfully dressed skiers on their way to the slopes. There were occasional horse-drawn sleighs with their tinkling sleigh bells, and at one point, to old Mrs. Rotherham's delight, a huge fluffy dog of indeterminate pedigree appeared, drawing a wooden sledge on which stood three milk churns. A countrywoman in a voluminous black skirt and matching head shawl accompanying the sledge completed the picture. "If only I had a camera!" Mrs. Rotherham sighed. And just at that moment the doctor's car appeared.

Marnie's heart sank. First she would be in trouble for taking up skiing, and then for allowing her patient to be out on the balcony—without His Royal Highness's permission.

But he seemed to be in a fairly good humor when presently he joined the two women on the balcony. "What a view you get from here of the village and the mountains!" he exclaimed. And not a word of reproach for his patient's unauthorized venture into the open air as he took her pulse and inquired about her night's sleep.

"It will do you good to have some sunshine," he pronounced astonishingly, and then turning to Marnie, suggested she should go with him into the lounge. "I have something to say to you," he announced ominously.

So the admonitions were to be made in private, Marnie thought apprehensively, as she followed him across the hallway. The big pine-gold room was empty at this hour, Stella and her parents having already gone out for their morning run on the ski slopes.

David Harford made a belligerent noise, clearing his throat. Like a dog barking to keep up his courage, Marnie decided disrespectfully. That was if he needed courage. Telling off helpless nurses would be to him a legitimate sport. So the throat clearing was just a male trumpeting.

He didn't invite her to sit down, though he himself perched on the arm of the settee. And you never sat down in the presence of a doctor on duty unless he condescended to suggest it. So she stood there waiting, while the bold hazel eyes surveyed her, a gleam in them that suggested he was enjoying her predicament.

"This skiing business..." he began. "I can't think why you didn't mention it to me before embarking on it."

"Mrs. Rotherham seemed to think it would be all right," Marnie put in quickly. "I thought she was going to talk to you about it. But it seems she didn't. Anyway," she added on a sudden burst of impatience, "I didn't realize I had to consult you as to what I do with my off-duty hours." The moment it was out she was sorry. It sounded pert, and David Harford looked hurt.

"It's not a question of dictating to you about your off-duty time," he returned with unusual gentleness. "Merely a matter of common sense. Skiing for a beginner can be a dangerous sport. You wouldn't be much use to your patient or to me if you were to break a leg, or whatever. And believe me, accidents on the slopes are not uncommon. You'll soon become accustomed to the sight of the clumsy vehicle on runners known as the 'blood wagon,' which collects the casualties. And naturally beginners are most at risk."

"Herr Praxmann is very careful with us at the school..." Marnie offered a trifle uncertainly.

The doctor frowned. "I expect he does his best, but with a couple of dozen novices milling around him he can't look after everybody."

"I'll be very careful," Marnie assured him, and continued anxiously, "please don't ask me to give it up. I found it absolutely fascinating yesterday and I think I can soon get my skis under control in the first elementary movements."

David Harford gave her a long considering look, and she was furious with herself as she felt her color rising. If he flatly forbade her to ski would she be within her rights to carry on? There were limits, surely, to the submission a nurse was supposed to show. Above her rebellious thoughts she heard Dr. Harford saying, "How would you like a private lesson? You would master the fundamental techniques much more quickly with a little individual tuition. I've got some time on my hands this afternoon and was thinking of taking the *téléférique* to the top of Mont Jolyon. If you would care to come with me I could give you a few tips. There's a plateau on the summit where you could learn to walk on your skis and generally manipulate them much more effectively than in a crowded class on the nursery slopes."

Marnie could scarcely believe her ears. David Harford asking her to spend the afternoon with him on the top of some mountain!

Where *is* Mont Jolyon?" she asked.

He stood up and beckoned her over to the picture window at the far end of the lounge. "Do you see that wooden structure to the left of the village? That's the *téléférique* station, the terminus of the overhead cable line which takes the *cabines* swung on cables up the mountainside. But of course you have the same sort of thing at the skiing centers in the Cairngorms."

"A long way from my part of Scotland," Marnie pointed out. "I've never been to the Cairngorms. If I had, I might have known something about skiing already."

"Quite." The word came out flatly and he was looking at her with an odd intensity. "Your home, I think you told me, is to the south of Edinburgh, isn't it?"

"Yes, near the Border country. The nearest approach to mountains that we have is the Lammermuir Hills."

"They breed sheep there, don't they?"

What an extraordinary question—having nothing to do with the matter they had been discussing. She wished he would get back to it—that amazing suggestion that she might go skiing with him this afternoon.

"Isn't that one of the cable cars starting up the mountainside now?" She leaned toward the window, watching the big boxlike vehicle, swinging dangerously in midair, swaying as it went. "How long does it take to get to the top?"

"About three minutes. You see that patch of pine forest about halfway up the slope?" He pointed. "Look straight above it and you can just make out the wooden platform where the cable car comes to rest. And it's right there we would find our nice safe stretch of trampled snow. There's a *piste*—that's a track—which winds alongside some woods, an ideally safe place for you to find your ski legs. So what about it? Like to come?"

"I'd love to! It's very kind of you." She tried to hold back the eagerness in her voice. But to get on more genial terms with her doctor-employer would make life at Arbois that much simpler and pleasanter. Besides, she was filled with a novice's enthusiasm for the exciting and perhaps dangerous new skill.

It was the danger, it seemed, which was uppermost in David Harford's mind, and stressing it now he said, "I'm not really being kind. It's just that I'm anxious to help you to avoid accidents. I wouldn't want you on my hands as a casualty. You are here, after all, to take care of my great-aunt."

She felt snubbed, deflated. Why did he have to spoil the afternoon's prospects by going all officious? Anger smoldered in her heart. But she must not show it. He had offered to take her skiing. Let that be enough.

"That's settled, then," he was saying. "Meet me at

the *téléférique* station at half-past two." This in his most autocratic tone. Doctor giving order to nurse, she thought. And the smoldering anger returned.

There was a mild sensation at the luncheon table when Marnie announced that she wouldn't be going to the ski school that afternoon, as Doctor Harford had suggested it would be a good thing for her to take her skis up to the plateau at the top of the Jolyon. "He says I'll be able to master the initial techniques more easily up there. He happens to be going up the Jolyon himself this afternoon and will give me a few tips." Put like that she hoped it might sound fairly casual. But Mark Rotherham laughed.

"David and his skiing lessons! He loves himself in the role of instructor—we've all been up the Jolyon with him in our turns, when we first came to Arbois. And I must say we found his hints very useful. I expect he'll be making the run down the Jolyon after he's put you through your paces... one of the steepest descents in the immediate district. Something I seldom attempt myself; a series of slaloms between the pine trees of the forest."

"And what happens to me?" Marnie asked in some alarm. "Am I expected to follow him down this precipice?"

"Good lord, no. He'll send you back safely to the valley by *téléférique*."

So Doctor Harford wasn't really going very much out of his way to help her. Marnie smothered a completely illogical sense of disappointment. Taking raw beginners up the Jolyon was apparently something the young doctor enjoyed doing. Perhaps he liked showing off his superior skill. Anyway, why should his motive matter to her? With a twinge of shame she smothered the memory of her delighted amazement when he had suggested the trip.

It was in a strictly practical frame of mind that she set

out for the *téléférique* half an hour later, carrying her skis professionally on her shoulder. Stella had advised her not to leave them in the ski-school hut. Once you got a pair that fitted you it was safest to keep a tight hold on them.

David Harford was waiting for her, and as a cable car was just about to start the ascent he hurried her unceremoniously. "I've got your ticket. Come along!" he urged impatiently. "If we miss this car we shall have to wait twenty minutes for the next one. I was beginning to be afraid you weren't going to make it."

Marnie resisted the temptation to remind him sharply that he had asked her to be at the station at half past two and it was not yet twenty-five minutes past that hour. But once in the cable car she forgot everything but the novelty of her experience: the preliminary jerk as the car was released from its anchorage, then the sense of swinging out into space as they rose swiftly and smoothly. It was a crowded car at this popular hour and Marnie found herself pressed close to David's side at the rear of the vehicle, right up against a perspex window, which framed great sweeps of sky and snow. The sense of soaring, of flying, was exhilarating. Soon the valley of Arbois and its village dropped away beneath them, a scatter of toy houses and a diminutive church. Away above the ski slopes with their skiers they rose—the skiers like little dots of punctuation on the white surface. And still they soared over pine trees, over gullies. It was much more impressive than being in a plane. Nobody spoke in the small crowded space, as if in this birdlike flight there could be nothing but silence. The only sound was the muted whirr of the oiled wheels on the great steel cable that bore them aloft. Marnie was only dimly aware of the man at her side, a limber figure in the regulation tight-fitting ski outfit, black stretch pants and a top to match, somber but very professional-looking, and he wore no cap.

Then suddenly it was all over and they were moving gently on the level into the cavernlike structure that awaited them. There was a valedictory jerk, doors were opened; everyone came to life, voices were raised, skis collected as the passengers poured out into the champagne-colored sunshine. The mountain air, too, was like champagne, stinging deliciously on the lips. Feeling a little dazed, adjusting perhaps to the difference in altitude, Marnie was glad of David's hand under her elbow, guiding her across a level stretch to the wide café terrace, which now dominated the scene. With the afternoon sunshine blazing down on it, it looked very inviting. Rendezvous des montagnards. Late lunchers still sat dawdling over a final coffee at the white tables under their colored umbrellas.

"Would you like some coffee?" David Harford offered—to Marnie's surprise. She had expected him to begin her skiing lesson without any waste of time. In the sort of life he led time would always be the enemy. Hence his moment of fuss at the *téléférique* station when he had feared they might miss the ascending *cabine.*

Barely heeding her murmured acceptance of his invitation to coffee, he was striding before her onto the terrace of the café.

"Actually I rushed off without my usual after-lunch cup of coffee," he was saying as they sat down. "So I could do with one now."

Everything he suggests is for his own benefit, Marnie thought with a stab of resentment. The whole expedition, she reminded herself, was planned to contribute to his peace of mind. He wanted to make sure she would be able to manage her skis in the tricky initial stages well enough to avoid some tiresome accident.

When the coffee came they drank in silence, Marnie absorbed in the beauty and novelty of the scene around her. The gay café terrace with the vista of mountains spread all around it; chain after chain of snowy peaks sparkling with the iridiscence of ice, the whole scene dominated by the majestic massif of Mont Blanc. It was breathtaking, intoxicating. She couldn't believe she was really here—in a world of beauty totally outside anything in her past experience. This time last week she had been plodding about her humdrum affairs in a Sussex seaside town...still a little preoccupied with Robert Tallant and his strange behavior toward her. How could she have let him matter? Caught by his superficial charm, she had lost for a time her basic Scots common sense. Now on her mountain top she felt as if she had come out of a dark narrow room into a great burst of sunlight and freedom. Unconsciously she drew in a long ecstatic breath and became aware of the hazel eyes fixed on her. She had almost forgotten her companion... but those magnetic eyes called her back to him.

"It's so beautiful up here!" she sighed.

"A little different from your Lammermuir Hills."

She laughed. "They have their quiet charm."

"And they're kindly, with their gentle green valleys. In this beauty there can be cruelty—valleys slashed out by savage glaciers instead of small singing streams."

And still the intense, compelling glance held her. As if with his eyes he was saying something to her for which he could find no words.

She thrust the exaggerated notion away from her. The altitude must be making her crazy!

"If you've finished your coffee," her companion was saying then, "let's be on our way."

They went down on to the level ground below the café terrace, where Marnie embarked on a struggle with her skis. Yesterday Rudi had helped her to fasten them. Now, on her own, the task seemed impossible. What a hopeless novice she was!

"Just lay them down on the ground and step into them," David Harford, who was watching her efforts, advised. "Stand on them firmly, pushing them into the snow."

But the moment she put a foot on the wretched things they began to slide away from her. Instinctively she clutched at her companion. Laughing, he supported her. "Lean on your ski poles," he told her.

"If I do, how can I fasten my ski bindings?"

He was down on his knees then in front of her, leaning over the tiresome skis, skillfully fastening the bindings around her boots, and he was still laughing, a young, gay sound. His bare head, bowed over the skis, was very close to her, the thick dark hair with the hazelnut gleam in it. She wanted to put her hand out and touch it. Mountain madness. I'm drunk with beauty, she thought... and I never thought to see the proud Doctor Harford kneeling at my feet! She suppressed a giggle and was flung back into a world of stark reality once more as her cavalier stood up and turned his back on her, stepping nimbly into his own skis and almost at once pushing off. Because that was how it was in skiing—literally—you always began by pushing your skis in front of you. Faced with the task of doing just this, Marnie was sobered.

"Come on," her instructor ordered brusquely. "Let's get going. Just follow me and take it easily. Don't forget to use your poles."

Nervously, but gaining confidence, Marnie obeyed him, pushing her way along the worn track beside the pine trees. Skiers flashed past them at incredible speed, using their poles as powerful levers, until they turned aside through the trees to find the descending *pistes*, which were their objective. Would she ever be able to move and control her skis like these godlike creatures, Marnie wondered.

Gradually she began to feel a sensation of gliding rather than pushing on her skis. Eager to learn, she watched David Harford in front of her—the broad shoulders, the narrow waist and hips, the long legs in their slim ski pants; every movement he made seemed effortless, perfectly controlled.

They came to a small rise and he showed her how to negotiate it by sidestepping. From the summit of the little rise she faced an equally slight descent, and David made her put the tips of her skis together, forming a wide triangle which, she discovered, made it possible for her to regain the level ground without falling. After that they concentrated on balancing exercises, lifting one ski off the ground and then the other. To do this without mishap gave her a great sense of achievement.

To finish the lesson he made her follow him down what was to her quite an alarmingly steep run. "Just take it slowly," he counseled. "Keep your skis in the snowplow position, and brake with your poles."

All went well until she was nearly at the bottom of the run, then confidence deserted her and she fell, tangling herself up hopelessly with her skis.

"That's right," David commended her unexpectedly, as he helped her up. "You must learn to fall—as one does in riding."

Upright again, rosy and bright-eyed with exercise, her hair tumbling over her brow, she leaned against him for a brief moment—a strangely vivid moment, there in the silence of the snow and the tall dark trees.

"You're not hurt?" he asked.

"Not a bit." But she was still clutching his elbow, hating, for practical reasons, to let him go. Their glances held. She was aware of the quickening of her pulse, a sudden feeling of warmth and life flowing through her. David Harford wasn't an aloof, rather annoying young doctor anymore, but a part of this wonderful world of snow-magic and mountain-magic that encompassed them.

"You're sure you're all right?" Gently he disengaged himself from her grasp. "Able to tackle the short way back to the *téléférique* again?"

"I'm perfectly all right," she assured him. "It's been a wonderful session. I've enjoyed every moment of it."

"We must do it again," he said, as she had hoped he would.

The run back to the *téléférique* was uneventful, and Marnie with every passing moment felt herself more in command of the two awkwardly extended pieces of wood on her feet.

"I'll be back at Arbois as soon as you, perhaps before," David told her as he helped her off with her skis. As soon as he had left her he would speed back along the plateau track and make his spectacular descent down Mont Jolyon. "Slaloming most of the way," he enlarged.

"I wish I could see you skiing like that!" she said impulsively.

He was human enough to look gratified at the admiration and awe there was in her tone.

"You shall see me," he promised, "when you're able to do the Jolyon descent alongside me."

But would she ever reach such proficiency, she wondered, as, having thanked the doctor for his lesson, she got into the cable car.

When she reached the valley it was still early. Old Mrs. Rotherham would not yet have finished her afternoon nap. So Marnie found an easy-looking stretch of snow, near the *téléférique* terminus, on which other amateurs like herself were tumbling around. Marnie determined not to look like an amateur and miraculously avoiding falls put into practice all that David Harford had taught her. He would be surprised to see how adept she had become when he took her skiing again.

But for the next few days there was no suggestion of this. Making his morning visits to his patient, the doctor treated Marnie with courteous but professional aloofness. It seemed impossible that he had ever knelt before her, fastening the bindings of her skis! He did not even inquire how she was making out at the ski school. In fact he seemed to have forgotten the whole matter. Firmly suppressing her disappointment at this, Marnie concentrated on enjoying her afternoon sessions with Rudi Praxmann. In a surprisingly short time her clumsiness was overcome and every time she made a successful traverse or kick-turn she would catch herself wishing foolishly that David Harford could see her. Rudi Praxmann, delighted with so apt a pupil, heaped compliments upon her. They were not empty compliments, he was genuinely pleased with her prowess, which endorsed his skill as a teacher.

"When can I do slaloms?" she asked him.

"*Alors, tenez*!" he laughed. "You must learn to walk before you can run."

Stella, furious at the amount of attention he was giving Marnie, made her infatuation for the instructor clearer every day—much to his embarrassment. Yet, in his vain male way, he encouraged her, or at least did nothing to *discourage* her.

One evening about a week after Marnie had been up the Jolyon with David, Stella, still in her skiing gear, arrived home late for dinner—not an unusual occurrence—and announced in a defiant tone that she was going out immediately after the meal. Rudi Praxmann was meeting her at the Splendide.

"What for?" her mother demanded helplessly.

"What do you think?" Stella replied pertly. "A drink, a dance. We might go on to Le Chat Noir," the liveliest and most notorious night spot in the village.

Denise Rotherham looked as if she were going to explode. But, anxious to avoid a family row, her husband put in quickly, "We'll all go to the Splendide and meet this fascinating ski instructor."

"Marnie must come, too," Denise declared resolutely.

Stella, taken aback, was silent a moment and then burst out, "I know what you're doing, all of you!" Her angry glance included Marnie. "You're trying to break it up between Rudi and me. I've seen the way Marnie makes up to him on the ski slopes, making him think her skiing is better than anyone else's. 'When can I do slaloms, Herr Praxmann?'" she mimicked in a ridiculous squeaky voice.

"Stella, be quiet!" her mother commanded.

"It was to have her dogging my steps, spying on me, that you persuaded her to join the ski lessons, wasn't it?" Stella shrilled.

"Stella!" It was her father this time. "Don't ever let me hear you speaking to your mother in that tone of voice again!"

Stella subsided, but sulked throughout the meal, and while the others were still lingering over their coffee, rushed out of the room. A few minutes later the front door slammed defiantly.

"She hasn't been long changing," Denise said. She stood up purposefully. "I think we should follow her as soon as possible. You are coming with us, aren't you, Marnie?"

"Of course she is," Mark Rotherham put in. "Grandma will be all right with Marie in attendance. Not even a martinet like young David could expect a pretty girl to come to Arbois at the height of the season and spend all her evenings in a sickroom."

"Being with Mrs. Rotherham isn't a bit like being in a sickroom," Marnie said quickly. "She's so cheery and so interested in everything."

"Chess and television," Mark said. "But tonight, young lady, you're going to have a change."

Marnie, now on her feet, glanced at Denise's smart après-ski frock. "Should I put on something else?" she asked, indicating the modest dress she was wearing. It was an amber-colored Paisley pattern with high neck and long sleeves, the neck and cuffs finished off with little lace frills—quaint rather than stylish. She had made it herself, choosing the color because it flattered her golden hair and warm creamy skin. Or at least so she hoped, but she wouldn't, she felt, cut much of a figure among all the smart après-ski set at the Splendide. Would David be there tonight, she caught herself speculating with a quickening of interest, which she instantly suppressed. If he was he would probably growl at her for having deserted her post.

CHAPTER FOUR

THE SPLENDIDE LIVED up to its name; it was a large modern hotel built on an eminence that overlooked the one long winding street of Arbois. Standing up from the road, which wound up to its wide entrance, its glass and concrete façade flanked a roomy terrace where small tables and chairs waited for the clients who would use them in the brief noontide heat the next day.

When Marnie and the Rotherhams arrived the foyer was a blaze of light. Palms and hothouse flowers filled every corner. Opening out of it on one side was the restaurant and on the other side, down a short flight of stairs, a small, discreetly lit bar on a lower level, the building having been erected on terraced ground, which had been cleverly incorporated into the design by the architect.

Stella and her escort were not in the restaurant or the bar, so the party went on to the ballroom where the lighting was flattering and the dance floor, surrounded by discreet sitting-out corners half hidden by potted palms, gleamed invitingly. On the platform above the dance floor sat a band of musicians dressed in Tyrolean costume—Rudi Praxmann's countrymen, Marnie thought. Just at that moment there was an exclamation from Denise, who had caught sight of Stella and her escort on the dance floor. Dressed in a high-waisted Kate Greenaway dress, Stella seemed even younger than her fifteen years, her hair hanging in curls around her flushed, lovely little face. The way she was looking up at her partner as they danced would have melted a heart of stone—and there was no doubt that Rudi Praxmann's heart was made of more vulnerable material.

"Will you look at her!" Denise groaned. "She's absolutely crazy about the fellow...."

"'Turned on,' is I believe the modern term for her state of mind," Mark said in an amused tone. But his wife was far from being amused.

"We've got to get her away from him...attract their attention," she urged, "and invite them to join us. That way we may manage to control the situation."

They seated themselves at a table on the edge of the dance floor and when Stella and her partner drew near, Denise called her daughter's name. Stella turned sharply, her expression one of anger and dismay, but Rudi Praxmann, hearing the summons, politely slowed down and guided the girl over to her parents.

"Won't you join us for a drink when you've finished your dance, Herr Praxmann?" Mark invited. There was a hint of command in his tone. Rudi clicked his heels, bowed low and said he would be enchanted. Stella scowled. It looked as if she was remonstrating with her partner as they resumed their dancing, but presently when the number came to an end the young man firmly piloted her to her parents' table where two seats awaited them. Small courtesies were exchanged, during which Stella sat in sullen silence. Rudi seemed pleased that Marnie was one of the party and said he hoped she would have the next dance with him. Nothing could have been more calculated to increase Stella's very obvious sulks. But Denise seized on the offer with deplorable haste, giving Marnie no time to speak for herself.

"Of course Miss Marnhem will dance with you, she loves dancing," she improvised wildly. It was almost too obvious. An embarrassed silence fell on the party, relieved only by the waiter with the drinks Mark had ordered. And it was Mark who rescued the conversation, drawing Rudi out to discuss the various methods of skiing which were in vogue. They both decided that the Austrian method, which of course Rudi favored, was the most practical for beginners. "And Mademoiselle Marnhem will soon be a skier *formidable*," Rudi declared, nodding approvingly in Marnie's direction—a tribute that pleased her, but which inevitably sent Stella deeper into her state of gloom.

As soon as the band began to play again her father stood up and firmly led her out onto the floor, Marnie and Rudi following. He held her a little too closely, but his dancing was perfection. The absolute control of movement he had acquired on the ski slopes gave him exceptional flexibility and grace. Marnie, trying not to think of the intimacy of his embrace, surrendered herself to his lead, enjoying the harmony of music and movement. It was almost too perfect to be real...like dancing with a dream figure in a dream.

Back at the family table they found Stella with tear marks on her cheeks, listening to a hastily whispered monolog from her mother. But as soon as she saw Rudi she jumped up and said, "I'm dancing the next one with you, Rudi," and just at that moment the band struck up.

"What *are* we going to do with her?" Denise groaned, as Stella hurried off with her escort.

"Come and dance with me and forget about her," her husband advised.

Marnie, left alone, breathed a sigh of relief. Family tensions were nerve-racking, especially when, as an outsider, one became accidentally involved in them. She watched Stella on the dance floor clinging to her partner in a way he must have found slightly embarrassing—it was so clear she was pleading with him. As soon as he brought her back to the table he invited Marnie out for the next number.

"*La petite*!" he began with some force as they circled to an old-fashioned waltz tune. "*Elle est folle!* For me it is difficult....she is so young, so *mignonne;* one cannot make her the hurt." He drew Marnie a little closer. "If you could help me, Mademoiselle Marnie? Stella wants me to take her to Le Chat Noir tonight. Could you perhaps come with us? This would make it more acceptable to her parents, who obviously do not quite approve of me as the child's escort. And they will certainly have doubts about our going to Le Chat Noir. But if you were to accompany us...?"

What could Marnie do but accept the equivocal invitation? Poor Rudi sounded so distressed. "Perhaps Monsieur and Madame Rotherham will come, too," she suggested hopefully. But when they got back to their corner it was to find the family in some disarray, Stella almost shouting at her parents in the course of what had clearly been a heated argument.

"You followed me here tonight, came on purpose to ruin my evening with Rudi, bring Marnie, making her dance with him. I know just what you're up to...and I'll never forgive you! Never!" As she flung the last word at them she jumped up from her chair. "I'm going home!"

"*Tenez*, Stella," Rudi offered soothingly. "The night is young."

Fiercely she rounded on him. "You asked me to spend this evening with you, but you don't really want me. You'd rather have Marnie. I bet you've asked her to come with us to Le Chat Noir."

"But of course," Rudi returned calmly, giving Marnie a polite little bow. "And she has kindly consented."

Stella burst into tears. It was childish, pitiful. Rudi

looked wretchedly confused, murmuring that she had "got him all wrong." Which just about covered the situation, Marnie thought wryly. She wished now she had refused Rudi's invitation to the nightclub, and wondered if she could get out of it. But already Denise, obviously pleased at the turn of events, was nodding at her approvingly.

"You go and enjoy yourself, Marnie," she urged. She put an arm about the weeping Stella, drawing her close. "Come along, darling. It's very wise of you to give the nightclub a miss tonight. We'll all go there together another evening. There'll be plenty of time for you to visit the various night spots before our holiday is over."

"That's not the point. Oh, you're all so *stupid*!" Stella wailed, and with a final despairing glance at the desperately uncomfortable-looking Rudi rushed off to the cloakroom where she could cry her heart out in privacy.

"She'll be all right," Denise murmured, hurrying after her.

Rudi, more ill at ease than ever, said he was sorry if anything he had said or done had upset "*la petite*."

Mark Rotherham shrugged. "I doubt if it's entirely your fault, young man, knowing my tenacious and emotional daughter. But she's at an emotional age, *n'est-ce past*? It might be wiser in future if you were to restrict your relationship with her to that of ski instructor."

"I'm sorry," Rudi offered again miserably.

Mark Rotherham smiled. "Think no more of it, my dear chap. Just wait until you have a teenage daughter of your own! Meanwhile what about taking Miss Marnhem along to Arbois's most-talked-about night spot?" He turned to Marnie. "It's all delightfully informal—pure country-style Savoyard with a rough wooden floor and people in ski boots stomping on it to the music of local fiddles."

Denise appeared at this juncture with Marnie's coat, saving her a trip to the cloakroom and a further encounter with the outraged Stella. "She's all right really," she answered Marnie's unspoken question. "You go and enjoy yourself." She leaned forward and dropped a light kiss on Marnie's cheek. "You're being *such* a help!" she whispered.

How clever she was! "Mother is using you." The words echoed uneasily in Marnie's memory as she went out into the frozen night with Rudi Praxmann.

It was only a few steps up the village street to the one-story wooden building that housed the nightclub. Small, intimate, overheated, it was crowded with dancers in every kind of attire, formal and informal. Many ski suits were in evidence and the heavy boots Mark had promised echoed resoundingly on the bare boards.

A swinging number was in progress, and joining the gyrating throng, ridiculously packed in the small space, Rudi drew Marnie into his arms. Ignoring the rhythm, he made the minimum of movement, remaining in one spot, swaying slightly to the rousing tune.

"Women!" he sighed into her hair. "With the women, young and old, I am always in trouble. Perhaps it is my own fault. At times I pursue them—at times they pursue me. It is a game, *n'est-ce past*? Not to be taken seriously. But with you there is no game. You are as kind as you are beautiful, and you give me rest."

Glancing over his shoulder, feeling trapped and slightly foolish, Marnie found herself meeting the somewhat astonished gaze of David Harford. He was standing by the bar at the far end of the room with a lively crowd of young people. Men and girls alike wore ski clothes, and their arrogant, confident voices ringing out above the general din were unmistakably English.

"Couldn't we sit down and have a drink?" Marnie

suggested. "It's really a bit too crowded for dancing at the moment."

Reluctantly her companion released her and led her to the chair where she had already deposited her coat.

"You would like perhaps a brandy, a liqueur?"

"A Campari," she answered, playing safe, aware that the doctor's disapproving eyes had followed her. He was dressed, like his companions, in ski clothes.

Rudi, returning with the drinks, took the chair by her side. As she raised her glass to her lips Marnie was still conscious of the doctor's gaze boring into her. She raised her hand slightly in salute and in return got a cool little nod of recognition.

"The medico from the clinic," Rudi said, noticing the communicating gestures. "You work with him, don't you? Nursing the grandmother of Stella...she told me."

Marnie mumbled her confirmation of this, wishing David Harford a hundred miles away, yet hating herself for being disturbed at his finding her in the nightclub with her ski-instructor escort.

"He is a first-rate skier, your doctor," Rudi was saying. "One of our brighter hopes in the races, which are to be held during the Mardi Gras Festival in a fortnight's time. That crowd with him at the bar will also be competing. A pretty good lot, from what I've been told—the English Ski Club. Arbois will have to look to its laurels."

"Do they have races for the women, as well?" Marnie asked, eyeing the group by the bar with mild interest.

"Mais certainement!" Rudi answered. "Some of these girls are more *formidable* than the men. The one Harford is talking to at this moment won several trophies at St. Moritz last year."

Marnie looked at the deceptively slim and fragile-seeming redhead, leaning close to David, laughing up at him. He looked happy and at ease.

"Don't be deceived by her looks," Rudi was saying. "She is tough, that one. I saw her in action on the slopes this morning. They hunt, these English types," he enlarged. "The fox." He made an expressive gesture with his hands. As usual he was wearing a bemedaled jersey that looked far too small for him, the sleeves revealing his broad, bony skier's wrists. "The—how you say in your country—the county set, they do the hunting, fishing and shooting, go in for show jumping, are indeed hardly ever out of the saddle. This gives them the well-developed knee muscles expert skiing demands. All ski control comes, as I've told you, from the knees." He took one of the little white paper serviettes from a tumbler on the table and began to make little sketches to illustrate his meaning. Marnie asked question after question, keeping him on his pet topic, hoping she wouldn't have to dance with him again in front of the watchful David. But when she looked over at the bar presently it was to find that he and his party had left.

Then it was time for the cabaret. There was folk dancing in country costume, which was delightful. Most of the songs and dialogs were in Savoyard patois, which went way over Marnie's head. But she enjoyed the wild music of an elderly accordion player. When it was finished she said that she really must go home. "I have to be up early in the morning to see my patient," she pleaded.

"I, too, must be up early," Rudi agreed. "I am taking a party up the Claveralp from Chamonix. We start from here at sunrise."

He walked with her through the icy, star-spangled night to Les Trois Chasseurs, where he kissed her good-night—an undisturbing kiss. She had got through the evening more easily than she had thought possible, Marnie congratulated herself as she entered the house. If only

David Harford hadn't been at the nightclub! The fact that he *had* been there loomed over everything else that had happened. Even Stella's outburst at the Splendide sank into insignificance. She would have given anything if only David hadn't seen her wrapped in Rudi's too intimate embrace on that cramped little dance floor. The coincidence of his presence assumed an importance beyond all proportion as, moving silently through the sleeping house, she crept up to her room. It was two a.m. and the Rotherhams, including the weeping Stella, would have long since been in bed.

What was wrong with her, Marnie asked herself, as she tossed on her pillows. What did it matter if Dr. Harford saw her dancing with every ski instructor in Arbois? What she did with her spare time was none of his business. Yet his cold-eyed, disapproving glances haunted her in her incoherent dreams. She dreaded the morning and his inevitable appearance in the sickroom.

Yet when she heard his car crunching over the frozen snow the following morning she felt calm and composed, and congratulated herself that she had put David Harford and his moods into perspective. From the first his attitude toward her had been critical. She wasn't the sort of nurse he had expected when he applied to the Seafleet Agency. He couldn't forgive her for not being middle-aged and staid, someone who would never want to learn skiing, or be likely to turn up in the village nightclub with a handsome ski instructor in tow.

I disturb him, Marnie decided, and the thought gave her a feeling of power over him that was oddly stimulating. When presently he marched into the sickroom she was able to return his stiff, "Good morning, nurse," without a tremor.

"Why do you keep on calling our nice Marnie nurse?" old Mrs. Rotherham demanded. "We all use her own name—Marnie. It's so much more friendly."

"No doubt," David returned dryly, and taking the old lady's wrist asked her how she had slept the night before. Then he tested her blood pressure and murmured in a technically worded aside to Marnie that he thought he could safely reduce the strength of the patient's tablets.

"You're getting better and better every day," he assured the old lady. "Soon I shall be allowing you to have a little sleigh ride in the sunshine."

"And I'll drive to your beautiful little chalet," Mrs. Rotherham declared. "Marnie will come with me and you'll show us your clever photography."

He laughed and patted her hand, but did not commit himself to any definite promises, either of sleigh rides or visits to his chalet. When he had said goodbye to his great-aunt Marnie dutifully followed him out into the wide central hallway.

"Come into the lounge for a moment," he ordered. "There's something I want to say to you...rather personal." He thrust his hands into his pockets, making it somehow an aggressive gesture, and strode before her into the sunlit, firelit room. Fortunately—or perhaps unfortunately for Marnie—there were no Rotherhams around.

He's going to tell me off for frequenting nightclubs with a ski instructor, Marnie thought furiously.

And that was precisely what he did.

"Your escort last night at Le Chat Noir," he began, marching over to the picture window, and displaying his adamant back. "I hope you realize the reputation your friend Herr Praxmann enjoys. One of the most popular of the Arbois ski instructors...with women. In other words he's adept at attracting them, especially the more foolish of them; handing them a line is part of his sales talk."

"Of course it is," Marnie agreed angrily. "And I really

don't see that it's your business who I may go to night-clubs with—or how I spend my off-duty time."

"Okay, Marnie! Hold your horses." He had used her "little" name, and his glance was conciliatory as he turned from the window. "I know it's none of my business. I was merely uttering a passing word of caution. Rudi Praxmann is a notorious heartbreaker."

"Thanks for the warning. But I've met his type before."

"In the Lammermuir Hills?" His tone was incredulous.

"I haven't spent all my life on a Scottish farm," she reminded him. "Poor little country girl flung out into the wicked world... is that what you were thinking?" She laughed in mockery. "I've had my three years at St. Chad's in big wicked London, don't forget. And Seafleet isn't exactly a backwater. The Rudi Praxmanns of this world are no novelty to me."

"I see. And you like them." His tone was curt. "Somehow I didn't think it of you. Sorry I spoke." He opened his medical bag and took out the new bottle of tablets he had prescribed for his patient. "The usual dosage." He put the bottle down on the table... and then he was gone.

Listening to him driving away, Marnie was conscious of the uneasy beating of her heart. Of all the impossible, interfering men! She was too angry now to admit to herself that she wished more than anything that he had not seen her in that too intimate dance with the handsome Austrian—an intimacy that hadn't meant a thing beyond friendship. Rudi at least was warm and kind and *human*, not cold-eyed and critical... like some people! The prim and proper Doctor Harford was way behind the easy-going times, working in monastic seclusion with his clinic full of nuns. Not that he had looked exactly monastic surrounded with those English skiing girls last night. And he would no doubt spend whatever time he could spare today skiing down spectacular slopes with them, while Marnie plodded up and down the little runs at the ski school, Rudi urging her on to persevere with impossible kick turns. For the first time it occurred to her that it might be to Rudi's advantage to be extremely thorough over the elementary lessons of his learners. Surely she was ready now to tackle something more than the boring daily routine with a bunch of novices. One of these days she would go up the dreaded Mont Jolyon by herself—and she would *not* come down by cable car! A daring resolve that pushed the thought of David Harford and his unwanted interferences with her private life into the background.

Lunch was an uneasy meal. Stella, pale-cheeked and red-eyed, scarcely spoke, and as soon as she had finished toying with her meal hurried from the room. A moment later the heavy front door could be heard to bang.

"There she goes! Off to her precious Rudi at the ski school," Denise sighed. "Will you be joining the class this afternoon?" she asked Marnie anxiously.

Marnie felt a stirring of impatience. How much longer could she be expected to act as fifth wheel to poor silly little Stella? She said, "I thought I might give the school a miss for once this afternoon, try out some exercises on my own on those easy slopes near the Mont Jolyon *téléférique*." She tried not to sound apologetic. After all, she had a perfect right to go skiing where she liked. This involvement with Stella's unfortunate attack of lovesickness was becoming a bore.

Shrewdly summing up Marnie's mood, Denise said in her sweetest tones, "It's just that I feel so much happier when you *do* go to the school with Stella. But I mustn't impose on your good nature. You were a wonderful help over Le Chat Noir last night. I hope your visit there wasn't too much of a bind?"

"Oh, no," Marnie returned politely. "It was quite amusing. The Savoyard cabaret and so forth...."

"I was really wondering," Denise interrupted, "what you thought of Rudi Praxmann. You didn't find him...troublesome, I hope?"

It was quite obvious what Denise really wanted to know, so Marnie humored her and told her that on the whole Rudi had behaved correctly.

Denise's sharp ears seized on that "on the whole," and drew her own conclusions. How far had Marnie encouraged him? "Did he speak of Stella?" she demanded sharply.

Marnie said, "Yes, he did, but he was very sensible about her, realizing her extreme youth and anxious not to hurt her. Though she doesn't make it particularly easy for him."

"Poor little Stella, doing all the running."

"Well, yes, that's about the way it is," Marnie admitted.

Denise shrugged. "What it is to be fifteen! I suppose I was just as silly at that age; I remember being completely infatuated by a good-looking gardener we had at home." She laughed at the foolish memory away. "But it's all very well to laugh," she qualified. "At the time it hurt tragically."

Marnie offered no comment...and thought of Robert. You didn't have to be a foolish fifteen to be hurt by abortive love affairs. Thank goodness she was heart-free again...and she intended to stay that way.

It was a relief presently to leave the house. With her skis over her shoulder she made her way along the beaten snow track to the undulating fields near the *téléférique* station. The air was sharp and invigorating, the sun warm. Colors stood out against the whiteness of the snow, the vivid jerseys of the skiers, the painted signs of the wooden building that housed the clumsy cable cars. At intervals a car would come rumbling out of its cavernous shelter and start on its swinging ascent. And soon its counterpart, passing it in midair, would speed downward and come to rest with a gentle bump.

Vaguely aware of the crowds that came and went in the vicinity of the station, Marnie made her careful little runs on the undemanding slopes, gradually becoming more daring, seeking out the steeper gradients. It was wonderful how much easier the braking and guiding of her skis was becoming. The air and the exercise and the beauty of the soaring mountains all around her made her feel light-headed with happiness. At that moment she felt she hadn't a care in the world. Stuffy nightclubs and amorous dancing partners did not exist. Neither did critical, disapproving young doctors. Skiing was fun, she thought, as with professionally bent knees she negotiated her steepest descent yet. Skiing was the nearest thing you could experience to actual flying; real flying under one's own power, like a bird, not just sitting in a great metal machine being mechanically propelled through the air. Skiing was being a seagull high over the beach at Seafleet, a swallow swooping through the summer-evening sky....

Then she saw Stella and her carefree mood collapsed. What was the girl doing here at a time when she should have been at the ski school? She was making for the *téléférique* station, her skis balanced on her shoulder, her blond curls tumbling around her white, set young face. The tense expression on it made Marnie call out to her. She looked both wild and desperate.

"Stella! Where are you going?" Marnie halted in her tracks.

Standing still, Stella turned her head. "So this is where you are!" she addressed Marnie bitterly. "Rudi wanted to know why you didn't show up at the school this afternoon."

As she spoke Marnie coasted slowly over to her side. "I thought I'd like to do a bit of practice on my own. It seems you had the same idea."

"No, I had *not*!" Stella all but shouted at her. Her blue eyes held a furious light. "Rudi sent me away when I tried to pay another week's fee in advance. He said he'd taught me all I could possibly learn in the beginners' class and that it was time I joined Monsieur Anton's more advanced group." Her voice had risen to a wail. "It's all your fault, Marnie Marnhem! You set yourself deliberately to take Rudi away from me—and you've succeeded. But I'll make you sorry. I'll make everyone sorry!"

She would have moved on, but Marnie put an arresting hand on her arm, alarmed by her wild words. "Where are you going?" she asked.

"Never you mind. Rudi says I'm fit to ski on my own—so that's just what I'm going to do... away and away far over the mountains. Maybe I'll never come back!"

The words ended in a hysterical gulp as Stella hurried toward the little office where tickets for the table cars could be obtained. Marnie, without thinking about it, knew she must follow her, keep her in sight. Stella was half crazy in her childish misery and rage, a child struggling with the emotions and the anguish of womanhood. Stooping to unfasten her skis, Marnie had some difficulty with the bindings, and by the time she got to the *téléférique* station the gates leading to the waiting car containing Stella were closed. The girl would have a good twenty minutes' start. Ought she to use that time in phoning Les Trois Chasseurs to let Denise know what was happening? But maybe it would be foolish to raise the alarm, and in any case Denise was most probably out on her own afternoon skiing ventures with her husband by now. Anyway, Marnie comforted herself, Stella's words had probably been mainly designed to frighten her, pay her back for going to Le Chat Noir with Rudi last night.

Procuring her ticket, she waited with what patience she could muster until at last she was on her way up the hillside. Swaying and rising over the dark pines, she was too preoccupied today to notice the dramatic dwindling of the features of the landscape beneath them, as they rose high above it. When they jerked to a halt at the summit terminus she hurried out of the car, and for one wild moment hoped she might find Stella having a cup of coffee at the terrace café. But there was no sign of her.

Almost everyone who had emerged from the car with Marnie was now fastening on skis and there was a general rush along the beaten *piste* towards the pine woods. Marnie, fumbling more slowly with her own skis, listened to the swish of the runners on the frozen snow. Everyone seemed able to travel so fast, and here she was lagging behind in spite of her sense of urgency. For she must strive to overtake Stella. Was this the way she had gone? If so she might by now have arrived at the point of descent—a slope that could only be taken by an expert. So her only course would be to turn back and go down in the cable car. But there was no sign of Stella, and already the light was waning.

Pushing her skis laboriously in front of her, Marnie plodded along the track, her eyes sharp for any sight of the missing Stella. But there was only the eerie emptiness and silence. On the side away from the spectacular fall of the mountainside there was an expanse of more or less level ground, a kind of plateau, the white carpet of snow broken by occasional clumps of bushes, a white wilderness in the dying light. Surely Stella wouldn't have gone wandering off in that desolate direction. Or had that been her intention? "Maybe I'll never come back," she had threatened.

Leaning on her ski poles, Marnie looked around her. Why had she imagined she could find Stella so easily? Her search now seemed hopeless, and there was no one to whom she might have turned for help. Not another skier in sight. Turning her back on the descending side of the mountain, she went a little way into the wilderness of the flat whiteness. "Stella!" she called—without much conviction. The sound of her voice echoed uncannily in the dead silence. Oh, it was horrible—all this threatening snow, like a winding sheet in the darkening evening! Fear, cold as the ice beginning to be palpable in the quiet air, paralyzed her nerves. Numb with foreboding and anxiety, she made her way back to the café where lights now burned brightly.

The place was empty, the proprietor and his wife busy stacking tables and chairs together for the night. When would there be a descending cable car? Marnie inquired of them, and was horrified to learn the last car of the day had already gone down into the valley . "Always at sunset the *téléférique* ceases to function," the proprietor told her. But, he added, there was a chair lift about a mile along the *piste* and that would still be running. He and his wife would be making for it in a few minutes and Marnie could accompany them if she wished.

A chair lift. Marnie's spirit rose. Perhaps Stella had gone back to the valley that way. At all events it provided an alternative to the dangerous run down on skis which the child in her wild mood might have been tempted to tackle.

It seemed an endless mile to the chair lift, as she followed in the wake of the expertly skiing café proprietor and his wife. They reached the terminus just in time to catch the last lot of descending chairs. It was an eerie and chilly experience for Marnie sitting unstrapped in one of the shallow chairs, clutching her skis beside her. Hardly daring to look at the vacuum of twilit space beneath her, she closed her eyes and hoped for the best. It was a brief but harrowing ordeal, and matters were not improved when she discovered that the point at which they came down was a good two miles away from Arbois. There was a bus that served the route, but she had to wait half an hour for it.

When at least she reached Les Trois Chasseurs, cold and tired and unnerved, it was to find Denise Rotherham anxiously awaiting her. It had been dark for almost two hours and Stella had not yet come home.

CHAPTER FIVE

"WHERE HAVE YOU BEEN all afternoon?" Denise demanded angrily. "Is Stella with you?"

Disconcerted by the abrupt questions, Marnie stood hesitant. What could she say that would not throw the emotional Denise into a frenzy of alarm?

"She hasn't been at the ski school," the shrill voice went on. "And neither have you. I phoned Praxmann when she didn't show up at teatime...."

"He'd refused her re-booking," Marnie broke in, "told her he had taught all he could and it was time she joined a more advanced class."

"Yes, I gathered that," Denise nodded. "She went off, he said, '*un peu distraite.*' But off to where?"

"To the Mont Jolyon *téléférique*," Marnie disclosed. "I happened to be near there as I'd decided to do a bit of skiing on my own instead of going to the school this afternoon. I was making little runs on the slope near the *téléférique* station when I saw Stella approaching it. I spoke to her." There was no other way; she must tell the whole story now, or at least the less sensational parts of it. "She said she was going up the Jolyon and might try to ski down, since Rudi had evidently decided she was now an expert skier."

"Oh, God!" Denise moaned. "She isn't expert enough for the Jolyon run. Why did you let her go?"

"I couldn't very well stop her," Marnie pointed out, swaying a little where she stood; cold, tired, exhausted—

as worried as Denise herself. "I tried to follow her. But by the time I'd got out of my skis and bought my ticket the cable car containing her was well on its way and I had to wait for the next one. When I got to the top I looked around for her, but there was no sign of her. I went as far as the beginning of the difficult run down, and by that time it was beginning to grow dark and there were no skiers about, no one who might have seen her. There was nothing for me but to return to the *téléférique*, only to discover I'd missed the last car down. So I had to ski back for about a mile and take the chair lift to Servenne. I got a bus from there."

"Why didn't you get in touch with us and warn us you'd lost contact with her?" Denise moaned. "You could have phoned from the Jolyon café."

"Only to alarm you," Marnie pleaded. "All the time I was hoping she would have got safely home."

"But she didn't. And if we'd known she was contemplating the Jolyon we could have started searching for her earlier. Mark went off about an hour ago to look in the cafés and patisseries in the village, and when she wasn't to be found in any of them he phoned me to say he was taking a couple of guides and they were to start combing the countryside. It would have been such a help if we'd known she was contemplating the Jolyon run."

"I'm sorry," Marnie murmured inadequately, her voice not quite steady.

"Sit down," Denise had the grace to suggest. "You look worn out."

"I've been so worried," Marnie admitted, sinking gratefully into the settee by the heartening log fire. "But I was so sure she would be all right, that I'd find her here when I got home."

Denise gave her a blankly despairing look. "I rang David at the clinic and told him the state we were in, and that you'd disappeared as well as Stella. He said he would come round the moment he was free."

Sounds from below brought Denise sharply to her feet. "A car stopping!" She rushed over to the window, her hands to her breast. "Oh, no! It's the blood wagon," Marnie heard her exclaim in a sort of whispered groan.

After that things happened quickly, Mark striding into the room, followed by two muscular mountain guides carrying a stretcher on which Stella lay, looking pale but defiant.

"It's all right, Dee!" Mark's arm was around his wife's shoulder. "Stella has only twisted an ankle, I think. But I phoned the clinic and was told David is already on his way here."

Stella by this time had been deposited on the settee vacated by Marnie, who stood looking on and feeling rather helpless and at the same time vastly relieved. Ankle or no ankle, Stella was safely home.

"I fell and lost a ski... it was dark up there on the Jolyon," she whimpered.

"It's all right now, darling. Don't think about the nasty mountain." Denise, kneeling by her daughter's side, went on offering foolish little words of comfort.

Mark, who had been seeing the mountain guides out, returned to the lounge with David by his side.

Stella burst into tears at the sight of him. "I don't want David. I don't want anyone. My ankle will be all right. I wish you'd all just leave me alone. I didn't want to be found, I wanted to stay there in the dark and the snow, letting the cold take me!"

"Darling, what nonsense!" Denise laughed, not very convincingly. "A nice fright you've given us. Marnie spent the whole afternoon looking for you. She went all over the top of the Jolyon plateau and missed the last cable car down. Had to walk all the way to the chair lift and then find her way back to Arbois by bus. All for your sake...wasn't it good of her?" She was rattling on, as one would soothe a fractious child, holding Stella's hands in her own. "What ever made you go off skiing alone? And trying to come down the Jolyon!"

"She was way off the beaten *piste* when we found her," Mark contributed. "If I hadn't had the guides with me I'd have missed her, hidden away in the pine woods. One of the guides spotted the marks of her skis...."

Stella's tears had turned into uncontrollable sobs. "I didn't want to be found," she repeated, the words coming out singly and in gulps. Hysteria was not far off.

"Better let me tackle this, Dee." David's voice was matter-of-fact, designed to produce a calming effect on the agitated parents as well as Stella. Denise got up from her knees, making way for the doctor who sat himself on the edge of the wide settee beside his patient and began gently to remove the ski boot from the injured ankle.

"Go away!" Stella screamed. "Don't touch me!"

"My bag, nurse," David said quietly, and Marnie handed him the slim black case he had left on the table when he came into the room. In a moment he had produced a hypodermic needle and almost before Stella had time to realize what was happening to her it had been plunged into her arm. The effect was almost instantaneous. The sobs turned into quiet weeping. David, his fingers on her pulse, said in a hypnotic tone, "What have they been doing to you, then...tell your cousin David."

"It's *her*!" Stella returned darkly, nodding her head in Marnie's direction. "And my mother. She and Marnie, between them, have ruined my life." The words began to slur a little and Stella's head fell back on the cushions behind her.

"We'd better get her to bed," David said in a careful whisper. He lifted the girl in his arms and with Marnie and Denise following took her to her room. A brief examination of the injured ankle revealed that no bones were broken. Then Marnie and Denise between them undressed the now semiconscious Stella and tucked her up in bed.

Back in the lounge they found Mark and David having a reviving drink. Feeling mangled and exhausted by the whole harrowing afternoon, Marnie would have been glad to disappear to her own room, but just at that moment, old Mrs. Rotherham, whom they had all forgotten, came hobbling in on her stick, wanting to know what all the commotion was about. "Where have you been, Marnie?" she demanded imperiously. "I've been waiting for you ever since teatime." She spoke with the querulousness of the somewhat pampered invalid.

They all sat around the fire, and had aperitifs, though Marnie would gladly have exchanged her Dubonnet for a cup of hot tea. But it was long past teatime, and old Mrs. Rotherham's repeated questions demanded answers.

"Why was Marnie so late in coming home? Why was Stella screaming just now?"

It was Denise's turn to sound hysterical as she tried to provide explanations. Stella had rushed off to do the Jolyon run because she thought she had been spurned by her beloved ski instructor. Marnie, seeing her, had tried to follow her, but had lost contact. "The whole thing is too ridiculous!" she wailed. "Stella and her craze for this Rudi Praxmann." She turned to David Harford. "What can one do to put sense into a girl of that age? We've been having almost daily scenes with her over it. I even forced poor Marnie to help me to break up the silly little affair; making her dance with Rudi at the Splendide last night, and then maneuvering her into going off to Le Chat Noir with him. He'd originally invited Stella, but I was determined she shouldn't go. And of course this Don Juan, Rudi, couldn't have cared less which of the girls accompanied him—as I tried to make Stella understand, telling her that it's part of Rudi's job to have mild flirtations with his lady clients. Marnie of course is not so easily taken in as my poor Stella, and she simply went off to Le Chat Noir to help me out. It was good of her. I can't be too grateful...."

Marnie went a little pink, taken aback by these unexpected words of gratitude. From the depth of the armchair in which she had taken refuge from Denise's rather embarrassing outburst she found herself meeting David Harford's intensified glance. It was as if he had suddenly come to life, his hazel eyes golden in the firelight. Not hard eyes any longer—and there was something in them that might have been relief.

"So that's the way it was last night," he was saying in a tone pitched for Marnie's ears alone, lost in the general buzz of conversation, old Mrs. Rotherham holding forth about a dancing master she had once had a crush on when she was fourteen.

"A good deed bringing its own reward," the muted, now quizzical voice went on. "You looked as if you were enjoying yourself."

Marnie gave what she hoped was a sophisticated little shrug.

"Lammermuir *savoir faire*," David grinned. But he had more or less forgiven her. She was ashamed of the wave of relief that washed over her. What right had he to forgive or not forgive her... how dared he set himself up as a judge of her actions?

Mark was now enlarging on the saga of his search for Stella in the dark mountain forest with his guides. "It was lucky I was able to get hold of them so quickly," he remarked. "They were on the terrace of the Splendide when I went down to the village for help... hobnobbing with the English Ski Club lot."

The talk switched to the visiting skiers and the part they would play in the forthcoming races. David spoke of his modest part in the contest, and keeping the family firmly on the subject of the looming Mardi Gras junket successfully diverted them from Stella's mishap. Old Mrs. Rotherham, pricking up her ears, hoped she might be considered convalescent enough to watch some of the races. Marnie waited anxiously for the doctor's reply; she would love to see him in the exciting atmosphere of the advanced skiing competitions. But he was a little doubtful about the wisdom of old Mrs. Rotherham sitting in a wheelchair on the edge of the snow-bound course.

"I don't want you catching a chill," he said.

"I'm so tired of being confined to the house," the old lady wailed. "What about those sleigh rides you promised me?"

"Much better idea than being a spectator at the races," he agreed. "You can start your sleigh rides tomorrow afternoon if you like. What about coming to my chalet? Marnie will bring you, I'm sure. With any luck I'll contrive to be there to give you a cup of tea. If not my housekeeper will make you welcome."

"Oh, goody!" the old lady clapped her hands like a child. "And you can show us your pictures. I'm sure Marnie will be enchanted with your beautiful little house... I've been telling her about it."

"Indeed!" The doctor's tone was dry—the look he threw at Marnie curiously defensive. But at least he had included her in the afternoon's invitation. It looked as if the hard things he had said to her about her association with Rudi Praxmann were to be forgotten. In spite of herself and her rigid control, her spirits lifted. Perhaps now he would remember his promise to give her another skiing lesson on the Mont Jolyon plateau.

Stella, he pronounced, when he was leaving the house later, had better stay in bed for a day or two. He would look in on her in the morning when he paid his routine visit to her grandmother. "Who really doesn't need my attention anymore," he added, at which the old lady made a coquettish grimace.

"You mustn't desert me, David, dear. You have no idea how I look forward to your daily visits. And I'm sure," she added with a glint of mischief in her bright eyes, "Marnie does, too."

"Then I most certainly must show up!" David said with a mocking laugh. Marnie went crimson, and was furious with herself for her weakness. The hazel eyes fixed on her mercilessly did not miss her confusion. A few minutes later he rose to take his leave. "I'll order that sleigh to call for you," he called out as he ran down the stairs.

STELLA OBEDIENTLY STAYED in bed the next day, gratified at the fuss that was being made over her. Denise, abandoning her skiing plans, stayed at home and devoted all her time to her daughter. As is the way with families, the bitterness engendered by the Rudi situation seemed to have been forgotten. Only Marnie was still in Stella's bad books and she firmly refused to have any nursing attention from her.

After lunch a large piebald horse drawing an open landau-type carriage on sleds appeared at the front door of Les Trois Chasseurs. The seats were buried in piles of woolen and fur rugs. Marnie, with the driver's help, lifted old Mrs. Rotherham into a nest of covering, from which her small pointed face peered out, eager as a child's.

It was a perfect afternoon, sun drenched and windless. Marnie, too, felt a childish thrill of excitement as they set off, pulled by the plodding old horse to the gay sound of sleigh bells. There were several stops in the village. Old Mrs. Rotherham, thrilled with her first sight of the shops for some weeks, sent Marnie to make small purchases for her, including a sheaf of pink roses that had been flown to the ski resort from some Riviera flower farm. "Roses in the snow," the old lady murmured poetically. "Isn't it romantic? And they aren't hothouse roses, but grown outdoors on one of those lovely sheltered southern slopes behind Grasse, I expect. Many's the time my husband and I have bought them at the roadside as we drove through Provence."

A glimpse of the sunny, affluent life this lucky old lady had lived, Marnie thought with a mild pang of envy. But life, she reminded herself, couldn't be all sunshine and roses for anybody, no matter how affluent. Old Mrs. Rotherham had no doubt had her ups and downs bringing up her family, and in the end losing her lifelong companion—the husband with whom she had lightheartedly traveled the Provençal countryside. And now in her old age she was facing the shrinking years and her disabilities with a gay courage.

They were out of the village at last, climbing a winding, shadowy road with snow piled high on either side of it. Houses were left behind as the road angled its way through a pine forest and out onto a flat terrain bathed in sunshine. And, there standing high and alone on the hillside, was David's fairy-tale chalet. It was built of rough local stone with the inevitable steeply pitched roof. Wide wooden shutters flanked the windows. Heart-shaped openings had been cut in them and they were gaily decorated with painted alpine flowers; blue gentians, golden crocuses and white edelweiss.

"Isn't it charming?" Mrs. Rotherham exclaimed as it came into view. "David adores it; I imagine he has quite settled here with his beloved mountains. All he needs now is the right sort of wife to keep him company." She gave Marnie a considering sidelong glance. "It's not easy for him, surrounded as he is by foreigners," she said with old-fashioned prejudice. "And the nuns he works with are not much help when it comes to marrying—excellent women though they are."

Marnie, finding the conversation for some reason embarrassing, was glad when they drew up at the gate of the small formal garden and it was time to help her patient out of her cocoon of rugs.

There was a cleanly swept path between the snow-covered flower beds. "You should see this garden in the spring!" Mrs. Rotherham exclaimed. And then David was emerging from the house to greet them. Helping the old lady to alight from the sleigh, he conducted his visitors into a small tiled hall, beautifully heated. The lounge where tea awaited on a lavishly spread tea cart was filled with afternoon sunshine and the view from the window, like most windows in Arbois, was superb.

Marnie looked around her with interest, noting the bright chintz curtains, the rose-colored edge-to-edge carpet, scattered with white fur rugs, and the armchair in which she sat was luxuriously sprung. The home of this despotic young man was unexpectedly comfortable. And the pictures on the walls were arresting; a still life painted by a master hand and several large framed colored photographs of skiers in action.

"Some of David's efforts," Mrs. Rotherham pointed to the photographs with pride. "But his best work is kept in his study across the hall. Prize-winning photographs, many of them. You must show them to us presently, David."

Busy with the tea cups, he shook his head. "Not today, Aunt. I'm afraid I only just have time to give you tea, then I must hurry back to the clinic again."

"You left your work just to entertain us!" Mrs. Rotherham marveled.

"Just that." Flashing Marnie a warmly smiling glance and making a little bow to his aged relative he said, "I was honored to have you."

It was all very easy and friendly. David Harford in his home was charmingly approachable.

The conversation reverted to his photography again. "He's had several exhibitions," his great-aunt boasted. "Even one in London."

"In my youthful past," David interrupted. "Now I have little time for such diversions, what with a house to look after as well as my practice at the clinic."

"You manage very well for a confirmed bachelor," Mrs. Rotherham said, watching him preside over the tea cart.

"Not all that confirmed, I hope," David laughed. "Give me a chance! After all, I'm barely thirty." He was looking directly at Marnie as he spoke—a mischievous challenging glance. To her intense annoyance she felt herself blushing. She must watch herself, she decided sharply; she was becoming far too sensitive to the words and glances of David Harford.

"How does my mountain chalet compare with your farm in the Lammermuir Hills?" he was asking her then. She felt a twinge of surprise. Several times he had mentioned those hills.

"You're interested in the Lammermuir district?" she probed.

"Once, during my Edinburgh days," he told her, "I had a brief walking tour through that part of the country... with a friend."

Something in the way he added the last words made Marnie imagine that the friend had been a girl. She was more than ever convinced of this when he continued on a note of nostalgia to say it had been early June. "The whole countryside was at its best; the rolling green fields, the stone walls, that clean uncluttered scenery one finds only in Scotland. And there was May blossom everywhere. I can remember the haunting scent of it to this day."

A very special girl companion, Marnie thought—all mixed up in his mind now with the May blossom of the Border Country's late spring.

"A part of the British Isles I've never visited," Mrs. Rotherham remarked. "But Marnie has told me about her home...the farm, the animals, and how she and her sisters used to help with them when they were growing up."

"How many sisters?" David asked in an oddly hurried tone.

"Two," Marnie told him. "Both of them much older than I am. In fact they were both married and away from home before I'd left school."

"She's a good girl, she writes home regularly," Mrs. Rotherham contributed. "And gets great long letters from her mother in return. Sometimes she reads me bits of them. I'm beginning to know quite a lot about farm life, and the dairy and the cats who bring up families of kittens in the barns. It's the lambing season just now," the old lady ended knowledgeably.

"Only the very early start of it," Marnie corrected. "We're later with our lambs in that part of the world than farther south. But it's all very ordinary," she added. "Sparse scenery indeed—nothing to compare with the majesty of your mountains, and Mont Blanc."

"A gentle land," David said softly.

A few minutes later he was reminding them that he had to get back to the clinic. "Also," he addressed his great-aunt, "I think you've had quite enough for your first outing. You're beginning to look a bit peaked ."

"And we mustn't keep that sweet horse waiting any longer in the cold," Mrs. Rotherham clinched it.

"To say nothing of the driver," David laughed.

AN UNEVENTFUL WEEK FOLLOWED. Stella, after a couple of days in bed, was enjoying the distinction of appearing in the village as a skiing accident, her wounded ankle bandaged, a soft shoe replacing her ski boot. And to make it all the more dramatic she walked with the quite unnecessary aid of a stick, borrowed from her grandmother. Outwardly she seemed to have forgotten her hysterics over the defaulting Rudi, who by accident or design kept out of her way. In any case he was busy not only with his skiing pupils but with preparations for the ski races, which were to be part of the forthcoming festival. Then David helped things along by introducing his young cousin to the English Ski Club members, where by a lucky coincidence she found a young man who was the older brother of a girl with whom she went to school. Soon she was clamoring to have her ankle released from its bandages and was off skiing with her new friend at every opportunity.

"You prescribe more than pills and potions for your patients, it seems," old Mrs. Rotherham observed to her great-nephew, nodding a wise old head. And Denise breathed sighs of relief.

"We call it psychotherapy," David laughed.

But whatever it was called, it appeared to be working.

Meanwhile Marnie and her patient went their uneventful way, the sleigh drives now being a part of the daily routine, which rather interfered with Marnie's afternoon freedom. Old Mrs. Rotherham, who insisted that she should not miss her fresh air and exercise altogether, saw to it that she had an hour's skiing during the morning. This meant that Marnie often missed David's hurried little morning visits. But whenever she did encounter him his manner was friendly, if somewhat impersonal. At least he had dropped his critical attitude.

She was still hoping that he might remember his promise to take her for a second trip up the Jolyon. But he seemed to have forgotten all about it, perhaps because he was too busy, as were most of the other top skiers in Arbois, practicing for the Mardi Gras races. It was foolish to make excuses for him, Marnie reminded herself sternly. The truth most probably was that the casually given promise had meant nothing to him. A conversational flourish—that was all.

The Mardi Gras festivities opened with a colorful pageant on the skating rink, held after dark, in a blaze of floodlighting and backed by canned music. The whole village was lit up and decorated with flags. Bands and processions paraded the streets. But Marnie saw little of all this. Unfortunately her patient had contracted a chest cold.

"Too much gadding about in that sleigh of yours," David pronounced, and prescribed a couple of days in bed. Marnie, who told herself firmly that she wasn't in Arbois to attend festivals, spent most of her day in the sickroom, keeping her patient's spirits up. The "couple of days" stretched to include almost the entire week of the Festival high jinks. Marnie tried not to envy Stella, rushing off every day to one or other of the exciting items on the week's program.

Then it was Saturday, the last day of the races, with the Festival reaching its climax. This was the day David was to take part in the difficult slalom run from the summit of the Jolyon to the *téléférique* station, the comparatively flat ground around the *téléférique* making an ideal site for the spectators. In spite of his preoccupations with sport David kept up his visits to old Mrs. Rotherham, treating her cold with such success that she was well on the way to complete recovery.

On the Saturday morning he asked Marnie if she was coming to the races that afternoon, and when she hesitated with a glance at the invalid he said, "My aunt will be quite all right without you for a while. You've more than earned some free time this week, and I've been hoping you would be able to come along and wish me luck."

"Of course I shall be all right," the old lady broke in. "Marie will bring me my tea and she always stays and chats with me if I want her to."

"So that's fixed," David sealed it, giving Marnie a satisfied little nod. Her heart gave a foolish leap. Was it really important to him that she should be at the races, or was he simply being nice to her because of her concentrated hours in the sickroom recently? But when, later, she was getting ready to leave the house, she forgot her doubts and thought only that at last she could join in the excitement which had pervaded the village and the ski slopes all week. She knew now that she had been hoping against hope that she would be able to see David taking part in his most important race—simply, she persuaded herself, because when you knew one of the contestants personally, watching a race became that much more thrilling. Like everyone else she would go in her ski pants—the accepted form of day dress in Arbois. But she added a bright blue parka she had bought at one of the smart little boutiques in the village and the afternoon sunshine was so warm that she needed no head covering;

her glinting hair was hanging loose around her face.

It was a little bleak setting off alone; most of the other spectators moved in groups toward the *téléférique* area. Denise and Mark Rotherham and Stella had been gone all day, watching the morning contests and lunching at the Splendide afterward with the English skiers. Now they would probably be taking up privileged spectator positions near the course, procured for them by David.

Marnie had to content herself with making the best of it in the crowd on the flat ground near the *téléférique*. She could see the course in its deep descent from the starting point high up in the pine woods, the flags for the slalom race blossoming like spindly, colored flowers all the way along the route. The finish line was not far from where she was situated—if only the thrusting, pushing crowd didn't hinder her from being able to keep her eyes on it at the critical moment that would end David's race.

Straining, she tried to pick him out in the group by the starting point. But of course it was impossible at that distance. If only she knew the number he would be wearing! She wished she had binoculars, like many of the people around her.

The first items on the afternoon's program were the jumps, which were exciting to watch but looked desperately dangerous. She was glad David wasn't taking part in them. After that there were straight races, the competing skiers flashing down the course at incredible speed.

The slalom race was the last on the list. It seemed endless, there were so many competitors taking part, each tackling the course singly. At last it was David's turn. Marnie held her breath as his name was called out over the loudspeaker. Then she saw him, speeding down the impossible mountainside. Slim and pliant as a willow, he swayed and curved, maneuvering his way through the slalom poles at an incredible rate, his pace never faltering. Not one false move could be afforded. It had to be skill and strength and quickness of mind from beginning to end. When finally he swung around the finishing post with a perfect Christiania there was an outburst of applause from the spectators, and Marnie in her elation called out, "Bravo, David!" and was instantly horrified at her temerity. But he had heard her, turning his head to find her and waving his ski pole in recognition. In a ridiculous glow of satisfaction she returend the salute. But he did not come over to speak to her, busy receiving the congratulations of the officials crowded around the finishing post. She heard the result of the race given over the loudspeaker and David had come second. She hoped he would be satisfied—for it was a considerable achievement, since he had been contending with so many skilled and more experienced skiers, including the champion-grade Rudi, who had come in third.

Feeling a little flat, she began to make her way across the field, moving through the dispersing crowd. Old Mrs. Rotherham would be waiting to hear how her beloved David had fared. Marnie gave a full account of his triumph as they had tea. They were still sitting with the tea cart by the pine-log fire when the phone rang. Marnie hurried to answer it, thinking it might be Denise with some household instruction. The family would be having dinner at home, she knew, before going to the ball at the Hotel Beau Séjour, which was to bring the week's festivities to an end. But it was David Harford's voice that came over the line. "Is that you, Marnie?" And she confirmed that it was.

"I'm so glad you managed to get to the races this afternoon," the disembodied voice went on—a vibrant, compelling voice, vividly conveying his personality. "And you brought me luck! At first I couldn't find you, then I spotted you in your blue parka.... But that wasn't what I rang up to talk about. I wondered if you would care to come to the ball with me tonight?"

Marnie's gasp must have been audible at the other end of the line. "I...I..." she began hesitantly, "would love to. But what about Mrs. Rotherham?"

"Oh, she'll be all right with Marie, and in any case you wouldn't have to leave her until round about nine-thirty— when, presumably, she would be well settled down for the night. The Beau Séjour is not far away and I could run you back to the Chasseurs during the evening—just to see that all's well with our patient. Do come, Marnie," he ended persuasively. "I've got a spare ticket and it would be a shame to waste it."

An offhand invitation, perhaps; and it would have been more polite if he had given her a day or two of notice. Her hair wasn't at its best, she reviewed hurriedly. And what would she wear? Confused thoughts raced through her mind. Annoyed with herself for having been thrown into such a tizzy, she told herself that any more formal or considerate approach from this young man would not have been in character.

"What about those nice girls in the English Ski Club group?" she found herself suggesting. "Wouldn't one of them be glad to make use of your spare ticket?"

"Oh, they'll all have made their arrangements by now," he returned casually. "They pair off in these clubs. Anyhow, I've asked *you*."

"Well, thank you," Marnie conceded, laughing a little wryly into the phone. It was such a last-minute invitation. Obviously he hadn't given it a thought until this afternoon. And now, discovering that he had to have a dancing partner, he had decided that Marnie would do.

"Good," he was clinching it. "I'll look for you then at the Beau Séjour. You can come with the Rotherhams."

So he wasn't even going to call for her.

"It's very kind of you, Doctor Harford," she murmured, on a sardonic note.

"David," he prompted. "I use your Christian name on occasion—and I noticed you used mine today at the races."

"In a moment of excitement," she explained. "It was a terrific race."

"Sufficient to bring that spontaneous, 'Bravo!' One of my nicest congratulations."

Concession after concession; she thought. His success this afternoon had certainly mellowed her autocratic and aloof superior!

"Who was it?" old Mrs. Rotherham wanted to know when she had returned to the fireside. "Did I hear you say Dr. Harford?"

"Yes," Marnie confirmed. "He was phoning to ask me if I would like to go to the dance with him this evening. It seems he has a spare ticket."

"I'm so glad," the old lady pronounced forcefully. "You deserve a bit of fun after all the dull days you've had nursing me through this silly cold. It will do David good, too. Be a change from his nuns!"

Very soon after that the Rotherhams came home and in the buzz of conversation that followed Marnie escaped to her room and surveyed her wardrobe. There was only one obvious choice for the ball tonight—the dress she had bought when she went with Robert Tallant to his parental home that ill-starred weekend. It was flimsy, flowing, multicolored and vaguely oriental; beautifully trendy, in fact. She had hesitated about including it in her luggage when she came to Arbois, but just in case some exciting ski resort night life came her way she had decided to bring it along.

There were exclamations of admiration from Denise and the old lady when she appeared in it at the dinner table. Stella, in her Kate Greenaway dress, remained disapprovingly silent. She hadn't yet forgiven Marnie for what she regarded as her interference over the Rudi Praxmann affair. Indeed she consistently ignored the older girl, only speaking to her when she was forced to do so.

"I'm so glad you are coming to the ball," Denise ended her commendations of Marnie's toilette. "Aren't you, Stella?" she unwisely inquired, a little ashamed of her daughter's sulky demeanor.

Stella shrugged and offered the unkind suggestion that David danced so badly he would be hard put to get any girl to partner him. "Nurse Marnhem," she added nastily, "couldn't very well refuse."

"Now, Stella, don't be so catty!" Denise tried to laugh it off.

But Marnie took it in good part. Stella's summing up of the situation was no doubt so near the truth that it was no good resenting it.

CHAPTER SIX

THE BEAU SÉJOUR was a large ultra-modern hotel on the outskirts of the village, recently erected to cater to the increasing influx of winter-sports visitors. And there was, too, a growing number of aspiring mountain climbers who now came to Arbois in the summer months.

David was waiting in the foyer when the Rotherham party arrived. He looked bronzed and aggressively muscular in a dinner jacket that was a trifle too tight for him, as if he had, since purchasing it, acquired an extra width of shoulder in his efforts on the ski slopes.

Very soon Marnie found herself on the dance floor with him. Denise and Mark were waltzing together and Stella had found her English boyfriend, Paul. The orchestra was playing the "Skaters' Waltz." "As if we didn't get enough of that day in, day out from the amplifiers on the skating rink," David grumbled.

The ballroom was hot and crowded and David danced rather absentmindedly, holding Marnie in a casual grasp. Nevertheless she was a little too tinglingly aware of his nearness. It made her feel breathless and silly—for which she despised herself.

"I'm no good at this sort of thing," he apologized, as even before the number had quite ended he escorted her back to the table reserved by the Rotherhams. Soon Denise and her husband joined them; then Stella and Paul. So that was the kind of evening it was going to be. Marnie hadn't envisaged it as a family party. But what else had she expected, she asked herself impatiently.

Mark ordered champagne with which they drank to David's success on the ski course. A group of young people from the English Ski Club at the adjoining table added their contratulations to the victor, and presently one of them asked Marnie to dance with him. Halfheartedly she complied; David, deep in conversation with Mark over technicalities of the afternoon's competition, didn't seem to notice her going. After that she was kept busy dancing with the various young men among Stella's acquaintances. David, her escort, still engrossed with Mark, took no notice of her. Until suddenly, about eleven o'clock, he reminded her that they ought to go back to the Chasseurs and have a look at old Mrs. Rotherham.

"We'll go by sleigh," he decided, when she had fetched her cloak from the cloakroom. "I've left my car in the hotel garage and it might not be easy at this hour to disentangle it from the congestion of guests' cars which have come in since then." As they drove off to the music of swinging sleigh bells he leaned over Marnie to tuck the inevitable fur rug more closely around her. "Can't have Nurse Marnhem catching cold!" he said.

"I thought we were using Christian names."

David laughed. "Perhaps formalities might be safer. Sleigh bells and moonlight...." He left the sentence unfinished, settling down close beside her with a contented sigh. "This is nice, isn't it? After the hubbub of the ballroom. How is it that human beings have to make such an unearthly din whenever they get together in any number?"

A question, Marnie decided, that did not need an answer. In any case it was difficult to think clearly with David's taking up so much more than his share of the narrow seat, making her too vividly aware of his physical presence. The scene all around them was enchanting; a great silver moon coming up behind the mountains, pouring its light onto the snowy rooftops of the village and the cold white slopes behind them. The occasional pine tree plantations looked like splashes of ink, and to the west Mont Blanc soared in majestic serenity. When they stopped outside Les Trois Chasseurs they sat still for a moment, as if by common consent, and there was no sound in the world but the murmur of the stream, which rushed through its gulley at the side of the house.

As soon as they got indoors Marnie hurried up the stairs to tiptoe into old Mrs. Rotherham's room. She was sleeping peacefully. Silently withdrawing, Marnie crossed the hallway into the lounge, illuminated by a single deeply shaded floor lamp. David was busy putting fresh logs onto the pile of glowing embers on the hearth. He looked very domesticated, kneeling there coaxing the fire back to life again with a pair of bellows. In a few moments the golden flames were licking up the chimney and the sweet odor of burning pine filled the room.

With a satisfied glance at his workmanship, he sank down onto the settee. "Come and sit down," he invited Marnie, patting the cushions at his side. But no sooner had she obeyed the summons than he sprang to his feet impulsively.

"Would you be very disappointed if we didn't go back to the Beau Séjour?" he asked. "It's so much better here...." Without waiting for her answer he added that he would run downstairs and tell the sleigh driver not to wait. "What do you say?" he had the grace to inquire.

She was startled and a little hurt. "It's just as you like," she murmured. "You don't enjoy dancing, do you?"

"Not really. But if you're keen on going back to the ball I'm sure you'll find lots of willing partners...."

"No, no," she put in quickly. "Let's stay here." The

implication that he would not be one of the willing partners added to the hurt that was building up inside her. "Why did you go to the dance if you hate dancing so much?" she asked.

"Noblesse oblige," he returned. "The complimentary tickets were more or less thrust on me, since I was one of the welcoming committee for the English Ski Club. It wouldn't have gone down well if I'd refused them, or having accepted them, failed to use them."

So he hadn't even had to pay for the tickets. His presence at the ball was no more than a social obligation, Marnie worked it out bitterly, while David went to dismiss the sleigh driver. She listened to the diminishing tinkle of the bells as the horse was driven away.

It was a moment or two before David reappeared, he, too, it seemed, having gone to have a look at his patient. "Sleeping like a baby," he pronounced, and once more seated himself beside Marnie, spreading his hands to the now glowing fire. He spoke of his great-aunt and the wonderful progress she was making. It was thanks to her inherent vitality that she had thrown off that threatening chest cold so easily.

"Soon she won't be needing me anymore," Marnie hazarded.

He turned to her sharply. "In a hurry to get back to England, are you?"

"Oh, no!" The denial was a little too fervent. "But I came here to do a specific job, and if that job is nearly finished...."

"It's not," he interrupted sharply. "I'll let you know when it is."

He stretched his long legs out to the fire and laid an arm along the back of the settee, all but enfolding Marnie in its curve.

"This is good," he repeated. "The crackle of a log fire

instead of a babble of voices. Conversation is killed in a crowd. Just two people together can say so much more." And after a short pause, "Tell me about yourself, Marnie; your home in the Lammermuir Hills."

Odd how many times he had spoken of Lammermuir. Gazing into the fire, she felt a wave of homesickness. "It's beautiful," she said. "At least to me. A stone-built house at the head of a small green valley. At its deepest part it's such a sheltered valley that we keep bees there even in the winter. In the spring it's full of primroses and bluebells and cowslips. A little stream winds through it and there are steep slopes on either side of it that keep the cold winds away. Beyond the valley the land rises to the sloping fields where my father grazes his sheep." She broke off to turn to her companion abruptly. "Why are you so interested in Lammermuir?"

"I think I told you I once did a brief walking tour in that part of the country. It was a time of stress, during my early days at the hospital. Maybe I hadn't yet become accustomed to the constant contact with illness and death, and there was the pressure of working for exams. But whatever it was, the few days I spent in your quiet countryside seemed to me a haven of refuge. I've never forgotten it." He produced a pouch of tobacco and a rather ancient-looking pipe, which he waved at her with a casual gesture. "Mind if I light up?"

"Not in the least," she assured him.

"Somehow," he went on, "your being here reminds me so much of what I felt and thought on that holiday in the Lammermuir Hills. A background which, if I may say so, suits you better than the Arbois mixture of glacial Alps and sophisticated sporty-type holidaymakers." He puffed contemplatively at his pipe.

"The little Scots country girl," she mocked.

"I didn't say that. But it's not an unpleasant picture. I

don't find much wrong with it." He gave her a smile that she found annoyingly patronizing.

"Thank you, kind sir!" She hoped he would not miss the hint of derision. "But one is apt to shed one's youthful country ways as one goes along."

"Don't shed too many of them, Marnie." His voice was soft and for a long moment their glances held. He was very close to her in the firelight. Once more she was suddenly too intimately aware of his physical presence—the sheen of the lamplight on his hair, the strong good lines of brow and jaw, the clenched hand, holding the pipe away from him. What she felt she would have concealed from him, but his eyes imprisoned her, so that she could not turn away.

The spell was broken when he leaned over to knock the ashes of his pipe out on the hearth. "How is Stella's ill-chosen love affair coming along?" he asked. "She seemed quite content tonight without her Rudi."

"Oh, she was, I think," Marnie responded. "At all events she's consoling herself with this nice Enlgish boy you introduced her to. Much to the family's relief!"

"Poor Stella!" David smiled and shook his head ruefully. "The things one does when one is young and green!" He turned to her with that galvanizing look again. "Would you believe it, but once in my moonstruck days I fell in love with a photograph."

"A pin-up girl?"

He shook his head. "Oh, no, nothing so crude." She waited for him to go on, but he remained silent, gazing into the fire. What an odd mood he was in this evening!

"Have you been in love many times?" she asked, and was instantly alarmed at her daring.

But he didn't seem to resent the blunt personal question, shaking himself out of his reverie to answer lightly, "Oh, lots of times. Not very seriously. Doctors, until their careers are established, can't afford to be serious over their affairs of the heart."

The burned-out logs on the hearth collapsed noiselessly into a heap of white ash.

"What about your love life?" he challenged.

Marnie caught her breath. But she had asked for it. "Nurses don't have very much more time than doctors for falling in love," she fenced.

"Not even with yellow-haired ski instructors?"

She turned on him indignantly. "That's a silly thing to ask. And you know it is."

"You were just spiking young Stella's guns that evening at Le Chat Noir, putting a spoke in her wheels, or whatever the feminine equivalent is for such expressions?"

"I was trapped in an awkward situation, as Denise, if you remember, explained to you. The way she worked it I simply *had* to accept Rudi's invitation."

"Just a good deed in a naughty world...a very naughty world! And you came out of it unscathed."

She hoped that was a statement, rather than a question, and sought to change the subject. But the clock on the mantelpiece did it for her, striking midnight with insistent chimes.

David stood up, stretching himself. "Too late to build up the fire again, I suppose," he offered in a tone that settled the matter.

Marnie somewhat reluctantly got herself out of the seductive settee and stood beside him, waiting for him to take his leave. But he did not move. She glanced down at the evening shoes he was wearing. "How are you going to get back to the hotel to collect your car in those light shoes?" she asked.

"I'll borrow a pair of Mark's boots from the clutter downstairs in the hall," he replied, and still made no attempt to be on his way. "Thank you for the fireside chat, my dear, and for being my guest at the ball. I'm sorry I was such an unsatisfactory partner."

Before she could produce a polite protest to this he placed his hands on her shoulders and, stooping, kissed her gently but very effectively right on the lips.

"A salute to Lammermuir," he said strangely, and then he was gone.

She stood where he had left her, her hand to her lips, her heart hammering. From the hall below came the muted sound of boots being flung hither and thither as he made his choice, rooting in the untidy heap of footwear left by the family in transit. At last the hall door slammed and his footsteps crunched away over the snow into the night's silence.

Marnie sank back on to the settee. "A salute to Lammermuir." What an odd remark to have made! Who was it said there were two things that should never be explained—a joke and a kiss? Sometimes they were cruelly akin! She felt the prick of tears behind her eyes. What on earth was the matter with her? But it had been an oddly disturbing evening—turning out so differently from what she had expected. Just what *had* she expected? She didn't know. Only that there was an ache in her heart. Everything had mattered too much to her this evening, and now she was tormenting herself ridiculously over David's casual good-night kiss. But her lips seemed to burn with it—her whole being burned. She buried her face in her hands. She was falling in love with David Harford; she could no longer hide it from herself. And it was an insidious invasion of her will. Because she hadn't wanted to fall in love again for a long time, after that stupid affair with Robert Tallant. Only, the present assault on her emotions was totally different—deeper, more serious, containing a quality she had never experienced before—a strange compulsion, as if what was happening to her was completely out of her control, preordained. She shrugged off the pretentious word.

How long she sat there by the dead fire, fighting against the tumult within her, she did not know. It was the sound of the Rotherhams returning from the ball that sent her hurrying to her bedroom. The last thing she wanted was questions from Denise as to why she and David had left the party so early.

WITH THE SHROVETIDE FESTIVAL at an end the season at Arbois had reached its peak. In the weeks that followed the number of visitors would gradually diminish. Not that the decline was noticeable at first. Only the cable cars were not quite as full as they had been and it was easier to get a table at the Splendide in the evenings.

Old Mrs. Rotherham had now completely recovered from her cold and was indeed scarcely an invalid anymore, apart from the minor disabilities of her age. Already the family had begun to speak of their return to London. So her time at Arbois was rapidly running out, Marnie realized, and tried to persuade herself that her sharp pangs of regret were natural. It wouldn't be easy to leave this dazzling fairyland of snowy mountains and golden sunshine. At midday the temperatures were rising to springtime level and the music of dripping icicles could be heard everywhere.

There was almost no need for the doctor's visits anymore and Marnie did not set eyes on him for a whole week after her disturbing evening with him on the night of the ball. Then one day he arrived just as she was getting old Mrs. Rotherham ready for her morning sleigh drive, and suggested that they should include a visit to the clinic in their itinerary.

"I'd like to do an electro-cardiograph of my aunt just

to make sure that all is well before she returns to England," he told Marnie. "Also I think it might interest her to see where I work. And you, too?" he added on a questioning note.

Marnie said she would be most interested to see the clinic, a large white, balconied building she had glimpsed on the mountain slope the far side of the valley.

It was a longish drive through the village, along the valley road and then up the steep climb to the clinic. As soon as they arrived, Mrs. Rotherham was whisked away by two white-coifed nuns with sweet, placid faces, while David took Marnie to a small office on the ground floor to introduce her to the Mère Générale, the equivalent of a matron in this ecclesiastically run establishment.

"I'll leave you to have a little chat with the Mère Générale while I go and supervise my aunt's tests," David said, and vanished. The elderly nun smiled graciously at Marnie and after a few generalities asked her if she would like to see something of the clinic. As she led the way back to the central entrance hall she was asking Marnie interested questions about her nursing experience in England. Afterward Marnie realized just how pertinent those questions had been. Meanwhile she was taken around the comfortably appointed lounges, the television room, the games room where leisurely billiards could be played. "Nothing strenuous, you understand," Mère Générale explained.

They had twenty-five patients in residence at the moment, all chest cases of one kind or another. Most of them were up and around, sitting on the wide balconies outside their rooms, or taking gentle exercise on the spacious grounds. There were a few seriously ill people in bed. "Carcinoma and advanced heart cases mostly," Mère Générale said. "But we are full of hope here, even for the seemingly hopeless cases." She gave Marnie her strangely peaceful smile—as if the secret of hope beyond hopelessness was known to her.

There were two French doctors, she went on. Dr. Harford had been with them three years, originally engaged because of the increasing number of English patients coming to Arbois.

"But he is very popular with all our mixed nationalities," the old nun added. "*Très sympathique.* His patients adore him."

He was waiting for them when they got back to the little office, having established old Mrs. Rotherham in the sleigh outside.

"What do you think of our clinic?" he demanded of Marnie with a rather odd urgency.

"It's beautiful, set here in this glorious spot," Marnie replied—an opinion endorsed by old Mrs. Rotherham when they joined her.

"One wouldn't mind being ill in such surroundings and with such kindly nurses," she declared. "Only that I'm not going to be ill anymore.... David is delighted with the results of my tests, aren't you, my dear?" David agreed enthusiastically that he was.

Marnie was just about to climb into the sleigh when he put an arresting hand on her arm, the light touch sending a tremor through her nerves. "Will you have dinner with me tonight?" he asked unexpectedly. "At the Splendide? I'll call for you about eight? Okay?"

She hesitated, dumbfounded.

"I've a proposition to put to you," he went on.

A proposition. Something to do with work, no doubt. She hoped it didn't mean that Mrs. Rotherham's tests had not been as reassuring as the old lady seemed to imagine. But why did he have to ask her to dine to discuss...whatever it was? Concealing her agitation, she answered a little stiffly that she would be pleased to accept his kind invitation.

"That's settled, then," he sealed it, as he helped her into the sleigh.

"What's settled?" Mrs. Rotherham demanded inquisitively, having missed most of the hurried little exchange.

"Marnie is having dinner with me tonight. A little matter of business I have to discuss with her."

"Business?" the old lady echoed, sounding deflated. "How dull! I was hoping you were going to give the girl a nice lighthearted evening out. She deserves it."

David grinned. "I'll make it as lighthearted as I can," he promised.

"Allez-oup!" shouted the ancient sleigh driver to the ancient horse, and with a ringing of bells they were gliding away soundlessly over the snow, Marnie pondering on the latest turn in events.

Whatever business could David Harford have to discuss with her, she wondered again, and decided she would have to wait until the evening to find out. Meanwhile she must keep a stern control over her crazy emotions. It was quite clear that he was not inviting her to spend the evening with him for anything but the most practical of reasons.

Nevertheless when she dressed for her rendezvous she put on the glamorous oriental dress. A heavy gilt ornament hung around her neck on a slender chain, and she had gathered her hair into a knot at the nape of her neck. It gave her an old-fashioned air, but looked right with the flowing dress.

When she went into the lounge to wait for David, only Stella was there. Denise and Mark, having returned late from the ski slopes, were still bathing and changing for the evening meal. Stella, lounging on the settee, looked sullen and bored.

"My!" she exclaimed as Marnie came in, "David will be charmed, I'm sure. Giving him the works, aren't you? Après-ski wear of the *dernier cri.* But the hairdo, if I may say so, is a bit aging. No doubt you think that will appeal to my serious-minded medical cousin."

"Don't be so bitchy, Stella," Marnie returned quietly, and then couldn't resist adding, "You're just annoyed because *you* haven't got a dinner date yourself tonight. You'll be missing Paul."

"Now *you're* being bitchy," Stella accused. "And of course I'm missing Paul. But I shall be seeing him as soon as we get back to England." She studied her brightly colored nails with a sophisticated air. "Meanwhile there's always Rudi to fall back on. I had tea with him this afternoon."

Marnie groaned inwardly. Surely all *that* wasn't going to start up again?

Then the sound of David's car drove Stella and her troublesome affairs out of her mind. Gathering up her coat and bag, she ran down the stairs to join him.

"All well with the old girl?" he asked, as he opened the door for her.

"She's safely in bed, having her supper," Marnie assured him. "And afterward Marie is going to play patience with her."

"Right!" he nodded. "Now we can forget mundane chores and enjoy ourselves."

"Mrs. Rotherham isn't a mundane chore," Marnie couldn't help pointing out. "She's a darling and I've loved nursing her." How sad it sounded in the past tense!

"Mustn't get too fond of one's patients," the doctor warned.

"I know," Marnie agreed. "One of the first commandments."

"And a wise one."

And it applies equally to one's employer, Marnie found herself adding inwardly. Nor must one get too fond of beautiful mountain villages lost in a fairyland of sunshine and snow. The moment always came when you had to say goodbye.

"I've booked a table in the dining room," David told her as they entered the glittering foyer. "If you would like to dance later we can move over the café bar by the dance floor. But first let's eat."

Meals in the restaurant were, she knew, notoriously expensive. She was being honored indeed. But when, she wondered, as they went from one delicious course to another, was the "proposition" coming up... that lurking "matter of business"? It seemed to matter less and less as she eyed the dish of fresh strawberries and big bowl of cream the waiter was putting on the table. "You're spoiling me, David!" she couldn't help exclaiming. "I know this isn't the kind of thing one is supposed to say when one is a guest—but this meal must be costing you a package!"

"I owe it to you," David returned with something more emphatic than mere politeness. "In fact, to be exact I owe you a hundred pounds."

She abandoned her strawberries to stare at him. "Have you gone bonkers?" she demanded inelegantly.

His burst of laughter was reassuring. "No, I haven't taken leave of my senses. I *do* owe you just that sum. I know it sounds crazy, but it's not. One day I'll explain it to you." His eyes danced, enjoying her mystification. "Meanwhile shall we have our coffee in the less formal atmosphere of the café bar, and I'll tell you why I've lured you here this evening and softened you up with Chateauneuf du Pape—a wine even more fabulous than the food."

They found a secluded corner and as soon as coffee

had been brought to them David said, without any preamble, "How would you like a job at the clinic?"

Marnie put her coffee cup down so abruptly that some of the contents spilled into the saucer. "A job!" she echoed, in a stupefied tone. "At the clinic?"

"That's what I said. I took you there this morning so that Mère Générale might cast her wise old eyes over you...and she likes you, as I rather thought she would. We so often wish we had at least one English nurse to help out with our English patients. But there've been certain work permit restrictions in France, as you know. Now with Common Market conditions prevailing things are different."

She was still too taken aback to know what to say. Somehow, this was the last eventuality she had foreseen when David had spoken of his mysterious "proposition."

"It's such a surprise...." she began falteringly. "Something I'd never thought of."

"You like Arbois, don't you?" he interrupted.

"Oh, I do! The snow, the sunshine...." The words trailed away inadequately.

"And it can be even more alluring in the late spring and early summer when only the highest mountain peaks retain their snowcaps and the lower slopes are green and lush. As the snow retreats the flowers appear, whole carpets of them everywhere, climbing right up to the snow line. The colors are dazzling—it's a breathtaking sight. The *pistes* become pathways leading up into the high mountains. I could take you up a very different Mont Jolyon then...teach you the beginnings of real climbing."

He had warmed to his subject, his eyes glowing. He seemed to have forgotten the matter of a job at the clinic, carried away by his love for this mountain land.

"Do you wonder I choose to live and work in Arbois, rather than in some grimy English city? Even Harley Street, if I could attain to it, holds no attraction for me. Perhaps I'm lacking in ambition. At the clinic I can be sure of more or less regular hours, leaving me plenty of time for my skiing and mountain climbing. And Arbois out of season is miles away from the technological rat race of modern life, the noise, the pollution, the tensions. Perhaps I'm just a natural drop-out. The quality of life is more important to me than material success." He gave her a quizzical glance. "Maybe that's why I've never married. The sort of girls I've met so far wouldn't think much of a husband to whom mountains were more important than money. And," he ended rather disjointedly, "it rains quite a lot here during the summer." He broke off with a laugh. "Just listen to me rattling on about myself and my own interests! It was you we were supposed to be talking about, wasn't it? And that job at the clinic. You're not sure about it, are you?" He held up an arresting hand. "I can see I've startled you . . . you have a telltale face, Marnie. But there's no hurry. There will be lots of questions you'll need to ask me before you make up your mind. Let's have a round or two on the dance floor while you're turning the same questions over in your mind."

Then somehow before she had time to remind him how much he disliked dancing, they were on the dance floor. As usual at this hour the small space was crowded, so that there was very little room to move. David with his ineptitude for dancing was no doubt glad of this. But this time he did not hold her casually—as he had done the night of the Beau Séjour ball. He drew her very close to him as they swayed gently to the rhythm of the band . . . a rhythm and sweetness in which Marnie felt her very bones dissolving. Once more the sense of David's physical nearness was robbing her of all power of coherent thought. Powerless as a reed in the current of a rushing river, she laid her head against his shoulder. She felt his lips touch her brow and heard him whisper, "Dear Marnie! I don't want you to go away from Arbois."

It was just at that moment the shrill young voice hailed them, crashing in on Marnie's bemused senses.

"Marnie! Marnie!... David!"

It was Stella on the edge of the dance floor, beckoning to them urgently. The thought that came to them simultaneously was that something was wrong with old Mrs. Rotherham. In swift alarm they broke apart, and without a word, started to push their way through the hampering crowd of dancers.

Stella impatiently awaited them, her young face tense, her eyes enormous and filled with a strangely mischievous light, as though she gloated over some secret triumph.

She's glad of an excuse to break up my evening, Marnie thought in a hurried aside.

"Oh, Marnie!" Stella gasped as they drew near. "I thought I'd never find you. I've been searching in the restaurant, the lounge...I never imagined our staid old David would want to dance with you." She broke off to point excitedly over her shoulder.

"Your fiancé is here. He's just arrived in Arbois and came straight to Les Trois Chasseurs to look for you. So I brought him along.... he's over there by the bar, waiting for you."

CHAPTER SEVEN

"MY FIANCÉ?" Marnie repeated in an incredulous tone. "Stella, whatever are you talking about?" She was aware of David standing close to her in the crowded space.

"I'm talking about Robert," Stella was saying. "The gorgeous Robert Tallant himself. I recognized him the moment he arrived at the house, asking for you...clamoring for you." She giggled suggestively. "Aren't you the sly-boots to have kept so quiet about him? He said he'd got here as quickly as he could...that you knew he would be joining you. It seems he has a week off before his new play opens. But he'll tell you all about that himself," the rather breathless flow ended.

Marnie turned to give David a distracted glance. His face was a mask, his lips tight.

"There must be some mistake," she heard herself offer helplessly. The look he gave her hit her like a sword thrust.

"Do come along!" Stella urged. And it was just at that moment that Robert, having spotted them, pushed his way toward them.

"Marnie!" he cried ecstatically as he reached them. "Marnie, my love! What a hunt I've had to find you." The rest of what he was saying was lost to her as he folded her in his arms and kissed her.

Despair engulfed her as her hurried thoughts tried to take in the implications of the situation. Robert in Arbois! Something that in her wildest moments she hadn't expected. She had put him so completely out of her mind during the past few weeks that even having to accept that he still existed was an effort. But exist he did! And David had walked away, coldly, and in silence, losing himself in the throng around the bar.

Stella, giggling again, said, "Now look what you've done to my poor cousin!"

But Marnie hardly heard her, gazing up at Robert in frozen astonishment.

"Don't tell me you're surprised to see me," he reproached her. "It was you yourself who suggested my coming... remember? It was when we phoned our farewells, just before you took off for Geneva. 'See you on the ski slopes,' were your parting words."

With a stab of horrified recollection they came back to her. A foolish bit of backchat, which had meant exactly nothing to her. But for some reason, no doubt connected with his own self-interest, Robert had seized on them... and here he was! He looked so happy and expectant that good manners demanded she should make some effort at welcoming him. David had vanished. She didn't dare to think about David.

"It never occurred to me that you would take my remark about ski slopes seriously." She tried to laugh as she spoke. "It was nice of you to come all this way," she ended politely.

"I couldn't keep away!" he returned fervently. And then he was telling her about his week off before the opening of the new play, and how he had arrived in Geneva that evening and taken a slow country bus up through the snowy mountain roads. "I had no idea Arbois would be so far from the airport... it was quite late when the bus at last got me here, and as soon as I'd left my gear at the hotel where I'd booked I made my way to Les Trois Chasseurs and found your charming friend

Miss Rotherham there. She told me you were spending the evening here at the Splendide with her cousin."

"He's the doctor with whom I'm working," Marnie put in.

Robert made a rueful grimace. "You seemed to be on very good terms with him there on the dance floor," he commented dryly. "Sorry if I've driven him away! But no matter... I'm here now and *I'm* taking over. Aren't you pleased to see me, Marnie?" There was a note of desolation in his voice and for the first time Marnie noticed that he looked tired, oddly pale in this mountain village of sun-tanned, weatherbeaten faces.

"Have you had dinner?" she asked.

"No. I couldn't stop to eat until I'd found you." Oh, it was all very touching, typical of the charming things Robert always said. Once, she had taken them seriously.

"There's a marvelous restaurant here if you want a full meal," she began. But he said something from the cold buffet at the bar would do.

"I'll leave you, then," Stella broke in with an air of heavy tact mixed with coyness. Neither of them seemed aware of her going, the hungry Robert more interested in what the buffet had to offer, Marnie swamped by the turn of events.

They found a secluded corner and Robert provided himself with a tray containing an adequate assortment of light dishes and half a bottle of Burgundy, having first ascertained that Marnie had already dined with her vanished escort. "We ate in the restaurant," she said, for the sake of saying something, her powers of speech threatening to dry up completely. "A lovely meal," she murmured, watching Robert attacking a plateful of savory rice and prawns.

"The boyfriend did you proud, then," he remarked.

"He's not my boyfriend," Marnie contradicted with

unnecessary force. She couldn't speak lightly of David. The thought of him hurt too much. The look he had given her when Stella announced the newcomer as her fiancé still rankled.

"How did you get my address?" she asked.

"Your friend at the nursing agency in Seafleet gave it to me. I had to coax it out of her, assuring her that you would be glad to see me, had in fact suggested my joining you."

Oh, that flippant, "See you on the ski slopes!" What fiend of mischief had put the words into her mouth?

"You're still working at the Seafleet theater, then?"

"Only for the odd performance. They very decently waived my contract so that I could give most of my time to the London rehearsals for *Nought Else is Living*. And as I told you, I have a week off from the London company before we go into the final spate of rehearsals, and face the dreaded first night."

"Not dreaded, surely?"

"All first nights are dreaded. And this is a particularly difficult play . . . a bit of a gamble, in fact. I've got a hell of a tricky role to play in it. Hermione in the ingénue lead is wonderful. An extraordinarily clever little actress."

"Why didn't you bring her with you?" Marnie asked with the hint of a sneer.

Robert put down his fork to give her a swift, reproachful glance. "Marnie, what *is* the matter with you? I came to see *you*. I didn't want any infant prodigy actress tagging along. I see quite enough of the beautiful Hermione in London."

I bet you do, Marnie thought bitterly, and then was ashamed of her cynicism. Robert could no more help his philandering ways than he could help breathing. He just adored women, lightly, inconsequently, and if they adored him in return there was nothing he could do about it. Meaning no harm, he very often no doubt did a great deal. But feelings of remorse would sit lightly on the shoulders of the handsome, successful Robert Tallant. The world was his oyster.

"Why did you tell Stella you are my fiancé?" Marnie asked then.

"I didn't." He sounded puzzled, and then laughed. "Was that how she announced me when she called you from the dance floor? No wonder your boyfriend melted away in a huff. The word, you see, has a slightly different connotaion in France. It can, in fact, mean someone with whom one is having an affair. Though you could hardly call our few chaste embraces that! You aren't the "affair" sort of girl, are you Marnie?"

She gave him a desolate glance and did not answer. So "fiancé" in France could imply a lover—in the fullest meaning of the word. And what would the disapproving Doctor Harford make of *that*? She clenched her hands on her lap as the details of her evening with him came back to her. Not that she had ever ceased to be aware of them. It had all been so extraordinary: David offering her a job at the clinic, telling her he owed her a hundred pounds, finally dancing with her in a way that had robbed her of all her good sense. "I don't want you to go away, Marnie," he had whispered. And then... Robert Tallant had chosen to appear on the scene, apparently so sure of his welcome that he had traveled across Europe to join her. Even without Stella's unfortunate use of the word "fiancé" a situation would have been created. And it wasn't hard to imagine what David Harford's reaction would be. If only things hadn't been going so well with them! The way he had talked to her over dinner, making Arbois so beautiful for her. As if he needed to! If he had asked her to work with him in a slum instead of an Alpine clinic she would have been overjoyed. But now... sick with the sense of anticlimax, she forced herself back into conversation with Robert, listening to his accounts of his life on the stage with all its emotional storms and satisfactions. It was late when he had finished his snack and Marnie said it was time she got back to the Chasseurs to look after her patient.

"I am not altogether a lady of leisure," she reminded him.

"I hope you'll have time to show me the ropes in the morning?" he asked anxiously. "Tell me where I can hire some skis and so on. I'm by way of being quite an expert skier," he added with characteristic lack of mock modesty. "But I don't relish going off on my own, and the terrain is unfamiliar to me."

"Then you'd better come to the Chasseurs in the morning and I'll introduce you to Mr. Rotherham, Stella's father, the son of the old lady I'm nursing," Marnie offered. "He skis marvelously and knows all the best *pistes*. He might take you along on some of his own quite extensive expeditions."

Robert looked pleased. "What it is to have the right contacts!" he said. "A bit of luck I came here instead of dashing off to one of the other ski resorts where I wouldn't have known a soul."

Marnie accepted this offhand summing up of his presence in Arbois; it was so like him. Everything he did had for its first motive his own convenience. She wished David could have been listening—but he had gone off with the image of a devoted fiancé planted in his mind.

"Not that I want to spend *all* my time with this skiing friend of yours," Robert was adding magnanimously. "I want to see a lot of you, Marnie... when are you free?"

"Well, usually in the afternoons," she admitted reluctantly. "And I'm not an adept at skiing, I warn you. In fact I'm a most hopeless bungler, though the lessons at the ski school are helping me." If she was doing herself less than justice it was in the hope of putting Robert off. But it wasn't to be.

"All the more reason that you should have some practice with me," he said cheerfully. "And I'd like to do one or two of the tourist trips. Couldn't you get a day off and come with me on the cable-car run from Chamonix to Courmayer, which goes right across the Mont Blanc chain of peaks? I'm told it's one of the most spectacular of mountain panoramas. And we could do the Mer de Glace. You ought to see one of the great glaciers while you're here. How much longer will you be in Arbois, do you know?"

A question from which Marnie shrank. That job at the clinic David had spoken of...would it still be open to her? If he believed she was engaged to Robert everything would be changed. Explaining the situation wasn't going to be easy.

She said, evasively, "Old Mrs. Rotherham, my patient, is almost back to normal now—practically finished with my services. And the family will be returning to England in about ten days from now." Taking her with them, was the unspoken implication.

"That's grand, Marnie!" Robert covered her hand with his own. "You'll be able to come and see me in *Nought Else is Living*, he added with characteristic egotism. "I'll send you tickets."

She murmured her thanks.

A little later Robert took her back to Les Trois Chasseurs by sleigh, treating her to one or two rather automatic embraces on the way—too lukewarm to rate a protest. To her relief, he refused her invitation to come in. He was tired, he pleaded; it had been a long day and he wanted to be out on the ski slopes early. "When can I meet this chap, Rotherham?" he added eagerly. "I'm staying at the Roche-Brune hotel...perhaps you could phone me there."

"I'll see what I can do," Marnie promised, and kissing her good-night, Robert got back into the sleigh.

Going up the stairs Marnie hoped the family would not yet have returned from their evening activities. But Stella, who for once didn't seem to have had any engagement with her various friends in the village—apart from her trip to the Splendide with Robert—was stretched out on the fireside settee in a housecoat, drinking a nightcap of malted milk.

"Hello!" she greeted Marnie with animation. "Where's the dreamboat?"

"If you mean Robert Tallant, he's gone to his hotel. He's anxious to get out on to the ski slopes early. Perhaps," Marnie added on a sudden inspiration, "you could take him under your wing—show him where to hire skis and so on. He's an expert skier, by the way. I was wondering," she ended a little uncertainly, "if your father would take him on one or two of the more exciting runs."

"I'm sure he would be delighted to," Stella agreed enthusiastically. "And I'll look after him while you're on duty...if you'll trust me!" She laughed in a mocking way.

"I don't care what you do with him," Marnie burst out.

She flung herself into an armchair and stretched her feet out to the fire, the snow she had collected as she stepped from the sleigh melting on her shoes. "Whatever made you announce him as my fiancé when you brought him to the Splendide?" she demanded angrily. "He's nothing of the sort."

"I know," Stella giggled. "He told me he'd met you when he was in a nursing home for a week after a car accident. It all sounded fairly casual. Which figures. You'd hardly be wandering around nursing old ladies if you were engaged to be married to someone as fab as Robert Tallant."

"So...?" Marnie prompted icily.

Stella shrugged. "Oh, I thought I'd introduce a little drama into the situation. Especially when he said you'd suggested he might join you here, and when he got this unexpected week's leave he thought it might be a good idea."

"Better than going off to some ski resort where he knew nobody," Marnie muttered.

"Exactly."

"None of which makes him my fiancé."

Stella's face hardened, and she wasn't laughing anymore. "If you must know, it seemed to me rather a good idea to put a spoke into a beautiful friendship. You've been getting all tied up over David lately, haven't you? All of a tizzy because he asked you out to dinner tonight, getting yourself dressed up to kill. And you should have seen the look on your face when you were dancing with him." She shook her head in mockery. "Tut, tut, nurse! *Really!* Nor did my serious-minded cousin appear to be entirely indifferent."

She put her milk mug down on the floor at her side and sitting up on the couch hugged her knees. In the firelight the lines of her jaw were sharp, her mouth grim. "You deliberately broke it up between Rudi and me, didn't you?" she challenged. "Oh, I know mother egged you on, but that makes it all the more cold-blooded. It wasn't as if you gave a damn about Rudi; if you'd fallen for him there might have been some excuse. But no, you just wanted to spoil things for me out of pure spite. So tonight I returned the compliment, having a shot at breaking up whatever you imagine is going on between you and David. If you're hurt I'm *glad*!" Her voice rose shrilly. Then swinging her long legs off the couch she stood up, and with a curt, "Good night, Nurse Marnhem... happy dreams," she went off to her room.

Marnie felt a little sick. The sheer venom of Stella's attack was nauseating. She must know perfectly well that if there had been anything serious between herself and Rudi Praxmann the mild, mostly maternal interference to which it had been subjected would not have had the least effect. Nor had she been deeply wounded, finding rapid consolation in her friendship with the English boy, Paul. Yet the sight of Marnie dancing with David had reduced her to a state of sheer spite.

"You should have seen the look on your face when you were dancing with him!" Remembering the taunt, Marnie inwardly writhed. Had she really given herself away so obviously?

On her way to her room she looked in on her patient. The old lady was sleeping peacefully. How wonderful to be seventy-five, and finished with life's passionate turmoils, Marnie thought. Long after she got into bed she lay awake mulling over the evening's tragic confusion. David's offer of a job at the clinic; his whispered, "I don't want you to go away, Marnie." Then Stella's mischievous intervention. Would she ever be able to bring truth back into the situation—so cruelly twisted by the untimely arrival of Robert Tallant, and Stella's malicious use of it? How on earth could she explain it all away to David Harford, Marnie wondered. She could only wait fearfully for their next meeting... and take it from there.

There was no sign of him at Les Trois Chasseurs the next morning... nor the next. Marnie grew more and more edgy listening for his car, the sound of his footstep on the stairs.

"Young David is neglecting me," old Mrs. Rotherham grumbled, and phoned him at the clinic; only to be told he was being hindered by a spate of emergencies.

Were there really emergencies, or was David avoiding her, Marnie speculated. Perhaps even the drama of avoidance was too much to expect. He was busy, as he had said, the offer of a job at the clinic had been made more or less casually. If one English nurse didn't want it, there were plenty of other English nurses who would jump at the chance. Oh, she didn't know what to think anymore...only that her heart ached as it had never ached before.

Robert was very much in evidence at the Chasseurs, and the Rotherhams had succumbed to his charm. When he wasn't skiing with Mark and Denise, he was meeting them for dinner at the Splendide, Denise often insisting that Marnie should accompany them. "He is your friend, after all," she pointed out. "And soon enough you'll be leaving Arbois and its gaieties for the more humdrum scene in England."

Robert, in his element, declaring himself intoxicated with sun and snow and beautiful women, divided his favors equally between Denise and Marnie and Stella. And David consistently kept away. Dancing with Robert on the cramped floor of the Splendide...surely designed to induce the greatest degree of intimacy.... Marnie would wonder uneasily if he were somewhere on the crowded sidelines, watching her. But he never appeared.

Then one afternoon she caught sight of him in the village street. Unluckily—or did it matter—she was with Rudi, coming away from the ski school where she had had a specially encouraging afternoon. Gallantly carrying her skis, he had taken her arm while he emphasized some point in technique they were discussing. They must have appeared to be completely absorbed in one another. Then suddenly David was there—just across the street, giving her a cool little nod. After that she hadn't the faintest notion what she was saying to her ski instructor, or what he was saying to her. When she got back to the chalet she found old Mrs. Rotherham delighted because her beloved David had dropped in on her at last. Had he chosen the afternoon, instead of his usual morning hour, knowing she would be off duty, Marnie wondered bitterly.

"I told him that Robert Tallant is taking you on the Mont Blanc trip tomorrow and that you would be away most of the day. I insisted that I would be quite all right without you. After all, I reminded him, you haven't had a whole day off since you came here. But I needn't have fussed him with explanations. He didn't seem to mind where you went, or how long you were away. He knows I'm literally on my two feet again—not an invalid anymore."

He's finished with me, Marnie thought achingly. There would be no more talk of a job at the clinic. He was convinced she was all set to marry Robert Tallant—or at least deeply involved with him. Would she ever be able to explain to him how mistaken this impression was! But the longer it waited the more impossible such an explanation seemed to become. And this trip to Mont Blanc with Robert? Her impulse was to call it off, but pride intervened. Why should she let her foolish emotions influence her? If she had been silly enough to lose her heart to a man who had little interest in her that was no reason for letting the whole of her life turn sour on her. And the Mont Blanc trip was an experience it would be crazy to miss.

Chamonix at first glance was disappointing, a narrow street with shops on one side of it, darkened by overpowering mountains. But once in the cable car everything changed. The soaring flight in the early-morning sunshine was pure enchantment. She saw Mont Blanc, clothed now in morning light. As the tour continued the car, swinging vertically, floated over the needle-like peaks with their needle-like names: Aiguille de la République, Aiguille du Midi, Aiguille de Plan. It was on the plateau of the Plan that they lunched, sitting in the blazing noonday sunshine over a perfect French meal.

"The heat is fierce today on the upper snows," remarked the friendly waiter who lingered to comment on the exceptional weather after he had served their coffee. "The sort of unseasonable heat," he warned, "which can induce avalanches."

"Hardly a tactful prophesy to relay to sight-seeing tourists," Robert laughed when the waiter had left them. "Avalanches," he added knowledgeably, "are rare so early in the spring. It was in fact still winter, according to the calendar.

In the cable car descending to Chamonix he put his arm around her. Satiated with the sheer beauty of the sunshine, snow, food and scenery, Marnie did not resist him, and in the bus driving back to Arbois she let her head rest on his shoulder. He was, in many ways, a comfortable person to be with; warm, human, cheerfully unreliable and with absolutely no sense of guilt. It certainly made for a relaxed atmosphere.

"We must do the Jolyon run before I leave on Sunday," he urged. "If you can't get another whole day off we could do it in an afternoon."

She said she would love that. From the beginning the Mont Jolyon descent had stood out in her mind as the ultimate challenge. It would be a satisfaction if she could conquer it before she left Arbois.

The next morning David turned up at the Chasseurs bringing some special tablets for old Mrs. Rotherham to take back to England with her. In a matter of days now the family would be leaving. And what of her own plans, Marnie wondered. It was obvious that the clinic job was definitely off—but she couldn't just leave it like that, without a word of explanation. Though she hadn't much hope of it doing any good she wanted at least to try to clear up any misunderstanding David might be harboring about her relationship with Robert. She followed him when he left what was no longer the "sickroom."

"Might I have a word with you, Dr. Harford?" she asked, going with him to the head of the stairs.

"Yes, what is it?" he answered impatiently, continuing on his way down.

It was in the dark untidy lower hall with its clutter of skis and boots and coats that she stammered, "It's about the other night, when you took me to the Splendide. I haven't had an opportunity of thanking you for a very pleasant evening, and to say how sorry I was that you disappeared while I was talking to Robert Tallant, whose arrival came as a complete surprise to me. I would have liked to introduce him to you."

"Thank you," his tone was icy, "but that wasn't necessary. Naturally you would want to be alone with your fiancé who had just arrived. My presence at the moment of reunion would be of very secondary importance."

"But that's not how it was at all," Marnie returned breathlessly. "Robert Tallant is not my fiancé, merely a friend. I nursed him after a car accident he had."

"I see." The eyes regarding her were hard as stones. "A pretty intimate friend, I should have thought, if the way you greeted one another was any indication."

Robert's lover-like kiss in the bar of the Splendide, Marnie remembered sinkingly. And fiancé could mean so many things in France!

"Oh, that bear-like hug," she tried to laugh it off.

"That's just Robert's way. Actors are demonstrative people. It doesn't mean a thing, any more than the way they address everyone as 'darling'."

David shrugged, "It's not for me to speculate what your relationship to this chap may or may not be. I'm not interested. But if he's the sort of friend you like to have, typical of the circle in which you move in Seafleet and London, you would hardly be interested in taking a job at our quiet clinic. Arbois, out of season, wouldn't be your cup of tea at all. In summertime even the fascinating Praxmann would be absent, guiding and climbing in his Austrian mountains."

During this speech Marnie had colored. "If that's how you want to see me...." she began bitterly, and couldn't go on.

"It's not how I see you, but how Mère Générale would see you. I would hate to disappoint her. Naturally I feel responsible for having recommended you, giving the impression that you were—" he hesitated "—a much less frivolous person. What in fact we call in France *"une femme sérieuse."* Mère Générale is, I'm afraid, a little old-fashioned in these matters."

"And you share her standards, it seems," Marnie flung at him, anger coming to her rescue, delivering her from the humble attitude of apology that had been threatening.

"My standards don't come into it." There was a flicker of scorn in his glance. "Let's keep to the point, which is that I don't think you would fit very happily into the atmosphere at the clinic. You would be bored, out of place. So let's forget I ever suggested it."

Then he was gone. Blinded with sudden tears, she stumbled over a pile of boots and skates as she made for the stairs. What a prig the man was! Why on earth did she bother about him? He was right in one respect:

working with him at the clinic would be intolerable.

Now she was thankful that she was so soon to leave Arbois. With luck she might not see David Harford again. She would certainly do all she could to keep out of his way.

But the next afternoon Mrs. Rotherham announced in the middle of their customary sleigh ride that she had decided to drop in at her great-nephew's chalet, on the offchance of finding him at home. "I've seen so little of him lately," she said, "and by this time next week we shall be gone."

Marnie heard her with dismay. A social call on the unsociable, not to say coldly antagonistic David, was the last thing she wanted. She could only pray fervently that he would not be at home. But he was, and after the first moment of startled and obviously unwelcome surprise, he recovered himself and made the old lady welcome, ushering her into the small cozy lounge. Marnie, taken for granted in her subordinate position, followed meekly behind. It was only outward meekness, inwardly her spirit raged. As she helped Mrs. Rotherham out of her heavy fur coat and settled her in an armchair, her hands trembled.

"Will you do the honors, nurse!" David ordered rather than requested when presently the housekeeper appeared with the tea cart.

Nurse, Marnie thought bitterly. *I'm to be kept in my place from now on.* Well, so be it, she decided philosophically as she lifted the heavy silver teapot. The only way was not to care.

But suddenly, with an intolerable stab of pain, she was remembering how it had been between them the night they danced at the Splendide. He had talked to her of the brave early flowers that lifted their banners of color along the snow line. He had promised her mountain walks through the high meadows where in summer the grass would be deep and green, starred with scarlet poppies and big white daisies.

She realized, with a start, that David was speaking to her; asking her how she had enjoyed her trip to Mont Blanc. She answered inadequately that it had been "marvelous." How in this inimical atmosphere could she even begin to convey the wonder she had felt swinging in the lone cable car across the peaks of the great mountain range?

"It's a pity your Robert won't have time to take you to see the Mer de Glace," the old lady broke in. "The sea of ice, is the literal translation, though I always think river of ice would be more appropriate. David has taken a wonderful picture of it, sweeping in great white frozen curves through the gorges beyond Chamonix. I wish he would show it to you. It's with his best efforts in his study, along with the prize photograph for which he won a hundred pounds—*The Girl in the Green Valley*, it's called. Such a pretty title..." the old lady rattled on.

David stood up, giving Marnie a cryptic glance. There was mockery in it, and malice. "Would you like to see my 'etchings'?" he asked.

She rose to join him. "I'd love to!"

She followed him across the hall. The study was small and intimate, filled with books and pictures, deep now in afternoon shadow. He touched a switch as they entered and strip lighting brought the pictures to life. Mostly they were studies of skiers, in black and white. The Mer de Glace, perfectly composed, showed the jagged icebound flood, caught between summer banks of rhododendrons, a snow-covered panorama of mountain peaks in the background.

He pointed then to the single picture hanging in lonely distinction above his writing desk. It was a colored enlargement of a gentle country scene—no snow, no ice, no dramatic mountains.

Marnie caught her breath as she gazed up at the little green valley, sheltering its bee skeps, its flowers and its meandering amber-colored stream, her glance resting in final disbelief on the figure of the young girl who stood by the stream, looking down tenderly at the lamb in her arms.

"Hope Valley. *Our* valley!" she stammered, her heart beating as if it would burst. "How did you take it...when were you there?" And she remembered the lamb clearly; she had found the little creature trapped and alone in the valley—perhaps it had wandered away from its mother's side and slipped down the steep bank. She had gathered it up in her arms, pausing a moment by the stream to murmur words of comfort to it, before setting out to restore it to the flock. There in the picture above the desk she stood—immortalized—in her shabby cotton dress, her hair, more golden than it was now, tumbling around her slim shoulders, her face bent in tenderness above the lamb.

"The lucky snap that won me a hundred pounds," the doctor was saying. "Taken on that walking tour I had in Lammermuir. I told you I thought I'd seen you before...at a moment when you were too occupied with your picturesque errand of mercy to realize I was up on that high bank, looking down at you."

"Did you recognize me when I arrived here?" she asked through dry lips.

"Not at first. Your face teased me. I knew I'd seen it, or a face very like it, somewhere before, but it was a day or two before the penny finally dropped."

"I was younger then," she said on a note of unconscious regret. "Barely eighteen."

"And untouched, unspoiled. Seven years ago. A lot can happen in seven years," his voice was dry.

Seven years ago. Her thoughts seethed. She was remembering the night he had brought her home too early from the ball. They had sat by the fire, talking among other things of Stella's infatuation for her ski instructor. And David had said: "The crazy things one does when one is young. Would you believe it, I once, in my moonstruck days, fell in love with a photograph."

Was this the photograph? A question she could not possibly ask. She could only feel that it might have been and let the pain sweep over her.

"I didn't hang your green valley here in the place of honor above my desk because it had won me a hundred pounds, but because of what it meant for me," she heard David say. "Walking alone in those Lammermuir hills I think I first realized that I didn't want to be caught too deeply in the hurly-burly of modern life. The peace and tranquility of that beautiful unspoiled country appealed to me; the little gray stone farmhouses, the grazing sheep in the long rolling fields, the late northern spring coming to life all round me. Then at the heart of the valley there was the girl, her face filled with compassion for the little creature in her arms. I've looked at that face many times since."

There was a wistfulness in his tone that could have brought tears to her eyes, but she wouldn't let herself be moved by his romantic outpourings. That way lay too much pain.

"When did you first realize I was... the girl from the green valley?" she asked.

"It came to me gradually, mostly, I think, as I watched you with your patient. You had the same gentle compassion in your eyes when you looked down at her on her pillows, or made some small effort for her comfort, the same kind of tenderness you had that day for the lamb. You're a good nurse, Marnie."

"Thank you," she murmured, longing to say more, but not trusting herself. If she was such a good nurse could she not after all work in the clinic? But she wasn't going to plead with this adamant young man. He had idealized her, foolishly perhaps, in his youthful loneliness seven years ago. And her actual vigorous living presence had destroyed the shadowy image. The girl with the lamb wouldn't have been found dancing with an amorous ski instructor in a nightclub in the small hours of the morning. Nor would she have a brassy young London actor for her perhaps too intimate friend.

"I'm sorry," she offered, "if I've spoiled the picture for you by coming to life."

"You haven't spoiled it," he assured her with unnecessary vigor. "Nothing can spoil my girl in her valley. Because she doesn't live in a world of harsh reality. That June morning the girl and her lost lamb standing among the flowers by the stream were caught in a timeless moment." He gave her his strange impersonal look. "This picture that I treasure has nothing whatever to do with you."

"I see," she murmured. And as if the last word had been spoken between them he gestured toward the open door and ushered her from the room.

CHAPTER EIGHT

Now the shadow of imminent departure hung noticeably over the dwindling days. It was Friday. Robert would be returning to London on Sunday, and the Rotherhams on the following Tuesday, with Marnie accompanying old Mrs. Rotherham on her plane journey. It was all arranged. Marnie wrote to Jane at the agency telling her that the beautiful winter-sports assignment was folding up, and would she be looking out for another case for her as soon as possible. What she dreaded more than anything was having to hang around the hostel where she lived—idle, with too much time to think.

She also wrote her weekly letter home:

> One of my old patients, an interesting one, turned up the other day. Robert Tallant, the actor (I've told you about him before). He's taken me on one or two expeditions.

She tried to explain the beauty of that trip over Mont Blanc, and how generous the Rotherhams had been to her in the matter of free time. She added that the family had been good to her—she mentally excluded Stella—and that her stay in Arbois had been more like a holiday than work. But oddly she omitted any mention of the doctor who had engaged her services. Would she ever be able to tell her mother and sisters of the strange coincidence that had brought a medical student to Lammermuir...and then as a doctor and her employer to Arbois? The story of his prizewinning photograph of Hope Valley would galvanize them—but for the life of her she could not put any of this into her present letter home. Her sisters, she guessed, would seize on the mention of the glamorous Robert Tallant. Hadn't he been a larger-than-life figure at a recent Edinburgh Festival?

The sun was making its golden evening display over Mont Blanc as she returned from the village after posting her letters. She lingered on the way, savoring these last hours of magic in this enchanted place. There would be few more sunsets. Tonight Denise was giving a little farewell party to mark the approaching departure. Just Robert Tallant, and a Mr. and Mrs. Shawn, the couple with whom they had made many of their skiing expeditions. And of course, David. Mrs. Rotherham insisted, when he argued over the invitation, pleading work, that the evening would not be complete without him. Nor was Marnie to be forgotten. For once she found the friendliness of the Rotherhams embarrassing. If only they would leave her out of this family gathering! The thought of having to sit through a meal with David and Robert was daunting. Not that it would matter a whit to either of the men, she reminded herself bracingly, and went to help Mrs. Rotherham to dress.

Animated as a girl, the old lady discussed which of her evening frocks she would wear, and finally chose a soft petunia velvet. Marnie helped her into it and as a last touch of festivity pinned a matching velvet ribbon in the piled-up white hair. A lacy cream shawl for chilly shoulders completed the costume, and an ivory-handled cane for legs that were still not as steady as they might have been.

"And now what are you going to wear?" the old lady

challenged Marnie. "What about that nice floaty dress with the big gold flowers on it?"

The dress she had worn the evening David invited her to the Mardi Gras Ball.

"Isn't it a bit much for an evening *chez nous*?" Marnie suggested.

"No, it isn't. You wear it," the old lady ordered vigorously. "You look very pretty in it. It matches the goldy lights in your hair."

So Marnie did what she was told, and presently entered the firelit lounge with Mrs. Rotherham on her arm. With an instinct for an "entrance" the old lady stood still a moment on the threshold. Laughing, her son moved forward to meet her. "Mother!" he declared, "you put all the other women in the room in the shade... ribbons in your hair, and all!" He led her to the largest and most comfortable armchair, the other men in the room standing politely until she was seated.

"What a prima donna the theater has missed!" Robert exclaimed as he bowed to kiss her hand. "And Marnie," he added, turning to offer her his casual embrace. "You look marvelous this evening, darling!"

She felt her color rise... Robert's embraces and terms of endearment, which meant so little! She did not dare to glance in David's direction. But when they moved to the dining table at the far end of the long room she found herself sitting opposite him, with Robert significantly beside her. So markedly at all times the Rotherhams treated him as her special friend, and there was a touch of malice in Stella's remark during the meal that Marnie would be desolate when Robert had departed on Sunday.

"However," she added with a mock air of kindliness, "it won't be long before she's able to join him again in London. With luck she'll be in time for the first night of his play. You are counting on that, aren't you, Marnie?" It was so sweetly spoken!

Marnie murmured some kind of noncommittal reply, and it was Robert who took the matter up with a hearty, "Of course she'll be at my first night... in the very front row of the stalls... bringing me luck."

From across the table Marnie encountered David's cool, impersonal glance. There wasn't a flicker of feeling in it, indeed he looked mildly bored.

"Meanwhile," Robert was continuing, "I'm asking as a special favor if I may have her to myself tomorrow afternoon, my last day in Arbois. I want her to come with me on my farewell skiing trip on the Jolyon. She's going to make the run down with me, aren't you, Marnie?"

"I can try to," she replied, unable to think of any way of getting out of the arrangement, and indeed in her heart she was eager for this chance to conquer the great mountain *piste* before she left.

Robert turned to old Mrs. Rotherham. "Have I your permission, madame, to rob you of your charming companion for a few hours?"

"But of course," Mrs. Rotherham agreed at once.

"And yours, Doctor Harford?" Robert persisted, while Marnie inwardly writhed. It was all so falsely dramatic and unnecessary.

"It's quite immaterial to me how Nurse Marnhem spends her spare time," David answered coldly.

The seemingly endless meal went on. When the last liqueur and final cup of coffee had been disposed of Denise suggested they might drive down to Le Chat Noir and see the cabaret. But the old lady had had enough and was wise enough to agree when David advised bed. "Nurse will help you," he announced in an arbitrary way that made Marnie feel small. Which no doubt was his intention. Couldn't he see how unconcernedly Robert was accepting the fact that she wouldn't be accompanying them to the nightclub; saying an offhand good-night to her? "I'll call for you about two o'clock tomorrow afternoon, sweetie," he announced as he clattered down the wooden staircase in the wake of the general party.

Mrs. Rotherham insisted upon going out on the balcony of her bedroom to watch them drive off, Mr. and Mrs. Shawn in their own car, Stella in the backseat of the family car between Robert and David. Even after the small cavalcade had disappeared the old lady lingered, looking at the ghostly starlit white mountains. It was extraordinarily mild. "There's no frost tonight," Mrs. Rotherham marveled. "I hope the snow won't be too soft for your run down the Jolyon tomorrow. What a charmer your young man is!"

"He's not particularly my young man," Marnie pointed out as she guided the old lady back into her bedroom.

"He seems so fond of you," Mrs. Rotherham persisted, not to be done out of her romance.

"It's simply that he has a rather demonstrative way with him. Some theater folk are like that. Long ago I discovered that in spite of his affectionate mannerisms I don't mean anything special to him."

"Were you upset?"

"Not really," Marnie murmured evasively. "He's not quite my sort. I'd be far too dull for him."

"Nonsense," the old lady returned, emerging from her velvet dress with Marnie's help. "You couldn't be dull if you tried. You're far too pretty and charming. It would be more to the point if you said you're too serious for the merry Robert... he has that shallow, quicksilver temperament. It's what makes him such a good actor, I expect. And actors, I imagine, are not on the whole the most satisfactory of husbands."

"Who's talking about husbands?" Marnie laughed.

"I am," Mrs. Rotherham returned firmly. "Now

David... he would make a wonderful husband. I do wish he could find the right girl." The words were a little muffled, as Marnie was helping her into her warm cashmere nightgown. But the irrepressible voice went on. "Don't you think it was the most extraordinary coincidence that he should have taken that photograph of you with the lamb, all those years ago? And then suddenly you come out here and walk into his life!"

"He told you about the photograph?" Marnie asked a little breathlessly.

"The day after we'd been to his chalet to tea. I asked him what you'd thought of his prizewinning effort. And then it came out. It seemed he recognized you soon after you got here. You knew that, of course."

"Only recently," Marnie admitted, her voice barely under control.

"Well, I think it's all most romantic," Mrs. Rotherham declared firmly as she got into bed. "To think of you living in the beautiful little valley!"

"I didn't exactly live in it, but near it... it was part of our land."

"You know what I mean," the old lady asserted. "And David has always been so proud of that photograph, keeping it above his desk in his study. He must have looked up at it a hundred times. I've always fancied he was a little in love with that picture girl."

"Picture girls are pretty nonexistent things to fall in love with," Marnie said.

"But the valley is real enough, still there for you when you go home to it, with its bee skeps and its primroses. The mountains and their valleys here are terrifyingly beautiful... indeed terrifying is the word, for they can be very cruel. But your green valley looks so safe and so kind. A place of peace and love."

The old lady laughed at herself ruefully. "I am chattering a lot tonight, aren't I? It must be the celebratory champagne we had at dinner time." Snuggling down in her pillows, she drew a long, contented breath. "It's been such a happy evening." And then, holding out a hand to Marnie, "I shall miss you, my dear! You will come and see us sometimes in London, won't you?"

"Of course I will," Marnie promised, giving the frail old hand a little squeeze.

"And perhaps I can manage to have another illness next February. Nothing serious—but just enough to make it necessary for you to come with us again to Arbois."

Marnie laughed and switched off the light. "Now that *is* a champagne fantasy, if you like! You're not going to be ill again."

"But if ever I was," the old lady persisted, "Marnie, promise me you'll come to me if ever I need you!"

"Of course I'll come if you want me," Marnie ended it in her most matter-of-fact tone, and wondered if she ought to give her patient an extra sleeping pill. But a very short time afterward when she peeped into the room the old lady was peacefully sleeping.

THE NEXT AFTERNOON was disappointingly overcast. For the first time Marnie saw the village and its surrounding mountains starkly unlit by sunshine. Shadows in the valleys were gray instead of blue, the pine trees inky black and in the background the peaks of the Mont Blanc range looked sharp and cruel. But at least it was not cold, Robert pointed out as they walked to the *téléférique*. For once the cable car was not crowded. As they floated upward Robert put an arm around her. "It's been a wonderful week!" he whispered, his breath warm against her cheek. "I shall miss you terribly when I get back to London, Marnie."

She gave him a sardonic glance. Once such a remark would have put her in a flutter, but now she reduced it to its true value by pointing out that he had spent remarkably little of the wonderful week in her company. "You've been far too busy skiing with the Rotherhams and their friends... and I'm very glad you have. Skiing, after all, is what you came here for."

"Cruel Marnie!" His lips brushed her brow. "Once upon a time I thought you were a little in love with me."

"Once upon a time," Marnie retorted, "is the way fairy tales begin... and I've outgrown fairy tales."

"Oh, Marnie, *ma femme sérieuse*!" he said. "One should never outgrow fairy tales. They make life bearable."

The cable car ended its journey with the usual small jolt. Out on the wide plateau of trampled snow they fastened on their skis, moving off then at a leisurely pace, allowing the other passengers from the car to clear off ahead of them.

One of the gliding figures, a middle-aged man who was apparently one of Robert's nodding acquaintances on the ski slopes, slowed down to look back at him, saying, "I shouldn't hang about if I were you, Tallant. It looks as if we might be going to have a spot of snow."

"Now what's he on about?" Robert growled as the man hurried on ahead. "We're not going to hang about, but I would just like to put you through your paces before hurling you down that difficult slope. There's a miniature run on the right-hand side of this track that would do for the purpose. I just want to make sure you've got your braking and stemming right."

Marnie followed him along the way she had come that afternoon when she had been searching for Stella. The white wilderness stretched all around her, and once more she felt the tremor of fear it aroused in her. How dreadful it would be if one were to be really lost in that white waste!

"Come on!" Robert rallied her. "Can't you put a little more speed into it?"

She had never skied with him before. Perhaps he was finding her less adept than he had hoped. "If I'm hindering you perhaps I ought to pack it in and go back to Arbois in the next cable car," she suggested.

If he had agreed, she was to think afterward, the whole course of her life might have been different. But he was rallying her with a vigorous: "Nonsense! Of course you aren't hindering me. You're perfectly capable of doing the Jolyon. But just to be on the safe side we'll practice our braking here."

They went over some simple exercises several times. And this, too, Marnie was to realize afterward, was another factor that was to influence the course of the strange events that were to follow. If they had gone straight down the Jolyon instead of playing around with exercises everything would have turned out differently. Meanwhile the clouds overhead thickened and the air darkened, until even Robert agreed they had better be on their way.

There were no other skiers in sight when they reached the curve in the track where the descent of the Jolyon began.

"Just keep close behind me and follow my lead," Robert said. "Don't let yourself swerve off the track toward the pine trees."

He leaned down to test his ski bindings and then Marnie's, and it was as he straightened up again that what Marnie thought was a distant clap of thunder rumbled in the air. She saw Robert stiffen, with a sudden animal alertness, his face gray in the untimely twilight, his eyes wide. The rumbling that Marnie took to be thunder grew louder, seeming to draw near.

"An avalanche!" The words came from Robert in a

hoarse shout. "Quick, Marnie, quick!" He seized hold of her hand and was pulling her toward him, but she lost control of her skis and almost fell. By the time she had righted herself some terrible force had separated them, sweeping Robert away down the *piste*, and herself off in a different direction. A dreadful roar filled the air, drowning Marnie's cry for help. There was a froth of snow now, like breakers in a rough sea, rising around her knees. Turning her head with a last cry to Robert, she could see him far below, being half tossed, half carried down the side of Mont Jolyon by a great wave of snow. Then he was out of sight, while she herself went floundering in the direction the force of the snow was carrying her. *An avalanche!* Robert's words came back to her and her terror rose.

Later she was to realize that she had been caught mercifully on the edge of the avalanche, but for the moment there was nothing but her mounting fear. There were small rocks and branches of trees mixed up with the snow now, and like a river the white cruel wave spread out, carrying her she knew not where. The snow was up to her waist now, the icy cold penetrating her clothing, the weight of the snow almost bringing her down. But she knew that whatever happened she must resist collapse, keep moving. Then she realized that both her skis had gone—she had long since lost her poles. And all the time it was growing darker and darker.

Presently it began to snow, the clouds of snow pressing down on the mountains blotting them out. Marnie moved on doggedly through the thickening curtain of snowflakes. They clung to her hair, blinded her eyes; with awful gentleness and deadly persistence they lay upon her lips, her eyelids.

How long she struggled on she didn't know. Only the horror of stopping, of abandoning herself to this nightmare of white shadowy landscape and whirling snow kept her going. If only she had some idea where she was going! If only it wasn't growing darker and darker—with genuine nightfall now as well as with the snow clouds. It seemed to her that she had been pushing her way through this waist-high snow for hours.

Her bewildered thoughts turned to Robert. Had he been caught in the main path of the avalanche? Or would his rapid descent and expert ski control have saved him? It came to her that when she had last seen him he still had his ski poles and had been using them. And by the way he moved he must still have had his skis.

She didn't ask herself if in that split second when the avalanche struck he could have held her hand more firmly, dragging her along with him. She could only hope that he was safe, and be thankful that in her clumsiness and slowness she had not held him back.

But coherent thought was rapidly deserting her. There was only the snow left in the whole world now, and her own panting, plodding figure pushing through it, her legs weakening, her powers failing with every step.

Just when she made her last effort she didn't know; only that she was sinking down into the snow and it was strangely soft and welcoming. Just to step struggling against it was a vast relief. A gentle lethargy began to creep over her, numbing her senses. Instinctively she knew that she ought to fight against it—that to succumb to her strange sleepiness would be fatal. But she couldn't resist any longer. She had reached the end. Remorselessly the soft arms of the snow enveloped her...and she knew no more.

CHAPTER NINE

THERE WERE NO DREAMS in that snow-drugged state, no sensations, no warmth or cold, no thoughts of life or death. Just a merciful nothingness. The hands clutching at her shoulder, dragging her clear of the drift in which she lay, were scarcely a disturbance. Then she was being jerked up into a sitting position, the hands were beating against her cheeks—cheeks so numb with cold that the onslaught might have been an attack made on insensate wood. Her head lolled against the rough snow-wet fabric of a parka, something was being forced between her lips. As the fiery liquid touched her tongue she swallowed convulsively and felt it running through her, kindling her very veins, bringing her to hazy consciousness.

Someone was bending over her, kneeling beside her in the snow. Now the hands that had so roughly roused her from her torpor were gently wiping the snow from her face, her hair. And the whirling blizzard had ceased. Light came from a rift in the clouds, even a sunset gleam of gold.

Cradled in the arms that held her, Marnie looked up into the face of the man bending over her. "David!" she whispered through lips that felt numb and swollen.

The memory of her plight began to return to her, the terror of her moments alone in the path of the avalanche, and she trembled. A sobbing breath tore her chest.

"It's all right, Marnie. You'll be okay now. I'm here!"

her rescuer assured her. "But I've got to get you out of this. Do you think you can walk? Here, have some more brandy."

There was the fiery liquid again, the sense of warmth running through her, reviving her a little. But when David took his supporting arm away she slumped sideways and would have fallen back into the snow if he had not caught her.

"Marnie!" he called, as if she were at a great distance. "You've got to try to overcome your drowsiness. Come along now... take a deep breath. Make yourself move."

There was snow on the dark peaked cap he wore, snow on his shoulders. She saw his skis standing a little way behind him, planted deeply in the snow so that they stood upright like bare tree stems. His face was clearer to her now: lean jawed and anxious, his eyes all dark centers regarding her... full of concern. She lifted a hand and touched his cheek, hardly knowing that she made the gesture. "David, dear David!" she whispered. And then on a glimmer of stirring self-consciousness thought... *I shouldn't have said that!*

Somehow it was the small surge of embarrassment that made her try to struggle to her feet, and instantly his arm was around her, helping her.

He said, "There's a refuge hut about a hundred feet higher up... if you think you can make it." She murmured her acquiescence, and leaning against him for support, put a tentative foot in front of her. It sank deep into the snow, but she persevered, forcing herself along, vaguely aware of the effort she was making. She only knew that David wanted her to move. Her mind began to clear and the wonder of his presence pierced its cloudiness.

"How did you manage to find me?" she asked, through her painful, strangely unmanageable lips.

"We'll talk about that later," he told her. "Save all your energies now for the climb to the hut. You're doing splendidly." His voice rang with exaggerated pride—as though he were encouraging a child.

The brief glimmer of sunset light had gone now, the clouds closing down on them once more. It grew dark. The hut that was a hundred feet up might have been a thousand feet distant—the way to it seemed endless. Raising her head, Marnie peered through the gathering gloom for some sight of it, but there was only the sharpening incline before them, its whiteness blurred in the dwindling light. Her brief burst of strength began to fail her. To press on seemed impossible. Her legs felt weak, her breath in her chest hurt, her heart pounded against her ribs. But at all costs she must keep going: David expected it of her. By some miracle he had come to her rescue. If she collapsed now into the snow what could he do? To carry her uphill to that invisible hut might well be a feat beyond his strength.

Doggedly she struggled on, until her vision dimmed, and her senses began to fail. It seemed to her at last that she was swimming, weightless, in a white glimmering sea of snow. Then her knees buckled under her, a wave of dizziness blotting out what was left of her awareness. As if from a great distance she could hear David's voice calling her, rallying her.

The next thing she knew was that she was being half carried, half dragged over the threshold of the dark hut, and deposited on the bare wooden floor. David was flashing a torch, and with returning consciousness she followed its beam as it picked out a table, bunk beds, shelves, a wide hearth on which pine logs were piled ready for lighting. An oil lamp hung from the low ceiling. Lethargically she watched while David lit it. She tried to rise to her knees, and in an instant David was beside her, lifting her in his arms and helping her on to the lower of the two bunk beds. It was bliss to sink back on to the pillow, her half-frozen hands feeling the roughness of the blanket David was wrapping around her.

He said, "I'll have the fire going in a few minutes, and then I'll be able to get you a hot drink."

He had taken off his cap and his thick dark hair lay damply against his brow.

"I'm sorry I collapsed on the way up," she offered weakly. "How on earth did you get me here?"

"I'm afraid I had to haul you rather unceremoniously the last few yards..." He was tucking the blankets around her as he spoke, his face tense with concern, his eyes bright with a tenderness she could hardly believe in. Yet it was there. All part of this strange experience—half-dream, half-reality. It was in the reality that physical pain lurked...the tingling of her hands as warmth and life began to come back into them. But not even pain could quite destroy the dream that was David bending over her, the lamplight a halo behind his head.

She hardly knew what she did, only that inevitably it was part of the dream that when she lifted her arms around his neck and whispered, "Oh, David, dear, dear, David!" he let himself be drawn by her embrace, until his warm breath was on her face and his lips came down on her poor frost-burned mouth. Gently then he disengaged himself, putting her arms under the rough brown blanket. A moment later he was kneeling before the hearth, and soon there came the crackling of kindling wood. Drowsily she watched as he took a bucket and went out into the snow. It was snow, she saw on his return, that he put into the iron kettle, which hung on a chain over the fire.

Lying there between sleeping and waking Marnie knew a strange disembodied happiness. Instinctively, unformulated by words, lay the knowledge that she had been close to death out there in the snowy wilderness. And now every moment of the life given back to her was precious. Even the increasing pain in her hands and feet was a part of the sheer relief of being safe in this refuge. She saw David opening a cupboard, producing crockery, a teapot. And soon he was holding a mug of hot sweetened tea to her lips. She winced away from it, as it burned her sore lips. He was all doctor then, finding remedies in a small cupboard marked with a red cross: balm for her sore lips, a pain-killing tablet to ease her aching limbs. Taking off her ski boots, he rubbed her cold, wet feet, wrapping them more closely in the blankets.

After that David was sitting by the fire with his own mug of hard-earned tea. Leaning forward, his elbows on his knees, he gazed into the flames, looking oddly at peace and contented, as if the magic of the strange adventure had caught him, too, in its spell. Warmth, blessed warmth began to circulate. The air was full of the resinous scent of the burning logs, and there was no sound but the flickering of the flames, the occasional sputter of sparks from the living wood.

Lying back on her pillow Marnie felt as if time had ceased. The world had retreated. Here in this lost little hut there was only herself and David. Foolishly, she wished they might stay like this forever. She would have liked to go on savoring the moment, luxuriating in it, but drowsiness was not far off—induced by the warmth, the tranquilizing tablet and inevitable exhaustion after her grim adventure. And soon she slept.

This time it was a natural, healing sleep. When she woke, refreshed, it was with all her senses alert. But for a few moments she was too comfortable and warm to move. It was enough to lie still watching David dozing in his chair by the fire. Poor David, what a time she had given him! Reluctantly she let the events of the afternoon come back to her—setting out with Robert for the Jolyon, delaying over that skiing lesson so that they did not reach the start of the descent until the avalanche was upon them. What followed was still confused in her memory—all but the one incredible miracle; David's appearance on the scene.

As if becoming aware of her wakefulness she saw him stir and rouse himself. Stretching his arms above his head, he yawned vastly, then he leaned forward and put some fresh logs on the fire.

"What time is it?" she asked, and somehow the matter-of-fact little question sounded very natural and comforting in the cozy firelit hut.

David glanced at his watch and said it was close on midnight. "You've had a splendid sleep," he told her.

"I know. And I feel all the better for it. Quite recovered, in fact."

She moved as though to get out of her bunk, but sharply he told her to stay where she was. "You've had quite a shock one way and another, and as your doctor I'm ordering you to rest." But already she had discovered she was not quite as strong as she had thought and gladly sank back onto her pillow.

"I've had my supper," he said, "and now you ought to have something. There's some tinned ham here, if you think you can manage it."

When he put the food before her she found she was hungry and in spite of the chapped lips she managed to eat some of the meat and a slice of crispy bread. There was more hot tea to follow. Hot sweet tea, a simple remedy for shock, he said. Was she in a state of shock, she wondered—if so it was quite a pleasant condition, except that her head was still a bit muzzy.

"Do all refuge huts have food and fire and medicines?" she wanted to know. David told her they did, most of them being used not only in winter, but in the summer by climbers.

"Sometimes they use it as a base, returning to it for the night. There's a rough lean-to through that door—" he indicated a latched door "—where there are the usual facilities. So that if a rescue party doesn't catch up with us you'll be able to spruce up in the morning when I go down to the village for help."

"You mean I won't be able to ski down with you?" she asked.

"Of course you won't. It's absolutely out of the question. They'll take you down on the sled stretcher."

"The blood wagon!" she protested. "Surely that won't be necessary?"

"You'll soon find it is when you start to move about. You had a pretty close call out there in the blizzard." He passed his hand across his eyes as if he were wiping away the sight of her lying in the snowdrift. And she was remembering how in her return to consciousness she had called out his name in love. He had not repulsed her, even touching her poor frozen lips with his own—a kiss of life perhaps rather than a kiss of love. It could hardly have been that. An impulse, which had come to him in the extremity of the moment. Naturally he had been relieved when he found her. Supposing he had not? She thrust the alternative away from her with a shudder.

"How did you find me?" she asked. "What were you doing on the Jolyon in the middle of the awful snowstorm?"

"I was looking for you, of course," he answered simply. "As soon as warning of the approaching avalanche came over the village loudspeaker I hurried off to try to reach you. I knew you'd planned to make the descent on the Jolyon with Tallant and that you would have set out some time before the avalanche threatened. I found the cable car had packed up, so I started to climb, keeping well to the east, out of the predicted path of the avalanche. I was part of the way up when I saw Tallant, schussing down the Jolyon piste, which was still open. I could hear the roar of the avalanche coming from the west, where you must have been. I could hardly believe that he'd left you." His tone was icy and filled with scorn. "But that, it seems, is what he did."

Now the firelit peace of the little hut was shattered.

"He tried to take me with him," Marnie offered hurriedly, coming to Robert's defence. "But I stumbled. The snow pushed us apart. It was like a strongly running tide in the sea. He couldn't help being separated from me."

"If I'd been in his place I wouldn't have let you go." The words came a little unsteadily. "No avalanche in existence would have sent me skiing down that hillside, leaving you alone to face the incalculable danger."

"Robert isn't a mountaineer like you are. He hasn't got your experience of this part of the world and its storms."

"You can still make excuses for him?"

"I'm only trying to be fair to him."

"This man who pretends to be your friend, something more than a friend, but in a moment of crisis deserts you!" He stood up and kicked savagely at the logs on the hearth.

Marnie turned her head away, tears on her cheeks. "You don't understand." The whisper was half a sob.

"He's not worth your tears, Marnie."

She forced herself to face him. "I'm not crying for him, but because it's all such a muddle. You've got everything all wrong and I don't know how to explain it to you."

But here in the solitude of the mountain hut in the

middle of the night the words began to come to her. She found herself relating how she had at first been too easily attracted to the young actor, misled by his charm.

"The poor little country girl from Scotland," she mocked herself. "But I soon realized the charm was...wholesale...not for individual consumption." There was no bitterness in her little spurt of laughter.

"Yet you asked him to join you here." David pursued relentlessly. Did it matter to him that much? "He came here as your fiancé."

Oh, mischievous tongue of Stella! Marnie groaned inwardly.

"He was never in any sense of the word remotely my fiancé." She sat up in her bunk with sudden vigor. "As for asking him to join me here—that was simply a mindless quip I made when he phoned me the day I was leaving. It had no meaning in it whatever. I was in a hurry just setting out for the airport and I said, more to get rid of Robert than anything else, 'See you on the ski slopes.'"

Despair engulfed her. Weariness flooded every corner of her being.

"And when he actually did arrive in Arbois," the merciless voice went on, "you seemed delighted to see him. In fact from the embrace you exchanged it appeared to be quite a lovers' meeting."

"He was never my lover," Marnie cried, and turning her face to the wall gave way to her weeping.

Coherent conversation ended, David delving into the medical box once more to produce another tranquilizer. "I shouldn't have let you talk," he reproached himself. And even as he spoke weariness and the tranquilizer combined were producing their effect and Marnie let the drowsiness engulf her. How long she slept this time she did not know, but when she awoke she was alone. Feeling refreshed, she got out of her bunk and went to the door of the hut, opening it onto a lost world of snow and ice. In the distance she could see David, plodding over the wastes to where he had left his skis; they were dimly visible in the pale twilight of a setting moon. The air, sharp on her face, increased her alertness. Stars like points of ice glittered in the cloudless sky. It was awesomely silent. A world entranced, unearthly, forbidding as some uninhabited planet. And it was here she had passed the long night with David, safe in the kind little hut. It might have been so wonderful, but concerned as he had been for her, marvelous in his courageous journey to rescue her, he was still remote. It was a doctor, not a man who had laid her gently on the bunk, taking off her wet ski jacket, wrapping her in blankets. It was a doctor who had warmed her back to life with his hands, bringing her out of the deadly snow sleep.

Going back into the hut she found the lean-to with its primitive facilities, illuminated only by the reflection from the oil lamp in the main room. But there was a clean comb and brush on a small table over which hung a blotched mirror. It was a relief to tidy her thick tumbled hair and generally refresh herself.

Afterward she was glad to sink back onto her bunk. She was much weaker than she had thought, and strangely shivery. It came to her for the first time that the Rotherhams would be worried sick over her misadventure—for no doubt Robert would have gone straight to them with his story of catastrophe when he reached Arbois last evening. And Robert himself...how would he be feeling? Not knowing what had happened to her after his last sight of her as he fled in the path of the avalanche. Disturbing thoughts. It was a relief when David at that moment returned, stamping the snow from his boots on the threshold. She saw him prop his skis up against the outside frame of the door. A rescue party was on its way, he told her. He had spotted them toiling with the heavy sled up the steep slopes and had signaled them with his torch. There had been fresh snow while she slept, she learned, and this no doubt had delayed the arrival of the men who had come to look for them.

Methodically he began to put the hut in order, damping down the fire, washing the crockery they had used, emptying the teapot. "One is supposed to leave the hut as one finds it," he explained. And presently he was shoveling the hot wood ashes out onto the snow, and when the hearth was safely cleared he fetched fresh logs from the useful lean-to, and laid them ready for the next travelers to kindle.

She ought to be helping him, Marnie thought guiltily. But the drug he had given her was still working and she could hardly keep awake. She was dozing when a stamping of snow-clogged feet and a rush of masculine voices wakened her. The rescue team had arrived. Perhaps it was not surprising that Rudi Praxmann was among them, but Marnie was oddly dismayed when she saw him. He hailed her effusively , his white teeth flashing in his handsome mahogany tanned face. "The fright you have given us!" he reproached her. "Your English friend, Monsieur Tallant, alerted us, half out of his mind with worry over your safety."

"It might have been more to the point if he hadn't abandoned Miss Marnhem in the path of an advancing avalanche," David put in coldly.

"It wasn't quite like that," Marnie began, but was too weary to continue with the repetitive argument. If David wanted to think the worst of Robert's behavior there was nothing more she could do about it. If only she didn't feel so hot and cold all over and could stop this wretched shivering!

There was a brief interval while the rescue party rested, eating the sandwiches they had brought with them and drinking the brandy, or whatever it was in the flasks they carried. As they ate they spoke of the difficulties they had had in their ascent, and how they had had to improvise shelter for a time in the pine woods, while the worst of the night's snow storm swept over them. It would have been a poor lookout for the *mademoiselle*, Marnie heard them say, if the doctor had not reached her. There could have been only one end to a night spent in the mounting snowdrifts. A conclusion that would not have been expressed, Marnie realized, if they had not thought that she was asleep.

At last they were ready to leave, and Marnie, protesting that she would rather try to walk, was carried to the blood wagon. She was oddly reluctant to leave the warmth and comfort of the refuge hut, where she had spent so many hours alone with David. He had come to her out of the snow and darkness. He had saved her life.

CHAPTER TEN

IT WAS A LONG bumpy journey down the steep mountainside. Though the rescue team did their best to go carefully, the stretcher on its steel runners recorded every jar from the uneven snow, frozen hard in some places, dropping into ruts in others. It seemed to take hours. At intervals Marnie drifted into a state of semiconsciousness. But at last, in the first light of dawn there was the reassuring bulk of Les Trois Chasseurs before them, with Mark Rotherham standing in the doorway to greet them.

"Thank God you've got here at last!" he cried, hurrying forward to peer at Marnie on her stretcher. But she was already struggling to free herself from her coverings and sit up.

"Oh, Marnie, my poor child!" Mark greeted her.

"I'm all right," she assured him, a little too vigorously.

"The night we've had! Not one of us went to bed, or had a wink of sleep. Poor Robert, who came straight to us after his escape from the avalanche, was in a terrible way about you. At last about an hour ago we persuaded him to go back to his hotel and get some rest. I promised I'd phone him as soon as there was any news from the rescue team...." He was rattling on, garrulous with relief, while he helped Marnie to her feet. Rudi and David were also hovering helpfully.

"I'm perfectly okay," she repeated, on a wave of

strength born of exasperation. "Coming home like this on a stretcher!" she exclaimed. "I'm ashamed of myself. There isn't a thing wrong with me." It was true that for the moment she was filled with a spurious energy, her sense of guilt goading her on. She who had come to his house as nurse and comforter, now being brought to it as a helpless casualty! And she had kept her employers up all night, worrying about her. Heaven alone knew what the hours of anxiety would have done to old Mrs. Rotherham.

Thrusting David's offered arm aside, she hurried into the hall and began to climb the stairs. Even then her strange burst of energy did not fail her. Whatever happened she must recover her position as capable and reliable Nurse Marnhem. What she had done to the Rotherhams by her night's escapade was unthinkable.

Vaguely she was aware that the rescue team was refusing the drinks Mark Rotherham was offering them. They had been out all night, she heard the leader say. Now they must go to their respective homes and prepare for the day's work. Fresh guilt assailed her.

In the lounge with the curtains still drawn Denise and Stella awaited her—both in their dressing gowns and looking haggard from lack of sleep. Denise, near to tears with relief, put an arm around Marnie's shoulder. "What you must have been through!" she murmured, her eyes on the girl's swollen lips and blotched face. Stella simply stared and said nothing.

"Tell us what happened if you feel able," Denise urged when she had settled Marnie on the settee by the newly replenished fire. "How did David find you?"

Marnie's answer was vague. How hot the room was, and yet how cold. The shivering had begun again. Somehow she must hide from the Rotherhams how ill she was beginning to feel once more. And they must never know that when David came upon her she had been unconscious in a snowdrift, perilously near the fatal sleep of the snowbound.

Meanwhile David, who had gone straight to Mrs. Rotherham's room, appeared now to say that she had been badly shaken by her night of anxiety—but was overjoyed to hear that Marnie was safe. "I've given her a sedative and she should be allowed to sleep as long as she will," he ended. It seemed to Marnie that every word he spoke was a reproach to her.

"I'll go to Mrs. Rotherham ," she began, moving to struggle up from the couch. But David put an arresting hand on her shoulder.

"You'll do nothing of the sort. She'll be asleep in a few minutes, and as for you, the sooner you follow her example and get to bed for some real shut-eye the better."

But she had no intention of going to bed, Marnie asserted a little drunkenly. She had begun to feel very muzzy again, but somehow she must keep up appearances. And now Marie the housekeeper was entering the lounge with a cart on which stood a heartening pot of steaming coffee and a plate of sandwiches. She added her congratulations and commiserations to the wanderer returned and thanked *le bon Dieu* that the avalanche had not been a serious one. Most of it had crashed down on the far side of the Jolyon, the postman delivering the morning mail had just told her.

"So I was in no real danger," Marnie declared defiantly, ignoring blizzards and snowdrifts. Somehow she must get the atmosphere back to normal.

"It was simply that there was a bit of a snowfall and I lost my skis," she summed it up. "Then David miraculously appeared and took me to the refuge hut."

"It wasn't quite as simple as you're making it sound," David interjected tiresomely.

"Anyway, I feel fine," Marnie asserted doggedly, and forced some hot coffee through her painful lips.

The phone rang. Denise sprang to her feet. "That will be Robert," she guessed. It was. She held the receiver away from her, having called into it: "She's all right, Robert; she's here. She'll speak to you. . . ."

Marnie's heart gave a violent lurch at the thought of having to talk to Robert at this emotional moment with David and all of them listening. She couldn't forget the bitter way David had spoken of Robert.

Somehow she made her way over to the sideboard on which the phone awaited her and took the receiver from Denise's hand. "Robert? It's Marnie. I'm all right."Not a sensational opening, considering all there could have been to tell. It evoked a whole flood of thanksgiving and self-reproach from Robert. But he did not press for the more lurid details, which he must have known existed, concentrating instead on his own agony of mind after he had lost sight of her. How he had ever got back to the village, he would never know.

She tried to soothe him, aware that David was glaring at her from the far side of the room. Her senses whirled, her legs were weak. The shivering was almost uncontrollable by now, but somehow she must keep up the façade of well-being.

"Of course you must catch the morning plane from Geneva," she was saying in answer to Robert's anxious remarks about the importance of his return to London.

With a show of reluctance he was agreeing that this was what he would have to do. "But nothing would have dragged me from Arbois until I knew you were safe," he assured her. He would see her soon in London. "We'll celebrate on the first night of the play," he announced with blithe disregard for her nursing commitments. And if she knew anything about first-night celebrations he would be far too preoccupied with the theatrical celebrities such an occasion produced to have much time for the little nurse from Seafleet. But she made the appropriate acquiescent sound, wished him "Good luck and goodbye," and hung up. How she got back to the settee she didn't know. The room was whirling around her.

"So the bold Mr. Tallant couldn't even take the trouble to walk over here to see for himself how you are before setting off for his dazzling London triumphs," David was saying sardonically.

"There wouldn't have been time if he's to catch his plane," Marnie said, and overcome with dizziness buried her face in her hands. Would David think she was grief-stricken at the thought of Robert's departure?

"You're not so spry as you're making out," he said, hurrying to her side. Gently he lifted one limp wrist and took her pulse. "It's bed for you at once, young lady," he ordered. "And you'll stay there until I come back this afternoon to see how you are."

Obediently she struggled to her feet, but was so unsteady that Denise and David between them had to help her to her room. It was unfortunate that they had to go through Mrs. Rotherham's room in order to reach it. Not yet quite under the influence of the sedative the doctor had given her, she started up at the sight of Marnie being practically carried to her bed, and began pouring out agitated questions, Denise doing her best to reassure her. But it was so bad for her to be disturbed in this way.

Once more Marnie was filled with guilt. She had failed her patient, failed David, failed everybody. Just because she had gone skiing with Robert Tallant. Not because he was important to her, but because she had so badly wanted to make the testing descent of the Jolyon before leaving Arbois. But David wouldn't believe that. Blundering words of apology poured from her as she sank down onto her bed, a thermometer thrust between her lips effectively silencing her. Her temperature, it emerged, had soared. Which settled once and for all any nonsense about being perfectly fit and only needing a short sleep before resuming duties.

"Keep warm," David counseled. "Have plenty of hot drinks and I'll be back later on to see how you are."

It was a timeless day that followed, Marnie waking and sleeping, tossing restlessly through a series of nightmare dreams in which she struggled against white waves of soft smothering snow. Her limbs ached and there was a dull pain in her side. At intervals Denise appeared with the prescribed hot drinks. Down in the village the church bell rang. It was Sunday, Marnie remembered. And on Tuesday they were due to fly back to England.

"You'll never be fit for the journey," Denise mourned when Marnie spoke of it.

"Of course I will," Marnie declared desperately. "I've simply caught a chill from hanging about in the snow last evening, losing my silly way." Inwardly, however, she guessed it was something more than a chill and might have worried about it, only that she couldn't keep awake.

When David returned in the afternoon armed with his stethoscope, he diagnosed pneumonia, brought on by exposure. "It's nothing to worry about in these days of ever more effective antibiotics," he reminded Marnie. "We'll have you right as rain very soon. But I'm afraid there'll be no question of your returning to England on Tuesday. I'll make arrangements for you to be admitted to the clinic for a few days."

So there she was a couple of hours later, back on a stretcher again, being carried ignominiously out of the house and deposited in the ambulance that would take her to the other side of the valley. It was a dreadfully humiliating way to have to say goodbye to the Rotherhams and to poor old Mrs. Rotherham, who, still somewhat distraught by last night's worry, looked smaller and more fragile than ever. Marnie felt once more that she had hopelessly disgraced her profession. There were tears on her cheeks as the ambulance went on its lumbering way over the snowy roads and along the gay village street. Through the window at her side Marnie could see the carefree holidaymakers, their skis slung jauntily over their shoulders, making for the ski slopes and the *téléferique.* She felt more than ever an outcast and a failure.

But once installed at the clinic the calming routine of hospital life took over. Two Sisters in their white religious habits helped her into bed and gave her the tablets prescribed for her. Her room was small, but didn't seem enclosed, with its wide French windows open to the view of the valley and Mont Jolyon beyond. Lying propped up on her pillows Marnie could let her glance wander right out into the sparkling white space where the skiing slopes rose to meet the dark shadow of the distant pine trees, dense as black fur against the purity of the snow. She could, she thought, almost make out the high plateau where she had lost her way, and shuddering she recalled the terror of the avalanche. Though she tried not to dwell on it, there were moments when she remembered all too vividly her struggle against the snow, and how in the end she had let herself sink into that treacherous whiteness to sleep, a sleep that could so easily have lasted forever, if David had not come to her.

Dear David, with whom she had been unwise enough to fall in love. And now she was here as his patient instead of being back in England where she ought to be. The sense of reprieve brought a small sense of triumph. Just a few more days before David Harford passed out of her life.

Meanwhile he appeared at intervals at her bedside, very professional and aloof in his white coat, one of the Sisters invariably in attendance upon him. Marnie had to remind herself that the concern in his eyes and the gentleness of his touch were purely clinical.

Almost a week went by; the kindly Sisters coming and going, the sun rising and setting across the snow. . .and David's daily visits as the high spot to be looked forward to. Even if each one seemed more formal than the last.

I'm just a battleground of viruses and antibiotics to him, she thought sadly, and wished the same antibiotics didn't make her feel so sick, upsetting her liver. The liver, she decided, must be the seat of the soul, for when it was out of order the whole world was out of tune.

Then suddenly on the sixth morning she awoke feeling whole and complete and clear once more. For the first time food tasted delicious and she enjoyed her breakfast of honey and croissants and perfectly made coffee, topped with whipped cream.

The next day she was allowed to dress and sit in a lounge chair out on the balcony. And David did not pay his usual morning visit. Sadly she concluded that he was finished with her as a patient. But all at once in the late afternoon there he was; alone this time, having discarded his escorting Sister somewhere en route. Taking the small upright chair from her bedside, he joined her on the balcony with a leisurely air. When his fingers felt for her pulse they closed over her whole hand, holding it tightly. "You're really your old self again," he marveled. "The virus is vanquished!"

"Thanks to you," she told him.

"And the antibiotics," he reminded her reverently. "In a few days they've accomplished what would have taken week after doubtful week not so long ago in the annals of medical history."

"I was meaning something more than antibiotics when I thanked you." Her voice faltered. "Oh, David, it was such a miracle... the way you came to me that day I was lost in the blizzard... and the snow was almost the victor."

She moved her fingers convulsively within his grasp.

"I had to find you, Marnie," he said simply. It couldn't have been otherwise. I came to you as inevitably that day on Mont Jolyon as I did on the day long ago when I first saw you in the Lammermuir valley."

He laid her hand back on her lap, giving it a little pat. "Does it ever seem to you that there's a pattern in life at certain moments?" he asked strangely. "That things don't happen by chance?" And without waiting for her answer, he went on. "There's so much I have to say to you, and to ask of you, Marnie. But not here... not now. In a day or two—tomorrow perhaps if you're well enough—I might take you for a short drive; some time in the afternoon. I would make it right with Mère Générale."

She wondered if she was hearing aright, but managed a banal word of thanks and acceptance. It would be nice to get out in the sunshine again, she added; soon enough she would be back to the gray skies of an English March.

"That's one of the things I wanted to talk to you about," David returned, making her heart leap foolishly. Was he going to give her another chance of accepting the job here at the clinic? During her week as a patient she had enjoyed its tranquil atmosphere, and been touched by the kindness of the wise elderly Mère Générale who had twice visited her. But it was almost too much to hope that David would have modified his attitude to her involvement with Robert Tallant... and, less importantly, her ski instructor. Why did he have to be so stuffy and old-fashioned... as well as being completely mistaken in his judgment of her, she wondered impatiently.

Nevertheless she clung to the faint hope that his words had given her, hope of a second offer of the job in the clinic; she could not imagine anything more personal, nor would she let herself try to analyze the meaning of the things he had said about finding her on Mont Jolyon that snowbound evening, just as he had found her long ago in Lammermuir. He had been emphasizing the oddness of coincidence, that was all.

Yet the following morning when he pronounced her fit for the little outing and had promised to call for her in the afternoon, she could hardly contain her delight. Her luggage had been brought over from Les Trois Chasseurs when the Rotherhams left, and now, delving in her suitcase, she chose a golden brown woollen dress with a gaily yoked Fair Isle sweater to match. A very "Lammermuir" outfit, it occurred to her. And its warm coloring did something for her sickroom pallor. There was no need for eye shadow today to emphasize her large, too serious gray eyes with their long lashes. Indeed she had been stupidly self-conscious about using eye shadow ever since David had criticized it so rudely that first day at Geneva airport.

Then it was afternoon and he was coming toward her room, striding along the balcony—a masterful "here-comes-the-doctor" footstep she would have known anywhere. It was so characteristic of him.

A few minutes later they were driving down the hill toward the village street. The shops were as gaily set out as ever, the mountains in the background surrounding it as majestic, and the sky overhead was a brilliant blue. Snowstorms and avalanches seemed an utter impossibility in this tranquil scene.

"I'm taking you home to my chalet," he told her. "We can talk more comfortably over a cup of tea."

His elderly housekeeper was obviously expecting them and soon Marnie was installed in the small comfortable sitting room behind a well-laden tea cart. There were rather strained silences while they drank their tea and toyed with the dainty sandwiches and little French sponge cakes. For once David seemed oddly tongue-tied. And presently, in order to make conversation, Marnie began talking of Seafleet and the work that would probably be waiting for her there. "But whatever case I get next, it can't possibly be absorbing as the one I've just finished." She gave a regretful sigh. "I shall never forget Arbois."

"Then why don't you stay here?" David burst out, his words dropping into a sudden electrical silence.

"You mean," Marnie faltered, "that you might still, in spite of...everything...want me to work at the clinic?"

"Well, yes," he agreed hesitantly. "That, perhaps...and something more."

She gazed at him in mystification.

He seemed to have difficulty in bringing out what so surprisingly came next. "I haven't been very nice to you since you came here, Marnie, have I? But you annoyed me intensely at times."

Her heartbeats faltered. Hope flickered and died. He was going to remind her once more that she was not wholly suitable for work in the restricted atmosphere of the clinic.

"I'm sorry," she began.

He brushed the interruption aside, intent on what it was he wanted to convey. "Seeing you as you are," he went on strangely, "came as a bit of a shock. Careless and laughing, dancing in the arms of that handsome idiot Praxmann." He shook his head with a rueful smile, as if to banish the distasteful image. "Of course you had every right to dance with whom you pleased, even with Arbois' number one glamor boy! You weren't to know it was the eighteen-year-old Marnie I would have liked to see there before me, not the older, more sophisticated version. Ridiculous, wasn't it?"

He held out his hand to her. "Come into the study with me and let's look at that shadowy younger Marnie... a beautiful shadow from the past."

He led her the few steps across the hall into his study... his sanctuary, and there above his desk hung the colored prize photograph. "My girl in the green valley," he said softly. "For years that girl has been my icon, my image of all that was peace and tranquility. When life, as it invariably does at times, became confused and troublesome, or if I was tired and disheartened for some reason or other, I would would come in here and gaze at my picture. And I would see again, not as a photograph, but as a vivid memory, the beehives and the stream and the flowers; the grave compassionate face of the girl looking down at the lamb in her arms. It would seem to me then that my camera had caught a timeless moment, something that could never alter or be destroyed. There were other girls in my life, of course there were. But I never compared them with my girl in the green valley. She was alone, aloof, my secret resting place."

He had dropped her hand as he talked, and still gazing up at the picture, moved away from her a little—the real Marnie, she thought, who had blundered onto the scene, smashing the icon, breaking the dream.

"Foolish of me to feel like that, wasn't it?" He had turned back to her again. "Just how foolish, I realized that dreadful evening I searched for you in the snowstorm. When I found you at last and held you in my arms, trying to bring you back to life... I knew your life was my life, too." His voice had dropped to a whisper.

"What are you trying to tell me?" she cried, unable to believe that it could be what she longed for it to be.

He gave her a searching, hungry look. "It was the difficulty of adjusting, of accepting that the older Marnie was really the same as the younger Marnie. Only more real; warm, living flesh and blood instead of a beautiful shadow in a colored photograph. I wanted you," he said, "as I'd never wanted the shadowy Marnie. But I was angry with you . . . jealous of all the years in your life that I'd missed and jealous—oh God, how jealous, of the men you had known and loved. I wanted to be the first man in your life. Can you forgive me, Marnie?"

Scarcely able to take in what she heard, she held out her hands to him in a tremulous gesture. He took them gently, uncertainly.

"Do you think if we worked together for a while in the clinic and you got to know me a little better you might come to realize how much I love you . . . have in a strange timeless way always loved you? If I could make you understand. . . ."

It was so humbly spoken. Her arrogant David pleading with her! She couldn't bear it.

"There haven't been other men," she burst out explosively. "Not in the way you mean. You *are* the first."

"Marnie what are you saying?" His voice was wild, his eyes blazed. He had drawn her close, not gently now, but roughly.

"Oh, David!" she cried, "if you only knew. . . ."

But what it was he was to know was never spoken. There was no more need for words as his lips came down on her own. All need for explanations, declarations or promises melted magically away. In the kisses they exchanged there was promise enough—in the deep look that lovers give to one another, unclouded, clear with trust. Healing there was in that moment as well as passion.

And above the desk at their side the girl with the lamb in her arms stood in immemorial tranquility, the singing stream at her feet, the hopefulness of springtime all around her.

THE BEADS OF NEMESIS

FV 6310

The Beads
of Nemesis
Elizabeth Hunter

Pericles Holmes gave the beads to Morag at their first meeting—a talisman for protection. Soon afterward he asked her to marry him.

Morag knew he was thinking only of his young son and daughter. "They both love and need you, Morag. Would that be enough?" he asked. Willingly she agreed.

Pride prevented her from revealing that she had fallen in love with him and silently she vowed to be all that a Greek expected of his wife.

But in time, that wasn't enough—she wanted his love, as well. And she dreaded the arrival of her beautiful stepsister who had always taken everything Morag treasured. Could the beads protect Morag from her?

CHAPTER ONE

THE LITTLE VILLAGE of Marathon wilted under the hot sun. Even the breeze, such as it was, did no more than disturb the dust at the corners of the narrow streets, blowing its hot breath on the few plants that struggled in the heat, scorching the dry leaves into a uniform brown. Morag Grant stepped off the pavement and narrowly missed being run over by an army truck that came hurtling around the corner. It was the only sign of life she had seen.

Once more she consulted the guidebook in her knapsack, easing her shoulders from the strain of carrying the heavy bag. It would take her three hours to walk to Rhamous, she thought. Three hours in this blazing heat and on an empty stomach. She made a face at the printed word, which had not changed at all from when she had last looked at it. Would it be worth going all that way? She had thought so that morning in Athens, when she had thought that anything would be better than staying in the sultry atmosphere of the city. Now she was not so sure. These things were fun when one had company to complain to, and to laugh with at the shared complaints; on her own, she found she was lonely and dispirited even by the prospect of enjoying herself.

Morag picked up her knapsack again with her left hand and wandered into the relative coolness of one of the shops.

"*Kaliméra*," she murmured to the black-clad woman who sat behind the counter in the dim light.

"*Kaliméra sas*," the woman answered.

Morag pointed to a bottle of fizzy lemonade. "Please," she said, and then again, "*Parakaló*."

The woman picked out one of the bottles and opened it with a practiced movement of her wrist, pushing the lemonade across the counter together with a wrapped straw for Morag to drink from. "*Deutcsh?*" she asked.

Morag shook her head. "English," she answered. She wondered if she looked German, or if it was because by far the greatest number of tourists in Greece were from Germany, but the inquiry about her nationality seemed to have followed her around ever since she had arrived.

The woman favored her with a slow smile. "*Kalá!*" She blew out her cheeks and shook the front of her black blouse, signifying that it was hot. Morag nodded eagerly, putting off for as long as possible the moment when she would have to go back outside into the blinding heat.

But in the end she had no further excuse for delay and she stepped out into the shimmering whiteness of the street, blinking at the sudden excess of light. It was not very far down the Athens road where she had to turn off onto the smaller road to Rhamous, but by the time she had reached it she was already hot and sticky and the straps of her knapsack had rubbed her shoulders raw. With determination she gritted her teeth and set herself the next measure of the walk before she would allow herself to rest again.

So set she was on completing the distance she had decided upon that she barely noticed the car as it drew up beside her.

"Want a lift?" a masculine voice asked her.

She started, pausing to wipe the sweat out of her eyes. Of course she wanted a lift! But she wasn't sure if it would be wise to accept, all the same, and stood by the side of the road in an agony of indecision, trying to make up her mind. The two children in the back were a decided plus, and the right-hand drive telling its own story that this was a British car was another one. But the man didn't look English. Far from it. His black, curly hair gave him an exotic look that was further accentuated by the width of his shoulders and the cut of his shirt, which was only done up by the last button—revealing an expanse of tanned chest set off by a golden crucifix of the Greek type, with Christ regnant and vested on the front. He was a minus factor, she decided, though a mightily attractive one.

"Get in!" he said.

"But..." she began, then hesitated. "Are you going to Rhamous?"

"Get in!" he said again with increasing impatience.

She looked down at her knapsack, a little put out when the man merely grinned and, getting slowly out of the car, lifted it with an ease that made her own struggles with the thing seem pointless. "Do you want it with you, or shall I put it up on the roof rack?" he asked her.

She found herself saying something about putting it wherever it would be more convenient to him and hurried into the front passenger seat. "Hello," she said to the children. They looked very much alike, with practically the same hairstyle, though one was clearly a boy and the other a girl.

"Hello," they responded. The girl broke into a wide smile. "Were you afraid of daddy?" she demanded, her eyes twinkling. "I told him he ought to cut his hair before we get to grandma's house."

"Several times," the girl's father put in wryly, getting back into the car. "All right, I'm convinced, I look like Barbarossa himself."

"Not Barbarossa!" Morag said. "He must have had a red beard!"

"And mine, if I had one, is black," the man agreed. He smiled at Morag in a strangely intimate way, as if he knew her well, and she was surprised to discover a little fountain of excitement within her that responded to his look in a way she had not known for a long, long time. "Will you cut it for me, in exchange for transporting you to Rhamous?" he suggested.

Morag swallowed. "If you like," she said.

"I think I might like it very much," he answered imperturbably. "My name is Pericles Holmes. Most people call me Perry. The two in the back are Kimon and Peggy."

"How d'you do?" said Morag, still a little uncertain. Surely it hadn't been as long as all that since she had last sat beside an attractive man and talked nonsense with him. Surely she wasn't going to be shy. She took a determined hold on herself. "I'm Morag Grant."

She waited for him to recognize the name, but he showed no sign of having done so and she took a quick breath of relief.

"Pretty name," was all he said.

"It isn't English, but then I'm really a Scot," she explained. "Only I've always lived in England."

"We're a bit Scottish, too," Kimon informed her. "But we're more Greek. Grandma is Greek and mommy was half Greek, too."

"Was?" Morag said before she could stop herself.

"She's dead," Peggy said in carefully matter-of-fact tones. "I don't suppose one keeps one's nationality when one is dead, do you think? That's why Kimon said she was half Greek. She was half British, too." Morag thought she heard a faintly wistful note in the last few words and smiled at the little girl, turning her head to see her better. "My mother is dead, too," she said. "I can't remember her at all. My father married again and my stepmother had a little girl, too. We were brought up together."

"Kimon and I are twins,"Peggy volunteered.

"That must be why you look alike," said Morag.

Peggy's eyes flashed. "We're not identical twins. If we were, we'd both be girls—"

"Or boys!" Kimon interrupted. "It would be better if we were both boys. Then we wouldn't have to live with grandma!"

"That's enough, Kimon," their father interposed. "Morag was telling us about her family. Go on, Morag."

"There isn't anything more to say," she answered. "My stepsister and I are the same age, so I suppose we might as well have been twins, too."

"Only you didn't like her much, did you?" Pericles Holmes observed. "Why not? Did she tell tales to her mother? Or was it something worse than that?"

The children giggled. Evidently that was considered the most heinous crime that either of them could commit.

"I didn't *dis*like her," Morag compromised. "I suppose we didn't have much in common."

Pericles lifted his eyebrows, giving his face a knowing look that disturbed her strangely. "No?"

She cast him a swift look from beneath her lashes. "You can't dislike someone you live with for years. You have to come to some arrangement so that you don't," she confided. "It's very wearing disliking people and it doesn't do any good."

Pericles' smile mocked her. "That sounds like a very profound thought. You have us all disliking her now on your behalf," he added with a laugh. "Tell us more about her. I like to know my enemy! Is she a blond like you?"

"No." Morag looked embarrassed. "Her looks are

more definite than mine, if you know what I mean. She's much better looking than I am."

Pericles laughed. "I prefer a pretty blond myself, being dark."

Black and beautiful she would have called him, Morag thought.

She struggled hastily back into speech before he could guess at her inner turmoil and wonder, as she was already doing, at the reason for it. "I'm not really blond, either! I'm nothing in particular!"

His eyes swept over her. "Perhaps in an English winter. But the sun has bleached your hair nicely since you've been out here. Perhaps you haven't noticed."

She ran a hand over her hair as if it offended her. "I've been camping. Does it look awful?"

His eyes twinkled. "I'd call that a leading question," he teased her. "I suppose you have a tent in that knapsack of yours?" He frowned as she nodded agreement. "Where are your companions?"

"I haven't any," she said.

"Greece is no place for a young woman on her own."

"Perhaps not. But it really isn't any of your business, is it?" she retorted.

"I'm making it my business," he drawled, ignoring her angry face. "What happened to your friends?"

She bit her lip . "I was...held up. The others had all gone by the time I was ready, so I came on my own. I *like* my own company!"

"Like hell you do!"

Morag glared at him, holding onto her temper with a conscious effort. Was it so obvious that she had hated being on her own? She pursed her lips and studied her fingers carefully, noticing that they were brown from the sun and that she had torn one of her nails.

"There's Rhamous just around the corner. I'd say

you've come to the right place, Morag Grant. Play your cards right and Nemesis will make it up to you for all you've had to suffer in the past."

Morag was startled out of her anger. "Nemesis? I thought she went in for retribution."

She considered rebuking him for his use of her first name, but something told her that she would probably regret it if she did. "I know what it is to be unhappy," she said, "Most of us do."

"Unfortunately," he agreed. "But most of us are older than you are when we make that discovery. You don't look much older than Kimon and Peggy!"

But she *was* older—aeons older than they! She smiled briefly, opting out of the conversation. "I think I'll read up on it before I go on to the site," she said instead. "I like to know what I'm looking at."

"You don't have to do that with daddy," Kimon informed her. "He tells us all about the places we visit. He knows them all without having to look at any book!"

Morag didn't look up. "How come?" she asked.

"It's my job," Pericles said simply. "I start work this autumn with the local archaeological society. Before that I had a job with the British Museum."

"But now we have to live here," Peggy sighed. "We have to live with grandma and it's perfectly horrid!"

"Oh, dear," said Morag.

"It's worse even than that," Kimon finished for his sister. "We wouldn't have to if Peggy weren't a girl!"

"Why should that make any difference?" Morag asked, genuinely bewildered.

"Daddy says he can't bring her up on his own," he said moodily. "She has to have a woman around. Only she wouldn't ask grandma anything anyway, because no one would." He broke off abruptly with a meaningful look at Peggy. "Daddy's bought the tickets, so hush up.

He doesn't like it when we go on about not wanting to live with grandma. He can't think of anything else to do with us."

Morag's sympathy was caught. She knew only too well what it was like to have to live with relatives who put up with you rather than loved you, and who plainly wished you somewhere else. She was touched, too, by Pericles Holmes's concern for his daughter. It showed, she thought, an unusual sensitivity to her needs to want to have a woman take a hand in her upbringing. Her own father had remarried for quite different reasons and had ended by preferring his stepdaughter to his own prickly child—but no doubt he was not wholly to blame for that!

He touched her on her arm and she pulled away from him as if his touch had burned her. "I'm sorry," she said. "I was thinking."

"You think too much," he observed. "In Greece you have to feel, not think all the time. Particuarly not sad thoughts. Here's your ticket. Come with us and I'll explain what you have to do to gain the favor of Nemesis."

He brought his hand from behind his back and grasped her arm firmly with the other one. With a seriousness that intrigued her, he put a shell necklace over her head and arranged it against the opening of her shirt. "The boy who sells the tickets was making them for sale," he told her. "I have one for Peggy, too. The beads of Nemesis. The plastic ones are a bit too modern to appeal, I imagine, but the shells should catch her eye. What are you going to ask of her, Morag Grant?"

"I don't know," she admitted. She felt uncomfortable about accepting the necklace, but he had made it very difficult for her to refuse it. "I hadn't really realized that it was her temple here. I just came."

"I expect she'll forgive you." There was no hint of a smile, so she couldn't be sure if he meant what he said or not.

"Are you sure she doesn't follow you around like...like fate catching up with you?" She wasn't convinced she wanted to gain Nemesis's attention. She didn't trust her, no matter what Pericles said about her.

"The head of her statue that used to be in her temple here is in the British Museum," he smiled. "I got rather fond of her." He flicked the shells on her throat with one finger. "I believe you're scared, Morag. That'll never do! The Holmes family are here to protect you, you know. You don't have to be afraid anymore."

She walked behind him up the short path, reveling in the cool wind that blew against her skin. "What makes you think I'm afraid?" she asked.

It shows in your eyes. What happened, Morag?"

"I was fined for dangerous driving," she heard herself say. She hadn't meant to tell him. She hadn't meant to tell anyone! She had been so sure that she could put it behind her and never refer to it again. Why couldn't she? Why did she have to go blabbing about her troubles to any stranger she came across? She could have bitten her tongue. She had wanted Pericles Holmes to think well of her. It had been important to her—though why, she wasn't prepared to think about. "I pleaded guilty."

Pericles sent the children running ahead of them with a single gesture of one hand. He might have an English surname, she thought, but his Greek name suited him far better!

"You've told me too much, or not enough," he said quietly. "If you were guilty, why are you kicking so hard against what happened to you?"

She was dismayed to feel the tears pouring down her cheeks and hated herself for showing such weakness. "My fiancé died in the crash," she said simply.

Pericles looked surprised. "I'm sorry. What kind of a man was he?"

"Does it matter?"

"I think it does," he said bluntly.

"Why? Why should it matter to you?" she demanded.

"You won't like it if I tell you," he said with a slight smile. "I suppose he was much older than you."

"Wrong! He was two years older, if you must know. He was a splendid person!"

Pericles looked doubtful. "I don't believe you would have married him in the end. He may have been the most wonderful individual on earth, but he didn't know how to awaken you!" He swung around to face her, looking straight into her eyes, his own alight with a brilliance that made her shake inwardly. "Did he?"

"I loved him."

"I don't believe you!"

"You don't have to!" she retorted. Her eyes fell before his. "We were both in love with him, only it was me he asked to marry him!"

"What a triumph for you!" His sarcasm made her flush with anger. It hadn't been like that! "Well?" he shouted at her.

"He went out with us both," she said.

"I'll bet!"

She sighed. Nothing could stop the flood of words that she knew was about to break out of her. She had kept silent for so long, but she couldn't resist the look in this man's eyes. If he had been one of the men who had questioned her repeatedly as to what had happened on that awful night, she would have been quite unable to keep silent.

"I did it for David. I knew he was regretting that he had asked me to marry him."

"Just as you were regretting having accepted him?" Pericles put in dryly.

"I don't know! I never thought of it like that. All I knew was that he was unhappy and that he didn't love me. If we had gone on as we were, he wouldn't have even liked me, and I didn't want that. I knew he wanted Delia. That was the hard part, because Delia will never love anyone very much. But he wanted her, so I made up my mind that he should have her."

Pericles shook his head at her. "Now that, Nemesis could not approve. That, my dear, is the sin of *hubris*, of thinking that you can manage your own life and other people's without any help from anyone else." He paused to allow her to take in the glorious view from the fallen stones of the temple, pointing out a handy piece of masonry in the shade of a pine tree where they could sit and stare to their hearts' content at the deep blue of the sea, enclosed by harsh, barren mountains slashed by purple shadows and, in the foreground, the ruined walls of the ancient town that had once had its own fort to defend it, and the dark green of the pine trees, the scent of which vied with the thyme at their feet to give flavor to the refreshing breeze.

"Were you driving the car?" he asked when the silence had begun to bother her.

Morag gave him a quick glance. "How did you know?"

He shrugged. "I could say you don't look capable of driving dangerously, but I think you are," he said slowly. "But then your sense of justice wouldn't be outraged. I think you might be silly enough to shield someone else, and feminine enough to resent it when you are believed."

"I'm not a complete fool!" she protested.

"Are you not?"

She was silent for a long moment. "I suppose I am," she admitted. "But if David loved her, the least I could do was to protect her—or so I thought. Delia was going to say David had been driving anyway and he had been drinking—they both had! Imagine how his parents would have felt if they'd blamed their dead son for the crash. I think I was right to spare them that."

"No matter what the cost to yourself?"

She blinked. "I thought the price would be worth it."

He pulled down the corner of his mouth. "My dear girl, you haven't begun to pay it. You'd better hurry up and pay your curtsy to Nemesis before you succeed in ruining your whole life! Come on and I'll introduce you."

He made no attempt to help her as she clambered onto the floor of the larger of the two temples, the one nearer to the sea, which was whiter and looked as if it had been built at a later date than the smaller ruin that clung to its side. She had expected some word of sympathy from him, a pat on the back because she had chosen such a hard path and had suffered because of it. But he merely thought her a fool, and that hurt more than it should.

"Mr. Holmes, I don't know what it has to do with you, but I'd do the same again. I heard them crash. It was just below our garden, and it was so easy to change places with Delia. Nothing mattered very much to me just then, with David dead. There didn't seem to be any future for me anyway."

"And what about your parents, Miss Grant? Didn't it matter that they would suffer on your behalf?"

She shook her head. "It would have been worse if they'd known it was Delia. It was all that they expected of me."

"That sounds as though you're feeling sorry for yourself," he observed, bending down to take a closer look at one of the fallen Doric columns.

"I suppose I am," she admitted. "I thought coming to Greece would solve all my problems. That I'd feel differently about things—about being me! But I don't. My father doesn't want me home and I don't know where else to go."

"Then that's one problem solved," Pericles told her. "You can tag along with us for a while."

But you don't know anything about me!" she said.

"What do you want me to know?"

She tried to marshal her thoughts into some sort of order. "I'm good with children," she said finally. "But I can't give you any references. And how will you explain me to your mother? And supposing the children don't want to have me tagging along? You'd do far better to let me go on by myself."

"Camping on your own in Greece? My dear girl, try to have a little sense! I meant to take you back to Athens with us anyway. It'll suit me very well to have you along."

"You mean the children might settle better if someone else were there?"

He looked up, smiling. "Something like that."

She sat down on a base of a column, made uncertain by the swift turn of events. Her heart was hammering, the fountain of excitement within her exploding into a new delight. "I'll try to act as a buffer between them and their grandmother," she found herself saying. "I'll do everything I can—"

"I'm sure you will!" he cut her off. He stood up straight, standing over her in a way that made her look hastily away from him. "You don't have to be grateful," he drawled, sounding amused. "As far as I'm concerned you're the answer to a prayer and I mean to take advantage of you and the situation your crazy stupidity has landed you in to make use of you entirely for my own ends. I can't offer you any references, either, you know."

"Oh, but you have the children!" she protested.

"And that's enough for you to trust me to look after you as well?"

She bit her lip, aware that he was teasing her. Then she nodded her head. "Yes," she said.

"God help you!" he grinned. "Someone ought to!" He held out his hand to her. "All right, Morag Grant, welcome to the Holmes family."

She put her hand in his and was immediately aware of the strength of his fingers and the smooth warmth of his skin. "Thank you," she said.

He bent his head and kissed her lightly on the lips. "That's to seal the bargain," he told her.

Her color came and went and she swallowed hard, trying to control her trembling mouth. But he had already turned away, striding across the marble floor of the temple to take a closer look at the smaller one that stood by its side. There was no doubt, she thought, that she was mad to go with him, but how lovely it was to be totally mad for once and to follow her own inclinations, without a thought for anyone else! David she had loved, but David hadn't scared her, nor had he made her feel as though she had run a long race and had finally come home. This one could hurt her as she had not been hurt before. The knowledge came to her as if someone outside herself had spoken the words. A warning from Nemesis? She smiled at the fancy. Hadn't David hurt her by preferring someone else, by preferring Delia whom she had never been able to bring herself to like? Why then should she be afraid of Pericles Holmes?

The boy who had let them into the site whistled to his goats to follow him across the rough ground to where his family kept their hives, weighted down with rocks on the top against the wind. The bells around the goats' necks set off a carillon of sound, deep and melodious, and the cicadas set up their shrill love song from the other side of a clump of bushes. It was very peaceful there, like an unexpected benison after the turbulent events of the last few months. It was a new beginning and she was glad. She was even more glad that she had taken it into her head to visit Rhamous.

KIMON AND PERICLES went down to the headland to look at the fort. Peggy refused point blank to go with them.

"I want to stay with Morag," she muttered defiantly to her father. "I like Morag!"

"I like Morag, too," Kimon chimed in. "But I'd like to see the fort. The view from down there must be terrific!"

"Do you want to go?" Peggy demanded, tugging at Morag's jeans. "Wouldn't you rather sit here quietly with me?"

Morag abandoned the strong desire that she felt to run as fast as she could to the headland—to get there before Pericles and to have him show her the ruins of the ancient town that had once made such an impact on the local life round about. "I'd love to stay with you!" she claimed warmly, smiling at Peggy. "Where shall we sit?"

Pericles cast a quizzical look. "Peggy misses Susan every now and then," he said.

Peggy frowned at him. "I don't. Not really. But I don't like looking at forts. People were killed there—and I don't like that."

"Animals were killed outside the temples as sacrifices," Kimon put in. "I like that even less!"

"But not nowadays," his sister retorted. "Nowadays we get things. If Morag's and my necklaces were a gift from Nemisis—"

"Daddy paid for them!" Kimon pointed out.

"He did not!" Peggy tore the shells loose and scattered them over the ground. "If he did, it's a cheat, and I don't want them!"

Pericles took a long, level look at his daughter and, without a word, strode away from her toward the fort with a rather hesitant Kimon at his heels.

"Now I've made him cross again," Peggy sighed. "He thinks it's because I can't get used to mummy being dead, but it isn't that. Did you know your mother?" she asked, picking up one of the shells and playing with it between her fingers. "Did you, Morag?"

Morag shook her head. "Sometimes I think I can remember her, but sometimes I know I can't. There was a photograph of her once, but my stepmother got rid of it."

She saw that Peggy's eyes were wet. "Did your father love your stepmother more than your mother?"

"I don't know," Morag answered. "Perhaps. My stepsister is very like her mother and he loves her very much."

The child sighed. "I can't always remember mummy," she confessed. "I tried not to remember her because grandma chose her to marry daddy. Only Kimon says it's wicked. Are you wicked, too, Morag?"

"Often and often," Morag agreed, smiling. "Would you like my necklace in place of yours? You could think of it as a present from your mother, if you don't like to have it as a gift from Nemesis."

Peggy accepted the shell necklace and put it around her neck. "Don't tell daddy," she said solemnly. "Nobody ever understood before. I hate grandma!"

"Why?" Morag asked curiously.

Peggy pursed her lips, looking far older than her ten or eleven years. "You'll find out! She's all right with daddy. She's even all right with Kimon. But if you're a girl, she's horrid!"

CHAPTER TWO

PERICLES TOOK ONE LOOK at his daughter's face and said something to her in Greek. The child looked gratified and smiled and nodded.

"Morag says she prefers being a girl," she said in English.

Pericles looked amused. His glance swept over Morag's heightened color. "I expect she does," he agreed, his eyes inscrutable. "Give her back her necklace, Peggy. Being given that sort of thing is one of the benefits—"

"She said I could have them!" Peggy protested.

"But I gave them to her," her father insisted quietly. "If you want another necklace yourself, I'll buy you another one. But that one was specially for Morag. Hand it over, there's a love!"

Peggy drew the shell necklace over her head and held it up with a reluctance that made Morag feel sympathetic. "It's true, I did give it to her. I can buy another necklace for myself. I'll go and find the boy."

"No, you won't," Pericles muttered. He held her firmly by the wrist, still smiling. Morag wasn't even sure that he knew how tight his grasp was, or even that he was touching her at all. "That necklace was for you. Those frightful plastic beads that spoil the shells go with the color of your eyes. It was the only one he had with green beads and those pretty, curving shells, and you're going to keep it. If Peggy's isn't as nice, it's her own fault. No one else broke the one she had."

"I didn't get one at all!" Kimon complained in an aggrieved voice.

"You aren't a girl!" Peggy retorted, somewhat smugly. "Only girls get necklaces."

"Grandma will give me something else," Kimon answered, completely put out.

Peggy gave Morag a speaking look that told its own story. Morag looked straight back at her. "I'd rather have my shells," she said with a firmness that surprised even herself.

"Grandma will give me a coin for my collection!" Kimon went on belligerently.

"I don't care!" Peggy decided.

Morag smiled at her and the child smiled cheerfully back.

"What is this?" Pericles asked. "Feminine collusion? A fine thing! Kimon and I will have to watch out to see that you don't get the better of us!"

Peggy blinked. "Not of you, daddy," she said carefully, "but it will be nice to get the better of grandma. She's always giving Kimon things, and it isn't fair. Morag will be on my side!"

"Is that so?" her father drawled. "Grandma does her best for you, Peggy. You need a woman on hand when you're growing up."

"Then I choose Morag. I like Morag!"

"But I can't be there all the time," Morag said, embarrassed.

"Why not?" said Peggy. "Why can't she stay with us, daddy?"

Pericles shrugged his shoulders. "Why not?" he echoed. "Let's kidnap her and take her home with us—"

"And keep her forever and ever!" Peggy finished for him.

"Yes," agreed Kimon. "I'd like that, too."

"But not forever!" Morag said firmly. "I can't stay forever. I have to go back to England at the end of the holidays."

"Why?" said Pericles.

"Why?" said Kimon and Peggy in unison.

Morag's eyes widened as she faced the three of them. Why not indeed? What was to stop her? "I have my own family," she began, sounding so unconvinced that Pericles laughed.

"You have now," he murmured, and sweeping aside any further objections she might have, he went on, "the Holmes family—at least for a while, until you're quite sure that you don't want us anymore."

And that was likely to be never, she thought in a bemused way. Her heart had always been far too swift to love and to hate, and she knew herself to be helplessly enmeshed with this family despite only just having met them. They seemed familiar to her, as if she had known them for years instead of minutes. Besides, there was the strange elation she felt whenever she looked at Pericles—an emotion she had never experienced before and which she didn't know now how to handle. It was a far remove from the quiet devotion she had felt for David, if devotion it had been. Perhaps he had been no more than a handy receptacle for her to pour her feelings into, and neither of them had really loved the other. She gave Pericles an oblique look from under her lashes and wondered what it would be like to be loved by him. It was a thought that couldn't help but dismay her.

Her feeling must have shown clearly on her face, for he laughed suddenly and said, "You'd already decided to come with us, remember? I'm not going to let you get out of it now!"

He opened the door of the car for her and pushed her

onto the seat with a rough gallantry that brought a smile to her lips.

"Where does your mother live?" she asked.

"Lagonissi. It's on the Apollon coast, on the way to Sounion. She used to live in Glyfada, but when they developed the international airport there, she found the noise a bit much and moved farther out of Athens. It's mostly hotels and tourist apartments and villas, and it's quite near where the president has his villa. The swimming is good, but the life is a bit unreal."

"You don't care for it very much?" she hazarded.

"No, my dear, I do not. But I can't persuade my mother to move, and as the object of the exercise was for us to live with her, we were landed with it." He gave her an amused look. "With your advent, if you last, we may find somewhere else for ourselves and leave my poor mother in peace."

"Oh yes, please, daddy," the children exhorted him.

"You can see why my mother doesn't enjoy their company much," he added dryly. "They have a distressing honesty—"

"Is that bad?" she interrupted him.

"Not when mixed with a modicum of good manners, but it can be rather devastating when naked and unadorned!"

Morag laughed, "I can imagine!"

His mouth twitched. "I suppose you've seen the results of a like honesty yourself, being the same sort of person," he said.

"Am I?" She was surprised first and then nettled. "I rather pride myself on my manners!" she objected.

"I'll remind you of that when you've coped with all three of us yelling at one another. We try to keep to a laid-down pecking order. The children can yell at each other, you can yell at them, and I yell at you! Okay?"

"Do we have to yell at all?" she countered. She wasn't sure that she liked the idea of being yelled at by him.

"There's nothing wrong with your lungs, is there?" he asked with pretended concern. "We all yell, Morag. Perhaps you never yelled enough as a child."

"It wasn't the approved method of expression!"

"How forbidding you sound," he teased her. "I didn't know you were so disapproving!"

She lifted her chin. "But then you don't know me at all, Mr. Holmes!"

"You can call me Perry, if you like," he invited her.

"I don't like."

"Then you'd better make it Pericles."

"I don't like that, either!"

He grinned, "You'll get used to it." He touched her cheek with his finger and shut the door on her. "You're beginning to yell quite nicely," he added. "Only you're not allowed to yell at me. You're only allowed to yell at the children."

MORAG WAS SILENT the whole way through Athens. She found the traffic nerve-racking and was ashamed of her fears, for Pericles drove both carefully and well. He even seemed to know where he was going, up and down the one-way streets, but then she supposed he had made the journey many times. For a while she wondered why the waiting cars invariably honked when the traffic lights changed from red to green, but then she realized that they were almost impossible to see from those in front, and amused herself by trying to will Pericles forward before anyone had time to honk at him. She was not sorry, though, when they had finally driven through the city, passing close beneath the cream-colored Acropolis, surely the finest monument that any city can boast as its central feature, and came out at last onto the coast road.

"Not far now," Pericles smiled at her.

She relaxed a little in her seat. "They drive very fast, don't they?" she said, annoyed by the note of apology in her voice.

"It seems faster to the uninitiated. It's a bit baffling at first, finding one's way around the city. Looking at a map doesn't help much, unless the one-way systems are marked. You'll soon learn them."

"I don't drive!" The sharpness of her tone made her bite her lip. "I mean, I can't just now."

"Banned as well as fined? It might be as well if you kept that item of information from my mother, Morag."

"I don't think I'd drive in Greece anyway," she said defiantly. "I'm not a very experienced driver. My father doesn't like women driving his car, and I haven't one of my own."

Pericles smiled faintly. "My mother expects all young people to drive, especially young English women. If you say you don't drive, it may even be a point in your favor. Susan didn't drive, either."

"Your wife?"

He nodded."Susan was brought up in Greece in a rather old-fashioned household. Women here are taught to obey their husbands and to leave all the decisions to them. Before that, they obey their fathers and learn all the domestic arts. Driving a car isn't often included in their education."

"Oh," said Morag.

"Is that all you have to say? I thought you'd start yelling at me again about the equality of women in modern society."

Morag laughed. "A bit obvious, Mr. Holmes!"

"Morag...."

"Yes, Mr. Holmes?"

"There's a Greek side to my nature that prefers women to be meek and obedient. I don't expect to have to repeat myself when I give you an order. You are to call me Pericles. Understood?"

She nodded. It occurred to her that she was a little afraid of Pericles Holmes and that she didn't entirely dislike the sensation. "I suppose it would be silly, as you call me Morag," she managed. It was not much of a last word, but it was the best that she could manage under the circumstances.

"I am in a privileged position," he said with a sardonic smile. "I'll call you anything I please."

"Isn't that rather unfair?"

"Life is unfair," he said.

He turned off the main coastal road shortly after that, apparently heading straight into the sea. "Welcome to my mother's house," he said formally. "Kimon, you can make yourself useful by carrying Morag's knapsack inside. That's one of the other benefits that we allow the girls."

"Kimon doesn't carry my things for me," Peggy said at once.

"I do that!" her father reminded her. "Who's carrying your necklace now?"

"Morag. You only carry heavy things."

Morag giggled unexpectedly. "I'm sure a Greek man wouldn't do that!" she said. "I thought it was the women who did all the work!"

"Would that they did!" he returned dryly. He smiled slowly at her. "You look quite pretty when you're amused," he told her. "We'll have to have you laughing more often."

She shook her head, her cheeks hot. "I'll never be pretty."

He touched her on the cheek, flicking her nose with

one finger. "You're right, pretty is the wrong word, but I could find you very attractive, Morag Grant, if you smiled a little more."

She tried to pass it off as casually as he had made the remark. "Then I'll have to be as sober as a judge," she said, and if her voice trembled, she was almost sure that only she had noticed it.

"You can try!" he said.

"I...I...." She swallowed. "David..." she began hesitantly.

He lifted his eyebrows in mute inquiry. "Yes?" he prompted her when she still said nothing.

"David thought I was pretty—sometimes."

He shook his head at her. "Morag! And that was enough to make you love him?" He put a hand under her chin and forced her to look up at him. She tried to back away, but the warmth in his eyes stopped her. "You don't know what love means, do you? When it does come to you, worrying about what might have been with David will seem a poor substitute for the real thing. You don't owe him anything." He touched her cheek again, half smiling. "Come in and meet my mother. She'll be very glad to see you, I promise you. She hasn't found it easy having the children here, any more than they have enjoyed being with her. Are you ready?"

She nodded, unable to find any words in which to answer him. She put up her hand to her cheek where he had touched her, wondering at the weakness that assailed her. She would have to pull herself together before she met his mother. What would she think if her unknown guest was quite incapable of greeting her in anything other than a foolish monosyllable, just because—because what?

Morag had no time to do more than brush down her tight-fitting jeans and try to smooth her shirt, which, what with the heat and the dust from the day, was scarcely looking as neat and fresh as when she had put it on in the morning. Pericles drew her inexorably into the house after him and out again onto the veranda on the other side. He let go of her there, bending over the elegant figure of the woman who sat, straight-backed, on a wooden chair, looking out toward the sea.

"You're home in time for the sunset tonight," Mrs. Holmes said. "I thought you might have gone to Sounion as the children have never seen our most famous local site—Poseidon's temple in the dying sun, when his famous blue hair turns to gray. Sometimes I can almost believe that he's real when I watch the sea taking on the colors of the heavens. That is why I love this house!"

Pericles kissed her lightly on the cheek. "I brought someone home with me. She's going to lend a hand with the children for the rest of the summer. Mama, this is Morag Grant."

His mother swivelled around in her chair, a look of shock on her face. "A stranger, Perry? How could you?"

I think you may come to like her," he answered calmly.

"But what does she know of our Greek ways?"

"We're not wholly Greek," her son reminded her. "Besides, I think you'll find her willing to learn. She's very amenable." The amusement in his voice stung Morag into speech. She took a deep breath and held out a hand to the older woman.

"*Héro poli*," she said in Greek, hoping that she had got it right.

Pericles' mother favored her with a long, searching look. "*Miláte Elliniká*?" she inquired, finally shaking hands.

"No," Morag admitted. "I tried to learn a few phrases

before I came. It seems only civil to try to speak to people in a few words of their own language, but most people seem to speak English, and I suppose I'm a bit lazy, too."

"The children both speak excellent Greek," Kyria Holmes said. "It's my wish that they should converse as much as possible in their own language. We have decided that both their lives lie in this country, and it is as well for them to learn how to be wholly Greek, whatever my son may say. Do you really think you can help us to achieve that purpose?"

"I can try," Morag answered her.

"No, no, it's impossible! Peggy especially needs to be taught that Greek women don't get their own way by throwing tantrums whenever they are crossed! When she grows up and marries, her husband will control her destiny, just as her father should be doing now. Wanting to do everything just the same as Kimon does will be of little use then!"

Morag looked quickly at Pericles. "Is this what you want for your daughter?"

"I'd like her to marry a strong man," he admitted. "As for the rest, I suppose it was the way her mother was brought up."

"Certainly it was!" his mother exclaimed.

Morag saw Pericles' lips tighten. "It might have been better for her if she'd shown more spirit," he remarked.

"I suppose you are referring to that foolish incident when she thought she was in love with Takis. Did she make you a less good wife because of that? Your slightest wish was her command right up until her death."

"Oh, quite!" he said.

Morag thought she detected an underlying bitterness in his words. "Who is Takis?" she asked, seeking to divert his attention from thoughts of his wife.

"Takis Kapandriti is my nephew." Kyria Holmes drew herself up. "He is staying with us at this moment. You will probably meet him sooner or later. He goes out a great deal, as he has business in Athens."

Morag looked around her, suddenly wondering what her own position in the house was to be. "Is... is there room...?"

Kyria Holmes rose to her feet. "It's a large house, Miss Grant. My son would not have brought you here otherwise." She nodded formally and went inside without a backward look, calling out to the children as she went.

Morag shrugged her shoulders.

Pericles looked amused. "She isn't really frightening once you get used to her," he reassured her. His face crinkled into a smile. "I think she was trying to warn you about Takis, in her own way. Stay clear of him, Morag. He isn't going to marry for a long time yet and he might not understand that there are some English girls who don't come here for the one thing only. Our Greek women are very closely protected by their families, and British freedoms are apt to be misunderstood."

"But I haven't even met him yet!" Morag protested.

"There's no harm in making things clear from the beginning," he observed dryly. "Takis is never serious and you are not to encourage him. Is that clear?"

"What do you expect me to do? Ignore him completely?" She faced him angrily. "It may not be very Greek, Mr. Holmes, but I make my own decisions of that kind no matter where I am!"

"Not very successfully," he reminded her. "It won't hurt you, while you're here, to do things my way. It's time someone put the brakes on where you're concerned. You are obviously warmhearted to a fault, but that can make for sloppiness if you're not careful. Takis would only take advantage of you—as easily as that David of yours, for instance."

She glared at him. "Thank you very much!" she stormed. "You don't know anything about it! How dare you—"

"Easily!"

"Well, you can stay out of my business once and for all! You can be as highhanded as you like with your own children, though I don't think you're at all fair to Peggy, but no one speaks like that to me!"

He actually chuckled. It was the last straw as far as she was concerned. "I hate you, Pericles Holmes!" she declared. "I'm going! I can't think why I ever came with you! Goodbye!"

He leaned against one of the veranda pillars, folding his arms across his chest. "What a fuss!" he mocked her.

"You can't keep me here against my will!"

"No?"

The single syllable seemed doubly insulting to her; first because it implied she didn't know her own mind, and second because it held a threat that she wanted to challenge but didn't quite dare to put to the test. She was afraid of Pericles Holmes, she thought, even while he attracted her.

"If I do stay," she began, "if I do, you must understand—"

"You'll stay," he said certainly.

Her lips quivered. "I won't be dictated to!"

"And I won't be yelled at by—"

"A mere woman, you mean?" she said easily. "I'll yell whenever I feel like it!"

"Not at me you won't!" He laughed suddenly. "I might have known your green eyes could flash with temper as much as any other emotion! But don't flash them at me, Morag Grant. You might get more of a reaction than you bargained for!"

She shrugged her shoulders, bitterly aware that she had somehow lost the battle and that he knew she had no intention of going anywhere. "Indeed?" was all she said.

"Indeed, *Kortsi mou.*"

She stood stock still, annoyed to find that she wanted to find out exactly what reaction she would inspire in him if she continued the argument. It was very tempting to her to find out. She gave him an uncertain look. "I'm not sloppy!"

His eyebrows rose. "All right," he said. "I take that back. You're not sloppy. You're just more feminine than is good for you." A mocking smile touched his lips. "But I won't tease you anymore. It's too soon for you to know what you want for the future and you need to keep a tight hold on your heart without any commitments until you know which way you're looking. Only don't tempt me, Morag. I'm only a man, and making love to you wouldn't be at all disagreeable to me, especially when you look at me as though you expect me to pounce on you at any moment!"

"You forget," she said quietly, "it's not long since I lost my fiancé."

He snapped his fingers, making an angry noise in his mouth. "Grow up, Morag! You didn't love David. He gave you a nice romantic feeling, no more than that! If I took you on, you'd find out what loving a man means. You wouldn't cast me off on your sister when you're tired of me!"

Morag gaped at him. "I don't know what you're talking about!"

"Oh yes, you do! Do you think Delia, or whatever her name is, would have succeeded in interesting David if you hadn't half wanted it that way?"

"You don't know Delia."

"It's got nothing to do with Delia. I'm sure she is prettier than you, more attractive, more everything, but that wouldn't have resigned you to losing David to her. What if she has always taken everything she thought you wanted away from you? If you'd really wanted David, you would have fought back, and you'd have gone on fighting until you had them both where you wanted them!"

Morag looked as surprised as she felt. "Would I?" she said. "I don't see how you could know that." Her eyes kindled with indignation. "If I wouldn't do it for David, I certainly wouldn't do it for you!"

Suddenly he took a step toward her and she panicked, almost running away from him to the far end of the veranda. "One day," he said, "I'll take you up on that, when you've had time to know me better."

An extraordinary, totally unfamiliar excitement ran through her. "You may have treated Susan to the masterful approach, but I wouldn't care for it at all!"

His laughter unsettled her badly. "Susan was well broken in long before she was chosen as a suitable wife for me. She obeyed, but she never loved, poor girl. They should have allowed her to marry Takis—she had more than enough money for them both! All I could do was to be gentle and to encourage her as far as possible to do things for herself. It was I who introduced her to the flying that finally killed her, but I don't regret it! At least it gave her a few moments of freedom from the quagmire in which she found herself."

The color rose in Morag's cheeks and she veiled her eyes from him, more than a little shy. "If you felt like that about her, why should you want ...." She broke off, not wanting to put the threat she felt from him into words after all. She might have misunderstood him, and then what would he think of her?

"To tame you?" His smile told her that he had read her thoughts exactly. "Perhaps because you'd revel in the battle as much as I. You're not like Susan in any way. She found marriage to me a prison, a comfortable prison for which she had been well prepared by a lifetime of submission to what her family decided was good for her. I was no more than her warder, carrying out the sentence they had passed on her. It would be different with you, Morag Grant. You would find freedom—"

She couldn't bear to hear any more. "Never with you!"

"Never with David!" he retorted. "Never with any man who wouldn't demand everything you have to give, who wouldn't make you wholly his, in every way!"

Morag swallowed. "I think that's a highly improper thing to say. I d-don't want to listen to you anymore."

He strolled across the veranda towards her, stopping so close to her that they were almost touching. Her breath caught in the back of her throat and she was more afraid than ever, not so much of him as of herself.

"Improper?" he repeated. "Why? Because I haven't known you long enough? It doesn't take time for me to know I'd like to kiss you, or for you to know that you'd like me to! Shall I give you a practical demonstration, *karthia mou*?"

"No!" The negative exploded out of her.

"Another time?" He put a hand under her chin and forced her to look up at him. "Cheer up, sweetheart, I'll try not to rush you. You'll be quite safe with me." He stroked her cheek with a gentle finger, bringing the burning color rushing in the wake of his touch. Then he bent his head and his lips met hers in a caress so fleeting that she couldn't be sure that it had actually happened.

The sound of footsteps coming onto the veranda made him take a swift step away from her. "Damn!" he muttered under his breath. Morag showed him a shaken face and he smiled straight back at her. "Perhaps it's just as well," he murmured. "You have to meet Takis sometime, and now is as good a time as any."

She had not time to say anything at all. Takis came out onto the veranda and stopped, blinking at them. He was a whole head shorter than his cousin, but he looked far less Greek. His hair was fair and his eyes were pale gray and rather hard.

"Thia Dora said we had a guest." His lips parted in a smile. "Has she something in her eye, or am I interrupting something?"

"Neither," Pericles said shortly. "Morag, this is my cousin Takis. Takis, Morag Grant. She's going to help with the children."

Takis took her hand in his and raised it to his lips. He smiled and winked at Morag, sharing with her the knowledge that he knew he was annoying his cousin by his too gallant greeting of her. Morag gave him back look for look and found herself smiling despite herself. Really, it was too ridiculous, but Takis Kapandriti was more like David than anyone else she had ever met!

CHAPTER THREE

TAKIS SELDOM ACTUALLY went into the water. He preferred to stand close to where the sea lapped gently at the shore, filling his lungs with the golden air and showing off his fine golden body to their neighbors.

"A few weeks and you'll have a fine tan yourself," he said to Morag, his eyes openly approving her neat figure. "Shall I put some oil on your back for you before you burn?"

"No, thank you."

"So shy! But you are not shy with my cousin Pericles, are you? Now why do you favor him, I wonder? You would do much better with me, little *anglitha*. I haven't two children and a secondhand love to offer you!"

Morag's eyes flashed. "Certainly not secondhand!" she murmured.

"What do you mean by that?" he demanded.

"What do you think! You've scarcely been out with the same girl twice since I've been here!"

"Does that offend you? But they are not serious girls, Morag. They are only to have fun with, you understand."

Morag shut her eyes, wriggling her shoulders into a more comfortable position. "I used to know someone very like you," she remarked.

"And that is why you don't like me?" he reproached her.

"I do like you. I liked him, too—very much!"

"Ah!" She felt his shadow come between herself and the sun. "Tell me about this interesting man you used to know!"

"There's nothing to tell."

"Nothing?"

"He's dead now, and you remind me of him. That's all there is to it."

"He must have been a fine man!" Takis exclaimed, naive with self-pride. "How long did you know him?"

Morag hesitated. "He was a friend of my family," she said at last.

"You were in love with him?"

"I thought I was for a little while. But he wasn't ready to love anyone, and I wasn't either. Just like you!"

"I am offended!" Takis told her. "You imply that I am childish. I'm not, not at all. There is nothing childish in liking women, is there?"

"No," said Morag.

"Then why do you imply that I am childish?"

"You don't like responsibilities."

"I like you," he said slyly.

She ignored that. She remembered that David had complained that she had thought him indecisive and how much he had resented her implied criticism of him. She had felt old in his company, older than he, just as she did with Takis. She turned her back on him, trying to still her sudden swift heartbeat as she reflected that Pericles didn't have that effect on her at all.

"Why do you do that?" Takis demanded. "I like to talk with you!"

"The sun's too hot and I'm too sleepy," she answered. "Besides, the children will be home in a minute."

"All the more reason to make the best use of this minute," he said with a laugh. He put his hand on her back and stroked her shoulders. "I told you you needed some oil. You are red now. When the sun goes down it will be very painful. Shall I put some oil on for you now?"

"I'd rather you didn't."

"Why not? It will be nice for you. You can shut your eyes and pretend it is this man you once loved who is doing this for you. It will make you happy and then you won't burn."

Morag gave him a determined look. "I don't want..." she began.

He smiled the smile that was so like David's, that touched his lips but never quite reached his cold, gray eyes. It was funny that she had only noticed that about David in the last few weeks she had known him.

"You will have a sore back otherwise," he reiterated. He put some oil in the palm of his hand and began to smooth it onto her back. "Isn't that nice?"

"It will probably come up in blisters!"

"No, no, my touch will prevent all such disasters. I have a very nice touch, *ne*?" He spilled some more oil straight onto her back and drew patterns in it with one finger. "Your hair is in the way. You have pretty hair. I like it." He pushed it away from her shoulders, and a second later she felt his lips on the back of her neck and turned indignantly toward him. "Ah, that is much better!" he said at once. "You like it? You like it very much!"

"I won't have it!" she said hotly. "Go away, Takis, and leave me alone!"

"But you like it! I am handsome and I know very well how to treat a girl! Why should you wish me to leave you alone?"

"Because I don't like playing at love."

"Only with Pericles!"

"Not with anyone!" she said. "I look after Pericles' children, nothing more!"

"That wasn't how it seemed the first time I saw you. Why do you dislike me? I am more handsome than Pericles. It is known that women prefer me to him!"

Morag jumped to her feet. "You're more conceited, too!" she said.

He grinned up at her. "I say only the truth! Even his wife, Susan, preferred me to him. Oh, she was very much in love with me! But her father said she must marry Pericles."

"I don't want to hear about it!"

He stood up, also. "I think you do. I think you are very curious about the woman Pericles married, the mother of his children. Are you jealous of her?"

"Why should I be?" Morag demanded.

"Because she knew both of us well. Shall I kiss you like I used to kiss her?"

"I don't believe you did kiss her!" Morag said, but there was no conviction in her words.

"Oh yes, I kissed her—before she was married, I kissed her. Afterward, she would not be alone with me. Pericles forbade it and Susan was a very dutiful wife. But we both knew that she wanted to be with me, and Pericles knew it, too!"

"I suppose you saw to that!" Morag said coldly. "You must enjoy hurting people to relish a thing like that!"

"But I don't wish to hurt you!" he claimed. "I want only for you to have fun with me. What's wrong with that?"

"Go away!"

"When you tell me why I must not kiss you. You see, you cannot! You will like it very much, my little English girl!" He tried to suit the action to his words, holding her tight against him and smothering her face with kisses, but Morag, lent strength by her own fury, pulled herself free and walked away from him across the beach toward the house.

Takis ran along behind her. "You have a heart like a stone!" he accused her. "You look like a pretty woman, but you have no feelings, or you would show me that you like me a little."

I don't like you at all!" Morag retorted.

"I shall make you like me!"

"Oh no, not that again!" she said desperately. But she was too late. He caught her to him and tried to kiss her again, taking no notice of her efforts to free herself from his restricting hands.

"Takis!"

The bruising grip of his fingers relaxed and Morag tore herself away from him only to find herself face to face with Pericles.

"It wasn't my fault," she said.

"The children are home," was all he said. "Go up to the house and see to them."

"Yes, Mr. Holmes."

"And, Miss Grant..." he added.

She turned toward him. "Yes?"

"I think it was your fault. I told you to stay away from my cousin."

"But he doesn't mean any harm, Perry!"

"How do you know that?" He bit out the words, strong angry lines etching themselves into his face. "How can you possibly know that?"

"He's like David. He has to show off. His beauty is all he has!"

Pericles' face softened a little. "How like David? Enough for you to fall for his feckless brand of charm?"

She shook her head. "I'll go and see to the children."

She wished she had something more to cover herself with than the towel she had brought with her to the beach. Takis had looked at her with an open admiration and she had hardly noticed, but Pericles had only to allow his eyes to drop to the smocked top of her swimsuit and she felt half-naked and shamed by the fact that she was vulnerable to his slightest change of mood.

He nodded shortly. "I'll speak to you later. If Takis is annoying you, I'll do something about it. But I won't have you encouraging him, Morag, no matter how like David he is! It's time you faced facts and grew up a little!"

She was determined not to cry. That would have been the final humiliation. But it was hard not to object to the injustice of that last remark. How could he think she would encourage Takis when—yes, it might as well be said—when *he* was living in the same house and when she couldn't think about anything or anyone else when he was around? She *had* faced facts—at least, she had faced the only fact that mattered, and that was that she was more than a little in love with Pericles Holmes. The trouble was that she had thought, that first evening, that he had found her a little special, too, but he had given no further sign that he liked her.

"I'm sorry," she said.

"You'll be more than sorry if I catch you flirting with him again!" he told her grimly.

"It wasn't my fault!" she declared again. The tears spilled over and ran down her cheeks and she brushed them away with an impatient hand. "I don't even like him!"

His eyes glinted as they caught the sun. "Remember that!" he advised her. "And stay away from him!"

She climbed the steps that had been cut into the rock leading up to the villa, doing her best to control her tears. She would not cry! She rubbed her face in her towel and tripped over a loose piece of stone, falling heavily against the rough side of the steps. The pain of the graze down the side of her leg put her tears to flight, but she felt that somehow that, too, was all Pericles' fault and that it wouldn't have happened if he had spoken to her more kindly.

"Morag, Morag, are you hurt?"

She looked up from her leg to smile at Kimon's anxious face. "I'll live," she told him. "It isn't very bad."

"You weren't looking where you were going," he rebuked her. He took a deep breath. "Did daddy tell you?"

"Tell me what?"

Kimon frowned. For him, there was only one important matter on hand at the moment. He hugged himself with glee, jumping up and down. "Did he tell you what grandma has given me? Did he? It's the most gorgeous thing you've ever seen. Can you guess what it is?"

Morag considered the matter. "A new fishing rod," she hazarded. She knew that Kimon had wanted one ever since he had come to Greece.

"No! That's quite ordinary! This is special!"

"I don't know," Morag said. "You'll have to tell me."

"It's a Spartan coin. You know, one of their iron cartwheels. It's terrific! All the other Greeks used to laugh at them because they wouldn't make their coins smaller and easier to handle, like the Athenians did. But the Spartans were the toughest people in the world and they didn't mind if their money did wear out their clothing. They seldom carried it around anyway. Do you want to see it? It's just like those you can see in the musuem."

Morag was caught up in his enthusiasm. "I'd love to. I didn't know you were interested in coins," she added as Kimon ran ahead of her toward the house.

"Oh yes, I've collected them for ages!"

Morag allowed herself to be hauled off into his room. "What about Peggy?" she asked. "What does she collect?"

"Girls don't collect things," he declared. "She used to like collecting different pebbles and stones, but grandma said they were rubbish and made her throw them away."

"I used to collect stamps," Morag remembered.

"Did you?" He was diverted for an instant from getting his precious coin out of its hiding place at the back of his drawer. "Peggy used to polish her stones. They were quite pretty. But it doesn't do for girls to get interested in men's things—they have to do other things."

"Can't they do both?" Morag asked innocently.

The boy shrugged. "Grandma doesn't think so," he answered. "When she was young, she wanted to paint more than anything. She used to do the most marvelous pictures, but my grandfather painted, too, and his paintings had to be better. He made grandma destroy all hers when she married him. She says it's much better not to get to like doing things if you can't go on with them."

"Your grandfather sounds like a bigoted old man to me!" Morag observed dryly.

Kimon grinned. "That's what daddy says to grandma when she goes on about Peggy. Look, don't you think it's the nicest coin you've ever seen?"

Morag did. She put the wheel-shaped coin on the palm of her hand and twisted it this way and that, marveling at the age of such a piece and the workmanship that allowed the spokeslike pattern to be seen so many hundreds of years later.

"What did Peggy get?" she asked.

Kimon had the grace to look a bit guilty. "Grandma didn't give her anything," he admitted. "Peggy doesn't mind!"

"I'm afraid she does," Morag said, returning the coin. "I think she minds very much."

Kimon thought for a moment. "Peggy will get a dowry when she marries," he pointed out. "She'll have a house and all sorts of things!" He put his precious coin back in his drawer. "She won't get married if she doesn't. Well, I suppose she might, to someone in Athens or one of the big cities, but not to an islander or someone more old-fashioned. Have you got a dowry?"

"No," said Morag.

"Mummy had one. Grandma says she brought a great deal into the family."

Morag pursed her lips together thoughtfully. "I think I'll give Peggy something. What do you think she'd like?"

Kimon went pink. "Have you still got your stamps?" he asked. "She'd like that. I thought I'd give her my scout knife, but grandma would only take it away from her. But she needn't know about the stamps!"

"They're in England," Morag said, feeling rather guilty that she should encourage the children to have secrets from their grandmother. "I could ask my step-mother to send them, I suppose."

"And meanwhile you could tell Peggy about them! Have you got many?"

"Not very many. But I've got some very nice ones. A few pretty ones from Africa, and a few quite valuable ones from all over the Commonwealth."

"You could tell her about those," Kimon enthused. "Peggy likes to know what things are worth."

Like her grandmother! But it wasn't fair that Kimon should receive so many valuable gifts and Peggy none at all. "You can tell her about the stamps, if you want to, Kimon," she said aloud.

"May I? She'll be thrilled to bits!"

He pushed past her with a whoop of joy, shouting for his sister as he went. Morag smiled after him. If everyone were so easy to please, how simple life would be!

KYRIA HOLMES BARELY looked up as Morag came into the room. "What is all the noise about?" she asked in her heavily accented English.

"Kimon was showing me his coin."

Kyria Holmes sniffed. "I fail to see why it should involve so much noise. You have little control over the children, although that is supposed to be the reason why you are here. I have told Pericles that I think it would be a mistake to allow them to become too fond of you. Children should be kept at a distance, Miss Grant, not made the center of things."

Morag stiffened. "I don't agree, *Kyria.*"

"Why not?"

Morag was astonished by the question. She had thought the older woman would merely have snubbed her for giving her unasked opinion, but then Pericles' mother seldom did the thing that was expected of her.

"I think children should be encouraged to be confident and sure of themselves," she answered. "No one should think less of himself than the best."

"That is a very Greek sentiment," Kyria Holmes said mildly. "It is all right for men, but it's harder when one is a woman. I would like to have been born a man! I would have shown the world...." She broke off, biting her lip. "I'm told you prefer being a woman, Miss Grant. Peggy says that you claim you have more fun as a girl. I find it unbelievable, but perhaps you have never wanted to do anything very much and then found you can't?"

"No, I haven't," Morag admitted.

"Then you don't know what you're talking about!"

"I suppose not, but if I wanted to do something very much, I'd do it!" She licked her lips, a little afraid of what she was about to say. "*Kyria*, why don't you start painting again?"

The silence stretched interminably between them, then Kyria Holmes said, "Pericles would not permit it!"

"What's it got to do with him?" The words were out before she could stop them, but Morag could not bring herself to regret them.

Kyria Holmes merely stared at her. "He is my son!"

"But he wouldn't stop you painting. Why should he?"

"His father didn't approve of my work. Pericles would think it disloyal of me if I were to start again now!"

"I've never heard anything so ridiculous!" Morag exploded. "I'll ask him! I'm not afraid of him, if you are!"

To her surprise, the older woman laughed. "Young people these days are afraid of nothing. But I think you are not quite so casual in the way you treat my son as you pretend, no?"

Morag colored faintly. "What makes you say that?"

"You are very brave on my behalf, but would you defy Pericles for yourself? I think not, my dear. You are not so different from your Greek sisters after all. You seek the approval of the man who controls your life, and that is good, very good."

"Pericles doesn't control my life!" Morag said.

"Does your father?"

"No one does!"

Kyria Holmes gave a superior smile. "The new liberated woman? My dear, how little you know about yourself. In England, when my husband was alive, I met many of them and they were none of them like you!"

Morag chewed on her lip, not enjoying the turn the conversation had taken. "Anyway," she said, "we were talking about you. Why don't you paint again?"

"You don't believe me about Pericles?"

Morag opened her eyes wide. "No."

"He is not my husband, it is true. Pericles would not stop me painting if he knew I wanted to do so, but I'm afraid that after all this time I'd be no good. Worse still, I might not know that I was no good. Do you understand me? My husband refused to allow me to paint on principle. Women, he said, could never be better than second-rate in the arts. I could not disobey him, so I did as he asked and destroyed my paintings, but not the desire, never the urge to paint!"

Morag wondered why, if she felt like that, she should seek to impose the same rigid ideas on women on her grand-daughter, but then she didn't begin to understand what moved the older woman. Perhaps Pericles did.

"Pericles would want you to try," she said certainly.

Kyria Holmes looked amused. "Thank you, my dear. I will ask my son when he comes in."

"Ask me what?" Pericles said from the doorway. His eyes were on Morag and she was very conscious of his gaze.

"Morag... Miss Grant...."

"I think you should get used to calling her Morag, mama."

His mother lifted her eyebrows, but she said nothing. "Morag has been trying to persuade me to start painting again. What do you think of that?" She threw back her head, challenging her son to renege on his father's ban. "She has impertinence, this young English girl!"

"Very impertinent," Pericles agreed. Morag looked up quickly and saw that he was smiling. "And a revolutionary in her own way. Peggy is jumping over the moon because she is going to collect stamps—yes, mama, she is. I have told her that she may! And now here you are, all set to start painting again!"

His mother compressed her lips. "I have changed my mind!"

"Because you don't want to be grateful to Morag?"

Morag was shocked that he should suggest such a thing. "She's afraid, Perry. Besides, why should she be grateful to me?"

"I'm not!" Kyria Holmes assured her. "To suggest that I am afraid!" She tossed her head. "If Pericles says I may start painting again, then I shall do so!"

"I'll buy you some paints next time I go to Athens," he promised.

His mother was far from pleased. "I shall buy my own paints! Afraid! Why should I be afraid of my own son?" She gave Morag a look filled with malicious amusement. "If anyone is afraid, Morag Grant, it is you, and well you might be if you always behave so freely with young men as you did with Takis on the beach. If you were my daughter, you would spend the rest of the evening in your room to teach you to be more circumspect! Such a sight! I'll leave you alone with Pericles and you can explain to him what you were doing!" She rapped Morag sharply over the knuckles with her open hand. "And then tell me you're not afraid of him!" she added in a low fierce whisper, and laughed a laugh so like her son's that Morag could only stare at her, hoping that Pericles hadn't heard her.

But Pericles had. One look at the mocking expression on his face was enough to convince her of that!

"I...I think your mother would be much happier if she could paint again!"

"Yes, I think she might be."

"And Peggy needs to collect something. If she can't collect stones, there isn't any reason why she shouldn't collect stamps, is there?"

"None at all."

"Then you don't mind?" she pressed him.

"Did you think I would?"

"N-no."

He came and sat down beside her. "Are you afraid of me, Morag?"

She looked away from him. "Of course not!" The color rose in her cheeks. "Your... mother thinks that all women should be afraid of some man. But I am not! Why should I be?"

He sat back, thrusting his legs out in front of him, looking the picture of ease and comfort. "Why are you?" he countered softly.

"I'm not—not really! I mean, it doesn't matter to me what you think of me. I don't have to stay here!"

She sought in vain for some kind of answer. "I don't know!" She threaded her fingers together, giving vent to her feelings in the only way she could think of. "I-I'm n-not!" she asserted.

His hand closed over hers. "Not at all?" She could feel his amusement and wondered why he could be so heartless.

"Why should I be?" she compromised.

"My mother is not unobservant," he remarked. He gave her a humorous look. "She likes you, did you know that?"

"She has a strange way of showing it! She needn't have mentioned Takis at all!"

He laughed and put an arm around her shoulders, pulling her close to him. "If she hadn't, I would have done. What did you mean, he's like David?"

She tried to ignore the feel of his arm around her, but it was hard when she could hardly breathe, let alone move, in case he should take it away again.

"He looks like David when he smiles," she said.

He was silent for a long moment, then he said, "Morag, will you marry me?"

Her heart pounded painfully against her ribs. She

struggled upward, but his arm pulled her back against him. "Why?" she whispered.

"You can't marry David, and I don't suppose Takis will oblige—"

"Why should I want to marry Takis?" she burst out. "I didn't want him to...to try to kiss me! I only meant that he likes to be admired, and David did, too! He couldn't bear it if people ignored him."

"Yet you loved him?"

She struggled with her conscience, more than half-decided to lie to him. "I...I thought I did. I don't think I know very much above love. He was nice, though, Perry, and very handsome—just like Takis!"

"I see," he said.

"No, you don't! I thought nothing mattered when he was dead. Nothing did matter!" She bit her lip. "I like it here. I don't want to go home. They were glad when I left. They didn't say so, of course. They didn't have to! David would have taken me away from them...."

"Then stay here and marry me," Pericles murmured.

"But why should you want to? Kimon and Peggy—"

"Exactly," he said. "I've never seen Peggy happier than since you came here, and Kimon is more thoughtful of her feelings. They both love you, Morag, and I think they need you. Would that be enough for you?"

It wasn't, but she could hardly say so. How could she begin to explain that she wanted his love, too? She shut her eyes and tried to imagine what it would be like if the arm that held her would tighten, and if he would kiss her, just once, as if he meant it.

"Yes, it would be enough," she said. "But I'd stay anyway. You don't have to marry me. I'll stay as long as you want me!"

He put up his hand and pulled on the lobe of her ear, much as he might have done to Peggy. "Oh, Morag!

Generous as ever, with never a thought for yourself!"

"Sloppy, don't you mean?"

"It's rather a nice characteristic when not taken to excess. If you marry me, there will be no more regrets for David, and no more romantic incidents with Takis. You will be my wife, do you understand that? In Greece, we take these things very seriously."

"But don't you want to marry someone you love?" He deserved so much better, she thought. First Susan, whom his family had chosen for him, and now herself because his children liked her!

"What about you?" He turned the question.

She took a deep breath. "I want to marry you," she said.

CHAPTER FOUR

MORAG FOUND saying goodbye to the children almost unbearable. "I suppose we have to go to England?" she said to Pericles.

"I think so. Your family will expect to see you safely married to me. It will only be a week before we're back here. It isn't very long."

"I know," she said. "But I wish we could be married here."

"I don't think my mother would thank you for the suggestion. All that trouble and fuss for an English girl she scarcely knows!"

Morag managed a smile. "I think she likes to embarrass me."

"You'll get used to it!"

Morag wasn't so sure. She found it difficult enough to come to terms with the idea of being Pericles' wife without her future mother-in-law's comments as to how her son would treat her once the ring was safely on her finger. Not that Morag believed that Perry was likely to beat her, or starve her, or even argue with her in front of his family, but he was half Greek and the Greeks expected their wives to be subservient to them, and who knew which half of his blood dominated in Pericles? He might be as Greek in that as his name!

Pericles looked at her doubtful face and laughed. "Don't you want to introduce me to your family?" he asked curiously.

She was immediately enthusiastic. "Oh yes!" A flash of amusement entered her eye. "I shall very much enjoy showing you off to them. You're much better than anything that Delia has been able to produce!" Her expression clouded over for an instant. "You don't mind, do you? You'll probably like her," she added stiffly. "Most men do!"

"I hope I shall, too," he drawled.

Morag felt despair around her heart. Delia would take one look at him and she would want him as surely as she had wanted anything else of Morag's, as she had wanted David. Well, she had taken David and Morag had cared, but she had not broken her heart over it, though for a time she had thought she had. But supposing Delia were to take Pericles from her? He was bound to find her beautiful and attentive and far, far more sophisticated than Morag could ever be. He was bound to prefer her to herself. It went without saying, and it was the one thing that she couldn't bear to happen. Pericles might not love her, but somehow or other he had stolen her heart from her, and that was the only reason she was marrying him, though she had agreed with every one of the practical reasons he had suggested to her, beginning with the children and ending with her own broken romance, the penalty the courts had imposed on her when she had taken responsibility for David's death, and the corresponding gossip that had so dismayed her family. What else could she do but agree with him when he hadn't once to her certain knowledge mentioned the word "love"?

"Pericles," she began. Her lashes swept down to hide her eyes.

"Uh-huh?"

"I wouldn't ask you to pretend exactly, but..." Her cheeks turned scarlet. "I haven't told them that you find it convenient to marry me, because of the children and

so on. Would you... would you mind very much ...."
She broke off, unable to continue.

"If I laid more stress on 'and so on" than on the children?" he suggested. There was amusement in his voice.

She didn't dare look at him. "They all knew that David preferred Delia to me. We all pretended for a while, but they knew, just as I knew."

"Perhaps we should get into practice," he suggested.

Her eyes widened and she shot him a swift glance. The brilliant laughter in his eyes did nothing to reassure her. "I only meant," she said hurriedly, "that... that I'd prefer them to think that we were getting married for all the usual reasons."

"I know exactly what you want them to think!" he said. "All right, *karthia mou*, we'll play it your way. I may enjoy stringing them all along—especially Delia!" He put a hand beneath her hair on the nape of her neck and drew her toward him. She felt a suffocating sense of excitement and was immediately afraid that he would know how he affected her.

With a little gasp she pulled away, but he would have none of it.

"You have to pay for your pride," she heard him say as if from a distance. "We can't have you getting in a panic every time I touch you or no one will believe I find you irresistible, or that you melt with desire every time I come near you. That wouldn't do at all, would it?"

She licked her lips. "No," she said.

The pressure increased on the nape of her neck and, perforce, she had to take another step closer to him. His body was hard against hers and his arms were like two steel bands holding her tightly to him. The excitement within her exploded into something she had never experienced before. She was trembling and she scarcely knew whether it was with fear of the unknown, or with sheer longing for him to initiate her into that unknown.

"You're a better actress than I thought," he said dryly, pushing her hair back from her face. "I could swear you were enjoying this!"

She hid her face against his neck and pretended not to have heard him. But she could feel his laughter and it made her tremble still more.

"Look up, little Morag," he said more gently. "How can I kiss you when you hide from me?"

She wished she had the courage to do as he asked, but she knew that if she did look up, he would see what lay in her eyes.

His fingers stroked the nape of her neck for a few more seconds, then they entangled themselves in her hair and forced her head backward, whether she would or would not. She shut her eyes, putting her hands flat against his chest, her body tense and waiting. "You have to kiss me, too, you know!"

"I can't," she breathed.

"Why not?" he touched her mouth lightly with his own. "You have two excellent lips just made for kissing. All you have to do is this and this...and this!" The first two kisses were meant to tease her, but the third was of a different quality. It began just like the others, but soon the pressure of his firm mouth parted her lips beneath his and she felt his male joy in conquest as her resistance flared and died, changing into a delicious surrender that wanted only to please him. Her arms slipped up behind his head and the tension went out of her. She felt his hands exploring her back and the soft curve of her breasts and she dug her fingers deeper into his hair. It was tough and virile like him and showed as little sign of bending to her will, and somehow that pleased her, too.

"*Yinéka*, for someone who can't kiss, you certainly would have fooled me!"

She took a deep breath, struggling to maintain a modiof dignity. "Don't call me Greek names! I don't know what they mean!" She longed to fling herself back into his arms, to plead with him to kiss her again, but she knew that she couldn't do that.

"I'll call you any names I please," he said, the mockery back in his voice.

She blinked. "I wouldn't mind in English." She bit her lip, thinking that sounded craven. "Perry, I never...never kissed anyone like that before—"

"I should hope not!" he cut her off.

"I didn't know—"

He stopped her words with his mouth. "Hush, I know that, too, Morag. I know it all!"

How can you? she wondered.

He kissed her hard and put her away from him, giving her a little push, even while he smiled at her. "Freedom is more dearly bought, sweetheart. That paid for your pride as far as your family is concerned. The payment I set on mine will ask more of you than that!"

"I don't understand," she said.

"You will!" he retorted, and she couldn't tell whether he meant it as a threat or a promise.

She bent her head. "I'll try to be a good wife to you." She thought perhaps his silence meant that he wasn't convinced. "I l-liked it just now—when you kissed me. If-if that's what you want...."

He tipped her head up until her eyes, dark with embarrassment, met his.

"But what do you want, Morag? What do you want so much that you'll beg for it? When will you take because you need to take more than you need the luxury of giving? That's what you have to pay for *my* pride!"

There was no answer to that. She had never gone down on her knees to anyone and she never would. Not even for the kisses of Pericles Holmes! But she felt cold when he took his hand away and colder still when he turned his back on her and left her alone with her own chaotic thoughts.

THEY LEFT ATHENS AIRPORT in bright sunshine with a temperature of more than ninety degrees and came down three hours later into a wet, windy day in London that made for a rough landing and a quick dash from the airplane to the nearby terminal buildings. Rather to Morag's surprise, her whole family had assembled to meet her, and while she was waiting for Pericles to collect their suitcases and carry them through customs, she caught sight of them waiting on the other side and she was struck anew by her stepsister's pale looks and the confident way she looked around her, sure that she was attracting every male eye in the place. Nor was her confidence misplaced. Morag watched, with what she told herself was amusement, as a good-looking young man brushed against Delia's shoulder, turned with a wide grin to apologize, and immediately stayed to make the most of the incident.

"So that is Delia," Pericles murmured in her ear. "What a very dishy young woman!" Stung, Morag wished she could deny it. "I told you she was," she answered. "I told you that you'd like her, too!"

Pericles looked amused. "So you did. Do you think it's too soon for me to give her a brotherly kiss of greeting?"

Morag didn't bother to reply. It didn't matter what she did, she thought, Delia was bound to take over, and Pericles would follow her lead, and it would be just like David all over again. Any man had only to see Delia to want to kiss her.

She cast Pericles a swift, reproachful look and was not surprised to see he was smiling. It was an anticipatory smile, as if he already knew just how much he was going to enjoy dallying with Delia. Well, if she had anything to do with it, he would not be given the opportunity!

"I don't think it would be at all suitable!" she snapped, her head held high. "Besides, you owe me something, too! Or have you forgotten already?"

His smile grew deeper and she thought it had a rather triumphant air to it. "I haven't forgotten," he said. "You won't have any cause for complaint—while we're in England. Afterward—"

"Afterward we'll be back in Greece with the children." She attempted humor. "It won't matter then!"

"I expect your family will come out and stay with us from time to time. I certainly mean to do all I can to see that we stay on good terms with all of them!"

I'll bet! she thought. And all this after one glimpse of Delia! What was it going to be like when he had spent a whole week in her company?

Delia settled the whole question of the kiss by coming straight up to Pericles and offering him her face. "I ought to congratulate you," she said huskily, "but I know Morag too well to do that. I think I'll congratulate her instead! How did she manage to find an Adonis like you, even in the wilds of Greece?"

"I expect she'll tell you herself," Pericles answered smoothly. He turned away to shake Morag's father's hand and to be introduced to her stepmother. When he felt he had made himself sufficiently agreeable to them both, he put an arm aroung Morag's shoulders and smiled down at her.

Morag was so busy reminding herself that he didn't mean what his smile was telling her that she was quite unprepared for her stepsister's sudden exclamation.

"My dear Morag, where did you get that dreadful necklace? Let's have a look at it!" She pulled at the shells that Morag had put on under her sweater and laughed out loud. "It would be quite pretty if it weren't for those terrible green beads! Morag, you ought to know better than to wear such rubbish."

"I like them!" Morag declared.

Pericles grinned at her. He pulled the necklace out from under her sweater and rearranged it around her neck, making, she felt, the most of the moment and plainly enjoying her own shy attempts to prevent him.

"I gave them to her," he told the others. "She's under the protection of the goddess Nemesis when she wears them—"

"Yes, but I don't believe that!" Morag protested.

"Then why wear them now, darling?" he said.

"I thought they'd get crushed in my suitcase." It wasn't true. She hadn't thought about it at all. But it seemed as good a reason as any other. She would not admit, even to herself, that it was because he had given them to her. She had worn them constantly ever since, hiding them under her dress, or with a scarf around her neck. It was the only thing he had given her!

"Nemesis?" Delia said vaguely. "Seem to have heard about her. Doesn't she creep up behind people, dropping swords on their heads?"

Pericles frowned. "Not swords, no. I don't think you can have the right lady." He sounded short to the point of rudeness.

"No," Mr. Grant said soberly. He gave his step-daughter an affectionate look mixed with admiration. "Delia's facts are always well chosen to suit herself. Nemesis sought out and punished evildoers."

"And compensated those who suffered," Morag put in, not looking at Delia. "I went to visit her temple in Greece."

Delia managed a very creditable smile. "What a good

thing she has no jurisdiction in England!" she shot at Morag.

Mrs. Grant giggled. "Goodness, yes! But we mustn't bring up any painful memories for Morag today. She has obviously forgotten all about David—poor boy! We must try to do the same, Delia. After all, he was *her* fiancé!"

Morag colored guiltily, seeking to evade Pericles' restraining arm while she thought of some devastating retort. But Pericles would not allow it. He gave Mrs. Grant a cool, considering look and then he smiled.

"Perhaps Morag had less to forget," he drawled. "Puppy love is painful at the time, especially when one's beloved is not particularly faithful, or particularly particular, come to that, but one grows out of such foolishness!"

Morag gave him a look of exasperation. "Puppy love?"

He raised an eyebrow, grinning. "Wasn't it?"

Her cheeks burned. "I suppose you know best," she managed to say.

He flicked her cheek with a gentle finger, but his attention had already wandered and she knew, without looking at him, that he was covertly studying her stepsister.

IT WAS STRANGE to be back in her father's house and to sleep in the room that had been hers all through her childhood. From the window she could see the stretch of road where that fateful evening the car had come weaving toward the gates, only to crash into the telegraph pole on the far side of the road. Morag stood at the window for a long time, trying to recall what it was that she had felt then that had compelled her to take Delia's place at the wheel, after hurrying her stepsister up into the house and telling her to call the police. She must have been mad! How could she have thought that David mattered so much to her that his lightest interest had to be protected at such a cost? She sighed, glad that it was getting dark and that it was time to change her dress. She had brooded for long enough. She had other things to think about now. Pericles, for example.

Coming home had had one unlooked-for advantage in that she was reunited with her wardrobe and no longer had to make do with what she had been able to carry in her knapsack. It took her all of ten minutes to decide which dress to wear. Her stepmother thought it was unlucky to wear green and so Morag had only one dress of that color, and she chose it now, knowing that it brought out the green of her eyes and made her hair look darker and richer against the soft glow of the silk. Having made up her mind, it took her much less time to slip off the clothes she had been wearing, to put on a long petticoat, and to slide the green dress over her head, letting the wide skirt fall to her feet.

A knock at her door interrupted her efforts to pull up the zipper behind her back.

"Come in," she called out. She heard the door open and went on quite crossly, "Do me up, will you? I think it's stuck!"

"Very pretty!" Pericles congratulated her.

She twisted around to face him. "I thought you were Delia!"

"Your father sent me up to fetch you. He wants to toast our health before dinner." His eyes looked her over with appreciation. "You'll have to turn around if you want me to fix your zipper."

She turned her back, shivering as his fingers came in contact with her bare skin. "I wish Kimon and Peggy were here," she said. "They might have enjoyed all the fuss."

"Meaning that you're not?"

"Not much," she said.

"Then you don't want me to leave you here and go back to Greece on my own?" She started undoing the few inches of zipper he had managed to do up. "Oh, Perry, you wouldn't! Please don't tease me! I'll do anything—"

"Anything?"

Her hands clutched at and found his sleeve. "Y-yes," she stammered. "Only don't leave me here! You can't! You said you'd marry me!"

"You said you'd marry me, but I can't help wondering if you know what you're doing, Morag Grant. You're not marrying Kimon and Peggy!"

"I know that!"

A gleam of amusement lit his eyes. "I wonder. I think you're more intent on having some kind of revenge on your family. But it will be you who will have to live with it, *karthia mou.* I don't want you to rush into something you may regret."

She turned her back on him again, finding it easier not to look at him. "It isn't only that," she said. "I won't pretend that I'm not enjoying—well, you know how it is! You're so modest that you don't know that you're better than good-looking and... very attractive! But I wouldn't make use of you like that!"

"Not even to get at Delia?"

Morag did not deign to reply as he finished zipping her up and turned her around to face him. "This is the last chance I shall give you to change your mind, Morag. I'll try not to rush you, but there can be no going back on your decision now."

She looked down, veiling her eyes with her long lashes. "I've said I want to marry you," she said quietly. "Isn't that enough?"

"I hope it will be—for you," he answered.

She looked up at him then, the color creeping up her cheeks. "I don't know what you mean."

He gave her a little shake. "I could beat you when you pretend to be obtuse!" he growled at her. "Don't count on my being patient with you forever! One day I'll make you say it, all of it! You make a mistake if you think you can lead me by the nose for long! I am a man, and I won't play second fiddle to any chit of a girl. Is that clear enough for you?"

She nodded. "But you did promise that you'd pretend to be in love with me while we're here—Pericles, please...."

"Yes?"

But she couldn't go on. "You promised!" she said again.

His eyes narrowed and she was once more afraid of him. "I didn't promise to pretend anything. I promised to save your pride."

"But it's the same thing!"

"No, *yinéka mou*, it's not the same thing at all. Come on, we'd better go down to the others." He opened the door for her and stood back to let her pass. "By the way, did I tell you that I like your dress?"

She made a humble gesture with her hand and was surprised when he captured it in his own. To hide her pleasure, she rushed into speech. "You said you liked green. I put it on for you!"

He bent and kissed her cheek. "Very pretty, *pedhi*, but it's the words I want, and it's the words I mean to have!"

IT WAS STRANGE to be married. Stranger still to find herself the equal of her stepmother and no longer the lesser loved daughter of the house. Morag enjoyed herself. She made the most of every moment of it from the time she walked down the aisle on her father's arm, for once the center of his attention, right up to the last goodbye from the last of the guests.

True, it was a peculiarly solemn moment when she promised to love, honor and obey him for the rest of her life, but the look in Pericles' eyes had started a blaze of hope that had stayed with her all day and even now had not quite died away.

"Happy, my dear?" her father asked her, easing himself out of his coat with a sigh of relief.

"Very happy!"

"You're a lucky girl. I don't mind telling you now that I was a bit worried about you and David. He didn't strike me as being your type—far more in Delia's line, if you know what I mean."

"No, I don't," Morag said, frowning.

"Bit flashier in her tastes than you," her father rejoined. "He would have ended up with her—if he hadn't already. You're like your mother, and Delia is very like hers. I'm a lucky man to have known both. Don't misunderstand me, darling, my second marriage is a very happy one. One could not hope for the same generosity a second time such as your mother had. Is that what this Greek man has seen in you?"

"He's only half Greek."

Her father chuckled. "He looks Greek, and I daresay he makes love like a Greek. Did you tell him the truth about the David business, or did he guess?"

Morag gave him a quick glance. "I didn't think you knew!"

"I didn't know. I thought it likely, no more than that. I should have spoken up, I suppose. I didn't know what to do! I'm glad you've found someone to look after you. Too many people were ready to take advantage of you and you would have given them all everything you had.

Pericles looks as though he knows how to keep you well in hand. I think you've chosen well there!"

Morag looked at him as though she had never really seen him before. "It was a lovely wedding, daddy," she said. "Thank you for that."

"It was the least I could do. Ah, here's Delia. Did you enjoy the wedding, too?" he asked his stepdaughter.

"Heavens, no! I thought it was rather pathetic, actually. Morag may think she's got Perry where she wants him, but it can't possibly last. I give her a year, and then he'll be bored with her as David was!"

"Delia!"

Delia smiled lazily at her stepfather. "Don't look so shocked! You know it's true! By the way, Morag, where are you going for your honeymoon? I suppose you are having one?"

Morag's eyes glittered dangerously. "I don't know," she admitted.

Delia laughed loudly. "Well, hadn't you better find out?"

"Do you know?" Morag challenged her.

"Of course!"

Hurt to the quick, Morag ran from the room, running straight into Pericles in the hall.

"How could you?" she demanded of him. "How could you tell her and not me?"

"Tell her what?"

"Where we're going!"

"But you know where we're going, Morag!"

"I don't!" she stormed at him. She lifted a hand as if to strike him, but he was faster, pinning both her wrists behind her back.

"We're going back to Greece, where else? Isn't that what you want?"

"Yes," she admitted uncertainly. "But why tell *her?*"

"Why let her know you mind?" he countered. He let her go with a suddenness that made her stagger. "How soon can you be ready to leave?"

"I haven't packed yet." She bit her lip. "I thought—"

He gave her a push toward the stairs, sighing. "Go and pack, Morag."

She met her stepmother coming down the stairs and stood aside for her to pass, hoping that she wouldn't notice how close she was to tears. It was a forlorn hope.

"Oh, Morag, I thought you would be gone! Crying already? I'm not surprised! It seems so strange for you to be the wife of a foreigner. I hope you manage to get used to their funny ways. Delia says it wouldn't do for her at all! Perry has been telling her some of the things that are expected of a wife in Greece. She says he only married you to look after the children anyway!"

Morag managed a light, amused laugh, helped on by the freezing anger that gripped her. She ran up the remaining stairs and threw her possessions into her suitcase, uncaring as to whether they creased or not. She shut the case with a bang and took a last look around the room. The necklace of shells lay on the bedside table and she picked them up, longing to smash them as Peggy had smashed her necklace at Rhamous. Pericles had promised, and he hadn't even told her the simple fact that they were going back to Greece. She put the shells around her neck, not knowing what else to do with them, and went downstairs again.

Pericles stood up the moment she appeared in the doorway. He took a step toward her, taking both her hands in his.

"Ready, darling? I have been trying to convince your father that we'll be pleased to see him anytime in Athens. You'll have to add your persuasions to mine!"

"But of course we'd love to have you," Morag heard herself say.

Her father chuckled. "When you've had time to get used to one another we might think about paying you a visit."

"Do, sir. Morag will like to see you, won't you, sweetheart?"

Morag felt hypnotized into agreeing with anything he said. She still felt cold with anger at his betrayal, but it didn't seem to matter very much. Nothing mattered, not even the acquisitive look in Delia's eyes that at another time would have filled her with despair.

"The car is waiting to take you to the airport," Mrs. Grant told them busily, her eyes snapping at the sight of Pericles holding Morag's hand. "I don't suppose you want us to come with you."

Pericles grinned at her. "Quite right. I haven't had an opportunity to kiss my bride yet, and where better than in a comfortable car?"

"Oh, but . . ." said Morag.

"She's shy," Delia said, sounding bored. "You'd think she'd never been kissed before!"

Pericles put his arms around Morag and hugged her tightly, kissing her still pink cheek. "That's what I love about her," he said. "I'm Greek enough to want to come first with my wife." He kissed her again, very gently, but as if he meant it. "Do I come first?" he whispered in her ear.

She buried her face in his chest and clenched her fists, but she couldn't bring herself to say it. It was only to herself that she could acknowledge that with her he would always come first, and all the time, no matter what he did.

CHAPTER FIVE

"IT SOUNDS like a funny kind of wedding to me," Kimon said.

"You look just the same as before," Peggy added.

She felt just the same, too, Morag reflected. The trip to England and the few days spent with her family were like the events of a dream. Pericles had hurried her into the car that had taken them to the airport, but he hadn't kissed her. All he had said was that she must be tired after such a long day and that he hoped she wouldn't find the flight back to Greece too much for her.

Morag had been aware of a dull feeling of disappointment, which had lasted for the whole length of the journey. She had felt like a puppet, having her passport stamped and her luggage checked, and even when she had sat in the car beside Pericles for the short drive to his mother's villa.

Once they had arrived there, she had been sure that everything would change for the better, but it had not.

She had got out of the car, stiff limbed and more than a little weary, but undeniably glad to be back in this lovely house with its private pathway down to the sea. It had looked gray in the moonlight and friendly, just as she had remembered it.

"Aren't you glad to be home?" she had said to Pericles as he had bent to pick their luggage out of the trunk.

She had been a bit surprised herself, but there had been no doubt in her own mind that this was home, whereas her father's house had been no more than a memory of childhood to her. She had nodded her head, feeling lost and a bit presumptuous for implying that Kyria Holmes's villa in some way belonged to her, too.

"I expect my mother and the children are already in bed asleep," he had said, catching up with her at the front door. "Which is where you ought to be. I'll put your things in your old room and you can stay there for tonight."

She had felt quite unable to argue with him about it, especially as she knew from experience how the slightest sound echoed up and down the hall, and the last thing she had wanted was to have Pericles' mother hear them. Besides she had reasoned, feeling more and more leaden by the minute, it would only be for the one night, or what was left of it, and she could make the change into his room the following day. She had known, of course, that she would never find the courage to suggest such a thing herself, but she had been confident that he would insist on it, if for no better reason than for the look of the thing.

But he had done nothing of the sort. In fact, he had done nothing at all. She might just as well not be married to him! She had hardly seen him in the last few days, and when she had seen him, she had found herself rendered almost completely tongue-tied, so nervous had she been of saying anything untoward. She was bound to admit that he had been more than patient with this sudden affliction that had taken her, but then perhaps he hadn't noticed that she had lost her tongue and that she started like a nervous rabbit whenever he looked at her! Oh, how she despised herself when she thought of it!

"I'M GLAD YOU WENT," Peggy assured her happily. "You wouldn't have brought back my stamp collection if you hadn't gone."

"It wasn't much fun while you were away, though," Kimon told her. "I much prefer it when you are here. Daddy says he does, too."

Morag's heart lurched within her. When had he said that, she wondered.

"What do you want to do this afternoon?" she asked the children. "We could take the bus somewhere, if you like."

"Athens," said Kimon with decision.

"It's too hot in Athens," Peggy argued. "I'd rather go swimming."

Kimon made a face at her. "You always want to go swimming!" He gave Morag a sudden smile that was very like his father's. "What do you want to do? You ought to choose sometimes, too!"

"You like swimming!" Peggy reminded her quickly, afraid that she was not going to get her own way after all.

"Yes, I do. But we went swimming this morning. I'd like to go to Athens, too. I meant to do some shopping—"

Both children groaned at that. "I hate shopping!" Kimon muttered. His face brightened, though, as a new idea struck him. "Yes, you go shopping, and we can go to the museum and see all the different coins there. I want to compare my Spartan coin with the ones they have there. We'd be quite all right on our own in the museum, truly we would! And we could all have an ice cream outside afterward."

"Yes," said Peggy. "I like to see the man there carrying a mountain of things on his tray. I don't know how he remembers who wants what. May we do that, Morag?"

Glad to have found a compromise so easily, Morag said they would go immediately after lunch. Kyria Holmes, when told of the plan, thought at first she would like to go with them, but in the end she decided against it.

"Since you talked me into painting again," she said to her daughter-in-law with a wry smile, "I have done little else. You must tell me if you think any of my canvases are good enough to show to Pericles."

"I don't know if I'd know," Morag told her. "I'd love to see them, though. Are they all landscapes?"

"No, not at all." The older woman's eyes glinted in the sunlight. "I've been meaning to ask you to call me Dora," she said. "I don't think I should care for mama—it's bad enough that Perry calls me that—and we can't go on being formal forever."

Morag's face was filled with surprised pleasure. "Thank you," she murmured.

Dora gave her an amused look. "I'm glad you like living here," she went on coolly. "Pericles is afraid that you may be lonely, as he had so much business to get through, but you seem to fill your days pretty well. I find it hard to believe as he does, that you want your family to visit you quite yet! But you have only to ask—you know there is plenty of room!"

Morag answered quickly, "I don't think they'd want to come quite yet!"

"No? Your stepsister longs to come to Greece, I'm told. Pericles says she's a raving beauty. Perhaps I should paint her sometime."

Morag swallowed down the comment that Beauty Is as Beauty Does with difficulty. She thought Dora might have some difficulty in understanding the allusion, but she couldn't possibly mistake the tone.

"If Pericles wants to ask her," she began , "I should... should have no objection."

Dora shrugged, unmoved by these wifely sentiments. "You'd better tell him that! But I should remember, my dear, that Pericles is a man like any other, and the Greeks have always found it very hard to resist physical beauty—especially when there is nothing else to distract them!"

Morag shrugged her shoulders. "That's not my fault!"

"No?" Morag, who had grown daily more at ease with Pericles' mother, had forgotten how imperious she could be. "It would only take a word from you—"

"No! He arranged things this way. I'm not going to ask him for anything!"

Dora shrugged again. "Have you ever thought that it's more generous sometimes to take than to give? Why don't you have it out with him once and for all? At least he'd know what you wanted from him, and not just what you are willing to give, no matter how willingly!"

Morag shrank away from her impatience. "I couldn't," she said in a small voice.

"But how is he to know you're in love with him if you don't tell him?" her mother-in-law demanded unanswerably.

"You don't think he's guessed?" Morag asked faintly.

"Oh, don't ask me! I'm only his mother! you'd better get on to Athens and do your shopping before I start giving you some very bad advice, which you won't take. I doted on my own husband, not that he cared whether I did or not as long as I was there to fulfill his needs. But Pericles is different. I'd say it was his English blood, but what else was his father? Susan's indifference worried him very much, though she could hardly have married young Takis, no matter how much in love with him she fancied herself to be. Love grows after marriage, if you let it, but Pericles won't see that. I can't think why he married you!"

Morag's eyes filled with tears. "Why don't you ask him?"

"My dear child, I keep telling you that Pericles is a full grown man! I have no right to ask him any such thing. A man's life is his own. It's quite different for a woman. It's her nature to respond and not to initiate, so she can be taught to love and to live her life subordinate to her husband's. That is the Greek way!"

"Perry is only half Greek!"

Dora laughed. "Maybe, but he's man enough for you, Morag Holmes, as you'll find out one of these days!"

It wasn't a very auspicious start to the afternoon, and by the time she had collected the children, they had missed the bus and had to wait for the next one in the burning heat of the afternoon, a prospect that didn't please any of them. Morag and Peggy sat on a low wall by the side of the road, but Kimon was made of sterner stuff and spent the time spotting the different makes of cars that flashed past him.

"Look, there's Takis!" he shouted after a few minutes. "He'll take us to Athens. Make him stop, Morag! He won't abe able to see me!"

Morag stood up and waved her scarf halfheartedly. She rather hoped that Takis would go by without stopping, but with a screech from his brakes he drew in beside them, grinning broadly.

"How can I serve you, Morag? Do you wish me to carry you away from all your troubles?"

"What troubles?" Peggy asked him, not at all pleased that he should have spoken only to Morag thus, ignoring Kimon and herself.

"What troubles? You and Kimon are the biggest troubles. Her other ones she prefers to keep to herself! Well, Morag, where do you want to go?"

"We want to go to Athens, but we missed the bus and the next one doesn't come for another twenty minutes."

"Then of course I shall take you! You see how I feel about you, that your slightest desire is my immediate command. You shall sit beside me and we shall forget all about the children in the back and have a nice time. Is that what you'd like?"

"Not much," she answered frankly. "I wouldn't ask you to take us at all if it weren't so hot!"

"You are unkind!" Takis complained.

"Very!" she agreed.

The young Greek exploded into laughter. "Unkind, but funny! Climb in, children. One is not allowed to stop here and a policeman may come at any moment. Have you enough room, Morag? You can come closer. *I* do not mind!"

Morag sat as far away from him as possible, trying not to notice the handle that was sticking into her ribs, or his straying hand that somehow found her knee every time he changed gear.

"We're going to the museum," Peggy told him. "I'd rather have gone swimming, but we're going to meet Morag for an ice cream outside afterward."

"Oh? And where do you spend your afternoon, Morag?" Takis asked.

"I've got some shopping to do," she said reluctantly.

He flashed her a smile. "What do you buy? A new dress? I shall come with you and help you choose! I have a very good eye for buying dresses."

"I'd rather you didn't."

"No woman should go shopping by herself," he declared. "They need someone to tell them that they look beautiful in one dress, or more desirable in another. You will see, I am very good at escorting women and I always know exactly the right thing to say! Besides, I can translate all your wishes to the assistants and make sure you get what you want."

Morag sighed. She decided complete honesty was the only way to deal with him and she scurried around her mind for the right words in which to tell him that she didn't want his company. "Takis, please leave me alone. P-Pericles wouldn't like it and I don't like it, either!"

His eyebrows rose in complete disbelief. "P-Pericles," he mimicked her. "Do you mind about him?"

"Of course I do!"

"He doesn't seem to return the compliment! If you were my bride, you would not be waiting for a bus under the hot sun! He deserves that you should look elsewhere for a little fun. Why doesn't he buy you a car?"

Morag hesitated. Then, "I don't drive," she confessed.

"Pericles could teach you!"

Morag felt more uncomfortable and hot than ever. "I can drive, only I don't, so it's my own choice to wait around for buses. Pericles—"

"Could drive you himself!"

"Why should he? He has better things to do with his time!"

"But I haven't? From now on I am your chauffeur. You have only to ask and I shall be there to drive you!"

"No, Takis, If I wanted anyone to drive me, I'd ask Pericles! It was only this afternoon when we missed the bus and Kimon saw you that we needed a lift. Usually we can manage very well by ourselves!"

"No thanks to Pericles!"

Morag glared at him. "I won't have you sneering at him!" she retorted. "He's very kind to me and I love him very much!"

Takis lost some of his bounce and began to apologize. "I hadn't realized that you felt like that about him," he protested. "I thought it was a suitable arrangement for you both. Though I still feel he could look after you better!" His smile came back, and he patted her knee. "You defend him just like a Greek wife!" he teased her.

"Are you as meek to Pericles as a Greek wife should be?"

Morag looked determinedly out of the window. She saw with relief that they were almost in Athens. "I try to be," she said.

Takis chuckled. "It would be interesting to find out if he defends you with the same fervor. He was never in the least bit strict with Susan." He drove in silence all the rest of the way into the center of Athens, only asking her where she wanted to be let out. "There's a place to park just by the temple of Olympian Zeus. Will that be too far for you to walk?"

Morag had no idea, but she was in no mood to argue with him. "Of course not," she said with a confidence she was far from feeling.

"But it is!" Kimon insisted, breaking abruptly into the argument he had been having with his sister ever since they had set foot into the car. "Can't you take us right to the museum, Takis? Or to Omonia Square?"

"If you like," the Greek agreed easily. He pointed out the Royal Guard outside the parliamentary buildings, dressed in the short white kilts, white stocking, and long shoes with their poufs on the toes.

"Along here are the shops," Peggy told Morag. "Grandma buys her clothes here. They're very good shops, but there aren't any department stores like in London—at least, I don't think there are. You won't get lost, will you?"

"No, of course I won't get lost!" Morag protested. "I'll come and see you into the museum first."

Takis stopped the car and leaned across her to open the door. "You're not still cross with me, are you, Morag?" he asked her, smiling straight into her eyes. "Tell me you are not! Please let me come back to the café outside the museum in an hour's time and buy you all an ice cream. Then I shall know that you've forgiven me!"

Morag hesitated and knew, even while she did so, that it was a mistake. "I think it would be better if you didn't," she began, but he had already noted her lack of decision.

"You couldn't be so cruel as to deny me!" he pleaded. "The children will like to have me there!" He rubbed his hand through Kimon's hair. "Don't I buy you the best ice creams?" he asked him.

"I suppose so," Kimon confirmed. He ducked away from his cousin. "But daddy doesn't like us to eat too much between meals," he added somewhat primly.

"Then I shall come and sit at the next-door table and hope you take pity on me!" Takis declared. He watched them climb out of the car, his eyes dancing with amusement. "See you then !" he laughed, and with a wave of his hand he was gone.

Morag frowned after him, but there was nothing to be done and so with a slight shrug of her shoulders she put him to the back of her mind and walked with the children through the formal gardens that led to the National Museum.

"Are you sure you'll be all right?" she fussed as she bought their tickets and gave them each some money to buy postcards or anything else they wanted.

"Of course we shall be!" Peggy insisted.

Kimon nodded. "We know what we want to see, you see," he pointed out. "I want to look at any coins I can find and Peggy wants to make a drawing of the little jockey now that they've found the horse and mounted him on it. He does look rather super—much younger than we are!"

Morag, who had seen the statue when she had visited the museum before she had met any of the Holmeses, was surprised. "I didn't know you liked to draw," she said to Peggy.

"Well, grandma didn't like me to talk about it," the small girl explained, "but since she's started painting again, she doesn't mind my wasting my time drawing things half so much. She looked at some I'd done the other day and told me quite a lot of useful things to help me get the perspective right. She wasn't cross at all!"

"Wasn't she?" Morag smiled with real pleasure. "She must think you're good if she took the trouble to look at your work. She hasn't much time for the second-rate."

"No," Peggy agreed with all the assurance of one who knew that there was no danger of her ever being considered that. "But I'm not as good as she is. She's done a beautiful painting of you!"

"Of me?"

"Yes," said Kimon. "She showed it to us while you were getting married in England. It looks quite like you, only I haven't seen you looking dreamy like she has. She said you looked like that when you thought about daddy."

Morag was completely disconcerted. She longed to question them further, but their impatience to be gone was so obvious that she hadn't the heart to keep them. "I'll be back in one hour exactly," she told them.

"Yes, all right. Don't fuss, Morag!"

Conscious that she was doing exactly that, Morag went out of the building again, reminding herself that, unlike herself, they both spoke excellent Greek and could always ask someone if they couldn't find their way back to the main doors. It would be far more difficult for her to manage her shopping than it would be for them to spend an hour on their own in the museum. She walked down one of the main streets that went between Omonia and Syntagma Squares, shamelessly window-shopping.

She thought she was justified in buying herself a new dress. She had not discussed money with Pericles, and she had no idea whether he eventually intended to make her some kind of an allowance, or whether she would have to ask him whenever she was in need. But this money was her own. She had brought it with her to finance her trip through Greece and she had only spent very little of it. It cost her nothing to live at Dora's villa beyond her few personal needs. Then the idea had come to her that she would buy herself a new dress. It had to be no ordinary dress, but something very special, something that would flatter her into a kind of beauty. She had not forgotten how Pericles had looked at her that evening that she had worn her green dress and she wanted badly for him to look at her like that again. Not even Delia's best efforts to divert his attention to herself had quite succeeded that evening. If, Morag thought, she could find herself a truly splendid dress, perhaps he would look at her again in the same way, he might even want to kiss her again, kiss her as he had not kissed her ever since their wedding.

The first shop she entered had nothing that caught her eye, but in the second shop was a dress made of cloth of gold and cut in a style that she knew immediately would suit her. She pointed silently at it when the assistant came to serve her and for a second they both gazed at the dress in silence.

"It's beautiful!" Morag breathed.

The assistant nodded sympathetically. "It is also expensive," she murmured in very creditable English. "Do you want to try it?"

Morag nodded. She didn't care how expensive it was, she had to have it. If *that* didn't have the desired effect on Pericles, she would write herself off as a total failure, and that didn't even bear thinking about.

"How much is it?" she asked timidly as the assistant gathered up the full skirt and threw it over her head. She held her breath and watched the gold cloth ripple down to her ankles. It shimmered, trembling just as she had trembled when Pericles had touched her. She didn't care how much it cost, she had to have it!

Even so, the price came as a jolt to her. "Are you sure?" she exclaimed, unable to take her eyes off her gleaming reflection in the glass.

"Yes, *kyria*, I am very sure."

Morag sighed. If she paid such a sum on a single dress, she would have nothing left of her own. It would serve her right, for it would be sheer extravagance to spend her all on a single dress, and a dress that she was not likely to wear often at that.

"I'll take it!"

She felt quite dazed with her own bravado. She had to keep looking at the dress to reassure herself all over again as she countersigned the traveler's checks she had brought with her. The assistant glanced at her wedding ring with a little smile.

"I hope he knows! Or is it to surprise him?"

"It's a surprise," Morag admitted. "It's my own money, so he can't be very angry—" She broke off as a decidedly male hand covered one of hers and Takis squinted at the bill beside the empty plastic cover of her traveler's checks.

"Phew!" he whistled.

The Greek girl picked the gold dress off the rail and held it up for him to see. "Your wife has chosen well. She looked magnificent—"

"She always looks lovely!" Takis cut her off.

Only Morag seemed to have noticed the Greek girl's mistake. "He isn't—"

Takis silenced her with a quick kiss on the side of her

mouth. "My wife thinks I'm marvelous! You see, I never question how much she spends on clothes!"

"A nice husband to have!" the Greek girl said admiringly. "Shall I wrap the dress, *kyria*, or do you want us to send it?"

"I'll...I'll take it with me," Morag stammered, her mouth dry.

Takis flashed his bright smile. "I'll carry it for her, so put a decent handle on it. I don't like it when the string cuts into my fingers."

The girl gave him a look of pure adulation and hurried away to fold and wrap the dress.

"I wish you hadn't come, Takis," said Morag. "I did ask you not to."

"And who would have carried your packages then?"

"And another thing," Morag went on, warming to her theme, "how dare you give the impression that you're my husband?"

He put a finger across her lips to silence her. "Better that than that she should jump to a different conclusion, my sweet innocent. You wouldn't like it if she thought I was *not* your husband, would you?"

She glared at him. "I'll carry my own package!" she snapped, almost snatching it out of the assistant's hands. "I can keep my eye on it then!"

Takis shrugged and winked at the Greek girl. "Tell me when you are tired and then I will carry it," he smiled.

Morag could hardly refuse his company back to the museum. It would have been silly to have walked ahead because she knew he would only follow on behind, making her feel a fool.

As if he had read her thoughts, Takis put a hand on her shoulder and smiled his little-boy smile. "You won't make me sit at a separate table for my ice cream, will you, Morag? I'm doing my best to please you!"

She gasped with suppressed fury. "Your best! Perhaps you should try your worst for a change!"

He grinned. "If you like. My worst would be to forget this foolish marriage of yours and kiss you a little myself. You're a pretty little thing, Morag *pedhi*, especially when you try to look cool and calm, and your eyes flash fire and promise."

"They promise you nothing! Takis, if you go on like this, I shall tell Pericles—and Dora!"

"Dora would blame you. No man is ever to blame for flirting with a pretty girl, in her opinion. I think you won't say anything to Thia Dora. And you are too afraid of Pericles to mention any escapade to him. No, no. You value his opinion of you too highly to risk his taking you to task for playing games with me!"

Morag hurried her footsteps, her indignation reverberating along the pavement. "I'll never speak to you again!" she told him furiously. "Why won't you go away?" But he only laughed and took her dress from her, tucking it under his arm as he put a hand on her elbow to guide her across the busy street.

If Morag would have preferred him to be anywhere else, the children were more than pleased to see him, however. They were already seated at one of the tables that had been arranged under the trees in the forecourt of the museum.

"We didn't order until you came," Kimon mentioned quickly. "We thought Takis might be with you."

"So I can pay, huh?" his cousin teased him. "Well, here I am! What are you all going to have?"

"Ice cream," they demanded unanimously.

Takis looked at Morag, his eyes bright—too bright. "And you?"

She would have liked to have refused to have anything, but she thought that that would be making too much of a silly incident. Besides, it was terribly hot and the cooling breeze that always seemed to be present beside the sea was absent form the stifling Athens streets. She looked down her nose, sitting very straight in her chair. "I'll have a pressed lemon," she said.

Takis laughed. "I'll tell him to bring you plenty of sugar!" he teased her.

Morag averted her face. She rescued the box holding her dress from beside his chair where he had put it and hugged it to her. He had spoiled her whole afternoon, but at least she had her dress!

It was a long time before their order came. The waiter, when he did come, was carrying a huge tray, laden several layers with drinks, ice creams, cakes and large, cool glasses of water that were served automatically with every order. Diverted for a moment from her anger with Takis, Morag watched the man making his way toward them and thought how well the Athenians laid out their cafés, making the best of every site, temporary or otherwise. Then, with a start of dismay, she realized that the waiter was not the only one who was coming toward them, for behind him came Pericles, a Pericles looking so grim that she clutched her package closer still for comfort.

"Daddy!" Peggy exclaimed. "Daddy, what are you doing here?"

Pericles' eyes rested on Morag's face. "I came to take you home. Are you ready to go?"

She nodded helplessly, as tongue-tied as she always was in his presence nowadays.

"But your haven't had you lemonade," Kimon reminded her, his voice tinged with indignation. "Nor have we had our ice creams!" he added.

Pericles put his hand on Morag's arm, the steely pressure of his fingers drawing her to her feet. "Then you two can come home with Takis," he ordered them. "Morag will come with me—now!"

Morag clutched her package and followed him in silence to where he had left his car. She wished that he would look a little less grim, or that she could think of something bright to say that would relieve the atmosphere between them.

"I thought I told you not to dally with Takis, or to be alone with him," Pericles said smoothly in a voice that brought a wave of panic to the pit of ther stomach.

"The children—" she began.

"The children! Were the children there when you went shopping together?"

In silence she shook her head. "I didn't ask him to come, Perry. He followed me to the shop."

He gave her a long level look. "All right, Morag," he said at last. "But I shan't tell you a third time. Stay away from Takis, or I shall make it my business to see that you do! Now get in and I'll drive you home."

She did so, the tears stinging her eyes. He got in beside her and started the engine, but he didn't drive off immediately.

"Tears, Morag? Then see that you don't give me cause to get really angry with you because, by God, you'll be sorry if you do!"

Morag gave him a frightened look and thought he looked grimmer than ever. She had not the slightest difficulty in believing him. she was sorry now, though she didn't see how she could have got rid of Takis under the circumstances, and if she had felt braver, she would have said so. Pericles lifted an eyebrow and smiled suddenly as if reading her thoughts.

"You could have refused to get into his car in the first

place," he told her. "That was where you made your mistake."

And looking back over the afternoon, Morag could only agree with him.

CHAPTER SIX

"HAVE I any money?"

The question as it came out sounded bald and ungracious, and she immediately wished it unsaid, as happened so often with her nowadays.

Pericles glanced at the parcel she was still hugging to her. "I hadn't thought about it," he admitted. "I'm sorry, Morag. I should have done so. What have you been living on all this time?"

"I haven't needed much. I don't need much now. I only meant that it's nice to have a little, to give the children ice creams occasionally, and things like that."

He gave her a wry look. "Is that an explanation of why you encouraged Takis to tag along? To pay for the children's ice creams?"

She colored. "No, of course not. I was only trying to explain why I needed money."

"My dear girl, if you buy all your clothes at that particular boutique you'll need more than a few drachmas to keep you going!" She found his amusement very hard to bear, but it was worse still when he added, "Did Takis suggest you go there, too?"

"No."

He cast her a quick, curious glance. "I thought you brought all your clothes back from England with you."

"Yes, I did," she admitted. She knew he was going to ask her why she found it necessary to buy anything more and she had no answer ready for him. How could she confess that she had deliberately gone out to buy a dress that would transform her into the woman of his dreams, and not just the girl whom he had married as a convenience to look after his children! "But one doesn't want to wear old clothes forever. I'm sure your mother must be sick of the sight of me in jeans. She's very elegant herself, isn't she?"

"I don't think she minds your jeans," he said, still looking amused. "Is this new dress to take their place?"

"Not exactly," she said. Was it likely that she'd wear an evening dress of cloth of gold in the middle of the afternoon? It made it all the more difficult to explain why she had bought it at all!

"Did you buy the dress for Takis?"

"Of course not!"

"I don't see that there's any 'of course' about it," he returned with renewed anger. "He has a way with women, as I know to my cost!"

Morag felt an impatience with the dead Susan that made her long to tell Pericles once and for all how stupid she thought his wife had been. But there are limits as to what one can fittingly say about the dead, and she bit back the words, her mind working furiously as to how else she could convince him that Takis meant nothing to her, whatever emotion he had stirred in Susan's breast.

"I'm not surprised Takis is so spoiled," she said in an amused, cool voice that pleased her well. "You all go on about him as if he were something fantastically special. No wonder he believes it himself!"

Pericles' mouth tightened. "You have to admit he is handsome."

"Do you think so?" Morag said in the same light tones.

"Don't you?"

Morag achieved a yawn. "In a way. Flashy good looks

like his have never appealed to me much. I prefer...."
She broke off. If she told him what she preferred, he would be bound to recognize himself in the picture she drew. "I prefer someone less obvious—stronger, if you know what I mean, who doesn't have to playact all the time."

"Does he playact?" He sounded as though it were a new thought to him, and one that he rather liked.

"All the time. He's the biggest ham I've ever met!"

"Well, well," he murmured. "And what makes you think you prefer the iron hand in the velvet glove? I haven't noticed you giving way to anyone or anything, except when one of those sudden impulses of yours takes you by storm."

"I may have been impulsive over David, but I've got over that." She glanced at him covertly through her eyelashes. "I wish I'd never told you that Takis is like him! You've been quite horrid and suspicious ever since! And anyway, David had more substance than Takis, even if he wasn't all that I'd thought him. You make me sound a perfect idiot!"

"Didn't you also marry me on impulse?" he said.

She refused to answer. Was that what he believed of her? It seemed to her only too likely, and it was a depressing thought to her that she should see no way of denying the charge without telling him why she had married him, and she wasn't ready to do that, even if she could have found the words to do so.

"Well?" he prompted her.

Morag bit her lip in displeasure, frowning out of the window. "You don't understand!" she said. "You don't understand me, and I don't think you understood Susan, either!" She put a hand quickly up to her mouth. "I didn't mean...."

His hands tightened on the steering wheel and he

slowed the car down to a crawl. "What did you mean?" he asked in the inflexible, dangerous tones that she knew so well.

"Only that I'm not as silly as you think!"

He stopped the car altogether. "Aren't you, my dear?"

She shook her head, swallowing hard. "I'm not a child!" she almost shouted. "You go on as if I do nothing but jump from one scrape to another!"

She knew he was looking at her and that she wouldn't be able to read his expression even if she could bring herself to look at him. She began picking at her fingers instead, unconsciously betraying the nervousness that she most wanted to hide from him.

"If you do," he said, "this is one scrape you won't get out of in a hurry! You had your chance to change your mind. It's too late for you to do so now!" He went on watching her, then he put a hand over hers, forcing her to be still. "Why don't you think I understood Susan?"

"I don't know," she admitted.

"You must have some reason for saying such a thing!"

She hesitated. Then, "I don't believe she preferred Takis," she said at last in a small voice. "Not unless you made her think she did."

"Oh?" his voice was wintry in the extreme. She made a restless movement with her hands, but he had no intention of releasing his hold on them.

"She couldn't have done!"

His eyebrows rose at that. "Why not?"

"Because she married you!"

One corner of his mouth turned down. "She didn't have much choice. Her family saw to that, aided and abetted by mine. Love and romance didn't come into the matter. It's not unusual in Greece, you know."

Morag bent her head. "I can't explain," she muttered. "I knew you wouldn't understand!"

"On the contrary, I think I do understand. I find it a very interesting point of view!"

She shrugged her shoulders. "Yes, well, aren't we going home? Takis and the children will be there before us if we don't hurry."

"Does that matter?" he drawled.

"Of course!" she said. "It's my job to look after them!"

She saw him smile. "As my wife, your job is whatever I say it is. The children will be all right without you for a few minutes. Now, let's talk about you. How much money do you think you'll need each month?"

She was so relieved that Pericles wanted to talk about money and nothing more personal that she looked up with a quick intake of breath. Her eyes met his and dropped to his hand, which was still covering hers. "It's very hot. Takis had ordered a pressed lemon for me, but you took me away before I could drink it. You might at least have waited until I'd had a sip from it!"

"Is that a hint that I should find a café and buy you a drink?"

She nodded, feeling more at ease. "If we don't have to worry about the children. And if you can spare the time." She turned toward him, suddenly aware that it was the middle of the afternoon and that he ought to be working. "Why are you here, anyway?"

His expression was indulgent. "Would you rather I went away?"

"No, but shouldn't you be working?"

He glanced at his watch. "I think I can spare you a few minutes. Besides, I could do with a drink, too."

He chose a café overlooking the sea. He pulled out a chair for her and sat down himself opposite her, watching her closely. When the waiter came for their order, he gave it in Greek without consulting her. Morag presumed that he had ordered another pressed lemon for her, but when it came there was a cottage-type bowl of yogurt, rich and creamy, which he pushed over to her side of the table. "It's very good for the complexion," he told her.

She found it very refreshing. It was cold and sour, but not too sour. It was much richer than the yogurt she had known in England, but she thought perhaps it was because this was obviously home-made and had no other flavor, or real fruits added. It disappeared quickly and she had practically finished it before she became aware that Pericles was still watching her with the same close attention.

"Aren't you going to have any?" she asked him.

"I was going to have half of yours. Didn't you have any lunch?"

"Oh," she said. "I'm sorry. You should have told me before." She smiled. "You're too late now, it's all gone!"

"I'll make do with my lager." He paused. "Why did you buy the dress, Morag?"

She licked her spoon thoughtfully and then took a sip of the ice-cold water, which had actually come with Pericles' beer but which she didn't think he was going to drink himself. "No particular reason," she said.

"Shall I tell you what I think?" He picked up the parcel that held her dress. "I think you plan to dazzle someone."

She retained her composure with an effort. "I plan to dazzle all of you!" she said quickly. "No one in particular!"

Pericles looked into the parcel, fingering the cloth of gold. "Dazzle is the word!"

"Yes." Her enthusiasm for the dress rekindled. "Don't you think it's beautiful? It cost every penny I had, but I can't regret it! I won't regret it."

He pushed the parcel across the table to her. "When are you going to wear it?"

"I don't know. I thought perhaps Dora would give a party for us, after the summer when most people start coming back to Athens." She looked up at him again. "Not a big party—just friends and relations."

"You mean my friends and relations?"

"Mine are all still in England," she reminded him, yet instinctively thinking of Delia. "Besides, they came to our wedding. I thought now that we're married, you'd want to introduce me to your friends. I didn't mean to take too much for granted."

"No, you don't ask much, do you? Why not, Morag? If you want a party, why don't you insist on one?"

She pulled her dress toward her, deliberately avoiding his eyes. "You might not like it."

"And that matters?"

She nodded, taking another sip from his glass of water. "I wish you wouldn't look at me like that."

A smile creased his face. "Why not?"

"I never know what you're thinking."

"Just as well," he commented.

She gave him a quick look. "I don't see why," she began. "It would be much easier if I knew what you wanted. I always seem to guess wrong!"

He laughed. "All right," he said, "I'll tell you exactly what I was thinking. I was wondering what you'd do if I drove up into the hills and made love to you. Would you like that, *karthia mou*?"

She pressed the dress to her bosom. "You...you wouldn't!"

Pericles rose to his feet with a nonchalant ease that she

could only envy. "You are my wife!" he reminded her. He picked up the bill from the table and put down a few coins to pay it. "Are you coming, Morag?"

"Pericles, you haven't said if I may have some money."

A gust of laughter broke from him. "There is a difficulty ," he told her. "If I open a bank account for you, you'd have to write out your checks in Greek. Will you settle for a joint account?"

"Oh, but I only want a few pounds a month!"

"Okay, I'll give you cash and you can let me know if you need any more." He took the parcel out of her arms. "I'll throw this in for good measure. How's that?"

She gave him a cautious smile. "It was terribly expensive."

"I knew that as soon as I saw the label!" he said. He lowered his voice to an intimate murmur. "If I pay for it, don't you think you might tell me why you bought it?"

Morag prededed him out of the café, glad of the opportunity to turn her back on him and thus avoid the mocking brilliance of his glance. "It was an impulse," she lied.

He shook his head at her. "You're a bad fibber, Morag. one day I'll have the truth from you, the whole truth!"

She gave him a quick look. "But—"

"I know," he said. "I said I wouldn't rush you! But don't take too long, *pedhi*, in finding the words, or I may decide to do without them before we come to terms. I don't think you'll hold out against me for long!" He put her into the car and handed her the parcel. "You shall have your party. I'll speak to my mother about it. You're right about that, too. I should introduce my wife to my friends." He bent his head and kissed her on the cheek. "It'll give you a chance to get used to the idea, too," he added meaningfully. "No Greek waits for long on the convenience of a woman—and remember, I am half Greek!"

As if she were likely to forget it! It was part of his attraction for her, that she also knew! She cursed her own cowardice that had stopped her taking up his offer to drive her up into the hills for the afternoon. How wonderful it would have been!

If she shut her eyes she could almost smell the thyme that scented the barren slopes behind the coast, and the pine trees, if one happened on a clump of them, and even the inevitable goats, their bells sounding as they scampered over the rocky outcrops that littered the brown-gray background of the Apollon Coast.

THE CHILDREN WERE HOME before them. "Where have you been?" they demanded of their father, suspicious that they had been left out of some treat.

"I wanted Morag to myself for a while," he answered. "We don't get enough time to ourselves."

Peggy smiled up at him in a peculiarly feminine way. "We've hardly seen you at all, either, daddy. And I particularly want to talk to you about something." She took his hand in hers. "Can I talk to you now?"

Kimon watched his sister and father disappear down the path toward the sea with a slight frown. "Did you get into trouble?" he asked Morag.

"Whatever for?"

"Oh, I don't know. I just thought you might have got it from daddy. He used to hate it when mummy went out with Takis—he doesn't like him, you know. They used to fight like anything about it, but mummy wouldn't pay any attention. She said we weren't in Greece often enough for it to matter."

Morag swallowed, a little shocked that Kimon should

have been allowed to see so much of his parents' differences.

"No, I don't think he does like Takis," she agreed out loud. "But I explained about his giving us a lift into Athens."

Kimon gave her a cheeky look. "Are you scared of daddy? You looked it when he took you away!"

"Certainly not!"

"Not even a little bit? Did you tell him that Takis helped you choose your new dress? I'll bet you didn't!"

"Then you bet wrong! He already knew that Takis had followed me to the shop." She flushed a little and smiled, too. "Your father likes my dress, if you want to know. He's going to give it to me for a present!"

"Phew!" said Kimon with dawning respect. "You must have spun him a yarn! Takis said he'd more likely beat you!"

Morag made a little gesture of distaste. "He shouldn't talk to you like that. I think Pericles is right. I don't like him very much, either."

"No, you wouldn't," Kimon agreed calmly. "Most people like him, though, especially girls, because he never seems to do any work and he has lots of money. That's why mummy liked him. She said he was good fun, but I think he's a creep! Only he does buy us a lot of ice cream, too!"

Morag merely looked at him and Kimon made a face at her. "Peggy likes him," he went on hastily, "because he tells her she's pretty, and she likes that."

Not for the first time, Morag thought how much shrewder Kimon was than his sister. She was glad to have won the liking and affection of them both, but it was Kimon's respect she wanted because she felt it was worth more than Peggy's. Peggy was too easy to bribe with pretty words and pretty things.

She looked down at the sea to where she could see Pericles and Peggy standing below her, and she tried not to mind that he had only chosen her so that she could look after his children.

"So WE ARE to have a party," Dora said. "Pericles says that it's your idea that we should introduce you to our friends." Her eyes lit with mocking laughter. "I hope you know what you're into! Pericles is not a party man by nature!"

"It won't do him any harm for once," Morag answered calmly.

"No, but I'm surprised he agreed to it all the same. He didn't give in to Susan so easily! Why should he indulge you?"

Morag, determined not to mind whatever her mother-in-law should say, merely smiled. "He wants to see me in my new dress," she explained. "He gave it to me," she added.

"So I heard," Dora said dryly.

Morag wondered what else she had heard and who could have told her. Takis? She wouldn't put it past him, for if he didn't get his own way, he liked to make trouble, rather as Peggy did sometimes; only Peggy did it far less now that she was happier in herself, and Peggy was only ten years old.

"Why don't you show some of your paintings at the party?" she said to give her mother-in-law's thoughts another direction.

"Oh, I couldn't!" Dora said immediately.

"Why not?" Morag insisted. "I want to see them and so does everyone else. I'm going to suggest it to Pericles, because I want Peggy to show some of hers, too, but only if you think she's any good. She thrives on praise!"

Dora was not pleased. "How should I know if her stuff

is any good? I don't know about my own any longer. I've got used to the idea that women have better things to do with their time than paint."

"I think you know," Morag said simply.

"And what do you know about it?"

Morag bit her lip. "Not very much. But Perry does! That's why I'm hoping he'll persuade you. It would be so good for Peggy to be taken seriously by people outside her immediate family."

"I suppose you think it would be good for me, too!" Dora said with increasing irritation. "Well, you'll have to do better than that to persuade me!"

Morag managed a smile. "I have another reason," she admitted, "but I don't think you'll like it very much!"

Dora's look was one of inquiry. "You're a surprising person, Morag. Would you go on with this if Pericles didn't like the idea?"

Morag wished that she could say she would. "No," she said.

"I thought not," Dora congratulated herself. "Then I shall have a word with Pericles, too. I think he's more likely to listen to me, don't you?"

Morag did, but she was not going to admit it. "Dora, please do this for me!"

Dora made a great play of rearranging her hair. "Are you asking for yourself?" She pulled her hair forward with a grimace. "Well, girl, what is this other reason I won't like?"

Morag came forward and began to scoop up the old woman's hair onto the top of her head, her fingers light and very gentle. "I want to see the picture you've done of me," she said.

"And how do you know about that?" Dora sounded so cross that Morag's spirits sank.

"The children told me about it. Please let me see it,

Dora! Nobody ever painted me before, not even at school!"

"Then you are asking for yourself!"

Morag finished doing her mother-in-law's hair. "I suppose I am."

"And it has nothing to do with Peggy's welfare? I thought not! But I should have thought you'd want to see it in private first, not at a party!" She turned around to look at Morag better. "You're a fool! Don't you see that if everyone is busy looking at my paintings, they won't be looking at you? Wear your dress, my dear, and be the belle of the ball for once! Wasn't that your first idea?"

Morag flushed. She couldn't deny that it had occurred to her that if Pericles should see others looking at her with appreciation, he might take a second look himself.

"I wanted to show off Peggy, too," she whispered.

Dora dismissed such nonsense with an earthy sniff. "My dear, I find it very irritating that you'll never admit to having a selfish bone in your body! All right, we've established that you want the triumph of having Pericles at your feet and so you bought the dress. What made you change you mind?"

Morag gazed at her in silence. Surely she hadn't been as brazen at that? "Not at my feet!" she gasped.

"Have I got the expression wrong?" Dora demanded. Morag shook her head. "Not that it matters! Are you afraid that Pericles will guess why you bought the dress?"

"N-no," Morag stammered.

"Then what is all this about the paintings?"

"I'm not much good at parties, either!" Morag said. "And I don't speak Greek. I don't see how I'm going to shine at this party at all!"

"Then of course we shall show my paintings—and Peggy's, too! Why on earth didn't you say so before?" Dora stood up and hugged Morag to her. "I didn't mean to say it now, but Pericles has had so much unhappiness, and a little bit of it was my fault. Now I want him to be happy with you and I will help you all I can, but you must help yourself a little, too!" She cast Morag a look of mock despair. "You must fight for what you want, not hide behind the rest of us! How can Pericles notice you if you run away and hide?"

"He knows I'll give him anything he wants from me," said Morag.

Her mother-in-law looked more than a little exasperated. "Do you think he didn't have that with Susan? She was a perfect wife in many ways. In every way, except that she had no need of Pericles himself, and he knew it! This time I hoped it would be different for him!"

Morag struggled to find the words that would reassure her, but as usual she was struck dumb when it came to what she wanted for herself. "I don't know how . . ." she began.

"Then you'd better find a way!" Dora snapped at her. She saw the tears in Morag's eyes and her expression relented a little. "Oh, come and see the portrait I've painted of you! When you've seen it, you may not want it to become public property. I can always put my others on show and keep this one as a wedding present for you and Pericles."

She led the way down the corridor from her room, into which she had called Morag a few minutes before, to the small room at the other end that she had turned into a studio for herself. Morag had not been inside the room before and she stood now in the doorway, staring at the canvases that met her eyes. How quickly Dora must work to have completed so many pictures so quickly! But then she saw her own features looking back at her and, fascinated, she studied the portrait of herself with a rising feeling of excitement.

Her mother-in-law had done the original drawing before Morag had married Pericles. She was sitting on the rough-hewn steps that led down to the sea and was wearing her oldest pair of jeans, a T-shirt that was none too clean, and the shell necklace that Perry had given her. The beads of Nemesis, she called them to herself. They were a talisman, assuring her of the goddess's protection, and she would keep them all her days. But she had not thought before that Pericles might need her services, too, to compensate him for a marriage that had been less than perfect.

She took a step closer to the portrait. Besides the casualness of her clothes, her hair was far from tidy and she had her hands clasped lightly around her knees. But it was the expression on her face that revealed exactly what she had been looking at when Dora had seen her. The desire in her eyes was a naked thing that made her embarrassed to look at it, and her lips were damp as if she had just licked them, as if she couldn't wait for Pericles to turn around and kiss her. For there was no doubt that Pericles was standing just outside the canvas and that he, too, could see how much she wanted him.

"Has Pericles seen it?" she asked, her voice husky and not very well under control.

Dora studied the picture in a critical silence. She seemed to have forgotten all about the real Morag beside her.

"What did you say?" she asked at last.

"Has... has Pericles seen it?"

Dora grinned suddenly. "He'd be a fool if he hasn't! Oh, you mean the picture? No, not yet. I did it while you were both in England, from a drawing I made of you the first day you were here. Do you want him to see it?"

"I don't know."

How could she want him to see it? It said far more than the words he had said he wanted from her!

Dora gave her a sardonic look. "Well, you have from now until the night of the party in which to make up your mind!"

Morag took a last look at the painting. "I have made up my mind!" She took a deep breath, hoping that she would somehow find the courage to go through with it. "I'd like it to be shown with the others."

CHAPTER SEVEN

THE GOLD DRESS was everything that Morag had hoped it would be. When she had seen the children into their best clothes and had helped Dora to dress her hair, as she often did nowadays, she went to her own room and sank into the luxury of a hot bath, appreciating it all the more because it wasn't often that she was able to talk the maid into firing the boiler sufficiently for the water to be anything more than tepid when it came reluctantly out of the tap into the elaborately fitted bath. Pericles said hot water wasn't necessary in the summer in Greece. It was a theory that had surprised Morag, for she wouldn't have thought that her husband was the kind of man to believe in cold showers, or anything that wasn't the last word in comfort. But then she had to admit that she still knew very little about Pericles Holmes, let alone about his personal habits.

She went about her preparations for the party with an orderliness that would have amused her if she had not been keeping such a tight rein on her thoughts and emotions lest she should tail and run away long before any of the guests had arrived. It wasn't often that she paid much attention to her appearance, but tonight was different. Tonight she had to build a brilliant shell between herself and her new family. It had been her own wish that Dora should show Pericles the portrait of herself for the first time in public, but she had determined that her real self would be as far removed from the vulnerable girl in the painting as it was possible for her to be.

Indeed, whenever she thought of her painted image her heart turned over with fright. How could she have looked at Pericles like that? He was bound to recognize the urgency of her need for him written clearly in her eyes, and what would she do then? No matter what he said, she couldn't confess how often she had longed for him to take her in his arms and kiss her as he had kissed her that once before. Was that what he wanted her to put into words? Her cheeks flamed at the thought. Surely not! Surely he would know how impossible it was for her to ask—suggest—make him aware that her whole being cried out for him with an urgency that had first shocked her and, even now, made her wonder if he wouldn't despise her if he ever guessed how she felt about him. She had always pictured herself as being won and giving herself to some man in response to his need for her. She had never imagined that she might have to ask, or worse still to plead with, any man to make love to her. Yet it didn't look as though Pericles was ever going to make her his wife in fact as well as in name. He had said he wanted all the words, but if he were kind at all, he would surely accept the naked invitation his mother had caught on her face when she had been looking at him and thinking herself unobserved.

She spread the gold dress out on the foot of her bed and turned her attention to making up her face, a task that took all her attention because for once she wanted to look sophisticated and to bear the image of "Swinging London" and, most of all, to put all the other women in the shade for the space of a few days. When she had finished, she was herself rather surprised by the result. Her green eyes, as bright as emeralds, stared back at her in the glass, looking as mysterious as two green pools of light. She allowed her eyes to fall and was pleased by the shadowy effect of her long eyelashes. She had never thought of herself as beautiful, but tonight, she thought, she looked quite as well as she had ever seen Delia look. Excitement flooded her veins, leaving a sensation of panic in its wake as she wondered if Pericles would notice and what he would do if he did.

Last of all, she dropped the golden dress over her head and smoothed down the skirt over her hips, marveling at the elegant cut and the glowing brilliance of the material. She turned swiftly as the door handle rattled briefly and opened to allow Pericles to walk into her room as calmly as if he did it every day—and with as little warning!

"I... I'm nearly ready," Morag faltered, wondering what he had come for.

"So I see."

The humor in his voice set the panic off again like fireworks through her blood. She glanced up at him, unaware of the appeal in her eyes. "Do you like it?" she asked him. His silence lent desperation to her next words. "You... did give it to me!"

"You look very lovely," he said at last, "but not quite the Morag I'm used to."

"You don't like it!" she exclaimed in dismay. "Oh, Perry, why not? It's the most beautiful dress I've ever had!"

"Very splendid!" He smiled slowly. "I hope you remember whose wife you are this evening! Every eye—every masculine eye—will be following you in that!"

"Oh, do you think so?" Her eyelashes swept downward. "I think I might rather like that!"

"Indeed?" he said dryly. "Well, keep your pleasure under control, if you can. You have no business attracting other men to want to make love to you, and I'm not the sort of man to stand by idly watching his wife flirt with other men!"

"Oh," she said. The excitement within her was almost unbearable. "Will you... will you flirt with me?"

"Do you want me to?"

She licked her lips. "I don't know." Her eyes flashed up to his face and dropped again. "D-do you?"

"That would be telling," he drawled.

"But Pericles..." she began.

Pericles raised his eyebrows. "Are you asking me to flirt with you, Morag?"

"No, no, of course not!" She smoothed down her skirt again and then stopped, thinking that he might think that she was trying to draw his attention to the very feminine line of the dress. "I wouldn't do that!"

He put a hand under her chin and forced her to look up at him. "Why not?"

"I'm not very good at it—and you might not want to!"

"Not very good at it? Oh, Morag! Don't let me catch you dallying with anyone else, that's all I ask! You'll regret it if you do!"

"Will I?" She tried to escape his restraining fingers. "I don't think you'd hurt me."

"Don't you?" The pressure of his fingers increased, though his thumb caressed her lips, which trembled beneath his touch. "I hope you're right!"

She pulled herself together with an effort. "What could you do to me?" she dared him. She put a hand over his thumb, pulling it away from her mouth. "You'll smudge my lipstick!"

"I'm sorry," he said automatically. He didn't look sorry at all. On the contrary, he looked as sure of himself and as autocratic as she had ever seen him. "No, dammit, I'm not sorry at all! Who has a better right to smudge your lipstick, anyway?"

"But not now!" she protested, hoping against hope that he would overrule her.

"No, not now," he agreed.

She winced, but he still didn't release her. "Please, Pericles," she whispered.

"Please what? Kiss you?"

Oh yes! Her heart thundered within her. "Please let me go."

He did so with a snap of his fingers. "Very well, but I meant what I said, and you would do well to remember that!"

Morag tried to hide her disappointment as best she could, making a play of looking at herself in the glass to see if she had to repair her makeup. But the tears in her eyes hardly allowed her to see her own reflection. Despair gripped her. The dress had made no difference! If it had, Pericles would have kissed her whether she had asked him or not. He wouldn't have been able to help himself!

"I'm not likely to forget!" she muttered.

His eyes met hers in the looking glass.

"See that you don't!" he said.

"Did you come only to threaten me?" she asked him.

"No, I came to see if you wanted me to zip you up again—and give you this!" He put his hand into his pocket and drew out something that flashed as green as her eyes. "Jade for a jade," he murmured. "I thought it would go with the dress." He made to put it on for her, but she took a quick step away from him, determined that he shouldn't touch her again. With a gesture of impatience he put his hands on her shoulders and pulled her against him. "Stand still," he commanded her.

She could feel his breath on the back of her neck, then the coldness of the jade against her skin as he fastened the chain for her. She shut her eyes, wondering what he would do if she were to turn in his arms and thank him in the one way she longed to do, with her lips. Then she felt the kiss on the nape of her neck and she had no choice in the matter, for he had turned her to face him and his mouth descended on hers with a force that lit the short fuse of her own desire and she was kissing him as much as he was kissing her.

"We must go and meet our guests," he said at last, putting her from him.

Morag nodded her head. "I suppose so." She half laughed, half sobbed. "Thank you for this, Pericles." She fingered the jade pendant, her cheeks pink. "I think I like my shells better, though—my beads of Nemesis."

He shrugged. "I think I do, too," he said, "though possibly not for the same reason."

She cast a questioning look at him as she was busily putting on some more lipstick, but Pericles only smiled and shook his head at her.

They went together into the sitting room. To Morag, it seemed the room was already filled to capacity and she was glad of Pericles' support as he put his arm lightly around her waist and introduced her to his many Greek friends. More of them spoke English than she thought possible, and after a while she began to enjoy herself, finding that almost everyone there was prepared to like her, and not only for her husband's sake, but because they found her likable for herself. Morag, quite unaccustomed to being the center of attraction, found it a heady experience.

Not even Takis, annoying as she found him, could disturb her new-found serenity. She took a step closer to Pericles, but she didn't really mind when Takis maneuvered her away from his side and over to the other side of the room where he could speak to her without being overheard by Pericles.

"You look beautiful," he congratulated her. "You see what good taste I have. Didn't I advise you that that is the dress for you?"

"Did you?"

"You know I did! Though I didn't know that you had such a beautiful pendant that would set it off to perfection!"

"Pericles gave it to me, he gave it to me just now."

Takis grinned at her. "So the dress had the desired effect?"

Morag shook her head. "I... I didn't want him to give me anything."

Takis took her hand and raised it to his lips. "Not many poeple would believe that, but I do. I am very hurt, Morag, here in my heart. When you first came here, you looked at me with your green eyes and I thought you liked me very well, but all the time you were planning the conquest of another!"

Morag smiled. "It was he who conquered me," she murmured.

"No, not yet," Takis contradicted her. "When that happens I shall totally give up hope. But until then I shall try to do to you what you have done to me!"

"I haven't done anything to you!"

"You have stolen my heart!" Takis returned, a gleam of laughter in his eyes. "I will revenge myself on you for that!"

"Will you?" Morag drew herself up, though she was still smiling. "Pericles will protect me from anything you can do!"

The teasing quality disappeared from Takis' voice. "Like he did Susan? He made no pretense to defend her!"

Morag felt suddenly cold. She had forgotten all about Susan for the moment.

"Did she need his protection?" she asked.

"She was his wife, too. He allowed her to do as she pleased. He did not protect her by calling her to heel."

"Perhaps he trusted her," Morag put in.

Takis favored her with a glittering smile. "Would you like to be so trusted?" He laughed softly. "Not by Pericles, you would not!"

She was saved from having to answer by someone coming up behind her. She looked around and saw that it was Pericles. She turned to him at once. "Did you want me?" she asked.

"My mother is getting ready to show her paintings. She wants you to help her to arrange them." He looked curiously at her. "She tells me our wedding present is among them."

Morag cast him an unconscious look of appeal. "Only if you like it," she began to explain. "You may not want it!"

"I shall hardly hurt my mother's feelings by saying so!" he said dryly.

"No," Morag agreed. "But Dora herself said you might not like it. She wouldn't want to hang it if you don't!"

Pericles put his hand on her upper arm, pushing her forcibly through the door and out into the hall. "Never mind that just now," he bade her grimly. "What was Takis saying to you?"

"Nothing!"

"I prefer you keep it that way! You have nothing to say to him, no matter how he flatters you and makes eyes at you."

"He doesn't mean anything by it!"

"Doesn't he?" Pericles' hand tightened around her arm until she uttered a cry of protest. "I warn you again, Morag, if you want to flirt with anyone, flirt with me!"

"Why should I?" she demanded, rubbing her arm.

He said something in Greek that she didn't understand, though she thought she recognized the words "*yinéka mou,*" which she knew to mean "my woman."

"You don't own me!" she said.

He laughed and pushed her before him into his mother's studio. "Don't tempt me, Morag."

Tempt him? She didn't think she could, otherwise she would have done so this long time past. Sometimes she thought she was fixing herself in his mind and heart, but mostly she knew better and that as far as he was concerned she was no more than someone he had found to look after his children. Of course, he liked to keep things normal on the outside, but it seemed she was alone in longing for love. He was able to do without it.

"Well, you don't own me!" she said with spirit. "If I like Takis, I don't see why I shouldn't talk to him all I want to!" She very nearly added "So there," but was prevented by the look on his face. It served him right, she thought rebelliously, to be a little less sure of her. Perhaps he would notice her more if she stood up to him.

She looked uncertainly at him and looked away again as quickly.

"Indeed?" he said coldly.

"As a matter of fact," she answered, "as a matter of fact I don't care for Takis."

"Then you don't need to talk to him."

"N-no, though I can't ignore him completely. He is your cousin, and seeing he's staying in the same house...." She broke off. "Perry, I do try not to be alone with him!"

"Try a little harder!" he advised, his voice tinged with ice. "I mean what I said about that young man. You're my wife, Morag, not his. See that you remember it!"

She blinked. "You have very Greek ideas sometimes," she said. "but I'm not Greek. You ought to remember that!"

The coldness left his face. "What do you mean by that?" he drawled, giving her an amused look.

"I mean I have a mind of my own!" she answered defiantly, taking a grip on herself. It wasn't the moment she would have chosen to have a row with him, but if he wanted it that way, she wouldn't balk at obliging him. His eyes glinted dangerously, reflecting the fearful excitement that still clutched at her stomach. "I don't take orders!" she added for good measure.

"You'll take mine," he answered. He still looked amused, and that added a fatal spark to her temper.

"Why should I?" she demanded.

"Because," he said quietly, "in the last resort, we both know that you would rather please me than fight with me. You may not be Greek, but you'll take your lead from me and be pleased to have it so. Don't be silly, Morag! Would you rather have it the other way around?"

Fortunately for Morag, she escaped having to answer because her mother-in-law came rushing into the room, her hair standing on end, and looked with surprise at the two of them.

"What are you doing in here?" she asked Pericles. "I keep telling everyone that I'm not going to show the paintings in here! The light isn't right. All I need is a litte help in moving the few that I want seen into the other room. If you carry these, Morag can manage the one with its face to the wall, and I'll bring in any others I've decided on while you're shifting those."

Pericles grinned. "Which one is our wedding present?"

Dora shrugged her shoulders. "We'll leave you to guess." Running a hand through her hair, thus making it wilder than ever she turned to Morag. "It'd serve you right if Pericles humbled your pride for you in front of all those people!" Her expression softened at the look on Morag's face. "You look beautiful in that dress, my dear. I'll have to paint you again in that one day, but not until you've found yourself." Her enthusiasm grew as she thought about it. "Yes, it will be a splendid counterpart to the first one! I'll give them both to you!"

"So that's what our wedding present is," Pericles remarked.

"But you're not to look at it yet!" Morag put in hastily. She was surprised to hear that her voice sounded quite normal. Even so, she couldn't quite bring herself to look at her husband in case he, too, should know what Dora had meant both by her finding herself and by the hope that Pericles would humble her pride. Dear God, it was uncomfortable enough to be in love with a man without having to tell him so in words, when one had no idea if he even liked in return, let alone felt any of the hurricane of emotion in which she found herself.

"Why not?" Pericles asked.

She made no answer, but turned her attention to struggling to lift the heavy canvas to take it into the other room.

"Here, let me have it!" said Pericles, taking it forcibly away from her. He turned it around and placed it back against the wall, standing well back and taking a long, thoughtful look at the painting.

Even Dora stood quite still, awaiting his verdict. Morag's eyes went straight to the painted image of herself. Perhaps it wasn't as revealing as she had remembered. And if it was, perhaps Pericles wouldn't notice the naked invitation in her eyes, or the strength of her desire as she looked quite obviously at him. The silence stretched on and Morag longed for the floor to open and swallow her up! Couldn't he say something, anything at all?

But then he did speak and she wished just as passionately that he hadn't. "I didn't think anyone else had seen her like that," he said.

"Like what?" Morag asked in a whisper. She cleared her throat. "Like what?" she said again.

His eyes swept over her face, but without the tenderness she had been hoping to find in them. "As though you wanted to be loved," he said frankly.

The hot color stormed up her face. "I don't! I mean, your mother is a very clever artist. I was just the model."

"Come," said Dora, "we must take the paintings into the other room. Peggy has done a sketch of Morag, also. Perhaps Pericles will find more to like in that likeness of you."

"I like this one," said Pericles. "But I'd prefer it not to have a public viewing tonight. It is not a view I want other men to have of my wife!"

"Oh, arrogant!" Morag began, feeling a good deal safer by his decision. "Just because you think—"

"So would any man!" he retorted.

She turned away from him. "But you do like it?" she asked.

"Yes—" He cut himself off as he heard footsteps coming towards them. "Ah, Takis, have you come to help carry the paintings?"

The young Greek looked around the room, his eye falling on the painting of Morag. "Very pretty!" he commented. He gave her a wicked look, his smile wide and innocent. "Who were you looking at, *pedhi*? Ah, but I remember now when you sat there and dreamed your dreams! You were looking at me, Takis Kapandriti!"

Morag wanted to deny it, but there were no words that came to her. She struggled vainly to defend herself when all she wanted to do was run away and hide. She owed that much to Pericles! She had to say something! This time she couldn't let them think what they liked about her. This time it was Pericles who would suffer.

"I remember it well, too," she said in a small voice. She clenched her fists and drove herself on relentlessly. "Pericles had just said I'd never be free...." But her husband wasn't even listening. He had picked up a pile of paintings and had walked out of the room.

MORAG THOUGHT the party was going on forever. It was time the children were in bed, she thought, and wondered if they would think her very officious if she suggested that they should take themselves off. Peggy was flushed with success from the praise she had received for her drawings and probably wouldn't mind too much, but Kimon was deep in conversation with a man Morag had not previously noticed. Judging by the boy's absorbed expression, they were talking about coins. Any moment now and Kimon's precious Spartan "cartwheel" would be passed from hand to hand, while he told yet again why it was so heavy and why it was made of nothing more valuable than iron.

But, rather to her surprise, the children were glad to go and disappeared without a murmur. Perhaps they knew that the party was about to break up anyway and that they weren't going to miss anything. Morag stood beside her husband and mother-in-law and wished good night to all their friends, a fixed smile on her face. She knew now that she would never be happy with Pericles, and she thought the knowledge would destroy her, so badly did it hurt to know that he would never love her but that, on the contrary, he wasn't even sufficiently interested to know that it was he who held her heart and not—nor ever could be—Takis Kapandriti!

What a relief it was to divest herself of her golden dress and put on a cotton nightdress and a thin, filmy negligee that barely covered her at all. She went to take a last look at the children and found Kimon in tears.

"Morag, I've lost my coin! I took it into the garden to see what it looked like by moonlight and I dropped it on the path and I can't find it!"

She put her arms around him and hugged him tight. "I'll have a look," she offered.

"But supposing you don't find it?"

"I shan't go to bed until I do!" she assured him. "I'll give it to you in the morning. Don't worry about it now!"

But her confidence took a dive when she had crawled up and down the path on her hands and knees and still hadn't found the coin. She didn't even mind when she heard Takis humming to himself as he came up from looking at the sea and found her there, stopping only a couple of feet away from where she was kneeling.

"Don't just stand there!" she said crossly. "Help me look for Kimon's coin! He'll be desolate if he's lost it!"

Takis obediently fell on his knees beside her and began feeling around for the coin. "Why do you make yourself the servant of these children?" he asked her.

She answered deliberately. "What other role have I here?"

"*Morag!*"

With a sinking heart she knew that Pericles had already seen her and, worse still, that he had seen Takis with her. "Kimon's lost his coin!" she explained.

Pericles bent down until his eyes were practically on the same level as hers. "I warned you, Morag," he bit out at her. He lifted her bodily to her feet. "Go into the house at once!"

She looked down at the inadequate negligee she was wearing and hurried to obey him. He came after her almost immediately, catching up with her in the hall.

"While you are my wife, you will not entertain your lovers at my front door!" he told her.

"But I wasn't! I was looking for Kimon's coin!"

For a long moment he stared angrily at her, then he opened the door to his bedroom and thrust her inside before him. "If you want to be loved," he said tautly, "you can make up your mind to be loved by me!"

She backed away from him, almost falling onto the bed behind her. "But I didn't go out to meet Takis—I wouldn't!"

His hands slipped her negligee off her shoulders, ignoring her protests. He pushed her back against the pillows, his lips taking possession of hers with a fierceness that took her breath away. She made a last effort to prevent him from taking her more firmly into his arms, but her own need to give way to him was too strong for her.

"Oh, Pericles!" she breathed.

She felt him against her and she clung to him, welcoming his warm hands against her flesh. She didn't care how it had happened, she didn't care what happened afterward, but to belong utterly to her husband was the fulfilment of everything she had ever dreamed of for herself.

Pericles was no longer beside her when she awoke. She started up, afraid that he had left her alone, but then she heard him splashing in the bathroom and knew he would soon be back, and that she would have to say something to him when he did. The door swung open and he came through it, his eyes brilliant as he looked at her. Reddening despite herself, she looked away from him and her eye fell on Kimon's Spartan coin on the bedside table. She reached out for it, her heart pounding out a new, unfamiliar message within her.

"You found the coin!" she accused him. "You knew I was telling you the truth all the time!"

Pericles came over to the bed. He leaned over her, putting a hand on either side of her slim body.

"Yes, I knew," he said.

"Then—" she blushed vividly "—I think you might have told me you knew," she said.

There was a curious look in his eyes and she found herself thinking how white and strong his teeth were, and that his mouth was every bit as strong and firm as it had felt against hers.

"Are you expecting an apology?" he asked her, the look in his eyes deliberately mocking. "I don't have to apologize for making love to my own wife!" he told her, as arrogant as she had ever seen him. "Not even to her!" he added. He bent his head and took an unhurried toll of her lips. "Especially not to her!"

CHAPTER EIGHT

PERICLES HAD GONE OUT. Morag passed a restless half hour trying to persuade herself that she didn't care where he had gone, but she failed so dismally in this that she was all the more pleased to see her mother-in-law coming into the dining room for her breakfast. Dora gave her a long, interested look as she sat down, smiling suddenly with all the warmth that made some people say she was the most charming woman they had ever met.

"You have a glow this morning, my dear. I think I shall have to paint you again like you are now. Perhaps Pericles would like it better. Positively complacent!" Her smile lit her eyes and died again. "It has happened to other women before, you know!"

Morag was getting used to Dora's odd, slanting shafts of humor. "But never to me!" she said. She eyed her mother-in-law across the table. "Nobody can take that away from me!"

"Why should anyone want to?" Dora asked dryly.

"Always before, someone has."

"Delia!"

Morag nodded. "Did Perry tell you about her?"

"Not really," Dora said with disinterest. "I think he mentioned her name once."

"Most men prefer her."

"Oh? I thought she had always been jealous of you. Didn't she try to take your young man away from you?"

Morag stared at her. "How did you know?"

"Kimon told me," Dora said simply. "He had heard you and Pericles talking about it. Children hear far more than they are ever meant to. I can't say that young man sounds much of a loss. Do he and Delia intend to marry?"

"No," Morag said. "David is dead. He was killed in a car crash."

Dora yawned. "I suppose she was driving?"

Morag maintained an uncomfortable silence. It was odd to think about David now. She knew that she had never loved him, and that her liking for him had been rather uncertain, bred of habit and the comfortable certainty that sooner or later they would come together in a more permanent relationship, as other people did.

"Well?" said Dora.

"I never thought of it before," Morag wondered at herself, "but Delia never did have any particular boyfriend of her own. Do you suppose that was why she wanted David?"

"Quite likely!"

"David wasn't really in love with me. He took one look at Delia and that was that. I might just as well not have existed!"

"You must have been very young to have minded so much," Dora commented. "He sounds a very dull young man, with not much understanding of life if he thought this Delia would suit him better. I hope you told him so."

"Well, no," Morag confessed.

"But you decided he should have what he wanted?"

"If it was Delia he wanted."

"I must say you were quite as stupid as Pericles says you were! It was she who killed him, I suppose?"

Morag bowed her head. "Did Pericles tell you that, too?"

"Pericles tells me nothing! And Kimon, who would tell me, did not know that! But now you are not so young and silly, *ne*? You give this young man away, but that was an extravagance of youth! You would not give your present happiness away so easily to your sister, or to anyone else. Have you told Pericles that?"

Morag avoided the question. "She's my stepsister."

Dora made an exasperated gesture. "It is only an excuse to say you are shy!" she muttered. "I hope he beats you if you don't tell him very soon! It was bad enough that Susan should only tolerate what she should have seized with gratitude, but with you it is quite different, and I am glad it should be so! I want my son to be loved above all else! Whether he in turn loves you is a matter of indifference to me. It matters to me only that you should love him and that he should know it!"

"I love Pericles very much," Morag said simply.

"Tell that to him!" Dora retorted.

"How do you know I haven't?" Morag burst out.

"Have you?"

"No." Morag wished she had cultivated the art of telling lies better and were not quite so naturally truthful. It was true enough that she had not told Pericles anything, but surely, sometimes, actions spoke louder than words. She sighed, knowing that it was the words that Pericles wanted, and words never came easily to her, and were now harder than ever to find when they mattered so much. She lifted her head. "Not that it's any business of yours!" she added to her mother-in-law.

Dora gave her a quick look of appreciation. "Quite right!" she applauded. "It would have been much easier for you if you had a proper honeymoon away from us all. I have tried to keep out of it, my dear, but it's a bit difficult when we are all in the same house and on top of one another the whole time. I apologize."

It was the last reaction that Morag had expected. "It doesn't matter," she said awkwardly. "I don't mind... much. Only don't hope for too much. Pericles only married me to look after the children. I can't...can't expect that he should want me to hang around his neck all the time!"

Dora frowned. "Don't be too unselfish!" she warned. There was a short silence while Morag digested this, and then the older woman went on casually, "By the way, I thought I might take the children out tonight. They want to see the *son et lumière* of the Acropolis, and I want them to see the Dora Stratou Theater of Greek Dance. It's right that they should take a proper interest in their heritage. Would you care to come, too?"

Morag looked as confused as she felt. "I don't know," she said. "Won't Pericles think it odd if we all go out without him?"

"Pericles is going out himself," his mother let fall. "He won't be back till very late, if at all."

It was typical, Morag thought, that she should be the last to know! "Where is he going?" she asked.

Dora smiled faintly. "In Greece a man often goes out alone and it's seldom that he tells his womenfolk where he's going. Pericles is no excception to that!"

"But he's only half Greek!"

"He is living here," Dora pointed out. "So I take it you will come with us?"

Morag nodded. "Thank you," she said. But she didn't feel like thanking anyone. Her pleasure in the morning was quite destroyed. She sighed and poured herself some more coffee, just as Kimon and Peggy came in from the beach.

"Did you find it? Morag, did you find my coin? Please say you did! I would have come back and helped you look, but I heard daddy talking to you." His eyes grew round at the memory. "He sounded awfully angry!"

Morag's features took on a calmness she was far from feeling. What else had Kimon heard? Pericles' angry accusation that he wouldn't allow her to entertain her lovers at his front door? Really, it was quite impossible to hold a private conversation in this house!

"He found your coin," she said aloud.

"Daddy did? But he didn't spend any time looking for it at all—"

"He...he came upon it immediately!" Morag cut him off.

"Oh," said Kimon. "Well, I'm glad it's found. It's my most precious possession in all the world. Do you think I should thank him?"

"Of course you should!" Peggy chimed in. "Wasn't it a super party last night? I thought I'd die when grandma showed all my drawings with hers, but they didn't look too bad, did they? There was one man there who wanted to take one of them home with him, but daddy said no. It was the drawing I did of you, Morag. Did you look at it properly?"

"It depends what you mean by properly," Morag teased her.

"I mean, did you think it looked like you?"

Morag had thought so. She had her head flung back and she was laughing. She had been surprised to find herself thinking that the girl in the picture was more than a little bit pretty. She was striking to look at, and quite different from the way she thought of herself.

"I suppose it does. I don't see myself very often—except in the looking glass."

"No, one doesn't," Peggy agreed. "I thought," she went on happily, "that grandma was going to show the painting she did of you, too. Why didn't you, grandma? I think it's terribly good!"

A sudden bark of laughter escaped form Dora's throat. She put up a hand to her mouth as if to prevent it from happening again. "Daddy said no," she said dryly.

"Daddy did?" the children said together. "Why?"

"You'll have to ask him," Dora suggested, but her eyes were on Morag's flushed face, and underneath she was still laughing. "Meanwhile, will you hurry up and finish your breakfast or we shall never get anything done today! Parties are all very well, but they do disorganize one so!"

Morag didn't see Pericles all day. Not that she would have known what to say to him if she had. She would have liked to have known, quite as much as the children, why he had refused to allow the man to take away Peggy's drawing of herself. Whichever way she looked at it, it seemed an odd thing to do. She wished with all her heart that she could think it was because he wanted it for himself, but she knew that to be an idle hope before she had even voiced it to herself. Why should he? All he had to do was ask Peggy to do another drawing of herself any time he chose.

It was not until they were all in Dora's car on their way to Athens that evening that she thought to ask Peggy who the man had been who had wanted the drawing.

"Adoni. He's a cousin of ours." Peggy stretched lazily. "He pretends to be Takis's twin, because they're almost the same age, but he isn't, of course. They aren't even brothers, though they've always done practically everything together. Kimon and I are the only real twins in the family!"

"I don't see why he should want a drawing of me," Morag went on worrying at the point. "I've never seen him before!"

Kimon looked kindly at her. "He would have given it to Takis," he explained as if he were speaking to a simpleton. "Takis said he wanted it to put up in his room."

Morag gave him a quick glance. "Are you sure?"

Kimon nodded. "I don't suppose Takis really wanted it," he consoled her. "He probably thought it would annoy daddy."

Morag suppressed a strong wish to strangle Takis and his cousin. If it had been anyone else but Kimon to say such a thing, she would have discounted it as his imagination; but Kimon was not given to fantasies and his lack of interest in the whole subject was made clear when he changed the subject back to his beloved coin, eagerly telling his grandmother that he was sure it was one of the best examples of Spartan coinage still extant in Greece.

But Morag could not forget what he had said as easily. For the first time she began to wonder in earnest about Susan—what she had been like and whether she had really been in love with Takis. There had to be some reason why Takis should want to hurt Pericles any way he could. Was it because he hadn't been as sure as he pretended to be that Susan had preferred him to her own husband? Oh, well, no one could tell her that now. Just as she would never be able to ask David if Delia had only run after him because she had been unable to bear the fact that David preferred her stepsister. What unhappiness such conceit in one's own attraction could cause! Was that the sin that the ancient Greeks had called *hubris*, the crime of thinking that one could be master of one's own destiny, of presuming to think that one could take anything merely because one wanted it? Morag fingered the shells around her neck with a faint shiver. It was Nemesis whose duty it was to punish all such presumption. On whom would her vengeance fall next?

"I'm tired, grandma!" Peggy complained, breaking into Morag's train of thought. "Why did we have to come tonight? I'm tired!"

"You slept late enough this morning," her grandmother told her.

"But I'm tired!"

"Hush," said Morag. "You can sleep afterward."

"But not for ages! The *son et lumière* doesn't begin until nine o'clock!"

"Doesn't it?" Morag exclaimed. "But it gets dark much earlier than that!"

Dora compressed her lips, signifying her displeasure. "I thought you'd like to hear it in English. The children understand English better than any other language, too. Also, it fits in better with the Dora Stratou Theater."

"You see," said Peggy, "we shan't get to bed before tomorrow! And I'm tired now!"

So was Morag! She wondered what time Pericles would be coming home and wished she had never agreed to come.

"Don't whine!" Kimon rebuked his sister. "You know daddy doesn't like it! He says it makes things worse if you whine—they take longer to live through!"

Morag began to feel sorry for her mother-in-law. Really, it was too bad to have three reluctant guests on her hands! To make up for the children's lack of enthusiasm, she began to ask about the Greek dances they were going to see. "I seem to have heard of Dora Stratou...."

"Of course you have!" Dora snapped. "She's won all sorts of international prizes for her work." She turned her head so that the children also could hear what she was saying. "The Greek dance is one of the oldest in the world," she told them. "Much of it was lost at one time and all that there was to go on was the odd mention of it here and there in Homer. But Kyria Stratou has studied the representations of the old dances on ancient vases, on friezes, wherever they could be seen, and has faithfully revived them. The most interesting thing to my mind is that the Greek musical rhythms are based on the old poetic rythms: 5/4, or 5/8, 7/8, 9/8, the very same meters that are to be found in the plays of Aeschylus, Euripides, and Sophocles. You can hear the same beat in the Byzantine music of the Orthodox church, if you listen for it."

Morag smiled at the children's blank faces, realizing that they had not understood one word of their grandmother's introduction to the evening's entertainment. "I expect you'll like the costumes," she suggested, sounding more optimistic than she actually was.

Dora snorted her contempt at the very idea. "They must learn to use their eyes! Especially Peggy, if she is determined to paint anything worthwhile. She will do better if she considers where she may have seen the costumes and the musical instruments before. It may have been in a Byzantine fresco, or in a statue depicting one of the ancient gods, on a vase in the National Museum, maybe even on a Christmas card! One has to learn to relate the things one sees to other things. This is the secret of a good painting, or a good design. Sometimes I think it's the best basis for the whole of life!"

"But grandpa didn't think so," Peggy said in bored tones.

"No," Dora was forced to agree in unnaturally subdued tones. "It's sometimes difficult to see any use in any of the arts. Your grandfather was an essentially practical man and he thought anything that didn't have an immediate practical use was a waste of time. I think he forgot that the soul can get hungry, too!"

"Was he... was he like Pericles?" Morag heard herself asking.

Dora considered the question. "In some ways," she said. "He was a hard man, but he tried always to be gentle with me. I doted on him." She sighed. "I'd rather have him than my painting any day!"

Just as Morag would rather have Pericles than all the other gifts all the ancient gods put together could lavish on her. She rubbed her shells between her fingers in a quick, nervous movement. If Nemesis were real, would she think that Morag deserved Pericles? Somehow Morag couldn't think so. She had so very little to offer him, and someone like Pericles deserved only the best. She tilted her chin into an obstinate angle. Then she would have to become the best for him, because nobody else was going to have him!

The people who had just seen the *son et lumière* performance in German were still coming out from the natural theater that looked out and up at the rock of the Acropolis, surmounted by the Parthenon. Dora allowed the children to buy themselves some Coca-Cola, taking it for granted that Morag, like herself, would prefer to do without.

"The mosquitoes are bad at this time of year!" the older woman complained, slapping her arms. "Something ought to be done about them!"

Morag, who had suffered from various bites ever since she had arrived in Greece, wondered if the season really made much difference. "They're at their worst at night. I wonder why!"

Dora shrugged. "One notices them more. Can you see the children anywhere? It looks as though we are at last moving."

Morag found the children with some difficulty and firmly anchored them to her by holding them both by the hand. She knew that they resented being treated as younger than they were, but she had no intention of losing them in the crowd that pressed all around them. "It won't be for long, just till we get inside," she told them.

Kimon blinked up at her. "We're not going inside," he corrected her. "It's an outside theater."

"Well, it comes to the same thing," Morag retorted.

"I don't want to lose you and I don't want to get lost myself, either!"

"You won't get lost!" he said scornfully.

"I hope not," she murmured.

She was glad they were sufficiently high up in the line to be able to have a choice of seats. Dora selected the four seats she wanted with enormous care, making certain that the children could see before she sat down herself, her own shoulders sagging a little with fatigue. "Perhaps we shouldn't have come tonight," she said to Morag. "We're all tired!"

Morag smiled. "I find it rather exciting," she said. "Did you ever see anything more beautiful than the Acropolis, lit up like that? How fortunate Athens is to have such a monument right at the heart of the city. There's nothing like it anywhere else in the world, is there?"

"No," Dora said. "Compared to London, Paris or Rome, or even Washington or New York, Athens is little more than a village. But give me my village every time! It is my home and I love it, like a woman loves a man, or a man a woman."

Morag was surprised to find that she felt a little bit the same way herself. She supposed it was because so much that was the history of Athens belonged to the whole European culture, and therefore everyone was more or less at home there. But she liked to think it was a little more than that. She wanted to think that Pericles had somehow conferred a citizen status on herself, that it was because of him that it was her home, too.

Then the lights went out and the days of Pericles and the Athenian victory against the Persians at Marathon once more came alive before their eyes. It was, perhaps, rather a ragged history of that glorious era when the Parthenon had come into being and Herodotus, the father of historians, had labored to reveal the world he knew to itself, with an attempt at objectivity never before seen in the ancient world. The small gem of a temple, dedicated to victory, glowed with a great light as the messenger from Marathon brought the news of victory to the city, though nothing was said of the way the man had run, expiring as he whispered the glad tidings, or that this was the origin of the great marathon race that is still contested by long-distance runners to this very day.

Last of all came the voice of Athene, the gray-eyed goddess of wisdom who had given her name to the city and to whom the Parthenon was dedicated, and once again she lived among her people, Greeks and strangers, all of whom recognized her patronage, which had brought to life this first of Europe's great civilizations, the first and in many ways the finest of them all.

Even the children were silent when the last trumpet died away and Athene's voice faded across the centuries and into oblivion. They rose with the others and scuffed the sides of their shoes on the gravel path as they left the auditorium.

"Funny," said Peggy, "but I'm not in the least bit tired now!"

Her grandmother unbent sufficiently to say that she was feeling more like enjoying herself, too. "We haven't taken Morag out nearly enough," she said to both of the children. "Never mind, when her family comes out to visit us, we'll take them all to the Argolid, or Delphi. It's a long time since I saw the theater at Epidaurus myself."

Morag gave Dora a quick glance.

"Mmm. That stepsister of yours, whatever her name is. Didn't Pericles tell you? She sent a telegram saying that she was coming. The only trouble is she didn't say when!"

"But she can't come here!"

"Why not?" Dora sounded amused. "I suppose Perry didn't tell you about her because he only heard this morning. Your father wanted her gone for a while, or so she said."

"My father?" Morag exclaimed. "Now that I can't believe!"

Dora shrugged, fitting herself into the front seat of her car. "Well, we can hardly refuse to have her with us, dear. Perhaps it won't be too long!"

Morag pressed her point. "Couldn't you say it isn't convenient right now?"

"No, I couldn't." Dora hesitated. "Pericles did say she was to stay as long as she wants to," she said then. "I'm sorry, dear."

Morag's spirits sank. "I don't believe that my father would have asked her to leave home. He adores her, just like her mother!"

"Well, as to that, I couldn't say, but I think I shall be quite interested to see this stepsister of yours. If she's as lovely as you say, I may want to paint her. What do you think?"

Morag made a face and then pretended that she hadn't as she caught sight of the children watching her. "I wish she weren't coming!" she declared.

"Don't you like her?" Peggy demanded.

"She's my stepsister!" Morag said.

"That's no answer !" Kimon reproved her. "Is she silly or something?"

Morag affected some amusement she did not feel. "Very silly!" she agreed.

Kimon gave her a very grown-up look. "I'll be able to see for myself if she comes to stay." He smiled suddenly, in the same audacious way as his father did. "If you don't like her," he said, "I don't suppose we shall, either."

It was only a short drive to the Dora Stratou Theater in the Philopappou area. Once again Dora had selected their seats with immense care. She herself sat well forward, her eyes never leaving the colorful figures as they wove in and out of the various patterns of dance on the stage. Morag found it almost as much fun to watch her as to watch the dancers. Later on, she supposed, her mother-in-law would reproduce what she had seen in paint. Morag could almost envy her gift, for it must be wonderful to be so absorbed in any creative activity. Then, fleetingly, she remembered how Dora had said she would willingly not paint if she could have her husband back, and she wondered if Pericles was home yet, and her heart missed a beat as she thought of the moment when she would see him again. If she only knew what he would expect from her....

The dancing came to a sudden end and Dora bounced out of her seat, intent on getting the children home as quickly as possible. "You're to go straight to bed the moment we get home!" she bade them. "Morag too! She looks like a little ghost, especially under these lights."

There was no sign of Pericles at the house. Morag went to her room and undressed slowly. Perhaps if she took a bath, Perry would be home by then. But Pericles wasn't, and finding she couldn't sleep, she slipped into bed and tried to read her book, turning the pages every now and then, but taking in nothing of the story.

She was still reading when the door opened and Pericles came in. She started, smiling nervously at his inscrutable face.

"My wife sleeps in my bed," he said. "I thought I'd made that clear last night."

Morag's fingers tightened around the spine of the book. "I prefer my own room," she murmured.

He raised his eyebrows thoughtfully. "Come on, Morag."

She pulled the bedclothes more closely around her. "I'm not coming!" she managed.

She scarcely saw his hand as he whipped the sheet away from her, but she felt the hard strength of his arms all right as he scooped her off the bed and onto her feet beside him. Pericles opened the door and bowed politely to her. "After you, Mrs. Holmes!"

She cast him a swift look through her eyelashes and lowered her eyes hastily at the unyielding look on his face. She picked up her negligee and, when he took it away from her, began to search for her slippers, only to have them removed from her nerveless fingers as well. She hugged her book to her, but that too joined the growing pile of discarded articles on the bed.

"Morag," he said at last, "if you don't come now, I'll turn you over my knee and smack you."

She turned a scarlet face to him. "I hate you!" she declared. "Do you hear me? I hate you!"

"Do you?" He put a hand on her shoulder, allowing his fingers to trail down her back, caressing her even while he drew her inexorably to him. "If you want to fight," he said in her ear, "you can fight me decently in bed, with no holds barred, like a man and woman should. Then, when you've had enough...."

She clung to him, not trusting her knees to hold her up. "You can't make me!"

He held her closer still, running his lips across her eyes and slowly down to her mouth, kissing her so lightly that she stifled a sob and tried to hide her face from him.

"I think I can make you," he said. "You are my woman and I'll make love to you when and how I please, no matter what you think!" He put a hand on her heart.

"You need loving, Morag. Why won't you admit it?"

She hid her face in his shoulder. "If you *asked* me," she pleaded, "but you don't care what I think or feel! You had no reason to be angry last night, no reason to... to take it out on me!"

He dragged his fingers through her hair, pulling her head back and kissing her mouth again. "If I had thought you were playing with Takis in earnest, I would not have been so gentle with you, my Morag! And you would not be standing here arguing with me now! Be grateful that I did believe you! Are you going to pretend that you didn't want me to make love to you?" He gave her a little shake. "Well?"

She tried hard to tell him how much she wanted him, but the words would not come. If he only loved her a little .... But she knew better than that!

"I know I'm your wife and... and...." She swallowed. "Oh, Perry, I want to be more than just a convenience."

His laughter shattered what little pride she had left. "Not a very convenient convenience, as you won't come to bed," he teased her. "Come on, Mrs. Holmes, you may as well bow to the inevitable. Will you walk, or shall I carry you?"

She gave him a telling look that lost most of its sting as she gave way to the pressure of his arms with something very like relief. He pushed her hair back from her face, running his thumb down the line of her jaw. "Is it war or peace?" he asked her.

The hot color flooded her cheeks. "Peace." Her eyes fell before the look in his. "An armistice until—if that's what you want."

"All right." He looked down at her, his eyes quizzical. "An armistice it will be. But one day I shall demand a total surrender, *karthiá mou*, and there will be no half measures then! You'll tell me everything I want to know before I sign a final peace treaty with you!"

"But you know...."

"I want the words," he said very gently. "Is that so much to ask?"

She couldn't answer him. If she could have found the words, she would have said them there and then, but how could she when he had not offered her a single word of love? And it was that knowledge that brought a droop to her shoulders and a slowness to her steps as she preceded him out of the room, down the corridor into his bedroom, and finally under the hand-embroidered covers of his bed.

CHAPTER NINE

"PERRY, I WANT to learn Greek."

Her husband looked amused. "Are you asking my permission?"

"Not exactly," Morag said. "It's more in the nature of a warning. I don't like being called names that I don't understand." His laughter made her hesitate, but then she went on: "I don't like you laughing at me, either!"

His eyes took on a wicked brilliance. "There seems to be a great deal that you don't like this morning."

"You never take me seriously!" she complained. "It's not my fault that I can't speak Greek!"

"No," he agreed. "Why don't you ask for a translation?"

"Because you only speak Greek at the most inconvenient moments! You know very well what I mean!" she continued repressively.

"Indeed I do!"

"Well, I don't like it!"

"Poor Morag," he drawled. "I don't remember calling you anything very dreadful, however. What would you like me to call you?"

"I don't know," she said. But she did know. She wanted to be called "darling," and "beloved," and "his much beloved wife."

"Then you'll have to put up with my Greek names for you!" He slid out of bed, looking down at her. "*Karthiá mou! Yinéka mou! Agapi mou!*"

"Ah," she said, "I know what *yinéka* means, it means woman!"

"And wife!"

She ignored that. "And *karthiá?*"

He grinned at her. "*Karthiá?* It means heart!"

"Oh," said Morag, suddenly breathless.

"You see," he said, pressing home his advantage, "it's nothing very bad, is it? I don't think you have much to complain about."

She sat up, hugging her knees, tossing up in her mind if she would also ask him what *agapi mou* meant. She decided against it, realizing he was still staring down at her and seemed to be expecting something from her.

"You look doubtful," Pericles said dryly.

"I... I didn't kn-know," she stammered. "It could have meant anything!"

"Well, now you do know, I hope I have your permission to call you anything I please, in Greek or English, or any other language."

Morag licked her lips, trying to drag her eyes away from his. He looked so splendid, so dark and immovable, so very much the master of the situation!

"I suppose so," she said.

She thought she was going to drown in the brightness of his eyes and that she wouldn't be able to care that he didn't love her, but would have to confess her own love for him and beg him to be kind to her. But then another matter came to mind and the moment passed. Her eye kindled with remembered indignation.

"How long have you known that Delia is coming here? I think you might have told me, instead of leaving it to your mother!" she sighed. "Why has she got to come here anyway?"

"She's a member of your family."

Morag's eyes flashed. "I'd prefer her not to come," she said mutinously.

He sat down on the bed beside her. "And I prefer that she does come. I have no wish to be thought inhospitable by your parents."

"She's not my real sister," Morag said. "Surely, if I don't want her here—"

Pericles put a hand behind her head. "Can you give me a good reason why she shouldn't come?" he asked. "Come, Morag, I'm not unreasonable! Tell me why you don't want her here and perhaps I'll agree with you and tell her not to come."

"Isn't it enough that I don't want her?" She sounded almost as desperate as she felt. With Delia in the same house as Pericles, what chance would Morag have to make him fall in love with her?

His fingers stroked her neck. "No, I don't think so. I want your family to feel free to visit you whenever they wish to. Besides, when you see her again, I don't think you'll find you dislike her half as much as you used to. She's really a very attractive young woman!"

She sighed, hating to have another clash of wills with him so soon. "As your wife, I consider I have the right to have some say in whom we invite here," she burst out, wishing that she could sound as cool and logical as he did.

"As my wife," he retorted, "you will do as I think best...or take the consequences!"

"But that's barbaric!"

"Isn't it?" he agreed calmly. "Very Greek!" He pulled her hair gently, smiling straight into her eyes. "It won't do you any harm to have Delia here for a while. She can give you a hand with the children and give you a chance to have some time to yourself."

"Just because you say so?" she demanded. "Well, I won't—"

"You haven't much choice. She's coming and that's that." He pulled her hair again, rather less gently. "Unless you have a good reason as to why she should stay away."

She shook her head miserably."She'll make trouble!"

"Then you'll have to cope with her when she does," he answered quietly. "If you care enough to put a spoke in her wheel, instead of giving way to her!"

Her eyes widened. "Why can't you give way to me?" she complained. "Only this once! It can't mean very much to you whether she comes or not."

"Ah, but it does!" He pushed her back against the pillows, studying her mouth with an interest that made her catch her lower lip between her teeth and avert her eyes. "Besides," he added, so softly that she couldn't be sure he had said it, "I like it when you're subservient and anxious to please me, and very, very feminine—like now!" His lips took hers with an insolent freedom that made it very clear what was her place in his scheme of things. She tried to twist away, but his hold on her hair made her cry out. Instantly she was free. "Did I hurt you?" he asked. "Morag, you shouldn't fight me!"

"I don't!" she snapped. "I'm not bossy like you!"

"Bossy?" His concern dissolved into laughter. "Because I won't let you have your way over Delia?"

"Because you never let me have my own way!"

He leaned on his elbow, putting out a hand to touch her face, tracing the line of her lips with his finger. "I will when you really know what you want," he promised. "At the moment you still haven't the courage of your convictions to dare all because only one thing matters to you. So you might as well go my wayuntil you find your tongue, *karthiá mou*, because I know exactly what I want!"

Her lips trembled against his finger and her own hands came up around his neck to bury themselves in the virile black hair at his neck. "Pericles...." She shut her eyes and swallowed convulsively. Didn't he know how his touch awakened her own need of him?

"Well, go on, then," he said. "Why don't you ask me to kiss you?"

Her eyes flew open and she turned away from him. "I...I can't!" she said.

"Then you haven't any grievance because it's I who commands you, *agapi mou*, for I can, and will, take your kisses when I want them! With or without your consent," he added for good measure. He kissed her ear. "If you were honest you'd admit you were glad to have it that way, because you like my kisses, don't you?" He turned her face to his. "Don't you?"

"Yes, yes, yes!" She was almost in tears with frustration, and at that moment she thought she disliked him more than anyone she knew. Then his mouth came down on hers and she melted into his arms in an agony of love for him. It was an unfair advantage he had, she thought while she could think at all, for he could rouse in her this delicious ecstasy at will, whereas she couldn't even find the words to beg him to kiss her again.

"THERE'S A LETTER for you, Morag." Dora looked curiously at her daughter-in-law, but she said nothing. "Aren't you going to open it?"

"It's from Delia!"

"All the more reason to find out what she has to say." She smiled, revealing all the warm charm of which she was capable. "Do open it! I've been sitting here looking at it for nearly and hour, wondering if she's changed her mind and decided not to come after all. Even the children were up before you this morning!"

"Yes, I'm sorry. I thought they'd sleep late."

"They did!" Dora rejoined. "Only not so late as you did. I'd have brought you your breakfast in bed, but

Pericles said you were to be left to sleep it out." She raised a sardonic eyebrow. "In my day it was the wife who guarded her husband's rest, not the other way around. Have you been finding the children too much for you, my dear?"

"N-no," Morag said.

"Wait until you have three or four to cope with! Kimon and Peggy are of an age when they can mostly look after themselves, but it's a different matter when they are babies!"

Morag gave her a confused look. "I don't know what you're talking about."

"My dear girl, what do you think? Oh, don't bother to tell me that it's none of my business, because Perry has already done that! He actually said he wanted to have you to himself for a while! I think that's a very good sign, don't you? He looked so happy this morning! Just what I'd always hoped for him!"

But that wasn't because he loved her, Morag protested silently. It was because he didn't love her! He didn't want children while there were no solid foundations to their marriage. Who would? He might find someone he liked better than herself and he wouldn't want to feel guilty about leaving her and starting again with someone else. He was bound to prefer somebody else sooner or later. Someone like Delia, for instance. Someone who was gay and beautiful and very, very sure of her own attractions!

Morag turned her stepsister's letter over in her hand, trying to focus on the bright, purple ink in which the address was written. *Mrs. Pericles Holmes.* Her heart turned right over within her. Was that her? Pericles had called her Mrs. Holmes, but somehow that was quite different from Mrs. *Pericles* Holmes! That made her seem a part of him, such as she longed to be.

She tore open the envelope and pulled out the letter inside. It was seldom that Delia bothered to put pen to paper. She far preferred the telephone as a means of communication, and Morag could imagine that it must have been her father who had put his foot down this time or she would surely have placed a call to Greece with as little thought as she called the people next door. she read:

> Dear Morag, I don't suppose it makes any difference to you when I arrive, so I shall turn up when I'm ready. Everyone has been very cross ever since you left, and crosser still when I said I intended visiting you. But I *liked* Pericles, and why should you mind if I come and look him up? You're safely married to him! Anyway, I'm coming whether you want me to or not, because your father has been very odd lately and I don't want him to think we're less than good friends. Have you been telling him anything? Ma thinks you may have had a heart-to-heart when you were here getting married. It wouldn't be wise if you were to turn him against me, you know. Just thought I'd warn you! See you soon, Delia.

"May I read it?" Dora asked.

Morag colored. "I'd rather you didn't," she murmured. "Delia says lots of things she doesn't mean."

Dora held out an imperious hand. "If you want me for an ally while she's here, I may as well know the worst."

"All right," Morag said reluctantly. "It doesn't say anything anyway. I mean, it doesn't say anything much. It worries me about my father, though. He's always adored Delia and she could never do any wrong in his eyes."

"What about her mother?"

"She preferred Delia, too. Delia was her own daughter and they're very... very alike!"

Dora came to the end of the letter and flung it down onto the table in front of her. "What could you have told your father about her?" she demanded.

"Nothing very terrible. It was always I who got into scrapes and had to be rescued from them. Delia never did anything wrong. Anything I could tell my father would have been my fault, far more than hers!"

Dora's eyes met hers. "Have you told Pericles?"

"He knows," Morag admitted.

"Then we needn't worry! Let her come and do her worst!" Dora wrinkled her nose fastidiously. "I don't think I'm going to like her. You can congratulate yourself, Morag Grant, in having a united family behind you! I thought you rather negligible when you first arrived, yet you have all of us eating out of your hand: me, Kimon, Peggy—even Pericles! I wonder how you do it?"

Morag was absurdly pleased by her mother-in-law's praise. "I like you all," she said, "and I want you to like me."

Dora chuckled. "Especially Pericles! No, don't bother to deny it. Even Kimon recognizes that Pericles is the sun, the moon, and the stars to you. Quite different from Susan!" she added on a note of satisfaction. She looked back at Delia's letter. "I think we'll put her in your old room. It's nicer than the other spare room, which is smaller and rather hot at this time of year."

Was it her "old room" already? Morag supposed it was, although most of her things were still there, in the wardrobe and in the chest of drawers. It would be a good excuse to move in properly to the room she now shared with Pericles, she thought, knowing that she would never have found the courage to do so without such an excuse. It would also mean that there would be no going back there herself, and that, too, might have its advantages.

Dora had told the maid to get the room ready for Delia, but Morag was there before her, making sure that all her own things were gone before her stepsister arrived. She had not said anything to Pericles and she wilted inwardly when she thought of how he would tease her for taking such a liberty, but he didn't seem to notice at all. In fact, he had obviously taken it for granted that she would move into his room as a matter of course. He had said he expected her to sleep in his bed and apparently he thought that was the end of the matter and that she would obey him without any further argument. And she had, though not without a great deal of inner conflict. If he thought it had been easy for her, it hadn't, and one day she would tell him exactly how difficult it had been. Perhaps, one day, she would find the words for that at least!

When the room was ready, she went down to the beach with the children. Kimon could swim quite well, but Peggy was still at the nervous stage when she alternated between wild boasts as to her prowess and shrieks of fear if the water happened to go over her head by accident.

"Will you come in, too?" she asked Morag, looking longingly at the bright blue that lapped amiably at her feet.

"Yes. Shall we swim out to that rock?" Morag suggested.

"I can't!" Peggy yelped. "I can't swim as far as that!"

"You said you could yesterday," Kimon reminded her. "Daddy said you couldn't, and you said you could easily!"

"So I can, if Morag comes, too!" Peggy claimed, casting a nervous look at the rock in the distance. "She can help me if I get tired."

Kimon squinted a look at Morag. "What are you going to do if Morag needs help, too?" he asked, and was off down the beach, feet flying, with Morag in hot pursuit. "You can't catch me!" he jeered over his shoulder.

Morag increased her pace, determined not to be beaten. In doing so, she failed to see Pericles coming towards her and ran full tilt into him.

"Oh, I'm sorry!" she gasped.

His arms caught her up and swung her around in the air. "Don't be! Shall I catch that young devil for you? What do you want him for?"

"He implied that I couldn't swim out to that rock and back without getting into trouble!"

Pericles looked amused. "Can you? Let's see you do it, then!"

"I'm going to swim there and back, too," Peggy said a trifle uncertainly. "Will you watch me, too?"

"Okay," said Pericles. "Kimon and I will sit on the beach and laze while you two prove yourselves!" He lowered himself onto the sand and lay back with a self-satisfied air. "Get to it, girls, I shall enjoy watching you!"

Feeling rather foolish, Morag pulled her cap on over her hair and began to walk out the first few feet until she had enough water to swim in. She was very conscious of Pericles making the most of looking her up and down as she took a header into the blue depths and struck out for the black shape of the rock in front of her.

"Wait for me, Morag!" Peggy cried after her.

Morag turned, swimming a few strokes on her back. "Come on, then!"

"I can't go so quickly!" Peggy pushed herself off and

began to swim a pedestrian, stately breaststroke toward Morag. "I'm coming!" she announced triumphantly.

Morag looked over her shoulder at the rock. It served her right, she thought, for wanting to show off to Pericles. She had always been able to swim well and she had wanted to make him admire her for that at least, by flashing through the water out to the rock and back again. But with Peggy slowly coming toward her she had no choice but to slow her strokes to match those of the little girl and to encourage her to do a few more strokes, and then a few more, until at last they reached the rock.

"Do you want to wait a while before we go back?" she asked Peggy.

Peggy nodded, gasping and spluttering as a small wave caught the side of her head. "I don't think I can swim back!"

"Of course you can!"

Peggy clutched at Morag's shoulder, pulling herself closer to th rock. "Daddy will give me a piggyback if we ask him. He won't mind! He often does it!"

But Morag was determined that they shouldn't have to call upon Pericles. There was no reason, she thought, why she shouldn't give Peggy a lift back to the beach herself. She was strong enough and she could swim as well as anyone she knew.

"You'd better hop on my back," she told Peggy.

The child looked dubiously at her. "You're too small, Morag," she said at last. "I'll push you under. I want daddy!"

"Of course I'm big enough!" Morag assured her. "I won't let anything happen to you!"

Peggy obediently put her arms around Morag's neck and sat astride her back, clinging on for dear life. Morag struck out for the shore, using her favorite Australian crawl. But Peggy was far from happy on her precarious perch and tightened her grasp around Morag's neck until she was practically throttling her. Morag put up a hand to release herself and they both rolled over and came up choking.

"You'll drown us both!" Peggy screamed.

"Then don't hold on so tight!"

Peggy began to cry in earnest. "I want daddy!"

"We'll try again," Morag said patiently. "We haven't far to go now."

"We have! We have!"

"We have not!" Morag snapped. She trod water, allowing herself to look over to where they had left Pericles sitting on the sand, but he was no longer there. For an instant she knew such a sense of desolation that she felt completely ridiculous. He wasn't really gone; he had probably only moved his position. But where was he?"

"Come on, Peggy, get on my back again!"

Peggy, suddenly silent, did as she was asked. "Daddy's gone," she lamented. "He might have waited!"

Morag thought so, too. "Never mind, darling. We can manage quite well without him!"

"We can't!" Peggy said with depressing certainty.

"Of course we can! Do sit still, Peggy! You're throttling me again!"

"I'm trying not to, but I want daddy! *He* doesn't sink so much when I ride on him!"

Morag forbore to answer. She swam on with a dogged determination, having long since abandoned any attempt at style. All she wanted to do now was arrive without too much damage done either to herself or Peggy.

"I think you could stand on the bottom now," Peggy told her. "I can see the sand through the water."

Morag tried to do as she was told, but the water was

deeper than Peggy had supposed and they both submerged and rose again, crosser and more frightened than ever.

"I told you, Morag, I told you! We're going to drown!"

"No, we are not!"

She seized the child under her armpits and, turning over onto her back, began to move with increasing pace toward the shore. Peggy was crying by now and she felt like tears herself. Then, just as she was beginning to give up hope, her shoulders grated against the rough sand and she realized that they were there. She looked up and saw Pericles standing beside her, looking down at her.

"I thought you'd gone!" she accused him.

"I did, but I came back to watch you two nits writhing around in old Poseidon's hair!"

"Don't encourage her," said another, only too familiar voice. "She's hoping you'll give her the kiss of life! Morag can swim like a fish!"

Delia!

Morag leaped to her feet in one swift movement. Her stepsister wore a cool white dress and looked as smart as paint, whereas she, she knew, looked a complete mess, her hair wet and straggly, and the swimsuit she was wearing so old that she couldn't remember when she had first had it, and without an atom of makeup to hide the freckles that the hot Greek sun had brought out on the bridge of her nose.

"Hello, Delia," she said in a strained voice.

Delia took a step backward and looked her up and down, managing to draw attention to the faded color of the swimsuit and the signs of wear on the straps that would soon fall into holes. "Hello yourself!" she drawled.

"VERY COZY!" Delia murmured, looking around the bedroom Morag had helped prepare for her. "You certainly knew what you were doing when you took off for Greece, didn't you, pet?"

"What do you mean?" Morag countered.

"I would have thought it was obvious. The only flies in the ointment are the children. Is that little girl always such a trial? I'm surprised Pericles allows her to hang around him like that."

"She'd been badly frightened," Morag pointed out. "She wanted to swim out to the rock with me and it was farther than she could manage."

"Showing off, I suppose, like you!"

This came uncomfortably close to the truth. "I'm very fond of both the children!" Morag claimed.

"Especially when their father is around? Oh, don't bother to pretend with me! I'd do exactly the same!" Delia sank down onto the bed and looked around her. "Where do you sleep? Or is that one of your little marriage secrets?"

"No." Morag wished that she had outgrown the habit of always having to answer Delia's questions, no matter how inconvenient they were to herself. "I sleep on the other side of the house. Our room looks over the sea, too, but it's at the other end."

"Our room? Well done, my dear. I thought you were here more or less as governess to those brats." She frowned, her eyes cold and hard. "That's the impression I received from Perry. He isn't in love with you—but I suppose you know that?"

"Did he say so?" Morag couldn't resist asking.

Her stepsister smiled slowly. "Now that would be telling! I must say he's the most attractive man I've seen for a long, long time. He makes David seem a wishy-washy shadow of what a man can be. But then I keep forgetting, you were in love with David, weren't you? Does Pericles know that?"

Morag fiddled with her fingers. "You were in love with David, too!"

"Was I?" Delia laughed. Morag remembered that laugh of old. It was supposed to sound like the tinkling of a distant bell and had hours of hard practice behind its soft, clear tones. To Morag it sounded like the knell of doom.

"You said you were. He thought you were, too. You know he did! He wouldn't...he wouldn't have taken you out otherwise!"

"Thus ditching you? My dear, I did you a favor. More of a favor than I knew, seeing you might have married him! It would have suited me a great deal better if you had!"

Morag was astonished. "Why?" she asked flatly.

"Why?" Delia laughed again. "Well, really, surely you don't have to ask. It would have suited Pericles a great deal better, too!"

Morag made no answer. She pointed out the towels the maid had left beside the dressing table, and the various other facilities of the room, and then she turned to go. "If there's nothing more you want, I'll be with the children," she said.

Delia yawned delicately. "Oh, but I was hoping you would unpack for me," she smiled. "It was all such a rush and you know how bad I am at folding things. I'm sure I've forgotten quite half of what I meant to bring with me!"

"Why did you come?" Morag asked.

"Why? I thought you knew. I came to see your husband—at his request—against other things!"

"Then what was all that about your falling out with daddy?" Morag said bluntly.

"He has been a trifle difficult lately. He was quite reassured when I said you would be home again soon. It was quite touching how worrried about you he's been, especially when you think how easily he took the David incident in his stride!"

"Oh?"

"Well, he did think that *you'd* killed David, and I don't suppose he enjoyed the trial and all the gossip. It gave him a shock to find that anything to do with your mother could be less than perfect." She slanted a look of pure dislike at Morag. "You always were naive about your father. I suppose you didn't know that he avoided you because you look like your mother. I thought not! What a fool you are, Morag Grant!"

Morag's hands clenched into two fists. "Morag Holmes," she corrected.

Delia got off the bed and went over to the window, looking out at the clear blue sea and the beauty of the headland.

"But not for long," she said to no one in particular. "Not if I can help it!"

CHAPTER TEN

DELIA HAD NO HESITATION in accepting the offer of the loan of Dora's car. Morag, already on edge because of her stepsister's attitude to her mother-in-law, tried in vain to suggest that she should rent her own, or should use the buses as Morag did herself.

"Why should I?" Delia had asked.

"I would have thought you'd know that!" Morag answered more tartly than she usually spoke to anyone.

But Delia only smiled. "It was you who was banned from driving!"

Morag bit her lip, hoping that Dora hadn't heard that. "I still don't think you ought to take Dora's car. It isn't easy driving in Athens and...and supposing anything should happen."

"Don't be ridiculous! What could happen? I don't intend to use the car often. Pericles has offered to show me some of the countryside and I'm not likely to turn down an invitation like that to drive myself!"

Morag stiffened. "Where is he taking you?"

"Oh, some place near Athens. Eleusis, or Elefsis, I think he called it. I suppose you've already been there."

"No," said Morag.

"Well, a governess can't expect such little treats, can she? Cheer up, I'll return him to you with a good grace when we get back."

Morag's eyes darkened. "Will you?"

"If he wants to be returned to you. Frankly, my dear, I

think he's more likely to have second thoughts about you—like David did—and make some comparisons between us in which you can hardly expect to show up very well. I nearly died when I saw you in that old swimsuit! How long have you had it? But then you never did put much value on glamour. David used to say you were the drab sister."

"I don't believe you!"

"About David? He wasn't the kind, simple young man you thought him at all! I came as quite a relief to him, I can tell you. At least I knew how to kiss and wasn't afraid to have a little fun! Do you bore Pericles, too?"

Morag flushed. "I...I don't want to talk about Pericles," she said. "Or David, either!"

"No?" Delia was plainly enjoying herself. "You wouldn't! You're the complete coward! Did you tell Pericles that you didn't want me here? Or did you pretend that we'd always loved each other, like good girls should? He didn't mind my coming here! I can stay as long as I like!"

Morag said nothing. She looked up as her mother-in-law, until now on the veranda outside, came in and smiled at them both. "Ah, there you are, Delia," she said with every sign of pleasure. "Did Morag tell you that my nephew is staying here for the time being? Pericles is so jealous of Morag that the poor boy has been feeling quite out of things, and he'll be all the more pleased to entertain you. I'm expecting him home anytime now and I promised him I'd be on hand to introduce you."

Morag stared at her mother-in-law in astonishment, only to recieve a fierce dig in the ribs and a command in Greek to sit up and behave herself, which she recognized as much by the tone of voice as by how often she had heard the same rebuke addressed to Peggy.

"Pericles has asked Delia to visit Eleusis," Morag said in a small voice.

Dora sniffed. "A very industrial site," she commented. "I suppose he wants the children to see it. They are beginning to interest themselves in growing things and it's time they learned the story of Demeter and how she gave the first crops to humanity. Of course, she was worshipped there more as the mother of Persephone, who came back from the dead. But I don't suppose you want to hear our old stories, do you? You look like a very modern young lady to me."

It was obvious that Delia wasn't sure whether this was a compliment or not. "I like to enjoy myself," she said, less sure of herself than Morag had ever seen her.

"With my son?" Dora looked faintly bored. "He looks more Greek than English, don't you think?" Her eyes narrowed. "Do his looks please you?"

"Why yes, I suppose so," Delia answered.

"In Greece, it is the woman who pleases the man!"

Delia managed a light laugh. "Isn't that kind of thing reciprocal anywhere?"

"Do you think so?" Dora, too, laughed softly. "No, a man may play with a pretty toy, but when it comes to his wife—then he will make sure that he is the only man in her life. Marriage, in Greece, is not a thing to be taken lightly. Every Greek wants a bride who will put him at the center of her existence. Morag makes the ideal wife for Pericles in that respect."

Delia opened her eyes very wide, looking the picture of innocence. "But didn't you know? Morag was engaged to another before she came to Greece!"

Dora looked at her with dry amusement. "You mean this David of yours? If Morag had been a Greek girl, she would have been protected from the attentions of a man like that! Girls of good family are not made use of by their relatives in that way here, not even by their worldly-wise sisters!"

"Ouch!" said Delia. "Sometime I'll tell you my side of that story, Mrs. Holmes. Morag isn't always very reliable when it comes to telling the truth!"

"Morag has yet to tell me anything." Dora rose to her feet. "She didn't have to. I know very little about her family, as a matter of fact, but she has a family here now and she is very dear to us all." She made a more familiar gesture of impatience. "Those children! For heaven's sake, Morag, go and see them! I will not have them making such a noise in the house. It's time Peggy learned a little restraint and didn't shriek like that!"

Morag needed no second bidding. She much preferred the company of the children just now. They knew nothing of the undercurrents Delia had brought with her, which swirled dangerously around Morag, threatening her happiness with the spite of years. It was good of Dora to defend her as she had, but it was Pericles' opinion that mattered, and still, he showed every sign of enjoying her company as much as David had before him!

Morag did her best not to encourage the children when they told her what they thought of her stepsister.

"She's awful!" Kimon said stolidly.

"Yes," said Peggy, "she's awful!"

"But she's very pretty," Morag said.

"I like looking at you better," Peggy assured her. "I don't want to draw *her*. Her eyes are awful! You have nice green eyes, hers aren't even blue! They're—" She broke off at a loss for words. "They're horrid!"

Kimon nodded. "Like pebbles," he put in.

"Some people think pebbles very pretty," Morag said, trying not to laugh. "Her eyes are gray, if you want to know!"

"They're not. They're not anything much—and she

changed into a blue dress and they still weren't anything much!"

Morag gave Peggy an exasperated look. "Don't let her hear you say that!"

"Why not?" Kimon asked. "If Peggy were to paint her, she would have to know, wouldn't she? It seems to me a reasonable thing to discuss."

"Oh, does it? Well, I think it's just an excuse for making personal remarks! She's my stepsister, don't forget!"

"But you don't like her, either," Peggy stated as a known fact.

"Do you?" Kimon added, his smile the image of his father's when he was most determined to bend her to his will. "You said you thought her silly, and so she is! You should have seen her when she arrived, running down the steps to the beach and practically sitting on top of daddy! I hope she knows that he married you," he added, giving the coin he was looking at a fierce jab with his finger. "You did tell her, didn't you?"

"Of course she knows!" Morag replied. "She was there when we got married."

"Oh, good!" the boy said with relief. "She can have Takis if she likes."

Peggy nodded soberly. "Good idea," she agreed.

"No, it isn't a good idea. It's a terrible idea, unless they both happen to want it that way," Morag protested. "Why were you making so much noise just now? Grandma doesn't like it when you shout at one another in the house!" It was bad enough that Dora should have decided that Takis could entertain Delia, without the childen getting the same idea! No, Morag wanted her stepsister gone as quickly as possible, not playing around with anyone as close to the family as Takis.

"We were having an argument," Kimon told her.

"About you," Peggy added.

"Me?" Morag asked.

Kimon turned and looked at her. "Did you invite Delia here, or did she ask herself? Peggy says that daddy asked her!"

Morag replied abruptly. "She asked herself!"

"That's what I thought," said Kimon. "But Peggy says she heard daddy and grandma talking, and that daddy said—"

"I don't want to know!"

"He said you'd never be free—" Peggy went on where her brother had left off "—not until she came. Grandma said it was an awful risk!"

"You shouldn't repeat other people's conversations," Morag quelled her. What had Pericles meant—she would never be free? She felt weak at the knees and more vulnerable than ever. Could he have meant free of him?

The children stared at her. "Are you all right, Morag?" Peggy asked.

"Yes, I'm all right. Will you be quiet now if I go and change for dinner?"

"Of course!" they agreed, full of injured innocence.

"What are you going to wear?" Peggy said almost in the same breath . "I suppose your gold dress would be too grand."

"Yes, I think so," Morag said, not thinking what she was saying. "I'm going to wear my jade pendant, though."

Peggy screwed up her face thoughtfully. "Yes," she approved. "And with you hair loose. Daddy likes it better that way."

Now when could she have heard him say that, Morag wondered. Had he really voiced an opinion, and if he had, what else had he said?

It seemed strange not to go to the room she had had

before, the one that was now Delia's. She had to restrain herself from knocking on the door of Perry's room. It didn't seem like hers at all. To her relief, it was empty. She turned on the light feeling like a burglar. She was glad to see that there was no trace of her possessions anywhere. At least she didn't have to feel she was imposing on him.

The dress she chose to wear was not new. Delia would have seen it hundreds of times before, she thought with a wry smile in the glass, but she looked nice in it and part of the pattern was green to match the jade pendant Pericles had given her. It made her eyes look greener than ever, too, and she thought how suitable that was. Green-eyed meant jealous, and that was exactly what she was. She was jealous of any other woman Pericles looked at.

She brushed her hair into a cloud around her head, ready to fasten it into the nape of her neck. Then she hesitated. Should she leave it free as Kimon had suggested? She fingered the loose ends and decided that she would, even if it did make her look younger and as vulnerable as she felt. Last of all, she looked for the jade pendant to hang around her neck, but she couldn't find it anywhere. Annoyed to think that she had left it behind when she had brought the rest of her things from the other room, she decided she would have to go back to Delia's room to look for it. She hurried down the corridor before she could change her mind, coming to a stop outside the door.

At first she could not believe her ears. It was Pericles that she could hear through the shut door. She stood completely still, unable to bring herself to move, just as Delia's tinkling bell laugh rang out. A second later the door opened and Pericles stood before her.

"What do you want?" he asked her.

"I—" She put a hand up to her mouth, found herself

quite unable to continue, and turned on her heel and fled.

She did not get far. His arm flashed out and held her hard against him. "Well, Morag? Are you reduced to listening outside doors now?"

"No," she whispered.

"No? Then what are you doing?"

It was ridiculous to feel so guilty. Surely it was he who was that! What had he been doing in Delia's room?

He let her go with a suddenness that unbalanced her, and she had to put out a hand against the wall to save herself from falling. "Well, I hope you liked what you heard!" Pericles shot at her.

"I didn't hear anything!"

"Then what were you doing?"

She tried to hide her face from him. "I wanted my jade pendant. I must have left it behind when I moved...moved my things...."

"Into my room?"

She nodded, rubbing her shoulder where she had caught it against the wall. "May I get past, please?"

There was an inscrutable look on his face. "I didn't know you'd moved," he told her. "I couldn't see any of your things around. Do you always keep everything so neat?"

"Please, may I get past?"

His eyes glinted. "What will you give me if I do?"

"Nothing." She was very sure of that. She gave a mutinous lift to her chin. "I wonder you should ask since you've probably already had everything you can want from Delia!"

His hand caught her around the arm and hauled her relentlessly back into the room she now shared with him. With his other hand he slammed the door shut behind them.

"Now," he said, "you can tell me exactly what you mean by that!"

She licked her lips nervously. "I only meant...."

"Yes?"

"Nothing," she said.

"That won't do, Morag. For once you're going to tell me just what's going on inside that head of yours. What would I want from Delia?"

She struggled vainly against his restricting hands. "She's... very attractive!" she said feebly.

"Yes, she is," he agreed readily.

The color came and went in her cheeks. Her eyes fell before his. "I know you find her attractive."

"And you're jealous of her? Is that what you're trying to say?"

"No, of course not! I think she's attractive, too!"

"Is that so?" he drawled. "It seems to me that you don't like her at all. Why don't you ask outright what I was doing in her room?"

"Oh!" she gasped. "You can do as you like!"

"I shall," he retorted.

She wept inwardly. As if she didn't know that! The first time he had seen Delia, he had wanted to kiss her—he had even asked Morag if she thought he could, as her future stepbrother-in-law. And it hadn't stopped there! He had insisted that she come to Greece for as long as she wanted, regardless of anything that Morag had said to him. And now he was visiting her in her room!

"You promised that you would pretend to my family that you... that you liked me!" she reminded him on a note of desperation.

"I promised I'd protect your pride while we were in England. But, if you remember, I told you the price you'd have to pay for my pride would ask a great deal more than a few kisses of you!"

"I... I didn't agree to pay any price for your pride!" she stammered.

"You haven't any choice—as my wife," he pointed out.

She wrenched herself away from him. "I've done everything you asked! I don't see what more I can do!"

He looked at her thoughtfully. "I can't remember that you've actually offered anything," he said. "If it had been left to you, you'd still be addressing me as Mr. Holmes!"

"Oh!" Her stifled gasp betrayed her consternation. "But I told you that... that I liked—" her voice dropped to a whisper "—you to kiss me."

"I might like being kissed by you!"

She was silent for so long that she thought he'd lose all patience with her, but he went on standing there, waiting. "Delia would like to kiss you," she said.

His mouth kicked up at the corners. "You don't say!"

Her eyes flew to his face. "You mean you knew why she came here?"

"I'd be a fool not to, my dear. I have a certain amount of experience of your sex, I am not in the least bit sorry to say. If she succeeds, though, you will have only yourself to blame."

She gave him a look of mute inquiry. If he could read Delia with such ease, could he also read the secrets of her heart, she wondered.

"You could compete with her," he told her dryly. "I find you attractive, too, as you very well know!"

Her heart jerked within her. "But I'm your wife!" she exclaimed.

He nodded soberly at her. "Yes, you are. Don't let me have to remind you of it again!"

He stood back and opened the door for her, a glint of amusement in his eyes. She couldn't bring herself to look up at him, but took to her heels and fled down the corridor, anywhere, just so that she could be out of sight of his mocking challenge.

DELIA'S TRIUMPHANT AIR was very hard to bear. Morag watched her covertly across the table and was astonished at the depth of feeling that consumed her whenever her stepsister's tinkling laughter rang out in response to some sally from Pericles. Delia knew exactly what she was doing. It was the old, old story, unfolding like a tired, seen-too-often film, of finding someone else's grass much greener than one's own. Morag had watched it all before, only then it had been David whom Delia had wanted, and Morag had been able to find all sorts of excuses for her, and for David, too, who had fallen flat at Delia's feet and had taken it for granted that Morag would understand.

She *had* understood, that was the trouble. Naturally David had found Delia more interesting and more fun than herself—everybody always did. It had been just the same at school, where Morag had once heard one of Delia's friends commiserating with her for having to live with such a dull person.

"Morag never says anything," the girl had complained. "How do you live with her silent criticism of you all the time?"

Delia had laughed. At the time she had still been practicing the tinkling bell laugh and it hadn't always worked. That time it had slipped into an off-key bray. "Nobody likes Morag," she had said.

It wasn't true, of course. There had been many people who had liked Morag very much, many who had preferred her vastly to her stepsister, but they had never been made welcome at the Grant house and Morag had practically given up asking them to her home. But such remarks don't have to be true to be hurtful, and it had been one of a whole series of pinpricks that had robbed her of much of her confidence, more especially when she came into contact with anyone new who had not known her since her babyhood, when her mother had been alive and had surrounded her with all the love she needed.

David had liked her at first. He had broken into her thirst for friendship like a glass of cool, clear water. He had particularly liked to dance with her. "You should always be seen when you're doing something," he told her. "Never sitting still!" She hadn't paid him much attention, but she had been pleased that he had thought about her at all.

After a while, she had even taken him home. It had been a curious, platonic relationship, with David making use of her notes and very often asking her to write his essays as well as her own for the tutor they shared at the college they both attended. "When we've done with all these exams," he'd said to her one day, "I'll put you out to work and let you keep me forever!"

It had seemed to Morag the most glorious moment of her life. "Do you mean you'll marry me?" she had asked him.

He had shrugged his shoulders, as shy as she. "Why not?" he had said.

It was only then that Delia had started taking an interest in him. In a moment of weakness when Delia had been feeling particularly charming, Morag had confided in her that she and David were getting married. "Not yet!" she had said, "but one day when David has a proper job." She had forgotten all about his threat to send her out to work for him!

Delia had smiled at David and then she laughed. "A man," she had said, with a flutter of her eyelashes, "would want more than the cool embrace of someone as innocent as Morag Grant. It takes an old man to want liking instead of love; a young man should be looking for fire and enthusiasm, something that Morag could never rise to!"

David had promptly thought so, too. He had tried to explain to Morag the excitement he found in being with her stepsister, when Morag had found the two of them entwined on the sofa in her father's study one Sunday afternoon. "One has to have a bit of fun!" he had ended, looking considerably ill at ease.

Well, they'd had their fun and Morag had tried not to mind. Once or twice she had tried to clear up her own position as far as David was concerned, but he had put her off with the occasional date, telling her that she didn't understand. Delia didn't mean anything to him! But that, she had thought, was a lie, for he had gone on seeing far more of Delia than he ever had of herself, right up until that last, terrible night when she had crashed the car and killed him.

"David always said you'd do anything he asked you to!" Delia had sobbed. She had looked remarkably unattractive at that moment, her face gray with shock and her clothes and hair mussed as much from David's attentions as from the crash.

"You'd better get into bed," Morag had said. "I'll go down to the car and wait for the police."

It had been better that way. It had been the way David would have wanted it. But Delia could not have Pericles, too! Morag sat back in her chair and looked at her stepsister with a cold, objective eye. She was attractive, of course, but it was a shopworn, Christmas decoration kind of attraction that looked tawdry in the full light of day. Little hard lines were beginning to crease her face from nose to mouth, and though she laughed frequently, her eyes were hard and never laughed at all. Morag had always known her to be selfish, but it had not previously occurred to her that Delia never gave anything away. She would take from any man, but she would give nothing that was worthwhile in return.

Morag stared at her as though she had never seen her before, and in a way, she hadn't. She had always thought of Delia as being beautiful and easy to love, but she wasn't. She was merely brittle and grasping and...and rather tedious! How odd, Morag thought, to find out now that Delia was scarcely worth the trouble of disliking, for she wasn't anything very much.

She most certainly wasn't good enough for Pericles!

"I'm sorry, what did you say?" Morag turned to her mother-in-law as though she were emerging from a dream. "I—I wasn't listening!"

"That, my dear, was quite obvious!" Dora rasped at her. "You ought to have something better to do than daydreaming at the dinner table! As Pericles' wife, you have a duty to help entertain your guests! Takis is still waiting to be introduced to your sister!"

Morag gave her a little shrug of her shoulders. "I'm sorry," she said again.

Dora shook herself irritably. "In Greece we prize hospitality very highly. You must learn to be a better hostess than that! My husband would have had something to say to me if I hadn't waited on his guests with my own hands! Pericles is too soft with you!"

Morag was not as afraid of her mother-in-law as she had been at one time. She smiled, tongue in cheek. "But you are still the hostess here!"

Dora picked up her spoon and rapped her smartly over her knuckles. In this mood, it was easy to see why Peggy sometimes disliked her. "This house belongs to Pericles, not to me."

Pericles leaned across the table and took the spoon

from his mother. "Leave Morag alone, mama," he said. He smiled straight at Morag, with such a look that her breath was taken away. "If anyone disciplines her, I shall!" he added. The glint in his eyes grew more pronounced. "I see you found your pendant," he added.

"Morag never took care of anything," Delia put in. "She would have turned my whole room upside down if I hadn't found it for her. My mother would never allow her to have anything of value in case she lost it. If she didn't lose it, she'd give it away! David said she'd have given away her engagement ring if he'd given her one!"

"Would you give away my ring?" Pericles asked Morag.

She fingered her wedding ring and shook her head. "Of course not!"

"She'll probably lose it!" Delia sighed.

"If she does, I'll definitely beat her," Pericles drawled. His eyes lingered on Morag's hot face with a faint smile, then turned away from her and gave all his attention to Delia, drawing her out with a charm that made her seem suddenly nicer and added a sparkle to her replies.

"I hope you haven't forgotten that I'm taking you to Eleusis tomorrow," he reminded her. "You'll have to ask Morag to tell you about the place, if you don't already know about it. She has all the old legends at her fingertips—an interest she shares with my mother."

"Are you taking the children?" Dora asked, obviously still annoyed at the way Pericles had taken her spoon from her.

"I don't think so," Pericles answered.

"It's good for them to see these places!" their grandmother declared. "You needn't think I'm going to look after them all day tomorrow, because I'm painting in the morning and playing bridge in the afternoon."

"Morag will look after them," Pericles said smoothly.

Morag looked up quickly. "But I'd like to come," she protested. "They say it isn't much to look at now, but it must have had terrific atmosphere at one time. The rites of Demeter and Persephone meant everything to such a lot of people. Persephone was the first one to come back from the dead, even in legend, as an ordinary person!"

"You can see it some other time," Pericles told her. "It will be too long a day for the children, and anyway, I want some time with Delia by herself."

Morag blinked. "The children will be disappointed."

Pericles threw back his head in an arrogant gesture. "But neither they nor you have been invited to come with us tomorrow. They won't be disappointed if you don't tell them about it."

But she did know, Morag thought resentfully. He might have married her to look after the children, but he didn't have to fling it in her face in front of Delia. And she was more than ever determined that Delia would have to go, and go quickly. The only thing she didn't know was how she was going to get rid of her.

CHAPTER ELEVEN

MORAG WENT TO BED before her husband. She heard him come in almost an hour later and pretended to be asleep. When he turned on the light she almost gave herself away, flinching from the sudden glare in her eyes. Her heart pounded, for she was almost sure that he wouldn't spare her feelings if he were to guess she was awake. When he came over to the bed she held her breath. He stood for a long time looking down at her, but he said nothing. He bent down and pushed a lock of her hair away from her mouth with gentle fingers. She almost, then, gave way to the urgent desire within her to open her arms to him and to whisper her love for him, but was stopped by the thought of how he had snubbed her when she had asked him if she, too, could to to Eleusis. Yet she might have changed her mind if he had touched her again, but he did not. He turned out the light and lay down on the bed beside her, pulling her into the hard circle of his arm. He must have known then that she was awake, but he still said nothing, and he was asleep long before she could still the loud beating of her heart and relax against him sufficiently to fall into slumber herself.

Her dreams when they came were muddled and confused. Dora had made her tell her stepsister the story of Demeter's long search for her daughter, and how she had served the royal family at Eleusis as nursemaid to their child and, becoming fond of the child, had decided to make him immortal by toughening him in the flames.

Not surprisingly, the queen had thought she had intended to burn the child to death, and Demeter had been forced to reveal herself as a goddess. In return for the royal family's kindness, she had made Eleusis the center of her worship. It was there, too, that Persephone came back from the kingdom of the dead, no longer a goddess because she had eaten the seeds of the pomegranate during her time under the earth and she was now fated to spend four months of the year with her husband, Hades, and the remaing eight in the service of her mother. Hence her new name of Kore, or Maiden, in token of her new position in the first sacred family of Greece. Morag had once seen a statue of Demeter, her arms outstretched, her face grieving for her loss, and she saw the heavy stone figure again in her dream and knew exactly who she was. The other figure, also a woman, came right up to her, a look of vengeance in her eyes, but when she saw the necklace of shells around Morag's neck she faded away again, changing her shape into that of a man, a man Morag recognized as Pericles, though it didn't really look much like him.

"Who are you!" she cried out.

"Hush, who do you think I am? I'm Pericles!"

It was Pericles all right, but she didn't know if she were waking or sleeping. "It was Nemesis," she said firmly.

"How do you know that!"

"She recognized my shell necklace."

"I think, my dear, that you have been dreaming."

"I suppose so, because she turned into you!"

"Into me?" He pulled her close and kissed her. "I hope that gave you joy!"

She hid her face against him. "Yes, it did," she said. "I'm sorry I woke you, Perry."

He pulled her closer still. "I'm not," he said.

IN THE MORNING her dream seemed very far away. Delia, on the other hand, was a very present reality. Morag saw her coming down the path to the beach, a little unsure in her fashionable platform shoes.

"I hope you aren't allowing that silly child out of her depth today," Delia panted. She looked very pleased with herself and Morag thought she knew why.

"Have you come down to swim?" she returned.

"Dressed like this? Really, I don't know how you can be so stupid! I'm waiting for Pericles!"

"Oh yes?"

Delia almost laughed out loud. "Poor Morag, but you didn't think he was in love with you, did you? You weren't as stupid as that? That was quite a snub he gave you yesterday, but you never learn! You ought to know by now why he wants to be alone with me!"

Morag kept her temper with difficulty. "Should I?"

"What have you to offer a man like Pericles? I can't think how you persuaded him to marry you."

Morag wasn't sure, either, but she had no intention of sharing her doubts with her stepsister. "I don't suppose you can," she said quietly.

"I thought you might have flattered him into it, but, knowing you, you probably haven't told him that you've fallen in love with him. He's very Greek, isn't he? Having a name like that would be ridiculous for most men, but it suits him in an extraordinary way. I suppose that's why he took you on. He can't have found it very lively living with his mother in semi-exile here. Anything would be better than nothing under the circumstances!"

Morag gave her a mocking look. "It's hard to tell!"

Delia frowned, for once uncertain how to deal with her stepsister. "Any man will take what's offered to him!"

"You should know!"

Delia's cold eyes glazed with anger. "You'll regret that! You're a fool, Morag! I hold your happiness in the hollow of my hand. You didn't mind when I took David, did you? But Pericles? You won't like losing him to me!"

"Pericles goes his own way!"

"My way," Delia rejoined. She stared long and hard at Morag. "Why, I believe you're even afraid of him!" she laughed, and there was very little of the tinkling bell about it. "So I'll be doing you a favor by taking him from you!"

"But why?" Morag asked. "Why do you want to hurt me?"

Delia turned away, putting one foot on a loose stone that slipped underneath her. If Morag had not held her upright, she would have fallen. "Don't you know why?" she said in a low and deadly voice. "I hate you, Morag Grant. I hate you for always being right and for doing all the right things! If I took your favorite toy, you'd offer me your next favorite after I'd broken it for you! The less you had, the less you needed. Even David—you couldn't be content with handing me him on a plate, but you had to sacrifice yourself to his memory and my good name. Who asked you to? Who asked you?"

"But I thought you wanted me to!"

"Well, you shouldn't think!" Delia pulled away from Morag, examining her shoes. "Why are you afraid of Pericles?"

"I'm not."

"But you said you were!"

"If you say so." Morag's face was controlled.

"Well, there you are then! What's the difference? I'll bet he knows it, too, and thinks he can treat you how he likes! I wouldn't put up with it! In fact, I shall quite enjoy teaching him a lesson. Of course, he's madly attractive, too. I like a man who doesn't mind taking the initiative.

And I don't think there's any danger of his not liking me, do you?"

Morag stopped herself from giving Delia a shove that would have sent her flying on those ridiculous shoes. That, she told herself, was not the way to deal with her. There had to be a better, more civilized way, if only she could think of it! "Pericles is a married man," she said, seething inwardly, because if that was the best argument she could find, she might just as well hand him over on a plate to Delia here and now.

"Oh, hardly, darling!" Delia's laugh was well in control now and sounded more bell-like than ever. "I don't suppose you'd have put so much as a foot in his room if I hadn't happened to be coming! It's obvious that he doesn't think of you in that way at all!"

Morag clenched her fists. "Why do you say that?" she asked quietly. A fine thing it would be if she were to burst into tears now and give Delia such an easy victory!

Delia smiled, savoring the moment. "Well, dear, David always said that you were too nice to be much of a temptation, and if you're very inexperienced, it's so easy to mistake good manners for anything warmer. I'm sure Pericles has lovely manners!"

"I don't see how you could know that," Morag protested.

The laugh came again. "Pericles and I had a lovely long talk together last night. I don't intend to waste my time while I'm here!"

Morag was scarcely aware of the cries of the children as they chased each other along the length of the beach. She watched them for a long pregnant moment, but she didn't see them at all. She took a deep breath. "I think it would be better if you went back to England, Delia," she said at last.

"I'm sure you do, sweetie, but I'm having too nice a time here. Life has been frightfully dull since David died—and he was rather dull too, or he would have been if he hadn't got involved with you."

"I don't think you understand me," Morag went on quietly. "I'm telling you to go. I'll see about your ticket myself, and my mother-in-law will drive you to the airport."

Delia's laugh was not quite so well under control this time. "And what will Pericles say to that?" she demanded. "He'll take my side! You know he will, just as he did last night!"

"My husband won't know until you've gone."

"Your husband? My God, that's rich! Don't you think that I might tell him? It was he who invited me here."

"Did he?" Morag asked coolly.

Delia's eyelashes flickered. "I wrote to him in the first place, but he wrote straight back and told me to come!"

"And now I'm telling you to go!"

Delia sat down hard, almost as though her knees had given way underneath her. Morag regarded her cautiously. It would be a mistake to think that after all these years Delia could be as easy to deal with as that.

"Aren't you afraid what Pericles will do to you?" Delia demanded.

She was, but there was no need to dwell on that, Morag told herself. "Perry won't hurt me," she said.

"He might, if that old woman is to be believed. She goes on as if Greek husbands were little tin gods and could do exactly as they liked to their wives!"

Morag smiled slowly. "Well, I don't see myself making Perry do anything he doesn't want to do, can you? Why should I? I like it very well that he's the boss and holds the reins, but he wouldn't hurt me. He's too big a person for that."

Delia gave her a condescending look. "You never

knew anything about David. What makes you think you can read Pericles any better?"

"I wasn't married to David," Morag answered with a calmness she was far from feeling. "Shall I help you pack?"

But Delia ignored the question. "What will you tell him? I mean about my not going to Eleusis with him?"

"I don't know," Morag admitted. "I may talk him into taking the children and me after all."

Delia narrowed her cold eyes, flicked a lock of fair hair out of her eyes and then pulled on it thoughtfully. "You haven't got rid of me yet. Really, Morag, I don't see how you're going to. You can hardly put me physically out of the house—I might fight back!"

Morag straightened her back, squaring her shoulders. "I'll ask Dora to drive us both to the airport," she began.

"And what about the children?"

Morag had forgotten all about her charges. What was she going to do with them? "They're not babies," she said aloud. "Peggy has a whole lot more stamps to stick in, and Kimon can always find something to do."

"Let's hope Pericles will agree with you!" The laugh rang out again and Morag was very conscious of the new note of confidence in Delia's voice. "You're storing up a terrible bustup for yourself with that so-called husband of yours! I think I'll stick around and see the fun. I came here to teach you a lesson, but I shan't have to lift a finger to do anything after all. You'll do it all yourself! Go ahead, Morag, it'll do you more harm than good!"

Repelled by the dislike in Delia's face, Morag clenched her fists. "I will!" she said wildly. "I'll get rid of you if it's the last thing I do!"

"It'll be the last thing you do as Mrs. Pericles Holmes!" Delia retorted.

Morag felt cold despite the hot sun beating down on her. "We'll see," she said grimly.

She turned on her heel and walked up the path toward the house, resisting the temptation to take the steps two at a time just in case she fell flat on her face, for she had no intention of granting Delia the satisfaction of such a spectacle. There was no sound of movement in the house. At least that was one problem out of the way, for to have run into Pericles at that moment would have destroyed the last vestiges of the courage that she had fought with herself for so long to bring to a steaming head. She had to make Delia go—there could be no turning back on that. If Pericles wanted her, it was too bad!

Morag wouldn't give herself time to change her mind. If she didn't do it now, in the heat of the moment, she knew herself well enough to know that she would never do it at all, and then she would deserve to lose Pericles. But Delia would not have him! No matter what Pericles had to say to her, Morag couldn't allow that. She was his wife, and even if he couldn't love her, she would try to be content with what he could give her. Indeed, she couldn't imagine how she could live without him now that he had taught her what it meant to love a man so much that all else paled into insignificance beside the wonder of it.

She swept into Delia's room and began to shove her clothing into her open suitcase. It was like her stepsister not to have found the time to unpack, not even her evening dresses, nor her toiletries, but then perhaps she hadn't felt the need to wash since her arrival the day before. It helped to stoke the fires of Morag's rage and she seized on it with relief. She banged the suitcase shut and dumped it onto the floor, pushing it across the floor. As she pulled open the door, she was confronted by her astonished mother-in-law.

"What are you doing?" Dora demanded. She had a paintbrush in her hand and was plainly cross at having been disturbed in her work.

"Packing," Morag answered briefly.

"I can see that. But can't Delia do her own packing?"

Morag wrinkled up her nose. "No." She sat down on the bed, trying to regain the pure flame of her anger. "I've told Delia she must go."

Dora started. "You haven't! What did Pericles say?"

"He doesn't know yet."

"Oh! Oh, Morag, do you think that was a good idea?"

Morag nodded. "I told her you'd drive her to the airport. Will you, Dora? I'll make it all right with Pericles. I'd drive her myself, only you know I can't."

"Yes, but, my dear, if she won't go, what will you do then?"

"She has to go!"

Dora sat down on the bed beside her. "Has she made you very unhappy?"

Morag nodded again. "She wants Pericles!"

"She may well, but does Pericles want her?" Dora waved her paintbrush in the air, uttering a small sound of annoyance as some of the paint fell on the blanket. "I think you're making too much of this. The Greeks have deep respect for the institution of marriage, and Pericles is entirely Greek in that respect. Believe me, if he hadn't, his marriage to Susan would have foundered long before her death."

"She hates me," Morag said simply.

Dora bridled, spattering yet more paint on the bedclothes. "Oh, my dear!" she murmured. "Are you sure?"

"I think she always has, only I didn't know it. I never guessed that it was that that lay between us. I can't think why she should have thought that I was any kind of threat to her, but it seems she did. Yet I always gave way to her in everything."

"But after all these years of putting up with her, why has she suddenly got to go?"

"She says she's come to take Pericles away from me."

"She said so?"

"I've never given her any reason to think I'll fight back, only—"

"Only this time you will?"

"This time I'm fighting for my life. I can't let her have Pericles even...even if he wants to go. Will you help me, Dora?"

"Shouldn't you be asking Pericles to do that?"

"Oh, no!" Morag shook her head vigorously. "I must do it all myself. You see, I haven't told him—I mean, I don't want him to know."

"Pericles has a right to know!'

Morag swallowed. "I'll tell him afterward. If he's angry with anyone, he'll be angry with me!"

"But he did say—"

"I don't care what he said! Delia is going. I'll have it out with Pericles afterward."

Dora looked less convinced than ever. "He's fond of you, Morag, or he wouldn't have stopped me yesterday—I would never have been allowed to speak to *my* mother-in-law like that—but it will be a different story if he finds you have defied him. His indulgence with your English ways will stop short at that!"

Morag found herself grinning. "I'll try to be very Greek afterward," she promised. "Perry will probably see to that!"

"I certainly hope so!" her mother-in-law retorted. "Has she got an airplane ticket back to England?"

"She hasn't got a reservation yet," Morag answered. "That's another thing I want you to do—telephone the airport and get her a seat on the plane."

"But what are you going to do for money?" Dora protested.

Morag's grin grew broader. "Take it out of the housekeeping!"

There was still no sign of Pericles anywhere. Morag took a look outside and was surprised to see that his car had gone as well.

"Where did daddy go?" she asked Kimon, who was coming running up the path from the beach. "Delia didn't go with him, did she?"

Kimon shook his head. "I'm afraid Delia got a little wet," he said in innocent tones. "Peggy and I thought we'd show her some of the jellyfish that the Greek children next door had fished out of the sea. She fell in!"

Morag hardly took in this information. "Did you see daddy?"

"Yes, of course. We told him Delia didn't want to go with him. Was that right?" Morag looked at him quickly. Surely the children wouldn't have deliberately.... If they had, she thought, it was very much better that she didn't know anything about it.

"Where's Delia now?" she asked.

"Down there." He jerked his head back down the path. "Peggy's helping her. She's all right, Morag."

Delia, however, thought she was far from all right as she came up the path a few seconds later. "Look what those brats did to me!" she shouted angrily. "Where's Pericles? I'm going to tell him how you've all treated me."

"I'm afraid Pericles has already left," Morag smiled. "I'm sorry."

"Are you?" Delia took a step toward Morag and slapped her across the face. "All right, I'll go! But you haven't heard the last of this, Morag Grant. I'll finish you with Pericles and I'll finish you at home, too!"

Morag was aware only of the expression on the children's faces. "It's all right," she reassured them. "She won't really hurt me. She's just a bit cross."

"She's silly," Kimon opined. "Silly and beastly!"

"And you're a horrid little boy!" Delia snapped back. "Look at me! Just look at me! They deliberately drenched me—they knew I was scared of those jellyfish! They were huge and...and ugly!" She turned on Morag. "Don't pretend you're sorry, because I won't believe you! You may have used those brats to get me out of the house, but I don't give up so easily! I'll write to Pericles and tell him how you've all treated me!"

"Daddy will be glad!" Peggy interrupted her. "He doesn't like you either!"

"Peggy!" Her grandmother's tone froze them all to the spot. "Peggy, you will apologize at once. It will be I who will be speaking to Pericles about this. I will not countenance such a disgraceful lapse in good manners in any grand-daughter of mine!"

"I'm sorry, grandma."

"It is Delia who will have to excuse you, not me, child!"

Peggy flashed a rebellious glance in Delia's direction. "I won't!" she declared. "She slapped Morag, and I'm not a bit sorry!"

Dora's look of distaste would have turned Morag's bones to jelly, but Delia was made of sterner stuff. "Sisters can be expected to have their quarrels," she said casually. "Morag and I always have had our differences."

"How fortunate that you didn't both turn out badly," Dora murmured with deadly charm. "My daughter-in-law has asked me to take you to the airport, Miss—I'm so sorry, I don't believe I know your name."

"Miss Price," Delia supplied.

"Well, Miss Price, I have booked and paid for your

seat on the next plane back to London myself. So, if you are ready to leave...."

"Like this? I shall have to change!" Delia flung a vindictive look in Morag's direction. "Morag, I can't go like this!"

Morag's face was expressionless. "I'll help you change," she offered. She picked up Delia's suitcase and carried it back into the house with Delia teetering along beside her, her high platform soles slipping out of control on the highly polished marble floor.

"You'll be sorry that you weren't nicer to me!" she threatened. "I shall tell your father."

"Tell him anything you please."

"Don't you care?" At another time Delia's bewilderment would have made Morag laugh. How odd, she thought, that this time she didn't care what Delia did! If her father didn't know them both by this time, he never would; and she didn't think he would judge her too harshly. After all these years, Delia's threatened tale-telling had lost its venom.

Delia saw that she had failed. "What are you going to tell Pericles? He won't appreciate having his guests bundled onto the first plane out of the country!"

"I don't know." Morag's tone was even.

"I suppose that mother-in-law of yours will tell him some story to save your bacon! I thought at first she didn't like you—it was all right when *she* hit you, I noticed—and yet she protects you. I wonder why?"

Morag was silent for a moment. "She has her reasons," she said then.

Delia looked up from putting on a clean pair of tights. "Oh? What?"

But Morag wasn't prepared to tell her. It was enough that she herself should know that Dora tolerated her simply because she worshipped the ground that Pericles walked on. Her stepsister would not view such a weakness with kind eyes. To her, love had always been a matter of taking, just as Morag had thought it meant giving and no more than that. She knew better now! Pericles had taught her that! Love meant loving and being loved, and one had to have both elements for it to be perfect.

THE CHILDREN WERE openly jubilant over Delia's departure.

Morag at first flushed with triumph, then began to worry. She felt depressed and shaky and very close to tears.

"What do you want to do this afternoon?" she asked the children.

They shrugged their shoulders. "Don't care," Peggy said. "Grandma said she might take us out somewhere."

"But grandma is playing bridge," Morag reminded them.

Kimon's eyes lit and he smiled the tantalizing smile that was so like his father's. "I think she's put it off," he said.

Dora, when she came back, took one look at Morag's face and told her with some asterity to pull herself together. "My dear girl, Delia's your stepsister. If you wanted her to go, you had a perfect right to get rid of her."

"Even against Pericles' wishes?"

Dora looked considerably less certain. "Well, I expect you'll be able to explain it to him," she said bravely. "But it's no good looking like a guilty shadow! What you need is a little time to yourself to put some spirit back into you."

"I can't leave the children."

"Really, Morag! You make me almost glad that stepsister of yours had the gumption to slap you! I have looked after my grandchildren before without any complaints from either of them!"

"But you're playing bridge!"

Dora favored her with a wry smile. "I told the other ladies I would not be playing at the same time as I called the airport. My powers of concentration are more than adequate for normal times, but I doubted that I would play very well this afternoon, somehow. I said my daughter-in-law needed me," she added, a glint of amusement in her eyes, "and of course they accepted that my duty to you came first!"

Morag raised a bleak smile. "You're very kind to me," she said.

"Go away!" said Dora, completely exasperated. "Go away and sort yourself out! It's more than time that you did. It isn't only you who likes to give and to be admired for your good nature. Perhaps even Pericles might like to be asked for something for a change!"

"Oh," said Morag.

"Try it!" her mother-in-law recommended. "Try telling him how much you want him to love you, and that it isn't enough for you to love him. Pericles has his doubts, too, you know." Dora rammed home her advantage. "He can't do it all by himself!"

Morag licked her lips. "He said I had to tell him in words...." She colored, suddenly embarrassed. "If you're sure you don't mind having the children, I think I will go out somewhere. I'll take some sandwiches and...and my tent, in case the buses don't fit, so don't worry if I don't come back tonight."

"*I* won't," Dora assured her. "But supposing Pericles wants to know, in which direction do you intend going?"

Morag opened her mouth, but no words came out.

She shook her head and pointed wildly away from the sea. "I don't know—somewhere!"

"Very enlightening!" her mother-in-law mocked. "Let's hope Perry can read your mind better than I can!"

CHAPTER TWELVE

MARATHON WAS HOTTER than ever. The light breeze that had stirred the dust the last time Morag had been there was absent, and there was nothing to ameliorate the burning rays of the sun as they beat down on the narrow street and the huddled white houses on either side. For a while Morag wished she hadn't come. She could have gone anywhere. She could have gone to Eleusis—she might even have found Pericles there before her! But then she still wasn't sure that she was ready to see Pericles quite yet. If he followed her, she supposed she would be glad. No, she amended that to herself, she would be more than glad; she would feel whole again. Her spirits leaped at the thought, only to fall again as she realized that she had no reason to think that he would come looking for her.

She went into the same shop she had been in before and was gratified when its black-clad owner recognized her and produced a bottle of bitter lemon, opening it for her with a flick of her hand. Morag offered her a bank note to pay for it.

"*Tehis psilá?*" the woman asked.

Rightly taking this to mean that she wanted something smaller, Morag searched through her pockets and produced a ten-drachma coin. The woman nodded happily and took it from her.

Morag drank the bitter lemon slowly, enjoying its chilled qualities as it slid down her dry throat. It was three hours to Rhamous, if that was where she was going, and there would be no one to give her a lift today.

When she turned to go, picking up her knapsack with one hand, the woman pointed to the necklace of shells around her neck and laughed out loud.

"I don't understand," Morag apologized in Greek. Those few words she had had reason to learn by heart from her phrase book.

"She said you had already been to Rhamous," a very familiar voice translated behind her.

Morag dropped her knapsack, looking so guilty that her husband laughed at her, touching her scarlet cheeks with an interested hand.

"I thought I'd find you here," he drawled. "Nemesis won't protect you today, however *agapi mou.* She's on my side in this!"

Morag murmured something quite incomprehensible even to herself, stopped, and made a dash to retrieve her knapsack from the floor. "Did Dora tell you...?"

"My mother was in no state to tell me anything! You've had a busy day, haven't you? Turning the whole family upside down and blackening my name with them for not treating you better! What she did tell me was that she was looking after the children for some reason, instead of playing bridge. Greater love than that, no woman hath!"

Morag stared at him helplessly. "I didn't ask her..." she began. Oh, lord, she thought, was she never going to finish a sentence again?" She allowed Pericles to take her knapsack from her and tried to conquer rising panic within her. "Are you...are you very angry?" she managed to ask.

"That depends," he said dryly. "It depends largely if you are prepared to talk. Are you, Morag?"

She nodded her head quickly, though what she was

going to say was beyond her. Her mouth felt dry again, all benefit from the bitter lemon having departed at his words. "Where are we going?"

He looked at her, his eyebrows slightly raised. "To Rhamous. Where else?"

"If you'd rather go home. . . ."

"Would you?"

She shook her head, fingering the green beads in her shell necklace as if they were some kind of charm that could protect her from her own inadequacy.

"I thought not," he said. "Rhamous will serve us both very well. Perhaps Nemesis will compensate both of us for what we lack in ourselves."

"But you don't lack anything!" she protested. "At least—" the look in his eyes made her feel hot all over "—I don't think you do," she ended, mumbling the words in an agony of embarrassment.

"Don't you, darling?" He lifted her knapsack onto his shoulder and exchanged a few words in rapid Greek with the shopkeeper, accepting a number of bottles of beer and bitter lemon from her. When he had stowed them away in the canvas bag, he put a hand on Morag's shoulder and guided her out of the shop. She could feel the strength of his fingers through the thin material of her shirt, and the same elated fear that she felt so often in his presence fountained up within her. "Bravely said," he whispered in her ear, "but it's only a beginning. This time we'll have all the words, if it takes us all night. Agreed?"

Morag wasn't in any position to refuse, even if she had wanted to, and she didn't know that she did. Wasn't that why she had come away by herself—to find the words that he had told her he wanted from her? The truce between them hadn't been enough for her—and perhaps it hadn't been enough for him, either. She looked at him uneasily as he opened the door of the car and flung her knapsack onto the rear seat, standing back to allow her to get in.

"I nearly didn't go to Rhamous," she told him. "I thought of going to Eleusis."

He grinned. "That would have been throwing down the gauntlet with a vengeance. I'll take you there one day, but today I think Rhamous will suit us better."

A truce was something that could be broken. Had she broken theirs by sending Delia away? She shivered, marveling at her own recklessness. But he had come after her, so perhaps he meant to make a final peace with her after all. He would hardly have come if he had only wanted to tell her that he couldn't forgive her gesture of independent defiance of his wishes. She wound her fingers together and her wedding ring glinted in the sun, startling her into a new line of thought. She was still his wife, and if she played her cards right, she might be able to tempt him into a final peace treaty that neither of them would ever want to break, not ever!

"Yes," she said. She put her head back against the seat and smiled at him. "I brought my tent with me. There's room in it for two—if you don't mind a bit of a squash."

"I think I could bear it." His eyes flickered over her, looking amused. "if you give me the answers I want in time. You won't put me off with a few kisses this time, though. Words are what I want, Morag, if I have to turn you inside out and squeeze them out of you!"

"You . . . you wouldn't!"

"I would, you know. In fact I'd enjoy doing it, so be very careful, *karthiá mou.* My terms will get steeper the longer you delay."

"The terms for your pride?"

"Among other things."

She looked out of the window, watching the famous plain slip past her. She tried to tell herself that she had nothing to be frightened about. Any fool could tell her husband that she loved him! Any fool but her! She didn't know how to begin. But if she didn't tell him, what then?

Pericles put out a hand and patted her knee. "Cheer up, Morag, I'll help you all I can. I don't want to be brutal with you, but neither will I balk at the last fence. I want us both to know exactly where we stand."

She averted her face, biting her lip. "You're not brutal!"

"No?"

"You know you're not!"

His hand brushed against her hair before returning to the gear shift. "I was afraid you thought I was the night Kimon lost his coin."

"Pericles!" she spluttered.

"What does that mean?"

"You know. . . . " She beat a hasty retreat into silence, hoping that he would let the subject drop.

"Know what?"

"That's why I bought the dress," she brought out jerkily.

"That's why I paid for it!"

Her eyes widened. "Was it? You didn't say anything! I thought. . . I thought you were being kind becuase I'd spent everything I had on it!"

"You didn't say anything, either," he reminded her, "except that you weren't going to dazzle anyone in particular, and that you'd bought it on impulse."

"But you were being kind, too, weren't you?"

"Maybe."

Morag wriggled uncomfortably. "I...I thought you didn't want me—only for the children. The dress was a symbol of...of...."

"Say it, Morag!"

She looked down at her hands in her lap. "That I was willing."

"Willing, Morag? You'll have to do better than that!"

"I can't!" she said.

She stared sightlessly out of the window, berating herself inwardly for her cowardice. He must know she loved him, so there was no point in not admitting it. She would, she promised herself, but not until she knew if he was angry with her for sending Delia away. Honesty compelled her to admit that this was a mere excuse for procrastination, and she knew that Pericles would recognize it as such.

He was silent, too, apparently waiting for her to take the next initiative in the conversation. Perhaps this was her moment for bringing up the subject of Delia. She cast him a speculative look, trying to persuade herself that he might find the story amusing rather than dwell on her own motives for removing her stepsister from his proximity as fast as she possibly could. The strength of his face pleased her, even while she thought it boded ill for her own immediate comfort. He was very good-looking, not in a commonplace way, but like a Greek statue with that curious tactile quality that made one long to touch, even to caress. She looked away quickly before she could give way to such a temptation.

They had left the Plain of Marathon far behind by now. A large flock of goats came running down a nearby hill and flooded across the road ahead of them. Pericles braked, slowing to a stop. The goat could well be the symbol of Greece, Morag thought. They came from nowhere, going nowhere, following the fluting call of their goatherd, their bells providing the counterpoint to the timeless music of the scene. They had such pretty ears!

"I love Greek goats!" Morag exclaimed.

Pericles eyed her lazily. "Well, you said that easily enough!" he observed.

Instantly she was all confusion. "That's different!" she murmured.

"So I see!"

"Oh, Pericles, don't be beastly!"

"The remedy is in your own hands."

She searched his face, looking for some sign that he understood how she felt, but apart from a fleeting flash of amusement in his eyes, he might have been carved from granite.

"I don't understand," she said faintly.

"Oh yes, you do!" He let in the clutch and the car moved slowly forward again. "I won't wait forever," he added, giving her a look that held so much in it that she felt a great rush of warmth for him.

"I—I love you, too!"

"Next best to the goats?"

That struck her as funny and she giggled. "No, I love you best of all!"

He pulled the car onto the side of the road, a pleased smile on his lips. "Now that," he said, "deserves some kind of a reward, don't you think? Bravely said, Morag! Was it so difficult?"

She was a little surprised to find that she had finally said it after all. "I love you very much!" she repeated.

He put a hand on either side of her face, smoothing back her hair with his thumbs. Her green eyes grew almost as dark as his. Then his mouth touched hers in a gentle salute. But almost immediately he put her away from him and started up the car again, giving all his concentration to the road ahead.

There was no one else at Rhamous. The ancient shrine slept under the hot sun, disturbed only by the occasional bird hopping over the fallen marble pillars, or soaring in the thermals that surrounded the headland. It was just as beautiful as Morag remembered it. The mountains in the distance rose in rugged grandeur on the other side of the ink-blue sea. The dark black-green of the pine trees offered a pleasing cool shade from where they could see right over the delightful view afforded by the ruined fort on the headland. Pericles, having bought the entry tickets, took Morag by the hand and guided her along the rough path toward the two abandoned temples that had once been the center of the worship of Nemesis, and Thetis with her interest in justice, custom and equity.

"I brought some sandwiches," Morag said. "They're in my knapsack."

He took them out, placing them carefully on a flat stone and arranging the bottles he had bought around them. "They're a bit squashed. My fault, I'm afraid. I put the beer on top of them. What else have you got in here?"

Morag looked away from him. "Not much. Just my night things and...and the tent."

"Ah, yes, the tent!" he grinned. "Weren't you going to get rather hungry if this was all the food you brought with you?"

"I have some money," she explained.

"I'm surprised. Did Delia pay for her own ticket?"

So it had come! The battle had opened with a vengeance, and although she had been expecting it, she felt quite unprepared to deal with it.

"Dora took it out of the housekeeping," she confessed. "I don't think she thought I had enough money to pay for it myself. I wouldn't have had if you hadn't paid for the dress! But you mustn't blame her, Perry, it was all my doing!"

"Was it indeed?"

Morag accepted the sandwich he held out to her, though when she bit into it she couldn't have told if it was ham or fish, or what it was. It was impossible to see what Pericles was thinking, for he had his face turned away from her and all she could see was his thick black hair and the way it curled up at his neck, as if it had a life of its own. What would he do if she were to reach out her hand and give that curl a pull? Would he know the delight she found in touching him and in having him touch her? Her face flamed at the thought.

"Why did you want to take Delia to Eleusis on her own?" she asked him. Her voice sounded husky and very unsure, and she gave herself a little mental shake in an attempt to pull herself together. This was no moment for dreaming, she rebuked herself. This was the moment on which her whole future depended.

"To annoy you," he said quietly.

Morag looked at him quickly. "But why?"

He turned his eyes on her, studying her gravely with an enigmatic expression. "I thought it might help you to get it all together. It did, didn't it?"

"I don't know what you mean!" she denied.

"Morag, if you say that once more, I'll take you home now and leave you to stew in your own juice! I'll give you five minutes in which to tell me all about Delia and then we can both forget about her. She never was as important as you imagined."

"She was to me!" Morag kept her tone even with difficulty. She was afraid that she was going to burst into tears. "I saw the way you looked at her when we arrived in England. But it was too late, wasn't it? You were already committed to me, but it was her you wanted to kiss and . . . ." She broke off, horrified by the sight of her own jealousy so plainly revealed to him.

"And she would be more than willing to take me from you. Is that it?"

She nodded in earnest now. "But I couldn't let her have you! I couldn't, Perry! I'm so sorry, but I couldn't!"

"Didn't it ever occur to you, my love, that I might have had some ideas on the subject? If I'd wanted Delia, don't you think I could have got out of marrying you? I'd had one marriage where neither of us cared very much for the other. Do you think I'd want to go through that again?"

She stopped crying and stared at him. "But you were—you did! I mean, you married me!"

He gave her a mocking look. "Exactly!"

"D-didn't Delia attract you at all?"

The corner of his mouth kicked up into a smile. "Not at all!"

Her eyes widened. "I don't think you should have made use of her like that. She might have got hurt."

"Unlikely," he decided. "Not that I would have minded inflicting a little pain in that direction. She had done so much to hurt you!"

"But that's nothing to you!" she protested.

"On the contrary," he assured her, "it affects me very dearly. You're my wife, and no one hurts you but me! David didn't matter. Anyone with half an eye could see that he meant nothing to you. He hadn't even kissed you properly."

"Who told you that?"

He laughed. "You did!"

She remembered that she had, that she had told him that no one had ever kissed her before he had done so, and the memory brought a sweet confusion on her face.

Had he known then that she had had no defenses against him, but had fallen headlong in love with him at first sight?

She put a hand up to her hot cheeks. "He wasn't particularly interested in that... that side of things," she explained.

"Just as well!" Pericles said. "I prefer to teach my own wife how to make love! But I had to be sure that you weren't being carried away by the emotion of the moment. I wanted you to love me enough to stand up and fight for me, my unselfish darling. And, you see, you did! Even if you had to get my whole family to help you do it, you got rid of Delia!"

"You mean you wanted her to go?"

"Well, she isn't my favorite person. I'm sorry to say it about your stepsister, but as a woman she's a pain in the neck!"

Unexpectedly, Morag chuckled and he looked inquiringly at her. "You sounded just like your mother," she said. "I'm sure you both think that a woman is a useless being unless she's subservient to some man!"

The gleam of humor in his eye grew more pronounced. "Don't you?" he mocked her.

"In a way," she admitted. Her eyes met his and her heart jerked within her. The laughter died from her voice and she averted her face hastily in case he should read there of her need for him. The silence stretched her nerves and made it unbearable not to look at him. "Perry..." she began. With a sudden movement she cast herself on her knees beside him. "Perry, I love you. I love you so much it hurts. Please, love me a little bit!" He made as if to speak, but she put up a hand and covered his lips with her fingers. "I know you want me, and...and if that's all, I promise you it'll be enough for me, but—"

His arms went around her in the most satisfactory way. "If that had been all, I wouldn't have made you my wife!" he mocked her. "Traveling around Greece on your own, you were fair game for any wolf who came along."

"I was not! I can look after myself perfectly well." Her natural honesty made her wonder if that was quite true. She might not have *wanted* to protect herself against Pericles Holmes, no matter what suggestion he had made to her. "Against anyone else," she ended meekly, veiling her eyes with her eyelashes and wishing heartily that she had retained a decent silence and had not let her indignation get the better of her. "I mean . . . " she began again on a gulp.

"Your meaning is perfectly clear," he assured her.

"Oh," she said.

His arms tightened around her as she halfheartedly tried to escape his embrace, "Sweetheart, don't you know yet that I feel the same about you? Long before the dress, or my mother's painting of you, I was plotting your downfall. I was afraid I'd put you off me once and for all, but I kept telling myself that you were my wife and that you must have expected me to take you sooner or later. If you were frightened at first, I thought I could overcome that."

"But . . . but I was quite willing." She remembered that he had said she would have to do better than that. "It was wonderful!" she forced out. The words that had always evaded her came tumbling into her mind, and they were somehow easy to say—at least to Pericles. "I couldn't believe it when I first saw you," she said. "You were so beautiful to me! N-not in a feminine sort of way, you could never be that and you know it, but a man can be beautiful, more beautiful than a woman, and I wanted you to make love to me then. You must have known that when you kissed me that time, but after we were married you didn't seem to want me. I thought you were wishing you hadn't, and then I thought perhaps you were Greek enough to think that any woman was better than none, and so I bought the dress and...and made Dora give us the painting, because I thought you'd know then, and it must be rather daunting to have a wife who doesn't—well, you know. But I didn't think it was going to work. It was such a relief when—"

"Then why did you go back to your own room?" he asked her.

"I wanted to be more to you after all. I wanted you to love me, too!"

He held her away from him looking deep into her eyes. "I think you were afraid, too," he said. "You looked scared stiff when I threatened to drive you up into the mountains and make love to you there."

Her eyelashes veiled her green eyes for an instant, but then she looked back at him. "I was afraid I wouldn't know how to please you," she confessed, "and I was shy. I'm still a little afraid of you. You see, I never knew that one could feel like this about anyone and...and it takes a bit of getting used to!"

His hand grasped the nape of her neck in a possessive gesture. "Darling Morag," he whispered, "I love you, love you, love you, like I've never loved any other woman, nor ever shall. But I had to be sure that you loved me, too. I knew my mother would tell you all about Susan, and I didn't want to be another lame dog for you to break your heart over because you're made that way! I was scared of being another David to you, someone you would give up in an excess of generosity, if Delia and I looked like we were attracted to one another.

I'll never get over the moment when I got home today and found you'd stood up to her and meant to cling onto me no matter what!"

She smiled, her eyes very bright. "Did that pay for your pride, Perry?"

He kissed her lips. "I hope you think it's worth it. My pride was lacerated by Susan's indifference. You are quite right, my love, it is daunting to mean less than nothing to the woman in your arms. But with you, not even a passionate physical response was enough for me. I wanted your heart and mind as well!"

"They're yours," she answered. "I only want to belong to you, Perry, nothing more. Where you lead, I want to follow—with love. Because I don't think I can live without you. Without you, everything is dust and ashes, and only you can make it all glorious for me like... like being born again!"

He held her close, a look that she had never seen before on his face. "Morag, *agapi mou*, for someone who is afraid of words, you can make them sing a lyrical song when you try." He kissed her slowly, his mouth lingering against her soft, parted lips. "Will you forgive me for making you say them?"

Her arms slipped up around his neck and her fingers buried themselves in his hair, luxuriating in the feel of it. "Oh, Perry, don't you know yet how it is with me? You said you wanted the words—all of them, and I nearly died at the thought, but your will is mine, and I knew I'd have to find them in the end if I wanted your signature on the final peace treaty. And I do! You don't know how much I do!"

"On my terms?" he whispered.

She nodded helplessly, scarcely aware of the gentle way he held her. "On your terms," she agreed. "Because I love you!" She tipped up her face for his kiss.

"On any terms," she said, and she was no longer ashamed of the hunger in her voice.

THE SUN WAS SETTING and the boy who looked after the site had appeared from nowhere, a knowing grin on his face.

"We close now," he said. "But you can come back in the morning. We very seldom have any visitors in the early morning."

Pericles grinned. "It sounds as though we've got our marching orders," he said. "Did you mean it when you offered me the sanctuary of your tent?"

"Yes, of course," Morag gave him a shy look. "But if you'd rather go home...."

"Certainly not! I intend to have you to myself for a few hours at least before we have mama preening herself that she did the whole thing on her own, and the children claiming all your attention, thinking that you belong to them."

"But I do!" she laughed. "I want them to think that. It wouldn't do to exclude them! Besides, I like them." She clamped her mouth shut, determined to say no more, but then she smiled and gave him the victory. "Kimon has a smile just like yours," she confided.

"My dear girl," he said, his eyes very bright, "if that's all it takes to make you happy, I'll have to see what I can do! Though I rather hope that we manage to reproduce that guilty look of yours as well."

"I'd like that," she murmured, determined not to let him see that he had embarrassed her. "But only if Kimon and Peggy don't mind!" She put her hand in his. "Every child should come first with both parents. It's horrible when you don't!"

His fingers stroked her cheek. "I don't think the twins have anything to worry about. You'll find room for them all in that loving heart of yours. I'll vouch for that. Shall we go and get a meal in Marathon, and then come back and make our camp on the headland, outside the old town there?"

She nodded, becoming aware of the boy who was still waiting for them to go. "There's something I must do first, though. I have something for Nemesis, as a kind of thank you, because she did give us a handsome measure of joy today. I wouldn't like her to think we aren't grateful."

"Are you afraid she'll take it all away again?" he teased her.

"No," she said, but she didn't sound particularly certain. "But I wouldn't want her to think me guilty of *hubris,* either!"

He laughed and said something to the boy in Greek. The two of them stood side by side and watched her as she mounted the high step onto the floor of the ruined temple that had been dedicated to Nemesis the many hundreds of years before. There was a place a little towards one end where probably once had stood her votive statue, the only one extant long enough for us to know what it looked like.

Morag stood quite still for a long time, savoring the moment. It was likely, she thought, that she would never be quite as happy as she was at that moment. No one could live on the peaks all her life, nor would she want to, but neither would she have been without this one day when Pericles had said he loved her.

She took the shells from around her neck and laid them carefully on the ground in front of her.

She stood up, and smiled at Pericles, and remembered a speech she had once learned from the *Eumenides.* She thought it was Athene's command to the Furies when they had agreed to settle in her land. She quoted:

> *Blessings, in harmony with a victory that has no evil in it: blessings from the earth and from the waters of the sea and from the sky. And you must pray that the wind's breath may pass across my land in sunlight; that the fruits of the earth and increase of grazing beasts, abundant, thriving, may not fail my citizens in time to come; and that the seed of man may be kept safe.*

Pericles came to the edge of the temple and lifted her down, with a smile as intimate as her own.

"Amen to that," he said.